The Maldoran Chronicles

The Unbreakable Will

Rhys Eynon

To Linda,
Thanks for buying
my book!
Enjoy
Rhys

The Maldoran Chronicles
Copyright©2023 Rhys Eynon
First Edition

ISBN: 978-1-7393179-0-4

Published by: Frost Bridge Publishing
www.frostbridgepublishing.com
Cover design by: Jonathon Vero Quintero
Images within by: Deborah Withey
Maps by: Rhys Eynon

The Maps

Maldora 1370 U.E
Zarmania
Mandleheim
Nordland
Hothland
Frankonia
The Ringspine Mountains
Gower
Alvaria
Satyrom
Aberemrallt
Prince's Bay
Old Argantis
Lapenthoes
Byzalia
N
S
W
E
1
2
3
4
5
6
7
8
9
10
11
12
13
14
15
16
17
18
19
20
21
22
23
24
25
26
27
28
29
30
31
32
33

Legends

Gower

1. Everdale
2. Gard Afon
3. Nyth Fran
4. Bryn Gwyrdd

Satyrom

5. Novadarci

Terradonia

6. Luvera
7. Paroy
8. Merine
9. Kosantos
10. Bourgiatta
11. Arivinium
12. Ravenno

Hothland

13. Albruck
14. Reikenburg
15. Stettow
16. Ostenburg
17. Luden

Nordland

18. Holmslond
19. Oslohm
20. Brekkur

Madleheim

21.Veldor

22.Myrgrad

23.Dimbuhr

Zarmania

24. Orni
25. U'Imolk

Frankonia

26. Saulogne
27. Belfort
28. Poilly
29. Frebonne
30. Ayos

Alvaria

31. Rheonne

Islands

32. Lapenthoes
33. Byzale

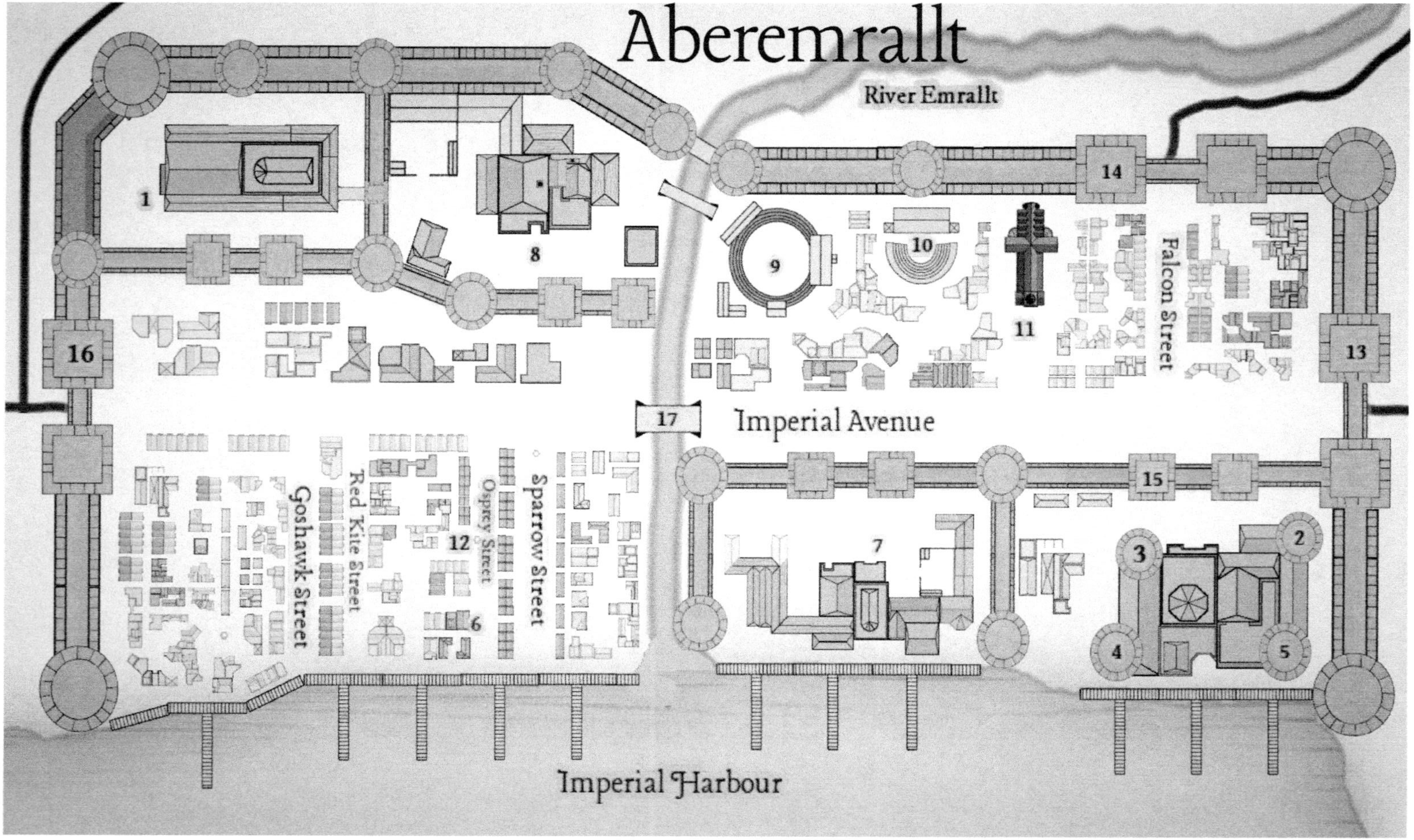
Aberemrallt
River Emrallt
Falcon Street
Imperial Avenue
Sparrow Street
Osprey Street
Red Kite Street
Goshawk Street
Imperial Harbour
1
2
3
4
5
6
7
8
9
10
11
12
13
14
15
16
17

Legends

1. The Imperial Academy

The Imperial Palace

2. The Sun Tower
3. Griffon Tower
4. Crow's Tower
5. Raven Tower

6. The Jolly Maid
7. The Stronghold
8. City Barracks
9. The Coliseum
10. Amphitheatre
11. The Panethedral
12. Markets Square

Gatehouses and bridges

13. Sun's Gate
14. Bard Gate
15. Bastion Gate
16. Merchant's Gate
17. Lion's Bridge

Introduction

THE CONTINENT OF MALDORA is a land of magic and secrets and is home to many great civilisations.

In the North is the Dwarven homeland of Mandelheim, neighboured by the steppe kingdom of Zarmania. To the southwest is the Kingdom of Frankonia. Across the narrow channel is the island kingdom of Alvaria, home to the wise and inquisitive elves. In the centre of Maldora, surrounded by mountains, is Hothland. On the far northeast coast is the proud nation of Nordland. In the south lie the architectural city-states of Terradonia and the humble neighbouring nations of Gower and Satryrom, the home of the satyrs.

For 300 years, these eight kingdoms enjoyed an age of peace and prosperity under the Maldoran Empire, ruled by the emperor and his grand council from the seat of power in Aberemrallt. But even under their vigilant watch, dark and ancient forces lurked in the shadows and below the earth. Those that control these forces, known as the Dark Lords, are erratic masters of brutality and sorcery. Commanded by Samael, the Lord of Darkness.

Leading the fight against these dark forces is the religious fighting order known as the Twin Blade Brotherhood. One of many orders exists; they are composed of brave warriors, renowned knights and the most potent mages from all corners of Maldora. They are tasked with finding and rooting out the influence of the dark power wherever it hides.

But a new conflict is arising, one that will shake the empire to its foundation and tip the balance of Maldora between the forces of light and dark.

Monsters will awaken.
Secrets will be revealed.
And heroes will be born from the chaos.
One such hero is Arran Connaught, the last to wield the Unbreakable Will.

Prologue

Tuesday 27th August 1370 U.E.
The Courtyard, The Academy, Aberemrallt

THE ACADEMY, a bastion of cultural knowledge, occupies the north-western corner of Aberemrallt, the capital of the Maldoran Empire. Sheltered from the rest of the city by its own walls, the main towers overlooked everything.

It was a cool night, with the full blue moon looking down at the Academy. Guards in groups of two patrolled the inner complex, with some on top of the walls watching outward for intruders. Most of these men were soldiers from the city barracks next door, sharing the same fortifications that separate the two buildings for the purpose of providing security.

Underneath the tower connecting the intersection was a small sewer hatch. Something was pushing the hatch from underneath. With enough force, the bronze top shifted aside, scraping along the cobbled ground.The stench of excrement mixing with the clean cold air. From out of the darkness, a hand reached up, followed by another, gripping the edges. A tall, slender man appeared from below, pulling himself up from the hole. He crawled away on all fours before rising to his feet, breathing in the cool, fresh air.

Gerald scanned his surroundings. Good timing, he thought. Nothing but a few torches hanging high from the walls. He turned back to the hatch.

"All clear," he whispered.

He stepped back and waited, a light breeze tugging at his cloak. Gerald listened as another pair of hands and feet ascended the ladder and another man pulled himself out of the darkness. This was Brodus. Short, but bulky in comparison, he wore a similar cloak to Gerald for concealment, though his was ripped in places.

"About bloody time," Brodus inhaled heavily. "Good to have some fresh air."

"We've only just got past the gate," said Gerald.

"Well then, let's not wait any longer. Which way?" Brodus asked as he tilted his head, catching the warts on his eyebrow.

At that point, Gerald heard the sound of plodding boots and murmuring voices that grew louder. "Guards are coming," he said.

"Right, let's put this hatch back then."

They gripped the bronze sewer cover and moved it. Gerald was holding his breath, struggling with his side of the disk. Brodus however, was handling his side with ease. They laid the top down over the sewer hatch. The disk creaked as it slid back into place. The oncoming footsteps were getting louder.

"Quick, over here!" Gerald pointed toward a wagon filled with barrels nestled in the corner between the archway and one of the towers. They rushed to hide behind it.

Gerald pressed his back against the wagon. He tried to slow his breathing, unaware that his hood had fallen back while running, revealing a young, fair face with freckles on both cheeks and a mop of ginger hair. Brodus was sitting next to him taking slower, deeper breaths. The muscley man had a deep scar that travelled diagonally from the outside of his left eye, down the side of his mouth. Not the nicest looking person to be around, Gerald admitted. But his strength, reliability and no nonsense attitude - according to the employer they both answer to - were the reasons for why he was assigned to accompany him. He crawled to the end of the wagon and peered around the side: two guards on patrol, talking obliviously to themselves. Their purple and yellow tunics stood out against the grey walls. Gerald glanced at them briefly before he pulled his head back up, and they passed by without even looking at the wagon. He watched as they walked down the route between the Academy wall and the gatehouse. Gerald quietly sighed when Brodus nudged him.

"So, where do we go from here?"

"Most of the doors outside will be locked," Gerald explained. "We need to get inside from the archway. Follow me."

Gerald, with Brodus in tow, circled around the cart and walked through the archway. *Well, so far so good*, he thought, but he still felt uneasy about being here. He doubted anyone else would feel any different to him, especially when you're infiltrating one of the most heavily guarded places in the city of Aberemrallt. Well, second only to the Imperial Palace itself of course. But he had a job to do, to get inside the Academy and acquire a specific item for his employer.

To his right, there was a spiral stairway into the tower that connected it to the walls. He climbed up the stairway, wary of any soldiers stationed above. Upon reaching the top, Gerald crouched low. Only one section of the tower was covered in a full wall, facing the direction of the river, with one small arrow slit. He gestured to Brodus to stay back and be quiet.

As the guard came closer, Gerald had to retreat back down the stairway but kept the guard in his sight. If he were spotted now, the whole complex would be alerted. The guard stopped inside the tower, unfastening a flask from his belt and taking a sip. Gerald held his breath as he watched. After taking a drink, the guard returned the flask to his belt and carried on patrolling, completely bypassing the stairway.

Gerald and Brodus watched and waited until the guard was out of sight. They crept out of the tower and followed the bridge to a doorway into the Academy.

Once inside, they followed a long corridor that went from east to west. On his left, Gerald could see the gatehouse through the windows as they progressed. He let his hand trail along the right wall, taking in the cold, dry and yet smooth texture that existed between each classroom door he saw. He was all too familiar with this place, this corridor in particular, for he was once a student and spent years learning the art of making potions. Now, he was here not as a student, but as a thief. He was chosen by his mysterious contractor to steal a black box that contained something of value was all his employer said. Something that should never be kept in the Academy in the first place, they said. Gerald didn't really care about the details, so long as the payment outweighed the risks involved.

Gerald knew where the object was concealed but needed to find the correct keys to access the room it was hidden in.

The pair turned right after reaching the other side of the complex. Gerald was now descending a flight of stairs. The wooden steps creaked with every light step he and Brodus made. Gerald found himself at the Academy entrance, where two oak carved doors towered over him, reaching up to the ceiling. There was another flight of stairs on the opposite side of the building's entrance just like the one he had been walking down. Gerald soon saw the silhouette of another guard heading in their direction. He dashed for the nearest pillar and hid, Brodus following suit. Holding his breath, Gerald listened to the footsteps. Peering carefully around the pillar, he saw the back of the soldier as he stopped by the Academy entrance and went up the right stairway.

This was Gerald's chance while the guard was unaware of his presence, he left the pillar and sneaked past then headed down the corridor, which was wider than the one up above. Ahead were the doors leading into the main hall where students and lecturers gathered for assemblies. He turned down one of the side corridors. Another right, past more classrooms, each quick step carrying the weight of memories to help him navigate his old schoolground and then he found himself standing before the most unlikely place to hide something important: the storeroom. Brodus caught up to him.

"Is this it?" he asked.

"Don't judge a book by its cover," Gerald whispered.

"Who said that?" Brodus tilted his head.

"My mother told me that, but the point is—nevermind. Just watch my back for me."

Gerald approached the door. He pulled out two keys attached to a small metal coil from one of his pockets .A simple twist in the lock followed by a click and the door was open. Once they were inside, he closed the door behind them. Before him was a small, compact storage room. From left to right, there were shelves upon shelves so stacked they looked like they were near touching the ceiling above. Every space in these shelves were crammed with essential items, books, bottles and boxes. Cobwebs stretched across the hard to reach corners of the room. The walls that compressed this vast itinerary were plastered in plain clean white, but Gerald noticed a section in the bottom left corner where the plaster had been peeled off, revealing the rows of centuries old brickwork that lay underneath.

Brodus stepped past Gerald to look around. He wasn't impressed.

"So, where is this secret entrance then?" He looked at Gerald, who pointed to the floor. Beneath them was a brown rug that was worn in places. Gerald grabbed hold of one end whilst Brodus took hold of the other. They pulled it over, revealing a long dark wood trapdoor.

"Alright," Brodus nodded his head, "I wasn't expecting it to be hidden down there."

Gerald suppressed a smile. "I guess they wanted to hide this black box where no one would expect to find it."

"How did you come to learn about this door, anyway?" Brodus asked.

"Well, before I was expelled," Gerald began, "I was in the middle of acquiring supplies for my studies."

"Hmm, yeah, your studies, right," Brodus chuckled.

"I'm serious. Next thing I know, I heard people outside, so I hid behind one of the shelves. I watched as the headmaster and some guards came in and uncovered this trap door. Anyway, I'll go down and investigate whilst you keep watch."

Brodus raised an eyebrow, "Really?"

"Look, we're here for this box your employer wants, nothing else, right? Just don't steal anything more."

Brodus grumbled. "Fine, but don't keep me waiting."

Gerald nodded to him before kneeling down to the trapdoor and used the second key. After opening it, Gerald found himself staring down a flight of steps descending into darkness. There was a lamp hooked underneath the trapdoor, a small candle encased in a wrought iron cage. He removed the lamp from its hook, ignited the flame inside and down he went. The timber planks creaked with every step he took. Gerald found himself travelling along a narrow corridor. It was plain, except for sconces every few metres apart. The walls were marked with brickwork patterns. No effort seemed to have been made to cover them up. The air was cold with a dusty taste. The journey felt like it was never-ending, until Gerald saw something glowing ahead. A green light that was pulsing, as if it were alive. Gerald picked up the pace and jogged toward the phenomenon, passing though a slim archway leading into a small chamber. The room was empty, except for a handful of crates in one corner. He scanned the room until he found the source of the light. A marble podium stood in the centre, with a small black box on top.

As Gerald walked closer, he took note of its details. The box was adorned with silver skulls, all human-shaped, with a glowing emerald on top. There was a lock on the box as well. He checked to see if any of the keys he had could open it, but none of them fit into its keyhole. He put his lantern down on the ground and reached out for the box. Was it boobytrapped? He clasped his hands around the box, touching some of the skull ornaments with his thumbs and acknowledging the metallic and smooth texture of them. Then he took a deep breath and closed his eyes as he gently lifted it off the podium. Gerald pulled it to his chest and waited. Opened one eye, then the other, but nothing happened. Relieved, Gerald held the newly acquired item under one arm while collecting the lantern in the other before turning back to the chamber archway and making his way to the surface. The emerald piece continued to glow ominously all the way.

He returned to the steps before the storeroom and whispered, "You there?" but there was no response. He climbed the steps and to his surprise the storeroom door was open. He looked around the shelves but there was no trace of his comrade. Had Brodus decided to abandon him? Or was he caught by the guards? He would've been trapped down below if the latter happened. It didn't matter. He did most of the work of getting in here himself, he was sure he could get out the same way. He didn't need that oaf anyway. Gerald put the lantern and the black box down on the floor, then he grabbed hold of the trapdoor. It was easier with Brodus's help, admittedly, but he managed to lift the door until it slammed down on the secret entrance. The sound echoed beyond the room. Gerald cursed under his breath, but didn't panic. He dragged the rug over the trapdoor, picked up his things, and rushed out of the storeroom. He was about to close the door when he heard-

"Oi, you! Stop right there!"

Gerald jumped. There was a guard with a torch in one hand and about to draw a sword. Gerald simply dropped the lantern and ran.

"Come back here!"

The guard pursued him down the corridor. Gerald held the black box under his arm as he ran. The sound of his shoes hitting the marble floor resounded down the hallway. His plan was to rush back up the stairway and make his escape before he could attract more attention, but he was too late. Another guard stood between him and the stairway. He was caught with nowhere to go.

"Before you come near..." he panted, "If you could just let me explain. We can let this slide… if you know what I mean."

"You can explain to the headmaster tomorrow morning, you little shit," the first guard said.

The one in front of Gerald walked closer to inspect him. "I know who you are. You're Gerald Gilles."

"The one who sold those illegal potions?" the first guard asked, raising his voice in interest and awe.

"Um, actually," Gerald gulped instinctively, "you mistake me for him but I'm actually his cousin, I know we look alike but..."

"Shut up, you lying little shit," the first guard bellowed. He grabbed Gerald by the shoulder and pointed his sword to his face, the sharp steel tip of the blade prodding and biting at his cheeks. "It's because of those potions that one of your classmates was fucking my wife!"

"Now, hold on! That wasn't entirely my fault. Whoever did that must have used too much of the stuff," Gerald protested.

“Oh, so you think you should be spared, huh?” said the second guard. “First you start giving out dangerous potions, now you’re intruding somewhere you don’t belong.” He noticed the glowing emerald of the black box still tucked under Gerald’s armpit. “And what’s that you got there?”

“Oh, this? Just a box of personal things that I forgot to reclaim before I was chucked out.”

“I don’t believe you one fucking bit,” the first guard snarled. “Come all the way here just for personal belongings, my foot! Time for you to spend the rest of the night in the barracks. We’ve got a nice cosy cell for little shits like you.”

“I’ll have that.” The second guard unsheathed his sword and grabbed the black box from Gerald.

“Oh, for fuck’s sake,” Gerald protested.

From out of nowhere, a knife struck the front guard right in the back of his neck. The box fell from his hands as he dropped to his knees. Gerald was taken by surprise and so was the man holding on to him.

“Who’s there?” the guard shouted. “I have your friend. Come out and face me!” The second guard remained close to Gerald and urged him to walk toward his fallen comrade. He lightly prodded his sword at him, but he was already gone, blood had begun to pour from the back of the man’s neck and created a red pool around the body. “Shit,” he muttered.

Gerald felt the guard’s grip involuntarily loosen. He elbowed him in the abdomen and followed with a quick stomp on the foot. That did the trick. Breaking free he made a dash for the black box. Gerald glanced behind; the second guard was attempting to pursue him but was tackled to the ground by a shadowy figure; the force knocked the sword out of his hand as he fell, clattering loudly. Gerald stopped when he realised the figure was Brodus. The stocky man was on top of the guard. He punched his foe in the face three times before pulling another knife, jabbing the man in the throat and pressing the blade in deeply. If Gerald wasn't shocked by the first kill, he was by the second. Brodus rose to his feet, leaving his victim gasping for air, blood erupting from the fallen man's neck and trickling down the sides of his body.

Gerald stepped back, the roar of his own blood in his ears, swallowing the sickness he grimaced at Brodus.

"What?" Brodus looked at Gerald.

"I can't believe you just did that," he said.

"I just saved your life, mate," Brodus answered back.

"This wasn't supposed to happen. We could've avoided this, you know."

"We could've this, we could've that," Brodus mocked. "You're not in charge here."

Gerald resorted to sarcasm. "Yeah, like no one's going to notice two dead bodies on the floor. Nobody will think something happened to justify the blood spilt here!"

At that point, Brodus walked past the bodies and grabbed Gerald by the collar, pinning him to one of the pillars in one fluid movement, showing the younger man the truth of his strength, and his badly arranged set of teeth

"What are you doing?" Gerald replied, feeling increasing discomfort as Brodus's massive hands wrapped around his throat.

"Listen, you little shit!" He growled, shaking him harder. "The only reason I agreed to have you with me is because you know your way around the bloody place."

At that point, they could hear footsteps and men calling out.

"Time for us to go," said Brodus as he released him.

"Oh, fuck me," Gerald muttered. He picked up the black box and tucked it within his cloak.

The pair raced up the stairway and used the same route they had taken into the building to make their escape.

Gerald hoped that they would be able to reach the sewer before getting caught again. Even whilst running for his life, doubt and regret crept within him. He hoped that the payment he was promised would justify all he had done to get hold of this damn box. He just had to keep going, no matter what. For there was no turning back.

Chapter 1

Wednesday 28 August, 1370 U.E.
The Andlan Forest, Province of Gower

EVER SO PEACEFUL was the Andlan Forest on a fair summer day. The woodland itself was named after the Andlans, a nomadic tribe who travelled from the far west and settled between the forest and the River Tor.

An exchange of songs from many birds could be heard in every corner of the forest. The day was warm, and the sun's rays pierced through the gaps between the dense pines.

Crouching among the bushes between the ancient trees was a hunter covered from head to toe in a long cloak, and with feet clad in a pair of brown leather boots pressed softly on the bed of grass beneath them. The hunter hid behind a tree that was thrice his arm width, gripping a spear in his right hand and slowly peeped his head around the large trunk just enough to see his prey, a buck grazing in the distance.

The deer raised its head, motionless for a moment before moving on to the next patch of grass. Remaining low, the hunter followed. Many hunters carried a bow when hunting; he recalled his friends saying before he left, *"You'll have a better chance with a bow than a spear to make a kill from a distance."* He had acknowledged this publicly, but privately the hunter begged to differ; he believed that closer to the game meant less effort to throw this spear. He had other weapons under his cloak should that fail. Besides, this hunter had been doing this for most of his youth when not occupied with more pressing tasks and duties. As a result he was calm wherever a first timer's heart would be racing with hesitation.

The hunter crouched behind a bush; his eyes still focused on the deer. It raised its head and ear twitching to its surroundings before continuing to feed. *Now is my chance*, he thought, a spear to its side should kill it. He steadied his breathing and rose slowly from the bush, turning the spear in his hand as he readied himself. With one breath, the hunter hurled the spear, watching its flight from the release to where it found its intended mark.

The impact of the spear into the deer's side left the beast in a state of panic, stumbling on the ground. The birds took flight in every direction over the trees following the deer's cry. Seeing the creature struggling, the hunter decided to end its suffering quickly, pulling out a short sword from his scabbard; he rushed in before the deer could flee. He stood over the buck, kneeled down before it and slit the throat. It flailed and kicked around desperately, but soon succumbed to its fate.

A moment of silence followed. The hunter pulled back on his hood, revealing the face of a young man. He had sharp features, a thin chin, and sported short brown hair that spiked outward. He pulled the spear out from the deer's side and tied the front and hind legs together with a rope before finally hooking the spear through the hoops he had made.

The sound of birds soon returned as the hunter carried his game out of the forest. Once free of the densely packed trees, the first thing he saw was a large tree, separate from the rest of the woodland. Grazing underneath its branches was a dark brown horse that was tied by a rope to the tree trunk.

The horse was called Basil and was too occupied by the fresh grass to wander off. Around the other side of the tree was a sledge, made of dark, smooth oak wood with a few cracks underneath, laid flat on the grass. Engraved on one side of the sledge were the words 'Belonging to Arran Connaught'. Arran placed the carcass of the deer on the sledge, the blood from its cut leaving a smear on the ground, turning the green grass to brown.

Arran pulled the sledge around to Basil as he untied his rope from the tree, then he attached it to the sledge. He pulled out a flask of water from one of the saddle pouches, swigging whilst looking down at the River Tor below. The water gleamed with the reflection of the summer sun as it travelled southward. So bright it was that Arran had to shield his eyes each time he gazed in that direction. He then looked past the river to the east. There lay the province of Terradonia, its plains made of hills and sparse pockets of trees.

To the north, he could see Aldbruck Castle in the distance, the gateway to the pine filled lowlands of Hothland. The heart of Maldora itself, surrounded on all sides by the mountain range known as the Ringspine. The birthplace of the ruling clan whose authority over the Maldoran Empire was known all over the continent.

Arran returned his flask to the saddle. He patted Basil on the back and ran his hand down the smooth mane, murmuring praise whilst he picked up one of the reins. Rather than add more burden to Basil, he chose to gently pull on them to encourage the horse to follow him and drag the sledge behind them. They travelled down the dry and dusty road alongside the bank of the River Tor to the farming town of Everdale.

The first thing he spotted was a large wooden windmill perched on a hill overlooking several acres of farmland. Beyond them was Everdale: home. Arran noticed a few farmers looking at him as he and Basil walked past their fields. He waved at them briefly. A flock of sheep in a single file made the pair halt. They were followed by an elderly shepherd who was about a head shorter than Arran, carrying a long-twisted stick with jangling bells hanging from the top. The shepherd walked past him, and stopped to look at the deer strapped to the sledge behind Basil.

"Big game you have there," the shepherd said. He was smoothing his beard as he looked at Arran's catch.

"Aye, caught the thing this morning in the forest north of here," Arran replied.

"Couldn't be a better time to hunt. Gods be good to those who give back and receive," said the shepherd.

"They must have been good to you for this flock of yours," Arran replied, pointing at the sheep. "Can't stay around though, I have to deliver this meat."

"Where are you going with that deer?" the shepherd asked.

"To Pwynt Afon Castle on the other side of town," Arran responded.

"Well then, may you feed many mouths with it. Good day to you," the shepherd replied before moving to keep up with his flock. Arran and Basil continued to the town.

Where the tended fields were sparse in people, Everdale was a very populated place for a small town. Arran and Basil moved as if they were a fish swimming upstream, swerving and dodging men and women that pass by going about their daily routines. Some stopped to inspect them and the sledge and its content, before moving on and continued with their gossip. Small pockets of children laughed and chased one another, weaving carelessly around everyone else.

Suddenly Arran's nose caught the scent of something baking, looking right, there was a small bakery with open doors. He could see the baker churning out loaves from the oven whilst two young girls dealt with folk eager to trade their coins for bread. Further ahead, the clanging of metal-on-metal caught Arran's ears as he looked towards the local blacksmith hammering away with his tools.

The houses he passed were of various sizes, but most were bigger and wider than the cottages outside the town. One was a shrine where people came and went for daily prayers. The front door was open and Arran breathed in the sweet scent of incense.

He carried on with Basil until they came upon the centre of the town, where a well stood. By the look of the cracked tiles on the roof, it had seen better days, but remained usable by the townsfolk. As he got closer, Arran recognised two men making the most of the freshwater. The first man was Gabriel, his face was fair and clean, with wavy blond hair that dangled past his ears. He had made himself comfortable lying on top of the stones eating an apple.

The second man, Callum, was somewhat the opposite, with a wider body and stocky legs. He had a round face and dark brown hair that took the form of a small bowl atop his head. Both men wore a blue tunic with red cuffs and an emblem of crossed swords on their chests.

Arran approached the men by the well. "Off duty are we lads?"

"You off hunting by yourself is why we're here. Your uncle predicted you'd come past here by now," said Gabriel, standing up and moving away from the well to meet him.

"More likely an excuse to get out of the barracks," Arran patted Gabriel on the shoulder.

"Aye. Was getting bored waiting for you to come back," said Gabriel returning the gesture with a squeeze to the shoulder and slap to the back, though Arran could see his attention was on a pair of buxom washer girls walking past.

"Glad to see you brought back some venison," said Callum. "Something else to eat instead of turnip soup."

"Always looking out for the interests of our stomachs are

we, Callum?" Arran teased.

"Well, more likely his stomach will come first," Gabriel replied.

He and Arran laughed out loud as they placed a hand on the shoulders of Callum, who gave a little smirk acknowledging the joke.

"We should head back to the castle, but first you better change, you look like a no-good ruffian." Gabriel handed

Arran a weighty sack and pointed to a large tavern, The Red Arrow.

"Thanks, Gabe. Couldn't go hunting and get away with making a mess of my tunic now could I?"

A moment later he came out wearing a blue tunic identical to his colleagues, the colour of the Twin Blade Order.

"Let's go, can't keep the commander waiting," Arran spoke, as he held the reins of Basil and walked with Gabriel and Callum through the rest of the town.

In the distance as the trio walked, Arran could see towers that looked tall enough to touch the sky and beyond. This was Pwynt Afon Castle, erected centuries ago to watch over the Tor in the times when the kingdom of Gower was at odds with the Terradonian city states to the east.

This was where the rest of the company of men and women belonging to the order were stationed. T*ime to put down the spear for a sword,* Arran thought to himself.

Chapter 2

The Sun Tower, inside the Imperial Palace, Aberemrallt

THE LIGHT OF THE MORNING SUN radiated down into the circular room of the Sun Tower, named so because it was the first place in the Imperial Palace where one could see the sun rise. The rays brought out the shine of the marble floor. Standing between the light from the window and the room itself was a man. His tall and slender figure cast a shadow that stretched the length of the room.

This was Gedric Hermann, Chancellor to the Emperor of the Maldoran Empire. He stared out the window that reached up to the ceiling, and enjoyed the warmth that came with the sun's rays. It allowed him to clear his mind and think. He hardly ever had time to himself these days. He stroked his black hair that was beginning to grey in places. Managing this city, let alone an entire continent, was not an easy job. Especially not today. He had received word about the robbery last night. With preparations to be made for the Imperial Games, this was not welcome news.

A robbery was not unheard of, but what piqued Gedric's interest and anxiety was what had been stolen from the Academy. Something no one should have had any knowledge of. With the emperor visiting the nearby city of Kosantos, it was left to him to resolve the problem.

Do these people even know what they have taken? He continued to stare out of the window, looking beyond the eastern walls to the road that clung closely to the cliffs over the sea. Flocks of seagulls cried and circled over the cliffs before shifting out to the sea in search of food. A knock was heard, snapping Gedric out of this phase of tranquillity.

"Enter," the chancellor ordered. He turned away from the sun. On the other side of the room, one of the doors opened. A young man entered the room, carrying a tray with several cups and a flagon. Gedric watched as the boy carefully placed the tray at the far end of the table. The boy's name was Duran. He had only recently been picked by the chancellor to be his assistant.

"Are they here, Duran?"

Duran replied, "Yes, my lord. The other members of the council are here."

"Good. Let them in and then wait outside once everyone is seated," said Gedric.

Duran bowed his head slightly as he held one of the doors open. Gedric took his place at his side of the table. He could hear the click-clack of high heels tapping on the stairway. Up the steps came a woman donning a well-made green and silver dress. This was Lady Eleanor of the Elven House of Toreen, hailing from the kingdom of Alvaria. She was the head of the Elven embassy here in Aberemrallt. She was flawless. Her blonde hair coiled up into small, neat buns cushioned underneath her elven ears. Her eyes were like the sparkling blue of the River Tor, complementing her long face. What little of her peach-like skin she allowed to be exposed portrayed her as youthful, but Gedric knew that beneath it all, there was the wisdom of a very mature Elven woman.

"Lord Chancellor." Eleanor spoke calmly.

"Lady Eleanor, as punctual as ever, even in such an urgent meeting. Please," Gedric said, pointing to an empty seat to his right. She was accompanied by one of her servants, a slim young male elf with short and neatly trimmed brown hair wearing a dark green jacket. He sat next to his mistress at the table, pulling a quill and parchment out from a satchel bag that slung around one of his shoulders.

Next to enter the room was Therin Wibele, Captain of the City Guard, a middle-aged man with curly black hair and a small beard. He wore a brown tunic, though the shirt was creased and unbuttoned at the top. Pinned on his right breast was a golden badge shaped as a shield that indicated his position. There was history behind his family name, notably due to their reputation as defenders of Aldbruck Castle, built on the only passageway through the Ringspine Mountains between Terradonia and Hothland. And his family had guarded that pass for countless generations.

"Lord Chancellor, my lady" the man spoke as he placed a clenched right hand over his chest and made a light bow. "I'm sure we're not here to discuss my appearance."

"I'm afraid today won't be a good day for any humour if I can help it," Gedric replied.

"I'm sure there is a reason for it," Therin pulled out the chair to Gedric's left and sat immediately.

The sound of heavy boots on marble told Gedric who was coming next -- Kleif Stonebearer, Master of the Masonry and Smith Guild. He was a dwarf with brown hair tied back into a single ponytail, and a beard reaching down to his chest. As with most of his kind, he stood at around four feet, even though he was of similar age to Gedric.

"My lords and lady." Kleif gave a small bow to those already present at the table before taking his place. He looked somewhat displeased at the available refreshments present. "No wine or ale today, Chancellor?" he asked.

"Sorry, Kleif, this meeting is very important. I would appreciate it if you all could remain sober until we conclude."

To acknowledge the decision, Kleif simply shrugged as he always did and begrudgingly poured himself a cup of water. More footsteps came. This time it was Erlend Bray, the Mayor of Llancaphrig, a stocky man with a hat that covered most of his head. Around his neck was a thick golden chain with three gems dangling in front of his chest. Following closely behind him was the opposite: a well- built young man wearing shiny dark red leather. His face looked as if it were perfectly carved out of stone, with eyes the colour of amber and short blond hair. This was Fredric Valorn, prince and heir to the Imperial throne, this young man reminded Gedric of his youth. While the emperor was absent in his retreat, his son would take his place in the council meetings.

"Morning to you all lords and ladies," Mayor Bray called out as he strode toward his seat. "I honestly cannot recall the last time we had a meeting this early."

"Yes, and you'll soon find out why. Now please, take a seat Erland," Gedric responded, "and Prince Frederic."

"Lord Gedric," the prince replied calmly. The young man preferred to refer to the chancellor by his first name out of respect when his father wasn't present. He sat at the centre of the table, where he stretched his hands upward to the ceiling before flexing them.

There was one more person to attend. Through the doorway appeared a thin man with pale skin wearing a black hooded tunic. This was Valeran Serpentine, the Master of Coin. The man unfurled his hood, revealing a flat face with black yet greying hair, and icy eyes that showed little emotion. He bowed his head before the council as his way of showing respect, before walking slowly to his seat, tapping the floor with his snake-shaped cane with every step as he sat on the far-right end of the table. Out of all the members present, he was the least liked.

"Well then, my lords and lady, and my prince," Gedric said when everyone was settled. He took a short breath and cleared his throat before continuing.

"The reason I have called this meeting is simple. You may have already heard of the robbery that occurred at the

Academy last night and was discovered this morning. What I'm about to say, you will find disturbing, and I recommend it not be spoken outside of this meeting, lest we upset the citizens before the Imperial Games. Can we agree to this?"

Gedric looked at everyone on the table who looked at each other with a mix of interest and wariness before nodding slowly in agreement.

"Very well. It is believed that there were at least two people involved in this robbery. What they have taken, however, is the more troubling issue. What was stolen from the secret vault within the Academy was a box containing the key to the undoing of everything we and those who came before us have achieved." The chancellor took a pause to breathe before continuing, his eyes focused on everyone present. He knew what he was about to say wouldn't be easy to swallow, but he had no choice and so continued. "This box contains what many will know from legend as the Heart of Darkness."

The last few words that left the chancellor's lips caused looks of shock and outrage across the faces of the council members. All save for Valeran, who remained emotionless.

Chapter 3

Pwynt Afon Castle, Gower

ARRAN WAS WASHING HIS HANDS in a basin. A rack of weapons next to him, all neatly displayed in order of size and appearance. He picked up and fastened a round silver shield to one arm, then pulled a short sword with a blunt tip designed for sparring from the rack.

Gabriel would be his opponent in this spar. Arran watched him pull out his weapon of choice: a long sword to be gripped with both hands. Within the walls of the castle, activity was rife. Others were in their own private circles, exchanging strikes and blocks with swords made of wood or blunt steel. There were men and a few women testing their skills out at the range with bows and javelins. There was even a satyr among them, standing out amongst the two-footed soldiers with his hooved feet and curved horns. He was throwing spears at a much greater distance than everyone else, seemingly with much less effort as well.

Pwynt Afon Castle was only this active prior to the Imperial Games, when a gathering of the finest warriors and sportsmen from all over the continent was held in the capital of Aberemrallt every five years. In the past, Arran had participated as a young banner boy for the Order. If he met the requirements of his superiors this year, then he would prove himself worthy of fighting in the Games. He walked up to a sparring circle marked out by rope.

Gabriel did the same, meeting Arran's eyes whilst holding his longsword pointing outward. Arran adopted a similar stance, his weapon behind the shield.

"Okay, Gabriel, you first," Arran said confidently.

"You're going to wish you went," Gabriel replied as he stepped forward.

He went for a direct thrust. The steel tip made a blunt thund as it impacted on Arran's shield. He followed it up with a sweep, aiming for the legs, Arran saw this and jumped back a step. Gabriel then raised his sword over his head and went for a downward strike. Again,Arran brought up his shield. He angled it so that the longsword would slide off to the side. Taking advantage of Gabriel's error, Arran thrusted his short sword to his chest, stopping just inches from his foe's tunic. The first point went to Arran, he withdrew, giving Gabriel a chance to step back.

"You're making it too easy for him to block!"

Arran and Gabriel paused as a tall man, with short black hair and beard that were beginning to grey approached. He wore the same tunic as Arran and Gabriel but in a darker blue and leather gloves as he approached the circle. This was Alaric Dorwin, the captain in charge of the company of men for the Twin Blade Order present at Pwynt Afon Castle.

"You need to aim for where the man can't protect himself. Here, let me show you, Arran," he gestured as he drew his sword from a scabbard around his waist and took up a neutral stance in front of Arran.

The young warrior moved an inch closer to the captain, keeping his shield just under his chin. He watched the captain's stance and the movements he made.The two circled each other slowly. Arran made the first move, leading with his shield in an attempt to pin the captain down. But the captain anticipated the move and stepped to the side, unleashing a chain of slashes that forced Arran to parry with his short sword. Realising that his opponent's sword outreached his own, Arran tried to change his stance to bring his shield to bear but was swept up under his feet. The young warrior thudded onto the ground with arms out wide. Before he could rise again, the captain stood over him pointing his sword.

"You need a longer sword, Arran." Captain Dorwin withdrew his sword, sheathing it back into his scabbard before offering Arran a hand.

"The right sword can make a difference in a fight. Remember that."

"Yes, Captain," Arran replied.

The captain looked at Gabriel and said, "You see. Don't aim for the shield, alright?"

"Yes, Captain."

"I'll leave you to it."

"Yes, Captain," they both acknowledged. Arran and Gabriel watched as Captain Dorwin turned around and left them to it.

"Oi, what kind of an attack is that? Do you even know how to handle a spear?" The captain's gruff voice could be heard behind Arran and Gabriel, addressing another group of men.

"Don't mind him, he can spot a flaw a mile off," another voice spoke just as Arran and Gabriel were about to renew their session.

They turned to a female walking up to them, she wore the same colour tunic as they did, but she donned two leather pads on her shoulders. Her hair was short and dark brown with a fringe at the front. Arran noticed that at her hips were two swords tucked in their scabbards.

"He likes to see those under his command improve," the woman spoke again.

Gabriel seemed curious. "And how exactly do you know this?"

"Well, let's say it takes a lot to convince a father to let his daughter join the Twin Blade Order."

"That's interesting," Arran replied, amused by her revelation. "And I suppose you find what we do is more interesting than being the lady from some far-off castle then?"

"That's obvious." She grinned at Arran. "My name is Anwen. Anwen Dorwin."

"Arran Connaught, and this is Gabriel Stowark." Arran gestured to Gabriel who seemed perplexed for a moment about her relation to the captain.

"Okay, I get it now. I guess you're here to share something else that your father wouldn't tell us?"' Gabriel enquired.

"If you're really that clueless," Anwen replied.

"Well, come on then. You're either here to show off your fancy knives or you're here to make us look bad."

"You think you're so manly? Carrying a large sword you can't even use."

"Right, you asked for it." Gabriel drew his long sword from his scabbard.

Arran grinned as he enjoyed the trade of taunts. "You seem riled up, Gabriel. Shall I go first?"

"I'll be fine, Arran," Gabriel grunted under his breath. "I could take the both of you on," Anwen replied confidently as she drew out her weapons.

Each sword looked like a fork as there were two curved needle-like prongs protruding upward from the cross guards.

"Never seen swords like those before," said Arran.

Gabriel's eyes narrowed upon seeing them, "Forks? Really?

Arran took a step forward, presenting his shield. Though his weapon was short, he intended to make full use of it. Gabriel lifted his sword up and held it diagonally in front of him. Like before, he made this first move expecting to clash with a downward strike.

Anwen stepped back before twirling around him. She then kicked him in the leg, at the same time striking him in the back with a backhand. Gabriel was forced down to all fours. Arran moved in to challenge the woman, but she immediately spun around to attack him. He presented his shield, but it didn't stop Anwen at all. She unleashed a flurry of strikes that forced Arran back a few steps.

She's good, Arran thought, as he lowered his shield momentarily to deliver a swiping arc with his sword in order to create some space between himself and Anwen. He could see that Gabriel was on his feet again, raising his longsword over his head in a high guard stance. Anwen noticed this and changed her position. She was now between Arran and Gabriel, her swords pointing outward.

Again, Gabriel moved first, he swung his weapon in another downward strike. Anwen anticipated this. She was able to catch the blade within one of her side guards. Gabriel tried to pull his sword away, but it was stuck. Anwen pulled him closer so she could kick him in the gut. Gabriel grunted hard as Anwen drove her boot into his abdomen. She's definitely not messing around, Arran thought as he watched. At that moment, an idea came to Arran. After the kick, Anwen shoved Gabriel back, releasing the long sword from her grip before turning to Arran. He only moved a step closer, maintaining his stance. She came at him again. This time lunging forward with one of her swords. Arran stepped back with his front foot, sidestepping her completely.

At that point, he tilted his shield and jammed it between the blade and the guard. Anwen's sword was stuck. Surprised, she tried to free herself, but it was of no use. She struck out with her other sword. Arran had predicted this and countered with his own sword; he applied the same tactic. Now he had control over Anwen's arms. Using his superior strength, he knocked one of Anwen's swords free.

It was then the two were looking at each other, breathing heavily, the scent of metal and sweat engulfing them.

Arran was within body distance of Anwen, her eyes were an emerald green. She appeared calm despite her situation; strands of hair streaked across her pale face.

"You're good," she said.

"You're not half bad yourself," Arran complimented as he slowly pulled his shield away, releasing her sword from his trap. Arran went over to pick up Anwen's other weapon from the ground. It was surprisingly light and felt delicate to Arran. He could see why these fork-like swords were her weapons of choice as he twirled it around his fingers.

"Interesting choice of weapons," he complimented as he handed them back to her.

"Thanks, I made them myself," Anwen replied.

"Yeah, not bad for kitchen forks," Gabriel butted in.

Arran and Anwen just chuckled. At that point, there was a smile across her face as she looked at him, but her expression changed as she looked behind him.

Arran turned around as well to see Captain Dorwin near the keep.

"I think I'm needed elsewhere," said Anwen. "Shall we continue another time?" Arran asked.

"Look forward to it," Anwen grinned, she nodded to Gabriel before walking past Arran to the keep.

"Well, that was interesting," said Gabriel, but Arran's eyes were on Anwen.

"Aye. She sure will be nice to have around, though not the way you would like it," Arran smiled.

"Haha. Yeah, next time I won't go so easy. Anyway, I want another round, the loser provides the first pint."

"If you insist on getting me drunk at your expense then let's go," Arran agreed. The two spaced out and resumed their ritual of combat.

Chapter 4

Back at the Imperial Palace

"Preposterous, outrageous!" Mayor Bray jumped out of his seat upon hearing Gedric's words. "Of all the things these fools could've taken, they steal th…th ... that accursed thing! Do they even know what they have in their possession?"

"It should never have been kept there in the first place. A place of study, with an inadequate number of trained guards, is no place to keep such a dark artifact," Kleif agreed before picking up his cup. He stared at the water inside, Gedric could see he was wishing it was something stronger. The dwarf took a sip anyway.

Further down the table, Captain Therin leaned back in his seat, both hands covering his face as he sighed. Mayor Bray looked back and forth along the table nervously, hoping someone would say something to alleviate the tension a little.

"I agree as well," Lady Eleanor followed.

It was then that Prince Frederick broke in, leaning forward and sweeping his gaze across the council and their ashen faces. "Forgive me if my position as heir makes you think I know of this, but I have only heard stories. Is it true that the Heart of Darkness is the remains of—"

"The Dark Lord Samael? Yes, yes, it is," Gedric interrupted.

"It is the only part of his body that exists beyond the Underworld," said Kleif.

Lady Eleanor joined in. "By using the darkest of his powers, Samael made his heart almost indestructible, while the rest of his body withers away when defeated,

whether by fire, steel or magic."
"Aye, even when he is being destroyed by the Unbreakable Will," said Therin, "when wielded by a worthy hero, as Lord Orion did centuries ago."
Eleanor replied, "The downside of this trick is that by doing so, he traps his spiritual form within his heart, rendering him powerless, unless by some unfortunate miracle he is resurrected by another hand."
"This leaves us the question of who the thieves are and were they alone?" Prince Frederick asked. "I'm no magician but there's no way they can bring back Samael by themselves, this must be part of some coordinated act."
The room fell silent for the second time.
"If I'm not mistaken, this box requires a special key to open it, yes?" The council looked at Valeran in surprise when he spoke. The Master of Coin was tapping a finger on the table whilst sipping his cup. He rarely spoke unless asked directly, but when he did, his words often left a pessimistic taste on the lips of everyone.
Gedric looked at him with suspicion, even as everyone else turned their attention back to him, expecting a response.
"What he says is true. This chest cannot be opened by any ordinary keys. Following the defeat of the Dark One, the forgers who made the box saw fit to make a unique key specifically for it so as to prevent the heart from falling into the wrong hands. If such an attempt to acquire the box continuing the Heart of Darkness was ever made, the key would be seperate, in a location only a few individuals know about."
Wise strategy." Kleif commented whilst stroking his beard.
Gedric nodded, he looked back at Lord Valeran, the

Master of Coin remained emotionally blank as he leaned back in his seat.
"We should send a messenger to whoever has this key to be on alert," Prince Frederic suggested.
"No, I wouldn't go that far yet," Gedric intervened. "We don't want to cause trouble. For now, we must keep this problem within the walls of this city. I shall contact the Grandmaster of the Twin Blade Order and ask them to assist in the investigation."
"So, what exactly are we going to do about this problem?" Mayor Bray asked.
"It is imperative that we find the box before it leaves the city by land or sea. Lord Therin, you will instruct your men to inspect the harbour and every house they come upon whilst on duty, and leave no stone unturned. Not a single ship is to leave without your men present. Is this clear?" He looked at the commander with stern eyes.
"I can do that. I'm already signing up more volunteers for watch duty due to the Games," Therin replied, "I will also be paying the Academy a visit today and ask around."
"Good, I'll join you at some point today," said Gedric.
"This won't be easy," said Kleif. "We are talking about searching the entire capital, it could be anywhere. We still don't know who the thieves are. What traces have they left?"
"Only a few bodies," the chancellor spoke, "but with the Twin Blade Order's help we will uncover their identities."
"And what about the emperor?" said Lady Eleanor.
Prince Frederic responded, "I wouldn't be surprised if word reaches my father whilst on route. We're going to have a lot to explain."
"I'll explain to his Highness myself when he returns," Gedric replied. "Now, I believe we have spoken enough

on this matter, action is to be called upon. If anyone finds any unusual activity, report it to me immediately."

Everyone nodded in agreement.

"Then it's settled. I call an end to this meeting. Dismissed."

One by one, the members of the council left their seats and departed through the door. Gedric remained, however.

"Hold on, Lord Valeran," Gedric called out. "A moment if you please?" Valeran turned to face Gedric. The door closed behind, leaving just the chancellor and the Master of Coin in the room.

"Tell me, what do you know about the key and the Black Box?" he asked.

"Well, what I know is that every kingdom in Maldora had a part to play in the creation of the Black Box and its key. Men supplied the iron, and dwarves forged it. The elves and warlocks were involved in the enchantments to prevent it being opened by other means."

"Very few people know about the Black Box and the key that opens it. How do you, Valeran?"

"I collect old books here and there. Every now and then I come upon a text from a source about the origins of certain... events and relics which I find intriguing. It allows me to see things from both perspectives." Valeran locked eyes with Gedric, his expression betraying nothing. "Does this answer your question, Lord Chancellor?"

Gedric stared at him for a moment before deciding there wasn't anything else worth questioning Valeran about on the matter. "Very well, you may leave now," he spoke softly, turning his back to Valeran to pour himself a drink. "Oh, and while you're at it. I would like to have a report on the current taxes and the expenses for the

Imperial Games by the next meeting tomorrow, if you would please."

"As you wish, my lord," Valeran turned to the door and made his slow exit from the room, his cane tapping away on the floor as he walked.

Gedric watched as the door slammed shut behind him. A small thud echoed in the room, then it was quiet once more. He had once again been left to himself in the Sun Tower. He could do nothing else but wait for the next move to be made and pray for the worst to never happen.

Chapter 5

The Jolly Maid, Aberemrallt

GERALD WAS IN HIS ROOM standing by the window, embracing the warmth of the rising sun whilst staring out at the market square. which was flowing with activity.

People from all walks of life: humans, elves, dwarves and satyrs alike were walking between the market stalls and the docks. Merchants stood ready to sell their goods to the overflowing masses. Fresh fruit and vegetables, meat, wool, tools, jewellery, even herbs, vibrant coloured silks and spices from faraway lands. Everything Maldora and beyond had to offer could be found here. Almost everything.

Downstairs in The Jolly Maid, it was business as usual, the sounds of men and women talking, laughing, and dealing.

It was all strange to him when he first came here. He was born and raised in a small village in Western Gower, a quiet backwater place in comparison to the vastness that is Aberemrallt. On that first cold night arriving, this was where he stayed. He was welcomed here, given food and ale, and a room with a warm bed to rest before his first day at the Imperial Academy. Since then, life in the capital had become second nature to him.

But everything around him, the sounds, the smells, the flow of everyday life did nothing to ease his restless mind. He continued to look up and down the street until one stall caught his eye. An old man accompanied by a young boy, probably no older than ten, was giving out medicine to a young woman. The sight reminded Gerald of what he had hoped to achieve. All he wanted was to be a physician.

Things had gone well in the beginning, but he struggled to pay his debts, and that was when he decided to delve into making love potions: an art form deemed too dangerous and was thus banned by the authorities. He hoped that no one would know of this. It wasn't his fault, really. Just one shady customer who got carried away using the stuff and the next thing he knew he had been expelled. He tried his luck to find other work outside the tavern but to no avail. That was when he came upon a mysterious man who wanted something from the Academy and offered him an unusual job.

It was supposed to have been simple, just get in and grab whatever his employer wanted and get out without leaving a trace. It almost went to plan, until Brodus decided to use less than subtle means to rescue him. The sight of blood flowing onto the marble floor still tainted his thoughts. The only reason he was chosen for this endeavour was due to having witnessed some of the tutors and the High Master access the secret room underground. He shuddered at the things he had to do to acquire the keys so that his contact could arrange for a copy to be made. Then there was the box, that mysterious black box ornamented with skulls that he was told to keep until when his master would tell him what to do next.

Gerald turned away from the window and walked over to his bed. He sat down and sighed. A great burden had been placed upon him. That was when he started hearing it. A heartbeat. At first it was quiet, barely audible. He turned to the source, a small desk with nothing on top but a mirror and an empty wine bottle, and there was a chair in front of it. Gerald had hidden the black box in one of the drawers when he returned last night.

The heart beats were getting louder in his head, eventually drowning out the voices downstairs. He thought it was his imagination playing tricks on him, but he began to believe that the sounds were real. There was something wrong about the box. Something evil was inside. And it was alive. Something he never thought possible. Now he was hearing voices from the box, quiet at first but steadily growing louder, though he could not understand any of them. This couldn't be happening. Gerald scratched his head. His vision blurred as his mind fogged. Blinking rapidly, he used both physical force and his will to shake back the feeling of mindless seduction. Among the voices in his head, one of them was calling his name.

"Gerald?"

A familiar voice suddenly broke the spell. In an instant, the sadistic rhythmic beating and voices stopped. He looked at the doorway where Nianna, the landlord's daughter, stood. She was dressed neatly as a barmaid. Her red hair barely covered her shoulders, and a short fringe over her pale forehead. As Gerald's gaze fell upon her oval face and hazel eyes, his worries momentarily disappeared.

"Are you alright?" she asked.

Gerald shook his head. "Uh yeah, just feeling light-headed."

"Really?" Nianna placed a hand on her waist. "I think it's more than that. You look terrible. What exactly were you doing last night?"

"Some odd jobs, that's all." Gerald was struggling to hide his nerves.

Nianna walked into his room which made Gerald sit up. "Like what? You haven't been hired to kill anyone, have you?"

"Wha–wait. Stop, don't be silly." Gerald put his hand in front of Nianna. "You know I'm not a violent person."

"Well, what about that time at the Boar's Head?" Nianna queried. "I heard you knocked out the landlord's son."

"That was different," he protested. "He and some other drunken sod started that fight."

"Alright, calm yourself," said Nianna. "For someone who doesn't like fighting, you can be quite hot-headed."

Gerald sighed. He turned away from her and laid down on his bed. His arms spread out wide as he looked up at the ceiling.

"You know, Nia, I only wanted to make medicine for those in need of it when I came here. Do something that my family could be proud of."

"And you are, Gerald," Nianna replied. "When my father was sick, you knew what he needed. Do you remember?"

Gerald nodded. "Mm, I do. You were scared back then. Your father was stuck in bed constantly vomiting."

"Of course, I was silly. You helped him pull through. Not before he chucked his breakfast on you, though." She gave Gerald a nudge on his shoulder and then laid beside him on the bed.

"Oh, gods help me," Gerald sighed.

The two of them were chuckling away at the memory. The whole thing seemed to have resurrected a sense of optimism within Gerald; a feeling that life wasn't as bad as it seemed because he had such good friends like Nianna by his side. Overtime, he came to appreciate her presence above everyone one else. To him, she was the one person in this city who he could trust with his secrets. Most of them, anyway.

"I better go back downstairs," said Nianna as she rose from Gerald's bed.

"Wait, don't go," Gerald reached out for Nianna's arm. "Please, can you just stay a little longer? I just wish you and I could stay here and not worry about the world."

"Oh, Gerald," Nianna replied.

"I'm serious. gods will it, I would want nothing but to find a quiet place away from here and live out the rest of my life in peace with you."

"Now where's the fun in that kind of life?" Nianna looked at him. "You worry too much."

"I know," Gerald admitted. Nianna simply chuckled as he looked at her.

"I'll let you relax for a bit, and then you can come and help us out. Don't be too long though."

"Okay." Gerald nodded happily.

He watched as the girl walked through the door, then laid on the bed and sighed. Gerald turned his head to his desk, choosing to ignore the throbbing heartbeat from the box. He rose from his bed and started to walk toward the door. He was about to close the door behind him, when he felt a hard hand grasp him on the shoulder.

"Jeez! gods almighty!" Gerald gasped.

He was surprised when he turned around to find Brodus.

"Shhh!" Brodus placed a finger over his lips. Gerald could see, past the stocky man, that the window at the far end of the corridor was open. Gerald also noticed he was carrying a sack over the shoulder.

"What do you want?" Gerald asked.

"You know what I'm here for. My… our master wants the box now."

"What? Now?" Gerald was confused. "A bit soon to be moving that thing around don't you think?"

"Listen, boy," Brodus raised his voice a little, "There are more guards out on the streets looking for the bloody thing. They'll be knocking on this tavern soon. Just you wait. It'll be you who'll get hanged for treason, along with your pretty girlfriend. Not me."

"Alright, hang on, I'll go and get it now. Just leave her out of this."

Gerald looked back down the stairs and all round to be sure no one else was listening and went back into his room. He immediately pulled out the drawers until he found the black box. The emerald encrusted on the top had long ceased glowing when he brought it home and stowed it away. It was then, upon seeing it, that the heartbeats and the voices returned. He pressed his hands on his head and gritted his teeth. This was his only chance of getting rid of the damn thing. So, he stepped forward, grabbed the box, and rushed out of the room.

"Here, take it!" Gerald presented the black box to Brodus.

"About time," he replied. "My master has something for you." Brodus pulled the sack from over his shoulder. He put the black box inside and pulled out a small bag.

"For your troubles, he says." Brodus presented the bag to him. "Oh, and one last thing. No one knows about this, you hear? Not even your girlfriend."

"I can safely say this is one job I hope never to share with anyone," Gerald replied.

"We'll see about that," snorted Brodus.

Gerald watched as his temporary partner turned his back and went toward the window and made his exit. As soon as he was gone, Gerald took a deep breath. He was finally free of the noise. No heartbeat other than his own, no voices other than those below in the tavern. He could relax. Hopefully no one would ever know of the part he played. Whatever was inside that box, it would be someone else's problem now.

He went back into his room, threw the bag he acquired onto his bed, and closed the door. Gerald could now return to his normal life. Maybe the box will simply be hidden somewhere else. Under a mountain or thrown into the sea. Who knows?

Chapter 6

The Imperial Academy, Aberemrallt

GEDRIC WALKED DOWN THE CENTRE of the Academy's meeting hall. Aligned at both sides were tables with benches on opposite ends. This pattern would stop before the podium at the other end of the hall. Above that was a large glass window, the shaping of each piece of glass and the colour selected portrayed a man that watched over the hall like a shepherd would over a flock. He was Orion the Saviour, God of the Wind; he who preached reason, truth and knowledge.

The Chancellor continued down the hall until he stopped before the podium, then he turned right. Before him was a pair of double doors guarded by two soldiers. Therin had been true to his word indeed, for there were more guards stationed in the Academy than before. The soldiers straightened up as Gedric approached. They bowed and opened the doors for him. He entered what was the Academy's infirmary. It was a small room. In front of him, there was a desk with a display of utensils. Some were hung up on the wall while the rest were spread out along the wooden surface of the desk. There were several beds positioned along the walls of the infirmary. Two of them were situated to the right by the door that led to the kitchen, each occupied.

Therin was standing between them, he was accompanied by two other people. One of them looked like the local apothecary, the other was a young man wearing a dark blue hood. They turned to Gedric as he approached them.

"Lord Chancellor," Therin addressed him.
"What progress have you made, Captain?" Gedric asked.
"Not much," Therin admitted. "As mentioned before, nothing aside from the Black Box was taken. The only clues we've got are right here." Therin pointed to the bodies. They were soldiers, unfortunate men whose fates met an unjust end at the hands of those who defiled this place.
Gedric turned to the man in the blue hood. "I believe you're the one the Order sent at my request?"
"I am, my Lord," he replied. "My name is Eafen Ulrin. Apprentice mage, at your service."
"Yes, introductions aside," Therin butted in, "you can now tell us what's so special about you."
Eafen looked at the captain and then at the chancellor with a look that conveyed secrecy.
Gedric turned to the apothecary. "Could you please give us a moment, Apothecary?"
"Yes, of course, my lords." The apothecary bowed and vacated the infirmary.
"Thank you, my lord," said Eafen. "As for what makes me special, I have what many of the elders in my order call Foresight. The ability to focus on an area, object, or person and see events revolving around them. Take this room, for example. I could tell you who has visited this room recently and how frequent they have done so."
"So, let me get this straight," Therin interrupted. "You could tell us what these men saw last night, even though they're dead?"
"Yes, it can be done," Eafen replied. "I can search the recent memories of the living and the dead alike. The problem with the latter, however, is that their final moments can be a bit clouded. More so the longer I delay my search."

"If you'd told me this earlier, I would've let you get on with it instead of wasting time talking," said Therin.

"I gave the instruction not to use this power without me bearing witness," Gedric intervened. "Proceed Eafen." He gestured to the bodies.

"As you wish, my lords."

Eafen turned his attention to the bodies. The mage stood between the two corpses, then he placed a hand on each of them. He took in a deep breath before tensing himself. Gedric and Therin watched as Eafen went to work. At first, nothing happened, but after a single blink, Eafen's eyes turned from hazel to icy white. The whole thing made Therin look uncomfortable as he took a step back, but Gedric stood his ground and watched on with fascination. His rank afforded him the privilege to watch mages from the Twin Blade and the various magics they performed. Some wielded fire or changed the direction of the wind, and others could heal all but the most grievous of wounds, but Eafen's ability was new to the chancellor. He found it frightening and yet intriguing.

A moment passed, and Eafen's eyes changed back, his hands pulled away from the bodies. He shook his head as he readapted his vision to his surroundings.

"Are you alright?" Gedric asked.

"I'm fine," Eafen replied. "I tend to forget how disorientating my vision can get after doing this."

"Take a seat before you lose your balance," said Gedric. "Therin, bring us some water please."

The captain went over to one of the desks whilst Gedric pointed to a seat. Eafen sat immediately.

"Here, have a drink." Therin handed Eafen a cup of water, the mage nodded before slowly drinking it.

"Can you tell us what you saw, Eafen?" Gedric asked.

"Yes. The guards were apprehending one of the intruders.

They were about to take him to the barracks when they were attacked by the other intruder."
"What do they look like?" Gedric asked.
"The first had scruffy brown hair, very slim figure. The one that attacked them was bald and shorter, but certainly knew how to kill."
"Did they recognise either of them?" Therin asked, referring to the guard's memories.
"The only name that was mentioned..." Eafen took a moment to recall what he saw. "Gerald… The name of the man carrying the box. One of the guards recognised him as Gerald. The other one could recall nothing about him."
"That name rings a bell," said Therin. "Caught someone who was using illegal love potions. Said he was the one who made them."
"We'll need to speak to the headmaster about this Gerald person. He's our best bet," said Gedric. "Thank you for your assistance, Eafen."
"Happy to be of use, my lord," Eafen smiled.
"I can trust you to keep this knowledge between us and your masters, right?'
"I will, my lord," Eafen nodded.
"Good, take your time and return to the Order. We'll take care of the rest." Gedric patted Eafen on the shoulder.
He and Therin left the infirmary. The apothecary was standing outside the door, waiting.
"You may return to your work," said Gedric. "Examine the bodies and deliver them to the barracks for burial."
The apothecary nodded and went back inside. "What do we do now, my lord?" Therin asked.
"I will go and speak with the headmaster, he should have records on him of every person who has studied here, past and present." At that point, Gedric saw the figure of

Duran running down the centre of the hall towards them.
"Lord Chancellor, Captain Therin," he started, but had to pause to catch his breath before continuing.
"What is it, Duran?" Gedric asked.
"I've received a letter from Kosantos, my lords. It's from the emperor. He… he'll be returning home tomorrow."
He pulled out a parchment from his surcoat and handed it to Gedric. He unfolded the already opened piece of paper and read it.
"That's wonderful," Gedric replied with sarcasm.

Chapter 7

The Mess Room, Pwynt Afon Castle

IT HAD BEEN A LONG DAY of training in the barracks. Arran walked confidently into the main hall, where everyone gathered at the request of Captain Alric Dorwin. The hall roof and its supporting pillars were made of fine wood sourced from the Andlan forest and other woodlands. Their shapes gave Arran the impression of being within the ribcage of a very large beast, like a whale. There were three columns of long tables that stretched from the doorway. Arran came from the other side, where another table half the size was positioned sideways. Here Captain Alric and the other high-ranking officers sat, feasting, drinking and talking.

From the middle of the north wall going to the corner of the hall near the lavatory was a wooden boardwalk with stairs ascending to the floor above where the solar and private chambers existed. The small, arched windows above the boardwalk allowed the light of the afternoon sun to beam rays into the hall, which was now bursting with conversations. Wild jokes were being told in one corner, while boasts of glory about the coming Imperial Games were made in another. He saw Anwen, the girl he sparred with today, sitting at a table with other female fighters present. She still wore her tunic but now without her shoulder pads. Gabriel and Callum were seated on the next table. The latter appeared to be engrossed in a large book, oblivious to the surrounding banter. Arran walked over to the last table and sat between them.

"What are you reading there, Callum?" he asked, but Callum didn't hear him, so he gave him a nudge on the shoulder.
"Huh? Oh, sorry Arran." Callum jumped in his seat. "Didn't realise you were there."
"He's been reading that book most of the day in between chores," said Gabriel who was polishing a badge with a piece of cloth. "Something about long-gone battles."
Callum closed the book and presented the cover to them. "The Greatest Battles of Maldora. Written by Roff Kisland."
"Never heard of him," Gabriel replied
Callum explained, "He was a renowned scholar, commissioned to write this book by Emperor Clovis I. Every battle from the Terradonian Wars, all the way to the Age of Strife, even the battles involving our Order."
"I've read that book," said Arran.
"My favourite battle has to be the First Battle for Soulman's Gate," Callum admitted with a grin. "What would be yours then, Arran?"
Arran paused before answering. He decided to test his friend's knowledge. "There are two that come to my mind, one of them doesn't involve our Order."
"The Battle of the Twin Forests?" Callum responded
"Which one exactly?" Gabriel asked.
"I thought you didn't care about history?" Callum enquired.
"I don't, but I do believe there were a few battles fought along the road between those woodlands."
"Nope, it didn't involve any woodland." Arran watched as Callum pushed back in his chair in thought.
"The Battle of Llyn Coch?" was Callum's next answer, but Arran shook his head.
Gabriel sighed. "I don't know why I bother with this? It's

not like we've had a war recently."

"There hasn't been a war for the last eighty years," said a fellow sergeant who sat next to Gabriel. This was Rhodri; he had short ginger hair and was slightly taller than either Arran or Gabriel.

"There, you see," Gabriel agreed.

"Ooh, the Battle of Old Argantis," Callum replied. "And to answer your question, Gabriel, yes there hasn't been a conflict recently, but that doesn't mean we shouldn't look back on the past and learn from it."

Arran simply smiled and nodded at Callum, who clenched his fist upon getting the right answer.

Gabriel looked at them with amusement. "Didn't know you had an interest in sailing, Arran?"

"No, I don't," Arran replied, "but the whole thing was well devised. Lure out the Northmen's fleet to where they couldn't manoeuvre easily and set them on fire. The ruins of Old Argantis are a tricky place for ships to sail through, let alone fight."

"And you think reading this book would provide all the answers for the next great war?" Gabriel asked. "Every battle is different, just like every woman and bottle of wine."

Callum shrugged, having nothing else to say.

At that point, a small bell was rung, the clanging sound eventually breaking up the banter until everyone was silent. Arran saw Anwen in the corner of his eye, her legs were crossed only by the ankles so as not to attract attention and she was brushing her fringe of hair back with one hand. She appeared to have noticed him, but her eyes seemed focused forward. Captain Alric was seated in the centre of the table, flanked by two other men in similar colour tunics to his own. When he rose, so did they.

"Right, enough chatter. It is time. Sir Gilbran, Sir Irfon

and myself have decided, based on what we have seen today, who will partake in the Imperial Games. Although we can only send forward a handful for each event, that doesn't mean there won't be anything for the rest of you to do. Most of you will be assisting the Capital's City Guard with additional security." He stopped to drink from his cup and clear his throat before continuing. "I hope that you will all act and behave in a professional manner as is expected by everyone. Now, Lord Gilbran, would you please read out the names?" He turned to the man on his left. He was completely bald but had a white beard reaching down to his chest.

"Thank you, Captain," he coughed before he began. "Let us begin with the archery events. First we have—" he stopped to pull out a scroll from one of his pockets

"They always start with the damn archery every time," Gabriel muttered to Arran.

Arran looked at him and replied, "Patience is a virtue, like they always say."

"Ygrin Crea," Lord Gildran called out. Arran looked over to Anwen's table. He saw one of Anwen's friends stand up and receive applause. A blonde girl with her hair tied back into two long ponytails, she sat next to Anwen who patted her on the shoulder. Half an hour went by, names were called out for various events.

"And now we finally come down to the free melee combat event. As our first ever female to participate in this event, Anwen Dorwin."

Arran looked over to Anwen. All her friends at the same table started patting her on the shoulders. Arran then saw a smile on the face of the captain. Clearly, it brought him joy to see his daughter succeed.

"Now, for the men's group," Gilbran coughed awkwardly before he spoke again. "Rhodri and Jon Morman." The man that Gabriel knew who spoke earlier showed a closed fist and shook the hand of his brother Jon who was sitting next to him.

"Gabriel Stowark," was the next name called from Gilbran's list. Gabriel rose up with a raised fist so that everyone could see him. Arran knew he was an attention seeker.

"Arran Connaught," Lord Gilbran called. *Finally!* Arran thought as he stood up so everyone could see him. He nodded in acknowledgment to the captain and the other two men, and then looked at Anwen who, with a smile on her face, gave him cause to smile back.

"Well, congratulations to the both of you!" Callum offered a hand to both of his friends

"I think a drink is in order here," Gabriel spoke

"Careful now, we've only just been accepted. No more than a pint," Arran warned, shaking their hands.

Even with all the cheers and clapping, he couldn't help but take an occasional look at Anwen. She was engaged with her friend Ygrin. Seeing her in action would be enjoyable, if not with him. Then came the voice of Captain Alric that made everyone cease their chatter for a moment.

"Right! Before we even think about celebrating, we will be leaving for the capital tomorrow morning. So, pack what you need and get some sleep. Anyone who's not ready will be left behind, no exceptions."

"I think we better make a start," said Callum.

"I'll have to tell my mother and father the news," said Arran.

"Can we come?" Gabriel asked.

"Sure, why not?" was Arran's reply. "They like having guests around."

"I'll go sort my things out and join you two by the north gate," said Callum before he climbed out of his seat and rushed for the doors.

"Take your time, Callum," Arran called.

"Where do they live?" Gabriel asked.
"Just outside of Everdale. You're going to like the place," said Arran.

Chapter 8

Falcon Street, Aberemrallt

AS THE SUN DESCENDED FROM THE SKY, Valeran Serpentine walked through the streets wearing a cloak to cover his head and shoulders, blending into the shadows. As the Master of Coin, keeping a low head was the best way to go about your business unimpeded. Following the meeting with the council, and then day of counting and collecting the taxes from commoners, merchants and the rest, he was glad to be heading back to his home. What he hadn't counted on was the chancellor questioning him. This troubled him but he pressed on regardless.

Along the streets, he could hear the voices of the common people, a cacophony of conversations as they went about their everyday lives. Most were concerned with the Imperial Games, a few were talking about the robbery at the academy. Every now and then, Valeran would look over his shoulder, just in case that dog Gedric sent someone to trail him, but there was nothing out of the ordinary. He finally arrived at his place of solace, an old, attached house at the end of a long street. There was nothing special about it on the outside, for its shady appearance made it unattractive to the other houses and it seemed that there was nothing to see through the windows due to the closed wooden panels from the inside. Most lords and masters who had the privilege of having a career in the capital aimed to secure accommodation worthy of their titles, but Valeran found this place met his needs.

The Master of Coin walked up to the front of the house, to a door that had seen better days as the wood was dark and unclean in the corners. He unlocked the door and entered the house before closing it behind him. The inside was only slightly more appealing than the outside: one single spacious room with a pillar in the centre to support the floor above it. To the left of the pillar was a plain oval-shaped table with two wooden chairs, wick, a couple of candles and a stool. The room was dim to the point where one couldn't see much until Valeran walked over to the windows to unlock the wooden panels. At that moment, the room was filled with a beam of light, exposing the trails of dust languidly dancing through the air before settling and accumulating in some places, so strong was the sun's glare that Valeran had to cover his eyes. Once adjusted, the old man took the wick from the table and lit the candles one by one, knowing the sunlight would soon give way to darkness. He turned away from the window and then looked down at a large green carpet decorated with a coiled snake. His most prized possession, the symbol of a formerly prestigious house that once ruled much of the province of Terradonia before the Empire came to be. The fates, however, had not been kind to House Serpentine, and their influence and power dwindled over time. The only thing that kept the name in existence was Valeran's position in the council.

Empires and dynasties may rise and fall, but that didn't mean their legacies were gone forever or were so easy to extinguish; this he greatly believed. He walked past the carpet to another table where two cups and a barrel of wine called to him. He took one cup and started filling it. When almost full, he stopped and started stirring the contents with one of his slender fingers before taking his first long sip. It was then he heard a hard knock on the door. Valeran put his cup down on the table and moved to the door. There was a peephole that allowed him to see who was on the other side. His eyes were focused on a large man hidden under a filthy hood. Brodus.

"Were you followed?" Valeran asked. "Wouldn't be here, would I?" Brodus replied.

"Very well," Valeran closed the peephole and unlocked the door. Brodus walked through into his home. His arms were crossed just below his chest; clearly, he was carrying something.

"You have what I want?" he asked. Brodus nodded.

"Good. Have a seat, you must be thirsty," Valeran gestured to an empty chair while he prepared another cup. They sat around the oval table, and from under his cloak Brodus pulled out the Black Box. Valeran was immediately drawn to the thing with its silver skulls and markings. This was what he was looking for.

"Ah, beautiful," Valeran murmured in awe as he put his hands around the object. "Just as the texts described. So, I take it the boy wasn't much of a problem, was he?" he looked at Brodus, who was gulping down his cup of wine and tapped it on the table when he finished.

"That Gerald was hesitant at first," Brodus replied,"but he eventually gave it to me. Little shit looked like he had seen a ghost."

"I see." Valeran took another sip of wine.

"So, his part of the job is done then. Which leaves…" Brodus gestured by rubbing together his fingers.

"Ah yes, I haven't forgotten." Valeran reached out from under the table and pulled out a small brown bag of coins and handed it over to Brodus. He watched as his pawn squeezed and gripped the bag in his hand.

"So, now what happens?" Brodus asked.

"This is the first step of many, my friend," Valeran replied. "I must now acquire the means to open our little box."

"Well, it can't be that hard to open that thing, just find the key that will open it," said Brodus.

"Ah, but this is no ordinary box, my friend," Valeran explained. "It requires a key that was forged and imbued with the same powers used to imprison all the contents trapped within it."

"And where exactly is it?" Brodus enquired.

"No need to worry about that," said Valeran. "All you need to worry about is keeping low and awaiting my further instructions."

"So long as you're paying me," Brodus replied.

Valeran focused his eyes on him. Perhaps his most reliable pawn was getting a little too greedy. He let the comment slide and continued.

"I believe we can call it a day with our arrangements. You may leave now."

Brodus tucked his bag of coins under his cloak and walked over to the door. Valeran watched him coldly.

"Oh, and one more thing, Brodus," he called to him.

"Yes?" Brodus asked.

"Keep an eye on our friend for me. Should the authorities realise his involvement or if he starts talking to the wrong people, you can do what you like with him. As long as he remains… quiet if you know what I mean?"

"Looking forward to shutting him up, my lord." And with that, Brodus opened the door and closed it behind him.

As the door slammed shut behind his servant, Valeran was once again to himself. He looked at the Black Box, his prize.

"Ah yes, time to put the next phase of our plan into motion." Valeran said as he picked the box up from the table, then turned around to the carpet behind him.

Without hesitation, he raised an open hand in front of him and with it the fabric was elevated from the floor as if pushed upward by a force from underneath. With his hand, he guided the carpet and lowered it down next the table with the wine barrel. Doing so revealed a small trap door made of dark wood with several black locks. Valeran muttered a small command, and one by one the locks were undone and the trap door opened itself up. Every action seemed to make the Black Box feel more alive somehow. Valeran could hear the heavy thudding sound of a heart beat other than his own, followed by strange voices. Of all of these, one was calling out to him.

"Only a matter of time, my master," Valeran whispered to the box, smoothing its surface like it was a pet in his arms.

He walked down the column of steps that awaited, descending into the lower floor of the house. As he did so, Valeran commanded the trapdoor to close itself behind him.

An hour later, at the Imperial Harbour

Gerald walked along the harbour as calm as one could try to be in his situation. Several ships were tied up at the piers. Some were so vast in size that they looked like they transported an entire army to wherever they needed sailing. Others were no bigger than the taverns like the Jolly Maid. Done were the merchants selling their goods and the sailors who had travelled far and wide to dock in this city. Now was the time for such people to flock along with everyone else toward the taverns and inns. Gulls squawk and cry above him; some circled around the docks in search of food. Gerald paid no heed to anything but to the route he was taking, slung over a simple grey tunic was a brown leather bag with the little sack of gold from Brodus safely inside. He also wore a straw hat, a spare that his father lent him upon departing for Aberemrallt to keep his head cool during the warm summers.

It was wide enough to cover his head and, therefore, his gingery hair, to make it harder for people to tell from a distance.

Although the deed was done and he received his payment, he felt he wasn't out of the re just yet. The words of Brodus this morning plagued his mind *"There are more guards out on the streets looking for the bloody thing. They'll be knocking on this tavern soon. Just you wait. It'll be you who'll get hanged for treason, along with your pretty girlfriend. Not me."* For all his rude and not-so-appealing appearance, he was right; the city council would not turn a blind eye to the robbery at the academy, even with the Imperial Games soon to be taking place in Aberemrallt. No one yet had reported or stopped him for questioning, and the city guards have only begun to double in patrols. It was only a matter of time before he would be stopped and questioned. He needed a solution to help him lay low and immediately. He turned away from the harbour and walked up to Red Kite Street. Every house to his left was made with reddish tiles for roofing that resembled the colours of the distinct bird of prey, whereas the houses on the other side in Goshawk Street were a mixture of black and dark brown. Most of these houses and their walls were either plastered white or were cobbled stones. After passing the first row of six houses, Gerald found who he was looking for. A man wearing a brown sleeveless tunic stretching down to the knees, was leaning on the wall of the next row of houses, ipping a coin in one hand.

"Delwyn", Gerald spoke.

"Ah, Gerald. How are you?" the man stopped flipping his coin to look up at him.

"Uh, well, you know. Same old stuff here and there."

"Except you wouldn't have come here to ask a favour from me."

Gerald took a step closer to him, "Shh. Keep it down."

"Why? Oh, I see, so you've gotten yourself in some trouble

then?"
Gerald sighed, "Yes, I have. I may have done something that might get the attention of the city guard. So, I was wondering if you have something that might help me keep low for a while."
"Most people tend to pack their things and get out while they can before anyone notices."
"Yeah, and leave Nianna and her father scratching their heads, wondering where I've gone to? A clear indication that I've done something wrong."
"Alright, genius, calm down. So, leaving the city is not an option. I know someone who can help us out. I hope you don't mind changing your appearance a bit?"
"I don't have much of choice, do I?"
"It will cost you a bit."
"You got us into trouble at the Boar's Head last time. So, this is you repaying me."
"Not letting that one go, are you?"
Gerald shook his head, "not yet."
Delwyn sighed lightly, "Fine. Come on then, follow me."
"Where are we going?"
"To the Dwarves Quarter, near Merchant's Gate."
"Alright, but no trouble."
"Who me? When have I got us into trouble?"
Gerald rolled his eyes, "You are either a magnificent liar or have a terrible memory."
"Hey, you're the one bringing it up, and you're the one who punched the landlord's son."
"Because you started that fight."
"Always living in the past, my friend, whilst I'm moving on to the next thing," said Delwyn; at that point, he stopped flipping the coin and stowed it in one of his pockets before pushing himself off the wall. "Come on".
Gerald sighed, "Whatever you say, Delwyn."
"Oh, how is Nianna, by the way?" he asked.

"She's alright, thanks."
"Did she suggest coming to me, or was this your idea?"
"Mine. I said it was a surprise for her. That's it."
"You sure she won't think this as a bit odd?"
"Well, yes. Nianna's not stupid, but I would rather not involve her. You know how she reacts when we get into trouble."
"Oh, I'm familiar," Delwyn then puts one hand by the waist and waves a finger from the other hand as he pretends to sound like Nianna, "'You boys really shouldn't be getting yourselves in trouble, you know.'"
Gerald shook his head and thought, *you never change, Delwyn.*

They walked through the gap of houses into Goshawk Street, heading north before turning left, navigating a small alley between two blocks of houses and entering the Dwarves quarter. Many of the homes the pair weaved through sported dark grey and finely cut stone walls with black slate tiles for roofing in contrast to the buildings of Red Kite and Goshawk Street. Chimneys belched out smoke continuously, an indication of dwarf carpenters and metal workers still hard at work even at this hour on their chosen craft.

Gerald and Delwyn eventually reach a small square on the other side of the Dwarves Quarter. At this square, Gerald saw a house with an extended area jutting out, resembling that of the letter L. Like most houses in this city, it was built with two floors. The walls on the outside were painted a pure and clean white, while the roof was made of clay tiles that seemed to resemble sea shells with their curved edges overlapping each other. Above the front door was a large sign painted in green, with the following in black writing, Guilloux's Barbers and Incenses. Past it was a large inn with stables, and behind that were the bastions of Merchants Gate, casting shadows over this side of the city. Gerald watched as Delwyn approached the door of the barber house, who looked over his shoulder and gestured for him to come closer; then, he rang a bell attached to the door. It opened and out came a person. Delwyn's figure obstructed Gerald's view of the person in the doorway.

"Good evening, Delwyn", a female voice answered.

"Lara, good to see you. Is your husband busy?"

"Just finished with a customer."

"I hope he has room for one more. My friend here needs a bit of a makeover, you see."

Delwyn sidestepped, allowing Gerald to see a tall lady in a long green dress leaning in the doorway, whose blonde hair was tied back in a long-braided knot behind her.

"Gerald, meet Lara," Delwyn said as he used his hands to convey the introduction of names.

"Hello there,"

"Uh, hello," Gerald replied, almost too nervous about getting the words out of his mouth.

"You must be Delwyn's friend from the Jolly Maid?"

"I am," Gerald replied.

"Let me tell my husband," Said Lara before retreating back into the house.

Delwyn stepped back and whistled whilst they waited. Gerald couldn't help but feel anxious. It was only last night that he broke into the Imperial Academy, stole a mysterious artefact, and was threatened by the thug who helped him get it. And here he was in plain sight, counting on whatever mad plan Delwyn had in mind to help him lay low. He could have packed his things and left Aberemrallt before the guards realised it. But that would be proof that he was involved in the robbery. Nianna and her father would suspect something was wrong, no matter what he told them. Gerald said to her before leaving the Jolly Maid that he had arranged for a surprise and needed to go out for an hour to get it.

Although the guards that knew who he was were no

longer alive, no thanks to Brodus and his brutal means of disposing of people, there was still no guarantee that the authorities wouldn't suspect him of being involved. As far as Gerald believed, all it took was one person observing him during the escape from the academy, and the authorities would have an idea of who they were looking for. He surveyed the surrounding area. No guards were searching this part of the city. Yet. He pulled his hat slightly more to the front of his head to make his face less visible to everyone else.

At that point, Lara opened the door wide open before them. "Come on in." She said as she stepped back and let Delwyn in. Gerald took a deep breath before following. *Here goes nothing*, he thought as he entered the house.

Upon entering the house, the main room was long and relatively wide. As he followed Lara and Delwyn, Gerald's nose picked up a sweet and delightful aroma. The closest he could compare it to was elderflowers mixed with some fruit, possibly pears, along with some honey. Tracing the scent, he saw a square table in a corner with a collection of incense candles arranged in a small circle and all lit. Next to this was a spiral staircase to the first floor next to this, and its rail was made of dark oak. Another table, oval-shaped, was positioned further into the room with four chairs around it. Opposite this were two small workstations, each with a wooden chair and mirror. A girl with brown hair wearing a blue tunic was by the first workstation left unoccupied, sweeping away strands of blonde hair on the wooden floor with a broom. At the second station was a man snipping away at a customer's beard before putting the scissors down.

"This is our daughter, Clarissa," Lara introduced the girl.

"Hello," Delwyn said as he waved a hand at Lara.

The girl simply waved a hand back at him and Gerald.

At the next workstation, Lara's husband was snipping away with the scissors at the beard of his current customer, a dwarf. Satisfied, he put down the scissors on the workstation, then removed the apron from his customer. The dwarf leaned forward into the mirror to inspect his yellow beard before giving his approval with a thumb up. Gerald watched as Lara's husband escorted the dwarf to a door on the other side of the room, chatting and joking away as he opened it for his customer to exit.

The barber closes the door after saying goodbye then turned around to face his new customers. He had a gangly figure, wearing a black apron that stretched down to the tips of his brown boots, covering what was likely to be a simple shirt underneath. The barber sported a mane of long black hair that was tied at the back of his head, and also had a thin, well-trimmed moustache.

"And what business have you with me this time of day, Mister Yale."

"Joran Guilloux," Delwyn spoke, "I hope you still have time for one more appointment."

Joran put a hand on his hip as he replied, "I prefer my appointments to be requested in advance."

"I know, I know. This won't take long. See, this is my friend Gerald Giles and he's in need of a change in his hairstyle. He would like to add a darker complexion."

What? Gerald thought as Delwyn nudged him on the shoulder. "Uh, yes, I need to change the colour of my hair as soon as possible."

Joran took a look at him, stroking his moustache, "Can it not wait until tomorrow at least? I have a few slots in the afternoon."

"Unfortunately, he can't wait," Delwyn jumped in, "It's a little surprise for his girlfriend, you see."

"Yes, for my girlfriend," Gerald replied, choosing to just go with whatever Delwyn said rather than further complicate things.

Joran took a step toward Gerald to take a look at him.

"Hmm, I've never done a man with ginger hair before. It can be done, though."
"Really?" Gerald asked.
"A challenge I shall happily undertake, for the right price, of course."
"Well, Gerald?" Delwyn looked at him.
"Alright, I intend to pay." Gerald reaches into his bag, pulls out the purse, and hands it over to Joran, who weighs up the amount of coins inside.
"You've been a very busy man then?" Joran asked.
"Yes, I have been hard working toward this," Gerald lied.
"Very well. What colour would you like?"
"I would like to go with brown, please," Gerald replied.
"To change all of your hair entirely, or just to apply streaks?" Joran asked as he opened the purse to look at the coins inside.
"All of it, please," Gerald replied.
"Very well," said Joran as he held up the purse and handed it over to Lara.
"Could you pass me the brown dye bucket, dear?"
Lara nodded and went to a cupboard in one corner of the house. Still holding Gerald's purse in one hand, she opens the door with the other hand and pulls out a small bucket of dye. She walked over to Joran and placed the bucket on the barber's chair.
"Thank you, my dear. Why don't you and Clarissa go to the Jolly Maid? I heard your brother Steffan will be barding and sharing stories between there and the Market Square tonight."
"Indeed, he is," Said Lara.
"We're going to see Uncle Steff?" Clarissa asked.
"Yes, we are. Let's go tidy ourselves up first, then."
Joran then turned to Gerald and gestured to the chair, "have a seat, friend."
Gerald walked over to the chair and made himself

comfortable. Joran then wrapped a large blanket around Gerald's body from the shoulders down. Delwyn made himself comfortable by sitting in a spare chair next to Gerald. He then pulled out the same coin he had from before and started tossing it in the air in front of him. Joran, meanwhile, opened a draw in front of Gerald and pulled out a small white comb.

"Could you lean your head back, please?" Joran asked.

"Sure," Gerald complied and leaned back in his chair.

"Ah, good, just relax, Gerald. This won't take long," said Joran, as he began to run the comb through Gerald's hair, separating it into two parts evenly.

He then placed the comb down and put on a pair of leather gloves from the top of the drawer before putting the bucket of brown dye onto a stool. Joran took a handful of the dye in one hand and then applied it to his customer's head. Gerald could feel the texture of Joran's gloved fingers threading into his hair.

"So, you work with Nianna and her father at the Jolly Maid then, Gerald?" Joran asked.

"Yes, I do." Gerald replied.

"How long for?"

"A couple of years now."

"He used to be a student at the Imperial Academy," Delwyn added.

Gerald rolled his eyes. *I wish you wouldn't steal my thunder, Delwyn.* He thought.

"Really?" Joran asked, "Studying what?"

"Medicine, I was planning to become a doctor."

"Was?"

"Unfortunately, my lecturers and I had a falling out. Resulting in my sudden expulsion."

"A pity," Joran replied.

"Ah well, at least you have a job," Delwyn replied.

"Yeah, I know."

"You can always try to reapply again."
"I don't know about that," Joran interjected, "It must have cost a bit to apply the first time."
"I did some favours back home, in Bryn Gwydd", Gerald confessed, "Was an apprentice to the town physician, who recommended me to the Imperial Academy. Even paid for my entry fee."
"Do you think he will be willing to help you get back in?"
"The last I heard, he passed away a few years ago," Gerald sighed.
"I'm sorry to hear about that," Joran replied.
"And there you go," Joran said as he pulled off the gloves and moved the blanket away. Gerald rose from his chair and took a look at the mirror. He was amazed at how quickly his hair went from ginger to brown.
"That's amazing," he replied.
"It looks good on you, mate", Delwyn replied.
"And with that, I shall call it a day," said Joran.
"Thank you, thank you very much," said Gerald.
"Pleasure, my friend, just make sure you let me know in advance next time, alright."
"We will next time, promise."
Joran chucked, "We'll see." He then opened the front door and ushered the two out.
Gerald picked up his bag, slung it over his shoulder, and took the hat from the coat hanger. Then he followed Delwyn, who was already outside waiting for him.
"Don't mess with your hair too much tonight. The dye needs to dry a bit."
Gerald nodded in appreciation of the advice as he walked out the door.
"Have a good evening," Joran said as the barber closed the door.
Gerald looked around the little courtyard. The sky

was now cloaked by a deep dark shade of blue that soon turned to black as the last light of today's sun lingered past Merchant's Gate, casting a vast shadow over the western half of Aberemrallt. Along the battlements of that gate, Gerald could see soldiers lighting up torches along both sides of the walls. The same was done down here, as some citizens were coming out of their houses, to light up the many lantern posts stationed throughout this area and the rest of the city.

"Well, that wasn't so hard, was it?" Delwyn patted Gerald on the shoulder.

"Yes, it was a new experience, I'll be honest." He admitted as he put his straw hat back over his head. Although he only had his hair dyed tonight and, to some extent, might appear silly to wear a hat at this time, Gerald still didn't want to take any chances. "I best head back to the Jolly Maid then."

"Guess now we're even then?" Delwyn asked.

"Yes, we are," Gerald replied.

"But listen, if you're in trouble and need a hand, you know where to find me."

"Sure, no problem," said Gerald, though he questioned how reliable he would be if he knew the truth about what he did last night. Just then, a pair of city guards appeared from the corner of Gerald's eye. He stopped in front of them.

Oh shit, Gerald thought.

"Evening, gentlemen," one of the guards spoke.

"Evening," Delwyn replied cheerfully whilst Gerald put on a fake smile.

"May we see what's underneath the hat, please?" the guard asked, holding a small lantern over his head.

Suddenly, all eyes were on Gerald. *You must be joking? Damn my luck,* he thought. At that point, this was the moment of truth. If he refused the guard's request and took off, he'll be arrested regardless of whether they realised who he was or not. Reluctantly, Gerald took the hat off, revealing his hair. The guard with the lamp brought it closer over Gerald's head whilst the other inspected, circling around to get a look.

"Weird smell," the first guard said, twitching his nose whilst the second guard and Delwyn watched.

The thought of having someone this close inspecting him felt nerve-wracking, but Gerald willed himself not to panic, even as the hairs on his arms rose slightly and his knees started to shake uncontrollably. Keep it together now, Gerald told himself.

Then the first guard took a step back.

"Alright, not ginger. You're good."

"Thank you," Gerald replied, putting the straw hat back over his head.

"Have a good evening," the first guard said before gesturing to his comrade to move on.

Gerald and Delwyn watched as the pair marched on down the street. When they were out of ear reach, he sighed.

"Gods Gerald, you looked like you seen a ghost then," Delwyn commented, "Whatever you been up to…."

Gerald raised his hands, "Look, let's just forget that happened, alright? Thank you for helping me get my hair dyed. Should go before any more guards take a look at me."

"If you say so, Gerald. I'll see you around."

"Yeah, have a good night" was the last thing Gerald said to Delwyn as he walked on.

After walking back, the way he came, he reached the doors of the Jolly Maid. From the outside, there were two windows at the front. The one on the right was for Gerald's room, whilst the one on the left was Nianna's room, closest to the chimney for the fireplace downstairs. Both windows were covered by curtains from the inside, but Gerald momentarily noticed a light was on in Nianna's room. *She must be tidying herself up,* he thought. Several people were chatting while standing around a lamppost near the front door; further ahead near the square, Gerald could hear bards singing away. He took a deep breath before pressing on. He pushed the door open and entered.

The Jolly Maid was a vibrant place. Along the walls painted white, were long tables whilst in the centre between two pillars, several small round tables where people drank and played card games.

Gerald scanned the room briefly, hoping there weren't any more soldiers close by before he walked to the bar. He squeezed and weaved his way between the round tables, stopping and letting other people pass before carrying on. When he got to the bar, he saw Nianna in the middle of filling two tankards of ale and placing them on a wooden tray before handing them over to another maid, pointing to where to go.

She then sees Gerald, "There you are,"

"Did I miss anything?" Gerald asked.

"No, just glad to have you back."

Gerald simply smiled at her.

At that point, Nianna's father called from the kitchen, "Nianna, I need some onions. Can you check the store room, please?"

"I'll get some now, father." She leaves the bar and heads for the storeroom. Gerald followed as she went around the corner. Before the two was a single door, with a coat hanger close by. Nianna opens the door and enters the store room, with Gerald following.

"Now, where are those onions?" Nianna asked herself as she searched between two neatly assembled shelves. Gerald, however, notices something that she missed, a small crate of onions down on the lowest shelf on the left.

He bends down and picks the crate up, and calls to her.
"Found them."
"What?" Nianna turns around and sees the box in his hands,
"I was sure I put them further in here last time."
"Clearly, someone else had other ideas of where they should be. Well, not me, of course."
"Alright, clever clogs," Nianna replied as she walked back toward him. She notices something about Gerald.
"You know you can take that hat off now?"
"Oh yes, of course." Gerald handed Nianna the crate of onions before taking the straw hat off. Revealing the freshly dyed hair.
Nianna's eyes widened suddenly, "What in the world did you do to your hair?"
"I dyed it just now," Gerald replied.
"This is your surprise?" she asked
"What? You don't like it?."
"N...no, just never took you as some who wanted to change the colour of his hair on a whim."
"I fancied a change in appearance. It's only a temporary change. The stuff will fade away in a couple of days."
At that point, Nianna puts the crate on an empty shelf next to her left and looks at Gerald.
"Alright, what has really been going on, Gerald?" She asked, but Gerald didn't answer.
"I'm serious. This morning you were flat-out tired and barely wanted to move. Next, you're talking to one of Delwyn's mates to relay a message to him. Now you have gone and changed your hair?"
"You saw me?" Gerald raised his eyebrows.
"I had a feeling he helped you arrange the hair dye."
"Yes, he did. But this wasn't his idea." Gerald lied, hoping it would convince her that this was his intention.
"So, what's this really for?" she continued.

Gerald briefly rolled his eyes, "I told you, I fancied a change. I'm just sick of being recognised for my ginger hair."
"This wouldn't be something to do with a robbery last night, would it?"
At that point, Gerald gritted his teeth. O*h no, now you done it, you idiot!*
"Ehh, what robbery?"
"Oh, my gods, Gerald. Haven't you heard? I have been hearing some of our customers talking about it. Someone walked into the Imperial Academy and stole something."
"Something?" Gerald pretended to be interested.
"Doesn't that bother you?" Since you used to study there?"
"What have you been hearing?" Gerald enquired.
"Apparently, they're looking for someone who has reddish-colored hair."
"Alright, yes, I have heard about it."
"The last thing I want is to be mistaken for someone else just because they have the same hair colour as me."
"Oi, you two," Nianna's father popped his head.
"Whatever you two are discussing, sort it out later. I need a hand here with these orders."
"We'll be right there, father," Nianna replied as she peered out the store room doorway.
Gerald, at that point, took a deep breath before replying.
"Listen, Nianna. I care about you more than anything else in the world. If I involve you, it'll only complicate things. Please trust me on this. I have it under control."
"Are you sure what you did last night has nothing to do with this?" Nianna asked.
"I promise, whatever was going on at the academy, I had nothing to do with it. I'm long past being expelled from that place."
"You sure?"

"Yes, absolutely."

"Alright," she picks up the crate of onions and heads out of the store room, but looks over her shoulder to him, "come on, the next couple of nights are going to be very busy."

"I'll be there in a second." He replied.

Just to himself for the moment, Gerald leaned back gently until he felt his spine touching the shelves behind him. He inhaled a deep breath and then sighed. It took much more to convince Nianna of his innocence than he anticipated.

"Yeah, no rest for the wicked," he muttered as he put a hand through his hair but then remembered what Joran said about not messing with it too much. Hopefully, the heat of the main room will help dry the dye faster. He pushed himself off the shelf and walked out of the store room. Realising he still held onto his father's straw hat, he placed a spare hook on the coat stand near the storeroom. *Won't be needing this for the rest of tonight*, he thought as he went out to assist at the bar.

Chapter 9

The Keep, Pwynt Afon Castle, Gower

THE NIGHT'S SKY WAS CLEAR and with countless stars surrounding the full moon, its illuminating blue glow reflected perfectly in the ever-flowing River Tor. Anwen could see the glimmering river past the castle wall from her open window. She was staying in a chamber under one of the keep's towers.

It was tranquil outside. There were pockets of soldiers out and about; a handful patrolled the walls, others kept warm around small fire pits. Leaning toward the window, Anwen looked down at her clenched hand, opening it to reveal a small, hollow wooden heart with a triquetra symbol of copper weaved within it and attached to a string. This amulet was the last gift from her mother before she passed away.

Anwen was the only living daughter and the youngest of her siblings, her brothers dying at birth. Life can be surprisingly cruel to mortals. Despite the presence of her father and the friends she had made in the order, Anwen couldn't help but feel a sense of loneliness as a result of her family's tragic misfortunes. She looked upward to the moon; it reminded her of the old folk tales her father used to tell.

Some said the gods lived up there in solitude, watching as mortals go about their lives. It made her curious. If Orion watched over them from the moon, then why was there nothing but a greyish blue surface? The kings of the past spent their lives living in castles and kept within cities such as Aberemrallt. Even the gods must surely need a roof over their heads.

At that point, she heard a knock on her door.
"Come in," Anwen called as she turned away from the window, hiding her amulet behind her back. Her father entered the room, still wearing his tunic and cape. He closed the door behind him.
"Father," she greeted him.
"Are you all set for tomorrow?" Alric asked. "Yes, Father," Anwen answered.
"Good, we'll be leaving here in the morning after breakfast. What about your swords?"
"Right here," Anwen pulled out a bag from under her bed. She opened it to reveal her swords tucked away in their scabbards.
"Good, good. We don't want any accidents on the way," said Alric.
Anwen nodded; it was then that her father noticed she was hiding something.
"What are you hiding there, Anwen?" "Nothing, Father," she replied.
"You know you can't fool me, come on."
Anwen sighed and pulled her hand out from behind her back, revealing the amulet and handing it to her father.
"Gods, I had almost forgotten about that thing," Alric chuckled lightly, running his fingers over the amulet.
"You haven't worn that since you started training."
"I just didn't want to risk breaking it," Anwen confessed as her cheeks turned red.
"I know. That was made by your mother's father, said Alric, softly. His voice was gentle as he recalled his lost love and handed it back to her.
"Spent a whole day and a half forging and crafting it himself as a gift for your grandmother. It was the one thing she treasured most from him before she passed it down to your mother."

Anwen looked down at the amulet again before speaking. "Father, I know this might sound silly, but do you think, if she were here, mother would she be against me taking up a sword?"
"What makes you think that?" Alric looked at her curiously. "Why this now?"
"I… Well," Anwen hesitated, "you know it took a lot to convince you to let me join you, to be trained by you. You wouldn't have said no if I was a boy."
"I was a different man back then, sweetheart," Alric replied. "I was brought up on the belief that a woman's place was not on the battlefield. Whether or not your mother wanted this life for you, I can't say. You chose this, remember? And I know she would want you to follow what's in your heart and commit to it." Alric wrapped his arms around her.
"You have come a long way already, Anwen. Don't let what other people think stop you from what you want to achieve. If you ever have doubts, don't be afraid to speak to me. Alright?"
"Yes, Father," Anwen replied, swallowing deeply and willing the hot tears in her eyes to disappear. She blinked furiously. "Your mother is watching over us as we speak, I know she would be proud of you. So don't worry about her." Anwen nodded. Alric slowly pulled away from her. "Right, I'm off to check with everyone else. I'll see you in the morning. Oh, and no fighting with the boys tomorrow."
"I was only testing how good they were, Father," said Anwen. "I could've beaten them. Gabriel could do with using his head more instead of charging in. What do you think of Arran?"
Alric stopped before the door to answer. "They're all

good fighters, so long as they don't muck about in front of his Highness. Arran just needs to get himself a better sword and he'll be fine." He looked back at Anwen.

"Have you seen him?"

"I saw him ride out with Gabriel and Callum to the town," Anwen replied.

"Ah, that makes sense." Alric replied.

"What does?" Anwen was curious, "Does Arran have family around here?"

"I know his father, a damn good carpenter. He paid for Arran to join the order. But enough of that, I'll leave you be. Get some rest." Alric opened the door.

"Good night, Father. And thank you," said Anwen.

Alric looked back at his daughter and smiled before leaving.

The door creaked shut and the room was quiet again.

Alone but reassured in what she wanted to do, Anwen went to her bed and kneeled down by its side and prayed:

"Dear Orion, God of the Wind, and Lord of Reason and Truth. May you and Mother watch over me and Father tonight and in the days to come. Thank you," she kissed her amulet. She went over to the window once again. Instead of the moon or the river, she turned her head north to Everdale. The town was lit with torch lights from one end to the other. *Hope you aren't celebrating too much Arran*, Anwen thought. Satisfied, she closed the window and made ready for bed.

Meanwhile in Everdale...

Beside a bright, warm fireplace made from stone that arched over it, Arran sat at a small oak table enjoying some good ale. He was joined by Callum and Gabriel at one side, whilst on the other side was the man of the manor. This was his father, Dafydd Connaught. He was a talented man, crafting and supplying furniture for the town of Everdale and to the Lords of Pont Afon Castle and whoever beyond that. His friendship with the order as a result allowed for Arran to apply to become a page for the Twin Blade Order. He was a tall man, and his hands bore little scars here and there, testament to his dedication to his work. He was ecstatic upon hearing that his son and his friends would be fighting in the Imperial Games. To celebrate the occasion, the four of them played cards, drank ale and listened to Dafydd's jokes.

"And so there I was," Dafydd began, "watching my best friend riding the biggest pig ever seen and it bucked like a bull. He ended up face first in the mud."

Everyone was left laughing.

"Well, this has turned out better than I thought," said Gabriel

"That's good to hear," said Dafydd. "We may not have all the finer things that you'll discover in the capital, but who needs them when you have a flagon of ale and friends to play cards with!"

Callum nodded. "I've always preferred the quiet life, personally."

"And miss out on the action? The clash of sword and arms? Where's the fun in that?" Gabriel quizzed.

"Swinging a sword may help in battle but it doesn't help keep a roof over your head' Callum responded.

"You have to admit, there are some things you can't learn just from a book alone, Callum," Arran added.
"Ha, that's it my boy, experience," said Dafydd as he raised his cup in front of him. "You need to see as much of the world while you can and learn from it."
"Before you get too old?" Arran said with cheek.
"Oi, watch it now. If it weren't for me, you wouldn't be wearing that tunic."
The three young men laughed in unison. Dafydd poured himself another cup and raised it again before them.
"Here's to all of you, my son most importantly, moving onwards and upwards."
"Cheers!" The other three raised their cups as one.
At that point, a mature woman with a slender waist entered the room. Her curly brown hair was tied back in a ponytail. This was Ariana Connaught, Arran's mother.
"Mother," Arran smiled at her.
"Don't you think you've had enough to drink tonight?" she looked at the array of cups and cards that lay strewn across the table.
"Haha! I could go on all night if I wanted to, my dear," Dafydd replied to his wife then looked at the boys again. "Did I ever tell you lads about the time I drank two barrels of ale? Part of a bet it was."
"I think you did actually," Arran recalled. "You won the bet, but an hour later you were found throwing up outside the stables."
Callum and Gabriel chuckled uncontrollably.
Ariana walked over and tugged Dafydd on the shoulder. "Come on you silly hog. Let's get to bed before you end up doing something like that again on our floor."
"We should head back," said Callum. "We have a long journey tomorrow."
"Don't want the captain flogging us" said Gabriel with a

wince at the thought.

"You two go on ahead, I'll see you in the morning".

"Alright. It has been a pleasure to meet you all," Gabriel addressed as he rose from his chair. "Same here," Dafydd replied.

"You're welcome to come here anytime. As long as you don't bring trouble with you," said Ariana with a stern motherly stare and the ghost of a smile on her lips.

Arran watched as his comrades left the hall. When they were gone, he turned to his parents. His mother stood before him, arms out wide and a big smile across her face. He rose from his chair and embraced her.

"My little Arran has grown up," she said.

"I'm not little anymore, Mother," Arran corrected her.

"I know. I never thought my son would be competing in the Imperial Games."

"Gods, I remember the day when you said you wanted to become a knight," said Dafydd.

"It's like you said, Father, 'onwards and upwards'."

"Just be careful out there, Arran," said Ariana as she finally pulled away from her son.

"I guess I should go. Basil's probably getting bored being stuck in the stables."

"Wait just a minute," Dafydd called. He rose from his chair to give Arran a hug. "Make us proud, Son."

"I will. Don't you worry," said Arran.

After saying a final farewell, Arran left the manor and made his way through Everdale. The town's streets were alight with torches at every corner. The pleasant melodies of a fiddle and a harp, mixed with the tune of the townspeople's singing as he passed the local tavern followed him as he walked.

He finally arrived at the stables. A reasonably sized building, the town stable was made from wattle and daub, with a roof thatched of straw. Many travellers who come afar on horseback would leave their horses here in the care of the stable hands. When Arran walked around to the back, there were five stalls, and where he could hear horses snorting and sleeping, at least three of them appeared occupied.

One of the stable hands was present, a boy half Arran's age was attending to the far end stall where Basil was allocated. Arran stood and watched as he poured water into the trestle within the door. Arran recognised the boy by his curly brown hair and pale skin; this was young Emmet Gwyn. Basil was rearing his head further out of the stall as Emmet put his bucket down to stroke him.

"I think he likes you, Emmet," Arran spoke.

The boy jumped upon hearing his voice. "Arran, I mean Sir Arran."

"Haha, sorry to startle you Emmet. And please, there's no need for formalities yet," Arran replied humbly.

"Father told me to always refer to a knight as a Sir."

"That's true," Arran nodded.

"How come you've not been knighted yet?" Emmet looked at him curiously.

Arran paused for a moment to collect his response; he walked closer to Emmet and started patting Basil.

"Becoming a knight isn't straightforward. A man doesn't just join an order one day and expect to become a high-born warrior or knight the next one."

"My sisters are always talking about their dreams of one day meeting a knight and being married and living in a fancy, far away castle. It's really annoying." Emmet sighed

Arran chucked briefly, "You should tell them not to count their eggs before they hatch. A knight may be a higher stature to a commoner, but it doesn't mean he's a richer man."

"Really?" the boy asked.

"You'd be surprised. If every knight and high-born warrior were made rich from the moment he took the oath, I doubt there would be enough coin to go around."

Emmet nodded. At point, a light breeze began to stir from the southeast; lamp posts above each stall shook back and forth.

"You better go back inside. You've done well with Basil tonight," Arran complimented Emmet.

"Okay," the boy nodded; a smile was on his face. He took his bucket and left Arran with Basil.

Just as Arran thought himself to be alone with the horses, he looked at Basil and noticed a strange figure reflected in his eyes. That figure, when Arran turned around, was a Druid clad in a grey robe, holding a lantern in one hand. Within it was a constant low pulsating blue light. The person's body was a smaller stature, so he guessed it was a woman even though he couldn't see much of the face underneath the Druid's hood, save for the chin.

"Can I help you?" Arran asked, but the Druid simply stood there, not a flicker of movement.

Arran then said, "If you're looking for a horse, my lady, you'd have to wait for the morning to see if one is—"

"I have no need for a horse, young warrior." The Druid spoke with a calm voice as she raised her head slightly.

"Well then," Arran wasn't sure what to say.

"Tread carefully when you set foot in the capital. For trouble will soon be brewing," the Druid spoke again.

"I don't understand. Are you from the local shrine?" he asked.

"You will find out soon enough." The Druid raised the lantern up high above her head and the blue light emitted a flash of white. Arran covered his eyes from the light.

Then it was gone. When Arran finished blinking his eyes, the wind had ceased, but there was no one else around.

The strange woman had disappeared, and Basil was on edge, stomping about in his stall.

"Shhh, it's alright Basil, I'm still here," Arran whispered in the horse's ear. He looked around again.

"That was weird," he muttered to himself as he looked at the night sky. Was she a bringer of an omen or just a strange woman? His instincts itched at him to heed the Druid's advice. He opened the stall door and grabbed Basil by the reins and they rode back to the castle, hoping that in the morning he would make some sense of what had transpired tonight.

Time to get a good night's sleep, he thought to himself.

Chapter 10

Valeran's place, Aberemrallt

VALERAN SAT COMFORTABLY in his chair in front of a table where he placed the Black Box. The cellar was small, the dark grey and grubby stone walls illuminated by the greenish glow of dimly lit lanterns. Two in total, one in each opposing corner. Next to the table was a wide cauldron, empty and dry as a bone. There were shelves on every wall all around. one of them with a few old books on magic that were deemed too dark by the authorities to practice in public. The other shelves were stocked with jars of various ingredients, while dust-covered skulls, human and humanoid alike, filled the spaces in between. Rats, roaches and other insects crawled, weaved and scuttled their way in and out of the skull's wide-open jaws as well as their empty eye sockets and nostrils.

Valeran was in deep thought. Beside the Black Box on the table was a miniature pot that oozed with a dark, sickly aroma that the old man inhaled and exhaled slowly to help in his concentration. He closed his eyes and found himself within the deepest part of his mind, nothing but pitch black all around, but he wasn't alone. Standing before him his gaze was met by two massive yellow eyes, scrutinising him with their blood-red irises like an alchemist observing the mixing of powders and chemicals in a pan of water. This was but a fragment of the Demon Lord Samael's true form, and yet Valeran could sense such a powerful presence emitting from his current form, the low droning sound of the beating heart pounded all around. For the first time in an age, a shiver ran down Valeran's spine.

"You have awoken me," the deep and dark voice of Samael echoed around the chamber.
"Yes, I have, my Lord." Valeran hesitated slightly. "My name is—"
"Valeran Serpentine." Samael called him by his full name. "Your family's name. I am long familiar with the serpent."
Valeran gulped before he continued. "Then you know why I am here."
"You want to see your house at its prime once more. To be the house that commands authority and respect. Yes?"
The old man simply nodded, for he couldn't have spoken about his goals any other way.
"I'm not easily impressed," Samael commented, "but tell me this, old man. Are you prepared to play your part in my return? Serve me to the letter and you will have that which you seek. Stray too far from my hand, however, and you will experience pain like nothing the Empire could ever inflict upon you."
"I am committed to no one but you, my lord," Valeran replied. "I have been so for a long time. Spending many years working my way up the hierarchy of the Maldoran Empire; I have people in places that will aid us. The Empire will be celebrating the coming Imperial Games. What greater opportunity is there to remind the living of your power?"
"Indeed. Very well," Samael commented. "For this to happen though, you must seek the key to release me from my prison. It lies hidden under the foundations of Bourgiatta Castle."
Valeran spoke again, this time with a sudden spark of flattery towards the observing eyes. "Yes, I know of the place, my lord. I have men already in place ready to assist me in retrieving the key, my lord. Soon you will walk

again among the liv—"

"Do not get too far ahead of yourself, Valeran!" Samael's voice thundered. Valeran felt another shiver down his spine. "I do not need flattery. You can gloat about your achievements when you've actually accomplished them."

Valeran composed himself, having realised just how foolish he had acted just now. "Yes, yes. Forgive me, my master."

"Oh, and one more thing, Valeran." "Yes, Master?" Valeran asked.

"For my resurrection to be assured, I will need a new body. See to that while you retrieve the key. I will have another task for you afterwards. Do not fail me. Now go."

At that point, the eyes of Samael blinked, and a flash of light followed, engulfing everything around Valeran.

His eyes shot wide open, if a jolt of lightning had struck him, for a sharp and tingly sensation raced up and down his spine, even the bones in his fingertips weren't safe. The sudden and violent return to reality caused his vision to blur. He was rocking back and forth in his chair, trying to readjust, until it collapsed under his weight. The frail old man landed flat on his back.

For a moment, Valeran lay there, staring at the ceiling. He was breathing quickly, his every muscle burned in agony, sweat trickled almost uncontrollably down his wrinkled face, and the throbbing sensation in his head was like that of a devil jabbing a needle constantly to his brain. Eventually, he slowed his breathing. He sat himself up in spite of the fiery sensation flowing through his limbs and wiped his forehead with a sleeve. He looked around to find his cellar as he had left it, with the exception of the chair that had given way. Sluggishly, he rose to his feet.

He looked down at the Black Box on the table before him. *So that's what it's like to have another being inside your head,* Valeran thought. He had never felt such power take hold of him before. Now he felt weak. His throat was a droughted river and he had no idea how long he had been within his own head. He turned to the steps and made his way up. His time of concentration had robbed him so much of his strength, he had to push the trap door with his own hands after undoing the locks.

He knew what he needed to do next. He was to go to Bourgiatta Castle, acquire the key and release his master from captivity. There was also the need to acquire a body, though his master didn't say specifically what he was looking for as a vessel. Valeran would have to keep an eye out for one whilst carrying out his next plan. And so, he slammed the trapdoor hard after him. Not bothering to lock it. Time for wine and rest. Tomorrow he would continue with his plan; tomorrow he would know how to go about what has been set before him.

And onward to power and revenge.

Chapter 11

Thursday, 29th August
The Imperial Palace, Aberemrallt

THE MORNING SUN SHONE BRILLIANTLY over the eastern half of Aberemrallt, the streets bathed in its warm rays. Gedric stood atop Bastion's Gate waiting for the arrival of the Emperor. He was alone, save for the Royal Palace Guardsmen that went about their duties. Each soldier wore a purple cloak with three vertical stripes of gold that draped down the backs of their full-plated silver armour. Most carried swords that were sheathed, but some carried long halberds.

From here, Gedric could see the entire northern half of the city, from east to west. Before him, stood the Panethedral, its spires stretching out toward the open sky. He soon turned to the coliseum that stood by the river that ran through the city. There he saw men on scaffoldings laying out the banners that would drape down from the top. Across the river were the city barracks and the Imperial Academy, separated by a small wall just as there is one between the Imperial Palace and the Stronghold, the headquarters for the knights Twin Blade Order. He was reminded of the case that was still unsolved. Even with the knowledge provided by the mage Eafen, finding the people who stole the Black Box in such a large city was proving difficult.

Gedric heard footsteps and turned. Prince Frederick had come to join him. He was accompanied by one of his servants, a boy with short cut black hair who looked similar in age to him.

"Have you heard from them?" Frederick asked.

Gedric replied, "Nothing yet."
The Prince asked, "So what will you say to my father about … you know?"
Gedric sighed, he knew the Prince would ask.
"Well, we'll just have to come out with it. Behind closed doors of course."
"But what if they already escaped with it?" Frederick gestured. "You know, there used to be secret tunnels beneath these city walls?"
"And every last one of them was sealed up by your great, great grandfather, Arnold the Second," Gedric replied.
"Yes, Arnold the Suspicious," said Fredrick. "It is said that he almost intended to sack every member of his father's council upon inheriting the throne because he didn't trust any of them."
Gedric chuckled beneath his breath. "I'm pretty sure half of them would have shitted themselves upon hearing such a command."
"If it comforts you in any way," Frederick cleared his throat, "I trust you, Chancellor. I know you will have a way to solve this problem."
Gedric turned and smiled. "You're too kind, my Prince."
At that point, the elegant figure of Lady Eleanor joined them on the battlements. She was accompanied not by her usual servant but by a young elf girl who followed closely in tow.
"Ah, Lady Eleanor," Gedric greeted her.
"My Prince. Chancellor." She bowed. "So, I assume no luck with you-know-what?"
"Still nothing, Lady Eleanor," Frederick responded.
Gedric then replied, "Therin and I have an idea of who was involved from what we've learned at the academy. But the real question is who they are working for and why."

"Hmm, at least we can take comfort in knowing that whoever they are, they can't really do much without the key you spoke about."

"That is true, my lady. But if given time, they will learn where it is hidden."

"So, what will you do, Chancellor?" Eleanor asked. "I'd say we should cast them into the sea," Frederick suggested

"Cast the box or the key?"

"Both. Well, not together of course. Have one dropped in an ocean here, and the other piece over the other side. Let the creatures of the deep guard them for us."

"That's not a bad idea, to be honest," Gedric admitted. At that point, a horn was blown from atop the Sun Gate, the closest of the city's gates to where they stood. "That'll be them," said Gedric. "Time to welcome His Imperial Majesty back."

Prince Frederick and Lady Eleanor nodded. Gedric watched as they descended down the steps, their respective servants following after them. He turned back to the city where guardsmen were out on the streets. They called out to the masses to clear the streets before forming up in a straight line either side. Down below, four figures approached Bastion's Gate. The first was Captain Therin, followed close by was Mayor Erland Bray, Kleif Stonebearer and bringing up the rear was Valeran. Though they all made it inside eventually, the chancellor couldn't help but notice that the Master of Coin was lagging behind more than usual.

The horns blew again. Through the entrance to the city came the first group of horsemen who led the column: knights clad in full armour, all wearing purple and gold- trimmed capes. These were the Emperor's personal bodyguards handpicked by himself and the royal family. Next came a column of infantrymen. Gedric counted twenty of them. They too wore purple capes over their armour as they marched in formation, four men wide and five deep. They were followed by the imperial carriage. It was red and white, with gold and silver outlines, pulled by six beautiful white stallions. Following closely was another group of knights. These were not more of the Emperor's personal guard, however, for they wore pure white tunics with pauldrons over their shoulders that resembled the heads of gryphons. These were the Knights of Hothland, the ancestral home of the ruling House of Vorlorn.

The citizens watched in awe as this parade moved gracefully through the city streets. Gedric made his way to the courtyard as the parade drew closer. He found everyone in the Imperial Palace standing, waiting. The stewards stood separately based on their roles. The members of the council stood in a row of their own in between all of them and in front of the Palace doors.

He strode over and took his place among them. He watched as the iron gate was heaved open and then entered the imperial carriage. The horses that pulled it halted in front of them. The man at the front of the carriage jumped off and walked over to one of the side doors. He opened it and out came his Majesty, Emperor Otto V. A man of similar height to Gedric with short, shiny brown hair that was beginning to grey. He wore a red cape over a purple surcoat adorned with a golden sun.

All the people within the palace knelt before the Emperor as he stepped onto the courtyard ground, followed by Empress Deidre, a woman of fine beauty, her strawberry blonde hair pulled back in a tight bun, and her person adorned in a green and white cotehardie. Intuitively desiring to greet them, Gedric rose to his feet and walked toward the Emperor. He was followed instantly by Prince Frederick.

"Your Majesty," Gedric opened the conversation

optimistically.
"Ah, Chancellor, good to see you," the Emperor smiled at him then looked at Prince Frederick. "And Frederick, my son."
"How were Merine and Kosantos?" the Prince asked.
"Good as ever. Always good to watch the sea from a different shoreline," the Emperor replied.
"And plenty of works of art to observe. We even met someone happy to paint a portrait of you," Empress Deidre spoke for the first time. Frederick blushed upon hearing her.
"Oh, Mother," he replied whilst giving her a hug. "Who has time to stand still for some painter?"
"It's a starting point. You'll need to consider establishing your image for generations to come," Emperor Otto responded.
Gedric smiled before he continued. "We should go inside; there are some things to discuss, Your Majesty."
"Yes, indeed, Chancellor."
"I'll have your belongings brought in." Frederick gestured to his servant to assist in the unpacking of the carriage.
"Ah, Your Noble Excellences," Mayor Bray spoke out admirably as he reached out to shake the Emperor's hand. "So good to see you return."
Gedric was the last only to Valeran to follow the group in when he felt Therin's hand pat him on the shoulder.
"Well, at least the mayor is sober for once."
"Aye," the chancellor replied.
"I hope you've come up with a good report, my lord," Therin whispered in Gedric's ear.
The chancellor looked around him; the rest of the servants and soldiers had returned to their posts and chores. Only Valeran was close by, slowly ascending the steps past them. He then looked at Therin.

"We'll discuss it inside," he replied. Therin nodded and walked with him.

This isn't going to be easy, Gedric thought as they climbed the steps. But he had a plan in mind and would need to convince his Majesty to let him carry it out as soon as possible. For their sake, and the future of the realm. He walked past the guards as they pulled the large palace doors closed behind them.

Chapter 12

Crows Road, on route to the capital

ARRAN SAT COMFORTABLY IN HIS SADDLE as He rode with Basil amidst a column of other Twin Blade knights, squires and servants. They travelled along Crows Road, its path following that of the river Tor and in the distance, he could see where it would split into two.

The hot sun beated down on him, but a welcome breeze cooled him as he lightly gripped the reins. The group had embarked from Pwynt Afon Castle after breakfast with the capital as their destination. The only other settlement between there and the capital was the village of Nyth Crow, named after the road where crows were often seen circling.

Behind him were sergeants and fellow squires, followed by a few wagons carrying supplies. Further up the column, Arran saw Anwen riding alongside fellow female participants, while leading the whole group was Captain Dorwin, accompanied by a handful of knights and veteran officers. And last, there was Gabriel and Callum just behind him. It all seemed safe in Arran's mind, despite last night's mysterious encounter. He made a brief visit to the town shrine but none of the local clergies matched the appearance of the ominous druid woman.

"You seem to be deep in thought, Arran," said Gabriel.

Arran woke from his moment of thought and looked at Gabriel and Callum. "Oh sorry. I'm fine, Gabriel.

"You haven't spoken much since we left the castle," said Gabriel.

"I'm just thinking ahead, that's all."

"I'm thinking of how much better I will be with my feet

on the ground," said Callum.

Arran and Gabriel grinned at each other.

"Is your arse starting to itch already, Callum?" Gabriel joked.

Callum's face went red with embarrassment. "Oh, come on. It's not funny!"

"It isn't funny that your horse has to bear your weight, let alone your lack of enthusiasm," said Gabriel.

"Oi, now look here—" Callum was interrupted when his horse stopped suddenly to shake its body before carrying on, causing him to feel momentarily unbalanced; "Oh, now you've done it, Gabe."

Gabriel chuckled to himself.

Arran intervened, "If you two keep this up, the captain will send us to the rear of the column."

Gabriel and Callum looked at each other, surprised at their friend's sudden warning.

"There's definitely something up with you, Arran," said Callum.

"`Sorry. It's just ..." Arran was unsure of how to explain the events of last night. But he cleared his throat and just went with it. "You probably won't believe this but there was this woman who spoke to me last night as I tended to Basil at the stables."

"A woman you say?" Gabriel's face lit up with interest. "Don't tell me. You wish you were still back there with her? Or did something happen with her that you wish didn't happen?"

"No, not really like that, Gabriel," Arran explained. "She was cloaked in all green; I couldn't even see her face. She said to watch my back in the capital."

"Probably she meant to watch out for either puddles or, more likely, whores," Gabriel carried on. "The latter will eat away at your money if you spend too long with them."

"Yeah, like a mysterious woman in robes would suddenly approach me in the middle of the night, just to warn me about whores before flashing her lamp at me an disappearing."

"Did you just say lamp?" Callum asked.

"Yes. It was a big lamp with a bright green glow," Arran replied as he turned around to look at Callum.

"Well," Callum went on, "there used to be stories of women who come out at night to guide those in times of darkness.

"That rings a bell." Gabriel pointed out. "Do you mean the Cult of Breia? The Earth Women?"

Callum nodded. "Yeah. You could say that, since they usually wear green robes and carry lamps."

"I'm not so sure about it myself," said Arran. "There has to be more to it. She disappeared before I could ask her anything."

Gabriel gestured with open arms at his surroundings. "If trouble was coming, I doubt we'd find it in the capital or even out here, other than perhaps crossing paths with some thieves. What is there to worry about?"

Arran looked at him thoughtfully. Perhaps he was right. At that point, however, came the sound of flapping wings The trio, along with everyone else, looked up and saw a flock of crows fly above them in an endless black stre across the sky. The entire column halted, with everyone in awe of the sight.

"By the gods," said Callum. "I've never seen so many birds flock like that before.

Past the column, Arran saw where the crows were flyin to. A large, lone oak tree close to the road only a few miles from them as the land before them was fairly flat with onl a handful of hills in places, where a hundred more crows nestled, a chorus of unsettling caws followed. An elderly man in a brown robe came rushing out of a cottage, toward the tree. At that point, Arran saw Anwen pull her horse out of the column, heading to the front to investigate. Wanting to see for himself what was going, Arran squeezed on the reins and pulled Basil out of the column and followed her.

"Arran, what are you doing?" Callum called out, confusion across his face.

"Going to find out," Arran replied, then he kicked Basil into action. They galloped past the column. When he made it to the front, he saw that Captain Alaric had dismounted and was talking to the man from the cottage. Anwen was close by, mounted on a white horse. He rode up next to her.

"It's happening! It's happening!" the elderly man cried out.

"Calm down you bloody fool," Captain Alaric answered. "It's just birds gathering."

Arran leaned toward Anwen. "What's happening?"

"It's the tree." Anwen pointed. "That man's been watching over it for most of his life. He's the local priest for that village. There's a saying that if you find fif crows perched on that tree, it is taken as an ill omen."

"There's more than fifty I can see. What does that mean?" Arran looked at her with curious eyes.

She paused momentarily then looked at him. "Means dark times are coming."

Arran raised an eyebrow. "You actually believe in this?"

"I'm not sure. There's never been a gathering of crows like this for a hundred or more years. My father doesn't believe in them. Still…"

They watched as the captain and the old priest argued. Alaric ordered one of his lieutenants to escort the priest back to his cottage. Further down the road, farmers and villagers from Nyth Crow paused in their daily routine. They stared dumbstruck at the tree; there was not a branch that didn't have a crow sitting on it. The birds seemed intent on remaining there, squawking away. Then, all went at once, they flew upward cawing awa , forming a massive black cloud before they flew west. Everyone was speechless including the elderly priest who eventually turned to his cottage and started muttering something. At that point, Callum and Gabriel joined Arran and Anwen.

"At least they'll be someone else's problem," said Gabriel as he twisted his little finger in one ea .

"Surprising how much noise a flock of birds can make. Arran and Anwen rolled their eyes at the comment. By then, the captain had marched back to his mount. His face was etched with annoyance.

"Well, what are you looking at?" He addressed them.

"You three get back in line now, nothing to see!"

"What about the tree, Captain?" Arran asked.

"Those birds are probably there because there's nowhere else for them to go. It's just an old children's story about that tree, nothing more." Not wanting to talk anymore about the subject, the captain marched back to his steed and trotted ahead.

Anwen rode away from Arran to join her father without looking back. He soon pulled Basil to the side of the road to wait to return to his place in the column, with Gabriel and Callum joining him.

"Well, that was interesting," Callum said.

"Arran meets a mysterious woman, now crows cawing in a tree. What next?" Gabriel said, amused.

Arran nodded, his face turning to the tree, now empty and motionless. There was something not right about it. Could this be the sign of dangers the mysterious woman prophesied? Or was this just a series of mad events that made no sense.

Could this day get any more unusual? Arran thought.

Chapter 13

Chapter 13
The Stronghold, Aberemrallt

IT WAS MIDDAY at the Stronghold of the Twin Blade Order. Eafen walked down the middle aisle of the chapel, where the order members come together for sermons and matters within. There, dominating the entire room and behind a podium, was a statue carved to resemble Lord Orion, Master of the Wind, God of Reason and Truth, the Saviour of Maldora. The figure reached so high it almost touched the domed ceiling. A replica of the Unbreakable Will was in its hands, the spear that Orion used to defeat Samael in their final battle nearly a thousand years ago. Eafen had spent half the day thinking about the visions he saw yesterday.

The other half of the time was committed to writing new manuscripts. Eafen often came to this place to relax and contemplate what chores to do next. He sat on a bench to the left of the statue, undoing his dark blue robe and laying it out before sitting. Then he took a deep breath.

How did these thieves know about the Black Box and what it contained? Who else could be involved? What motives were in play? His fiery gut and mind burned at the thought that this was but a fragment of something bigger, more sinister.

He looked up at the statue: there was a large cyan gem in the centre of the stone-carved spear it held began to gleam. He thought he was seeing things and couldn't help but stare at the gem. Suddenly, the stone that he wore around his neck began to shine as well. In an instant, his vision went white and the young mage could hear cries and clashes of swords all around him.

When the flash receded, Eafen found himself somewhere else. He tried to look around, but his vision was fixed in one direction. In the corner of his eyes, Eafen noticed his attire was different. On his hands as they gripped the balustrade, there was a gold ring on two of his fingers. Further down, the wrists were covered by the cuffs of a dark blue cotehardie complemented by a pair of black trousers. Eafen realised at that point that this was a vision of an event happening in the future, but told through the eyes of someone else.

He found himself staring down at the arena grounds at the Coliseum. There were several warriors there, staring at a shadowy figure, who stood before a massive portal. Suddenly, a thousand more shadowy figures emerged. Many were humanoid in shape and form, but a handful were like trees towering over the rest. Other figures entered the fray with wings, foul and incommunicable cries echoed around the arena as they flew and dived down at unsuspecting spectators.

The eyes soon turned with the rest of the body, now the person whose body Eafen was a host in was staring at the Emperor and the Empress, who sat on their makeshift thrones, their eyes and mouths wide open in utter shock. As was the collection of governors, guards and politicians present in the royal auditorium overseeing the unfolding chaos.

The person called out to the guard closest to him.

"Sound the alarm now, get the people out of here!"

Eafen recognised the voice, *Captain Therin?* The guard nodded and rushed away to carry out his orders. The captain turned to the dumbstruck monarchs as alarm bells rang all around the arena.

"Your Majesty, you must leave here at once"

The Emperor glared right back at the captain, "Leave? We have been betrayed and outmanoeuvred by this treacherous snake, and you want me to leave with my tail between my legs?

"Sire, it's too dangerous to stay here…" the captain of the city guard argued.

"I don't care, damn it! This is what he wants. Can't you see? I show my arse to him and everyone else, it'll justify everything that madman said. I am staying until you contain this attack immediately. That's an order."

"Incoming!" a guard was shouting.

Captain Therin's vision returned to the balcony in time to see a fireball heading right for them.

"Get down, now!" he shouted.

At that point, the vision flashed just when the fireball was about to impact.

Where am I now? Eafen wondered as the flash receded. The mage was now witnessing another event from another perspective. Through the eyes of the being he was a host in, he was running down some sort of tunnel. He soon realised that he was rushing down one of the corridors inside in the Coliseum, upon seeing pillar after pillar used to support the structure. Eafen noticed how the host was breathing lightly as they headed toward the main gateway into the arena. There were soldiers positioned at the gateway.

"Open the gates, now!" the host called out to them in a feminine voice.

Wait, I'm a woman now? Eafen realised. He heard of rare accounts of people who had received visions through the eyes of the opposite gender. While the host watched as the soldiers opened the gateway, he glanced down to see this warrior was wielding two swords and clad in full armour with the blue tunic of the Twin Blade Order over it. Just as the gate opened, Eafen's vision was blurred by another flash. *Not again*, he cursed.

Now he was witnessing the battle taking place right before his very eyes within the arena of the coliseum. All around him, fires were ablaze, and civilians were fleeing in terror. Soldiers and knights were locked in battle, not with other men but against strange, monstrous creatures. As he looked down at his own hands, one was wielding a sword and the other a shield. He could hear heavy breathing coming from this person.

In the corner of his eye, he saw a knight in full armour of silver lying helplessly on the floor, clenching at the massive hole in his chest. He wore a dark blue cape over his shoulders that went all the way down his hips. The material was changing to a murky brown as a result of the blood pouring out of his gut and was creating a massive pool around his body. Despite seeing all of this through the future eyes of another person - thus having no control over what they saw or what they felt, Eafen could feel nothing but utter shock at what he was witnessing.

Straight ahead, beyond the carnage, was a dark hooded figure standing in front of what appeared to be a portal. More monsters were spawning from it. He suddenly turned around and saw the Unbreakable Will standing atop a podium in the distance.

Eafen's vision flashed a fourth time, this time the host was holding the Unbreakable Will in his hands. The energy was crackling from the tip of the blade. He turned to face the chaos again. Before he could say or do anything, a fifth flash occurred. Now he was closer to the portal but still out of reach. Eafen wanted to move forward, but he had no control at all. The next thing that happened surprised Eafen. The warrior host took the Unbreakable Will in his hand and threw it. He could do nothing but watch the spear fly over the battlefield and enter the swirling portal. A moment later, a massive explosion followed by another white flash that engulfed everything around him.

And then it was gone. Eafen woke to find himself still on the bench. He felt pale, and sweat dripped down his face. He glanced around the hall, but it was still just him. He breathed a sigh of relief. He couldn't believe the vision he had foreseen. Why was this battle happening in the capital? And through whose eyes did he witness this terrible event?

Eafen rose from the bench, grabbed his robe and walked out the way he came. He stopped momentarily and looked back at the statue, but the gleaming light that projected the vision onto him had gone. Was he becoming paranoid? Was there something he missed that the gods were trying to show him? Only time would tell.

Chapter 14

The Imperial Palace, Aberemrallt

GEDRIC, ALONG WITH EVERYONE ELSE in the council sat around a large oval oak table at the centre of the Imperial Palace's main hall, with the emperor and empress sitting together. Their mood changed from one of welcome optimism to one of outrage when the chancellor had informed his majesty of the unfortunate news.

"You mean to tell me that the Black Box was stolen by a pair of ruffians, and you have yet to apprehend them?" Emperor Otto bellowed fiercely.

A moment of silence fell upon the council.

"Your Majesty, with all due respect," Gedric replied, "it has only been two days ago since—"

"I don't care how recently it happened, damn it!!" His Majesty interrupted, unimpressed and scowling as fury radiated from his every pore. "It is still an embarrassment. I leave this city for a week to visit a good friend governing Kosantos, and this is what happens?"

Therin swallowed, his eyes darting to Gedric and then to the emperor, the tremor in his voice evident. "We have doubled guards at every gate and are inspecting all ships present on the docks. Nothing suspicious has been reported yet."

"And what about the sewers? Have you inspected those as well?" the emperor demanded.

"We are putting together groups to investigate the sewers now, Your Majesty."

"Have you started searching the brothels and taverns?"

"Every house in this city, big and small, is being searched

and inspected as we speak," Gedric replied calmly.

The emperor pushed back into his chair and sighed whilst the rest of the council looked plainly at him. Empress Deidre placed a hand on her husband's shoulder.

"I think you are overreacting, my love," she spoke softly to him before addressing the council. "We appreciate your efforts."

Gedric nodded optimistically, though everyone was still on edge after Emperor Otto's immediate outburst. Mayor Bray was sitting closest to the Emperor and Empress. Sweat dripped down the sides of his face as he gripped the side of the table tightly. Lady Eleanor remained silent, though her face was etched with concern that she could not say anything.

"What the enemy possesses is only one half of a greater machination," Flint broke in, stroking his beard before gulping down a cup of water.

"There is still time to make things difficult for them," said Gedric. He looked around the table.

Everyone nodded confidently except for Valeran, who simply sat at the far end of the table with his back to the sun as usual, acknowledging the situation with a stoic pale face.

The Master of Coin held his own cup in one hand whilst gripping his snake cane in the other. *Time to change the subject and put some attention on that miserable snake*, Gedric thought as he cleared his throat.

"If I may suggest, let us move on from this matter at the moment to the Imperial Games."

"Ah yes, the games. Something more delightful and manageable," Mayor Bray gingerly agreed.

Emperor Otto scanned the room, his face tense with anger at his council's inabilities. Eventually, he nodded curtly and gestured to the chancellor to continue.

"Tell us, Lord Valeran," Gedric looked at the Master of Coin. "What are the current projected expenses for this year's event?" Everyone turned their attention to Valeran.
"Well, at this moment," the pale man cleared his throat, then he rummaged through one of his pockets and presented a parchment. Gedric watched as the Master of Coin ran a bony finger down the paper, reading the numbers. He looked at the Emperor, arms folded as he watched impatiently.
Valeran replied, "we are looking at around 245,000 gold for running the entire games, including the cost for hosting festivities afterwards, Your Majesty."
"I see." Gedric nodded.
"Continue, Lord Valeran," the emperor insisted, though everyone else seemed already bored of hearing Valeran's low voice.
"We have received payments from all the knightly orders across the continent that have put forth participants.
"Thank you, Valeran," the emperor acknowledged. "How many participants are we expecting?"
The question was left to Prince Frederick, who sat on the opposite side of his father, to answer. "According to the last report, we will be expecting around one hundred and ninety-two participants for the melee competition, thirty of whom will be female fighters. For the jousting, we have a total of one hundred and twenty-eight knights who have signed up and paid in advance, including myself. We should have quite a spectacle in the coming days."
"I'll see to doubling the security throughout the games," Therin broke in, "If I were going to smuggle something, the games would be a great place to do so when no one is looking." Everyone nodded willingly.
"I recommend putting in effect immediately double checkpoints at every entry," Gedric added as he leaned

forward for everyone to see him. "Every man, woman and child must have all their pockets checked at both points. All baggage must be looked into thoroughly. I also want every cart coming and going from the arena to be inspected, every nook and cranny. Leave nothing to chance."

"Agree there," Kleif nodded.

"Very well," Emperor Otto seconded the idea, "make it happen, Captain Therin."

"It will be done, my Emperor." Therin replied.

"What will we do if any of the guards come into contact with anyone holding the Black Box or being suspicious?" Lady Eleanor asked.

"We'll detain them as quickly and quietly as possible and hold them in one of the spare rooms in the Coliseum until after the civilians have left," Therin replied.

"As if these people will come quietly," Kleif mumbled.

"I'll check with Grandmaster O'Hare of the Twin Blade and inform him of the new security measures to be in place for tomorrow," said Geric.

At that point, Emperor Otto nodded. He then unfolded his arms and placed his hands on the table. "It seems everything else is in order for the moment," He said. You're free to go."

Everyone looked at each other before rising from their seats. Valeran was last, slowly standing and leaning heavily on his cane. Gedric saw this as an opportunity to speak about his plan.

"Your Highness, if I may have a word?" Gedric asked.

"You may," said Emperor Otto, gesturing to the empress and the prince to leave them.

Well, that was a short meeting, Valeran thought as he left the hall with everyone else. On his way out, he caught a glimpse of the chancellor speaking with the emperor just as the large, heavy double doors started closing.

Sharing something confidential, are we Chancellor? Valeran grinned. He scanned his surroundings; the rest of the council continued to walk down one of the corridors, oblivious of him. Only he and two guards stood by the closed doors behind him. He followed the same route as the others but stopped outside a storage room. He found the door—locked, as usual.

The Master of Coin glanced around before slipping an old skeleton key into the lock and muttering under his breath with a frown as the key refused to turn in the rusted lock. Seconds seemed like hours until the key finally turned. Valeran grinned as he quickly entered the room and closed the door behind him. The shelves of the compact room were packed with buckets, soap, and wash maid clothes. Alone, with the door closed behind him, Valeran reached into his robe for a tiny bottle.

"Now let us see what you're up to in there, Gedric," he muttered before drinking the bottle's contents, the bitter liquid burning his throat.

For a moment, nothing happened, but then vibrations engulfed his body. The world around him became larger. His hands soon became little paws, and the skin on his arms changed from pale white flesh to black fur. Whiskers stretching outward began to grow from his nose, and he could feel a tail sprout out from his rear with the sharp lick of pain. His transformation from a pale old man to a black rat was complete.

Visually, his surroundings had become dark and blurry. Valeran looked and sniffed around for a way out of this now large place before noticing a hole in the top corner of the room, reachable by one of the beams. He clawed onto the bottom and climbed vigorously all the way to the top.

Upon reaching the hole, he scuttled in and made his way through the gap in the walls until he found another beam to ascend. There was hardly any light, but Valeran continued to use his altered sight to navigate his way until he found himself crawling onto a horizontal beam above the very hall he was in just now. Down below were two blurry human figures. Valeran recognised them as Gedric and the emperor by his enhanced sense of hearing. He watched, unnoticed, as they spoke to each other.

"So, you intend to leave here tomorrow?" the emperor asked.

"Yes. I believe that even if the culprits find some way to escape with the artefact, it'll be useless to them when they realise that the key's been moved," the chancellor replied calmly.

"But Bourgiatta Castle is well fortified and guarded by the best men in the province of Terradonia," said the emperor. "If they seek the key, we should prepare to greet them there."

"But what if the enemy is someone we thought we knew?" Gedric raised the question. "This theft was clearly well organised. It was orchestrated by someone with knowledge of the Black Box and the key."

"But who? All known cults dedicated to the dark god have been hunted down and eradicated by now." Emperor Otto sighed, annoyed at the situation. "It's hard to believe that there still exist those who think it profitable to stir up forces beyond their comprehension."

"I know," Gedric nodded, "but if I can inform Lord Bastone of the situation, I will take the key to Myrgrad, keep it there for a few years, then move it back."

Valeran twitched with curious eyes as the emperor

paused momentarily before concluding.
"Alright, Chancellor, you have your mission. You will leave here tomorrow morning and head for Bourgiatta Castle," the emperor commanded.
"As you wish, my lord," Gedric half bowed with a closed fist to his chest before he turned to the doors.
"Oh, and Gedric?" the emperor called.
The Chancellor turned his head. "Yes, your Majesty?"
"Come back to us in one piece, old friend. I can't begin to fathom who I would have to replace you as my chancellor." "Understood," Gedric acknowledged. "Enjoy the games,
Your Highness." With that, the chancellor left the hall.

So, Lord Bastone has the key. Beneath Bourgiatta Castle? Curses! Valeran thought. At this rate, he would only have the rest of today to get there before Gedric did. Valeran scuttled along the beam and back the way he came, hoping no one would be in the storage room when he got there. He needed to act fast if he were to continue his plans. Valeran returned to the storeroom and reverted back to his human form. His vision became clear again, and his sense of smell deadened.

He departed from the room with a slight frown on his face. Bourgiatta, of all places. His family built that castle many generations ago to act as a place for their armies to attack the other city-states in the south, only to be stolen by the descendants of House Bastone. *At least I have a reason to pay Lord Aeolus a visit*, he thought as he finally walked out of the Imperial Palace, passing several soldiers and servants who barely paid attention to him. Not that anyone would care much about a pale, frail and miserable old man.

Fools.

Chapter 15

A few miles from Market Gate, west of Aberemrallt

IT WAS JUST A FEW HOURS since they passed by the town of Nyth Fran. The smell of saltwater and the sight of gulls indicated to Arran that they were now close to the southern coast, and there was Aberemrallt. From a distance, its walls loomed over the fields and cottages. Arran could see several buildings within the city towering over the walls, including the dome-like structure of the coliseum. Commoners and farmers stood by the side of the road watching the Parade of Arms. Banners with the Imperial insignia draped down from the battlements a few metres from the ground.

"Ah, Aberemrallt," Gabriel spoke for the first time since Nyth Fran. "The greatest city in all of Maldora."

Arran looked at him with curiosity. "You seem very patriotic, Gabriel."

Gabriel shrugged his shoulders and agreed. "Well, I look forward to the opportunities that the capital brings. The action, the glory and so on."

Arran simply chuckled and nodded.

"I'm looking forward to seeing the Stronghold's library," said Callum, who rode behind them, his enthusiasm for knowledge and the literate arts beginning to show.

"Did you know," he continued, "that the library in the Stronghold and the Academy combined have the largest collection of books and scrolls this side of the Empire? Possibly rivalling the one in Myrgrad in every subject except building and forging."

"How fascinating. I imagine it would require one's entire

lifetime to read all those books." Gabriel's enthusiasm seemed blunted by the excess knowledge that flowed out Callum's mouth.

It was then that Arran looked out at Princes Bay. "Hmm, that's odd. I don't see any ships leaving or entering the harbour."

Gabriel shrugged, "Never was into ships. All I see is the sea."

Callum replied, "Perhaps a storm has been predicted in the coming days, or maybe something has stirred the sailors of the Byzalian Islands not to sail today."

"You could be right." Gabriel nodded. "You never know with the sailors of Byzalia and Lapenthos. They claim to be the best at what they do, and yet they're so fussy about how far they're willing to travel to trade."

Arran shook his head. "I don't think it's anything to do with trade. I have heard stories from sailors who brave storms almost every day at sea. What would make today any different?"

Gabriel scoffed, "First crows amassing around some old tree, now the Fish Heads not showing off their fancy ships. I think they're scared that they won't do so well in the games and have forfeited."

"I wonder if you will still say that when you find a Fish Head about to stick his trident up your arse," Arran grinned.

Callum, out of nowhere, burst into laughter.

Gabriel strangely looked at him, "What's so funny?"

"That might happen, Gabriel, if you're not careful," Callum chuckled. He had rocked himself so far back that he almost fell off his horse when Arran grabbed him by the shoulder.

"Easy there, Callum," said Arran.

"Sorry about that."

"I thought you didn't enjoy combat?" Gabriel asked.
"Yes, but I can imagine you being chased by a Byzalian marine with a trident around the arena."
"Yeah, right," Gabriel huffed to himself.
The sun and its warm rays fell behind the trio as they rode closer to the gate.

The Stronghold, outside the Chapel

With no luck in deciphering the sudden and gruesome visions he received, Eafen decided to forgo the peace and quiet of the chapel for the bustling life beyond the Stronghold walls. The Mage walked out through the open doorway and entered the hallway, still doing up his robe as he walked, looking down at the marble floor when he heard a familiar voice call.

"Good morning Eafen."

Eafen looked up; from the other side of the hallway, confidently approaching him, a tall, well-built man with dark brown hair and a short beard, all well combed and wearing a dark blue garment draped with a cape. He wore the same dark blue cape as him. Eafen knew the man as Sir Ferrand Mosse, an experienced knight and a good friend. As he came closer, Eafen remembered something from the visions, the bloodied knight lying on the ground in the arena. *No... it can't be, not him.*

"You've been working without rest again?" he asked.
"Uh, yes indeed, Sir Ferrand," the young Mage replied as he straightened himself up.
"I heard you were called to the Academy yesterday,"
"Yes. Yes, I was called upon to assist the Chancellor in revealing those behind the robbery."
"Ah, and did you find what you were looking for?" the

knight asked.

"Most of it," Eafen replied. He looked up at the statue. "I find it odd, though; something doesn't add up."

"What doesn't?" Sir Ferrand was curious.

Eafen paused, picking his following words carefully.

"Well. I am not supposed to say what was stolen…."

"A Black Box, wasn't it?"

The question caught Eafen unaware. He looked at Sir Ferrand, then scanned the hall before he continued, "How do you know of this?"

"Ha, you think I'm not aware of what remains of the Dark Lord? I have been curious about the whereabouts of the Heart of Darkness the moment I heard the priests and mage elders speak of it in my lectures when I was your age. The chapter master at the time of Samael's defeat wanted to keep the thing within the proximity of the order's forces. It should've been in our vaults, but he had no choice but to hand it over to the Great Academy in exchange for funds."

"And now it is in the hands of thieves," Eafen sighed.

"I doubt it will be so for long. You've done all you can." Ferrand looked down and put a hand on the shoulder of the young Mage. "Give the fools another day, and the box will probably drive them mad to the point where they will come forth and return it to us. Hopefully, the council and the emperor will find a reason for it to remain in our custody instead."

"Maybe a little too optimistic," Eafen admitted, "but I hope you're right. For everyone's sake."

"Anyway, I would love to stay, but I have some duties to fulfil." Sir Ferrand patted Eafen on the shoulder before walking toward the chapel.

"Thank you," Eafen said. The knight looked back over his shoulder and raised a hand to acknowledge his reply.

The Mage just stood there and watched Ferrand walk on, oblivious to the sudden visions Eafen received of the coming fate awaiting him.

Now he was to himself again in the corridor. Eafen took a deep breath and gritted his teeth. *This is absurd. Three visions in a day and one of them depicting him of all people dying before me?* He shook his head. *No, no. It could've been anyone. Still...* Eafen snapped out of his frozen state and carried on along the corridor. He then turned left to another one where the front doors lay open ahead. The massive doors, made from darkest oak wood, were etched with the order's emblem. The Mage walked past and entered the courtyard.

Things were livelier out here, as servants went back and forth, carrying out the numerous day-to-day chores. Birds cackled and tweeted as they flew between the tops of the Stronghold's towers. To his right, Eafen could hear the whines and snorts of horses as they were led in and out of the stables. Next door was the blacksmith along with the armoury. Beyond that was the wall that separated the Stronghold from the Imperial Palace.

The Mage could see Gryphon tower stand out between the lower bastions. It stood as the tallest of the four towers that jutted out from the Imperial Palace, second only to the Sun Tower, based on the other side. The Sun Tower was where the Emperor and the Empress's private chambers were located, or was it Raven Tower?

Eafen had yet to set foot in the Imperial Palace himself, so he could only guess who resided in each tower. Each one resembled an octagon shape, complemented with a conical roof made from orange tiles that narrowed halfway as you went further up to the very tip. Whereas the towers of the Stronghold were built with a platform underneath the roof.

Eafen stopped right in the courtyard's centre to stare at the palace. *I wonder what the Chancellor is going through right now*, Eafen wondered. He couldn't guess which was worse, seeing disturbing visions portraying the world's end as he knew it or dealing with the pressure of maintaining order in a vast city whilst searching for an ancient relic without alerting the entire population.

Eafen took a deep breath and moved on, believing that the Chancellor had the situation under control. As he neared the gatehouse, another thought came to him when he looked back at the first vision. *Where was the Chancellor? Why was Captain Therin giving the orders?* Being one of the most influential men in the Empire and yet not being present at the Imperial Games for some reason troubled Eafen. Then there was the image of the Unbreakable Will being used before the visions ceased. *Who was that he that threw it? Where would the spear end up?*

Eafen gritted his teeth in frustration as none of the images made any sense. And here he was, passing through the gatehouse, leaving one enclosed world for another full of people going about their lives unaware of what troubles may soon fall upon them. The Mage pulled his hood as he stood outside the Stronghold right at one of the crossroads within the city of Abermerallt as carts and people travelled from left to right along Imperial Avenue. Ahead of him was Falcon Street.

Horns were blaring from Merchant's Gate, on the other side of the city. *That must be the participants from one of our outer garrisons joining us for the games*, Eafen thought. Might as well go take a look. He pulled his hood over him and followed the flowing river of people heading toward Market Square.

Meanwhile, down at the Imperial Harbour...

Gerald stared out at the ships that remained anchored. There were sailors either walking back and forth or lying around on the docks, utterly bored. He watched as the crew of one ship took down a white sail that was dirty and torn in places and replaced it with a fresh new one. *Their captain must've acquired it from the market,* he thought. The smell of fish at one of the stalls attracted the seagulls waiting for a merchant to drop something delicious for them to snatch. It was only yesterday afternoon when the mayor decreed that no ship may leave without a thorough inspection. Every vessel, big and small, was searched about twice, some thrice, in every nook and cranny.

Each market stall and tavern in the city was searched by men in arms accompanying representatives of the council. Not even the Jolly Maid was spared. Gerald couldn't help but feel as if this was his fault - especially now that there were more soldiers at every gate.

Thank goodness I got rid of that accursed box, he sighed thinking about that Black Box. Knowing that there would've been severe consequences for everyone. All the while, Gerald was still wearing his father's straw hat over his head, not just because he feared someone from the Academy would recognise him by his hair, but also to keep the heat of the suns at bay. Briefly, he took it off and put a hand through his hair, the brown dye should have dried off and taken effect by now, according to Joran. It took quite a lot for him to convince Nianna that he had a reason for the change in hair colour and had nothing to do with the other night's work. Gerald wondered if he should tell someone else of his involvement at the Academy, though the action would likely be followed by Brodus with a knife at his throat. Either that or he would be brought forth before the authorities. All he could do was keep his mouth shut and get on with his life, hoping that to never be called to do such dirty work again, and that whatever he stole the other night was nothing more than a glori ed jewellery box. Suddenly, the gossip stopped; men, women and children turned in one direction.

What now? Gerald wondered. He followed the masses as they moved with keen interest through Sparrow Street to Imperial Avenue. He made it to where the crowd had gathered as the sound of marching boots and hooves plodded on the cobbled ground. But Gerald couldn't see beyond them. He saw the statue of a man standing tall and proud, holding a large book under his arm. Gerald walked toward it and climbed up to the pedestal. The sun had warmed the sculture's bronze surface on one side whilst the other side was cool.

Gerald wrapped his arms tightly around the waist of the statue and looked over the crowd. He saw a column of horsemen parading through Imperial Avenue. They were followed by a group of foot soldiers and a few horse-pulled carts. Gerald could see from the colour of their tunics they were knights or men of the Twin Blade Order, and they were most likely heading to the Stronghold situated on the other side of the city. He realised that they were here for the Imperial Games when many people cheered them. He breathed a sigh of relief before hearing someone shout out his name.

"Gerald!"

He saw Nianna among the crowd, pushing her way toward the statue.

Gerald yelled down to her, "Don't know what you're getting excited about. They are just knights from the Twin Blade Order. We see them every day."

"I know!" she shouted. "You look like you were expecting something else."

Gerald glanced at the parade, then back to her and

said, "Trust me, this is better than watching miserable sailors lounging about on their ships. Come on."

He reached down to Nianna and pulled her up to him. She held onto him loosely, as they looked out at the parading men and horses. They noticed one horseman with brown hair. They waved at this man, and he waved back with a smile as he rode past.

Nianna looked at Gerald and said, "We better get back to the Jolly Maid. Father is expecting more knights to stop by for a pint."

Gerald nodded and slowly lowered her down to the ground. Nianna turned to look at him, nodding for him to follow. The young man glanced back at the parading knights; now, he could see the footmen and their carts as they brought up the rear. The crowd slowly dispersed, though many still chose to follow the convoy.

Then, from among the crowd, he noticed three men clad in the attire of the city guard. One of them, wearing a purple cape, appeared to be looking for someone. This one held out a poster in front of him, while the other two scanned the crowd as a hawk would observe a field for vulnerable prey to catch. Gerald's stomach tightened in fear of being caught. *I can't go back to the Jolly Maid with these men following me,* he thought. Instead, he dropped down from the statue and decided to mingle with the moving crowd as they crossed Lion's Bridge. He looked behind him. The three soldiers were a few feet away approaching the bridge, inspecting everyone they encountered. He looked ahead and saw an opening between two buildings on the left at the otherside.

He moved further among the masses, then broke away from the crowd and turned left into the alleyway as soon as he was off the bridge. He hid behind a stack of barrels and slowed his breathing. Popping his head out, he watched the soldiers pass by. He was relieved; Gerald had dodged a possible capture by the authorities. He rose and walked down the alley, but just then, he felt a hand grab him tightly by the shoulder. The stranger pressed Gerald against the wall. It was Brodus.

"Looks like they're on to you, Gerald, old boy." The stocky man grinned at him, gripping a long curved knife in front of him.

"Look, I haven't told anyone anything, I swear." Gerald gulped hard. "I thought we were done."

"Of course, we're supposed to be done, but as long as you're still walking around carelessly there's a chance you'll be caught. And we can't have that happen, now, can we?" He pulled Gerald closer to him. The smell of Brodus's acrid breath made him gasp for air. The sudden shift in movement had caused Gerald's hat to drop to the ground, revealing his hair to the brute.

"Well, what have we here?" Brodus stared down at the straw hat, before taking a look and sniffing Gerald's hair. "Bah," he pulled his head back in disgust, "What is that stuff?"

"I don't know," Gerald was confused, "Didn't think someone like you would notice."

Brodus gritted his teeth and growled in anger, as he squeezed him by the shoulder. Gerald winced as this brute imposed muscle and bone upon his own flesh.

"Ahh, alright alright. If you want me to leave, I can do that. Just get your hands off me, damn it," Gerald demanded.

"I'm afraid I can't do that." Brodus replied under the gritting of his poorly cared for teeth. "I'm sure my master will pay me well for shutting you up. Besides, you'll be stopped before you even reach the gates. Sorry, nothing personal."

"Wait, come on. It's only been a day since, and you're—"

"Too late, you worthless worm!" Brodus changed the

position of his hand, placing them upon his neck and began choking Gerald choke. The pain and lack of air forced him to his knees at the mercy of this rugged man.

"Oi, you there!"

Both men turned in surprise and saw a man on a horse. Gerald recognised him as the knight he was waving at.

"Shit!" Brodus cursed under his breath, he quickly pulled Gerald closer to him before sheaving a knife from his belt. Gerald was left staring at the knight dismounting from his horse, while Brodus hand one arm around his neck and the other gently proding his check with the knife.

"Another step and he gets it, you hear me!" Brodus threatened.

"Now come on, let him go slowly and maybe we can settle this properly." The knight answered.

"Like I'm stupid enough to listen to you," Brodus barked back with defiance. "You're just some fresh little shit that just arrived in this city. Things don't work like that here..."

Before he could say any more, Brodus was whacked in the back of his head by what appeared to be a rusty skillet. The metal object clanked off a wall and landed on the ground. The stocky man fell; Gerald was free from his captor's grip. He was as surprised by the metal object as the knight was. Looking behind him, he saw another figure, a young man, wearing a dark blue hooded tunic.

"Well, this seems to be my lucky day," the new face replied as he walked forward.

Gerald didn't know whether to be grateful or worried.

"Nice throw," the knight said.

"Thank you," the hooded figure replied.

The knight approached Gerald. "Are you alright?" "Uh, yes, I am fine," Gerald replied, "Thank you. I—"

"Just the man we were looking for," another voice spoke.

Everyone turned to the source. It was the man with the purple cape and the two soldiers that accompanied him. The man with the cape walked over to check the unconscious body of Brodus. He then noticed Gerald's hat and picked it up from the floor before looking at him, at his hair in particular. *Should've had a haircut instead,* Gerald thought. Suddenly he felt a pinch from the back of his head, "Ah, hey," he responded as he looked and saw the man with the hooded tunic holding up some strands of his hair. He looked closely at them, even giving them a sniff.

"That smells like bark, with a mixture of walnut, rusty iron and pitch," he said.

The man in the cape looked amused, "Clever idea to hide your true colours," he said.

Gerald attempted a lie, "I don't know what you're talking about. This has always been my normal hair colour."

"We'll see about that. Gerald Giles. You are under arrest for involvement in the robbery of the Imperial Academy," said the man in the cape.

"Oh no," Gerald muttered under his breath.

"Hold on," the knight intervened, "This man was just attacked. Surely you should go easy on him."

"Oh, don't worry, we'll just be asking some simple questions." The man in the cape gestured to the other two soldiers to pick up Brodus whilst still unconscious.

"Please, just keep him away from me, and I'll talk. I swear," Gerald begged.

"I hope you do so for your sake." The man in the cape pulled some rope, and then he took Gerald by the arms and tied them behind his back. They began to walk toward Imperial Avenue.

"Thank you for the help, knight," he patted the knight on the shoulder.

"Oh, I'm not a knight yet. My name is Arran Connaught.

I just arrived today."

"Therin Soulman, Captain of the City Guard."

"And I am Eafen Ulrin," the Mage spoke. "I, too, am a member of the Twin Blade Order."

"Right, I'll need to take these two to the palace for questioning. Enjoy your stay, Arran." Therin nodded and pulled Gerald with him.

This wasn't how he wanted his day to end, to be threatened by that brute Brodus and then caught by the authorities. He glanced back to Brodus, cuffed by the two soldiers and dragged by the arms. The only thing he could think of now, as he walked away, was Nianna, waiting for him at the Jolly Maid. How long would it take before she realised something was wrong?

Arran looked at the man he had just saved, only to be dragged away by the captain, along with the thug who just attacked him. *What was that all about?* he wondered. Eafen the Mage walked up to him.

"Those two men were involved in a robbery at the Imperial Academy."

"What exactly did they steal?" Arran asked.

"I'm not supposed to say. It shouldn't matter; hopefully, we'll straighten things out and deliver appropriate sentences for them."

"I assume that's the reason the ships were being anchored?" he asked.

Eafen nodded to Arran. "After today, they'll be on their way. Come, we should head back to the Stronghold."

"Yes," Arran nodded and walked over to Basil.

His eyes soon looked past the crowd to the coliseum. Its oval structure towered over the walls and every building in the city but the Imperial Palace. Flags adorned with many colours and symbols were being placed all round.

"It's more magnificent when you're inside," Eafen pointed out.

Arran only nodded.

"Did you know," Eafen continued, "that when Emperor Flavian married his first wife, the celebration that followed the wedding was the largest ever? They had to use the coliseum to accommodate the feast."

"I heard about that," Arran replied.

"I assume you're here for the Imperial Games?" Eafen asked.

"Where else can a man go to make a name for himself?"

"I suppose so." Eafen stroked his chin. "Since there's been no conflict for the last two hundred years, the games keep the kingdoms united and entertain the masses."

Arran nodded. "You remind me of someone I know. Always knowing something useful."

"It never hurts to learn of what has come before."

"It's what's happening now that matters." Arran stroked Basil as the pair walked on.

"That's a fine horse you have there." "Thank you. This is Basil."

"If you're not a knight, then how did you come upon that horse?'

"I served as a squire to another lord. Sir Rhodrik Wynne. He died a few years ago and left me Basil in his will. My father was a good friend of his and put forth most of his funds so that I could be tutored by him."

"I see," the Mage nodded.

They walked further into the city. As Arran looked around, he noted that its buildings were a concoction of various architectural styles. There were houses framed with timber and filled with bricks. Their roofs were like triangles, pointing sharply up to the sky. Other buildings were built with rows of arches supported by pillars and balconies erected on top. They soon arrived at their destination, the

Stronghold. A fortress within the city, its walls grey and thick. There was a large gatehouse with bastion towers much like the ones in Gard Afon Castle. Its windows were small slits, enough room for one inside to see out.

"And here we are, my friend," Eafen spoke, Arran saw within the gateway that Gabriel and Callum were waiting for him.

"Your friends don't look pleased," Eafen noted.

"We've been having a strange day since our departure," Arran replied

As Arran and Eafen walked past the guards, they were joined by the other two.

"Trying to be the local hero again, Arran?" Gabriel asked.

"I just noticed someone in trouble," Arran replied.

"Your friend just so happened to be at the right place at the right time," Eafen added con dently.

"Who are you?" said Gabriel

"Eafen Ulrin."

The Mage smiled.

"He's one of us, lads."

"I'm Gabriel and this is Callum. We should head inside. Captain Dorwin is waiting for us."

"Very well."

"I wonder what they'll be serving us tonight," Callum asked.

"Oh, believe me my friend, when you try our stew, you'll be back for seconds," Eafen replied.

"Sounds good to me," said Arran.

Chapter 16

Valeran's place, Falcon Street

VALERAN HAD ONLY JUST RETURNED from the Imperial Palace. He did his best not to look suspicious to others when walking quickly, yet he knew that time would soon be against him. The Master of Coin slammed the door shut and sighed. He wiped his forehead with his sleeve. Next, he walked over to the table and pulled out a large map from the drawer. He rolled the map out, using books and other loose objects to hold down the corners. The entire continent of Maldora, its cities and landmarks illustrated with ink, was laid out before his eyes on the map.
He placed a bony finger at Aberemrallt, located south of the mountains with the River Tor running through it. Then he dragged that it with him along one of the many routes that Gedric would take. The quickest way for the chancellor to get to Bourgiatta Castle would be to head out east and cross the River Tor to the town of Paroy. Then ride northwest to Luvera Castle, which was on the other side of the river to Pwynt Afon, before going east again to reach Bourgiatta. T*hat should take Gedric at least two days to get there,* Valeran thought. Just then, he heard three knocks on the door.

Valeran wasn't expecting anyone to visit him today. He picked up a small knife next to the map and hid it behind his back. The door banged again in quicker succession, this time, there was urgency behind each rat-a-tat-tat. He opened the peephole to see who was outside. Before, he was a slim young man who wore simple clothes and sported short black hair. This was Dowri, Valeran's servant.

"What is it, Dowri? Why are you here?" Valeran asked sharply.

"I bring unfortunate news, Master," the boy whispered, "I've seen—"

"Stop!" Valeran commanded. "Wait until I open this door." He placed his hidden knife under his belt as he closed the flap and unlocked the door.

"Inside now," he hissed, and Dowri entered immediately. Valeran then closed the door behind him.

"Right." Valeran took a breath. "Whatever news you have, boy, spit it out. I have important things to do."

The squire gulped nervously before he replied, "Gerald, your contact, has been captured, my lord."

"What?" Valeran looked at him dubiously.

"He was apprehended by Captain Therin by the bridge."

"Wonderful," Valeran sighed; this was not good news. He walked over to the table. "And where was Brodus? I told him to keep an eye on him."

"Unfortunately, he was captured as well," Dowri replied.

Valeran turned and stared back at Dowri; his narrowed eyes terrified the boy so much that he took a step back. He returned to the table, where he thumped the surface with both of his hands,

"That bloody buffoon!"

"My lord," Dowri replied. Valeran continued to curse.

"That inbred idiot couldn't even do a dirty job in the middle of daylight without even a dog catching a scent, let alone the Captain of the Guard and his fucking lackeys. I swear I'd..." He exerted so much energy raising his disgust and frustration that he began to cough very hard. Dowri rushed to his master with a cup of water. Valeran swiped it from him and sipped it all, relieved as the cold fluid flowed down his throat. He breathed slowly to calm himself.

"It would appear that time is slipping much sooner from

my grasp than I thought," he sighed. "Where are they now?" Valeran looked at his squire for answers.

"Last I saw them, my lord, they were heading for the Imperial Palace."

"To be interrogated in the dungeon, below, no doubt," Valeran grumbled.

"Perhaps we can bribe the guards to let them go?" Dowri suggested. "Use some of the treasury to—"

"No!" Valeran shot back at his servant. "It is too late for them. Any investment in their release would only justify to Gedric that the true threat is here right under his nose. I will not compromise my plan for their worthless hides."

Dowri stood before him, saying nothing.

Valeran sighed again. He looked back at the map. It was only a matter of time before Gedric and Therin would learn more about his plan. He expected Brodus to put up more of a fight than Gerald, but Valeran would have to leave as soon as possible to avoid being questioned. He had the box and the knowledge of the key. All that he needed to do was cover his tracks. No witnesses.

Valeran turned back to his servant. "Fetch me some wine. Two cups, please."

Dowri looked puzzled by his master's request but did it anyway. He took two cups from the table and filled them with wine from the barrel. Valeran watched the boy as he did so. Dowri came from a poor family and had dreamed of becoming a knight. Valeran caught him spying as he used magic a few years ago. Rather than kill him, the Master of Coin had found a use for the boy as a servant, provided he told no one of his talents for the dark arts. He taught him how to read, write and count, so he could help him keep track of the Imperial treasury.

Dowri came forth. "Your wine, Master."

"Put them there," Valeran gestured to the table. "Now there is a box in the other room and a bag. Go fetch them for me, please." Again, Dowri did as his master ordered.

Valeran turned to the drinks his servant had prepared. He pulled out from one of his pockets a small vile. The contents were crimson. The Kraken's Curse: a poison made from the blood of a kraken beast mixed with other chemicals meant to bring swift and sudden death to anyone who drinks even this much. He opened the vial and poured it into one of the cups. He gently swayed the cup in his hand to mix the fluids. Satisfied, he put the cup with the poison down, ensuring he kept it away from his own.

"Is this what you wanted?" Dowri had returned, holding the Black Box in his hands.

"Yes, good. Put it on the table," Valeran ordered. The servant placed the box on the table.

"Do you know what this is, Dowri?" Valeran asked him.

"This is the Black Box," Dowri replied, unsure if he should continue as he looked around the room.

"Go on, don't worry, my boy," Valeran encouraged. "We are safe here."

Dowri gulped before he continued. "It holds the Heart of Darkness inside."

"Yes, good. And do you know who it belongs to?"

"The Dark Lord Samael. The one people shouldn't speak of." Dowri looked at his master. Valeran could tell he was uncomfortable talking about him.

"And why do people not speak of him?" Valeran asked.

"Because… he is said to be evil. That he embodies all that is wrong."

Valeran resisted the urge to chuckle at Dowri's answer. "`My boy, my boy. What is evil? Have you ever thought about it? If you think about it, evil is merely a construct of the living mind."

"A construct?" The squire was puzzled.

"In other words, it is a theory, or simply a word.

Something people come up with and put rules based around it to stop others from conducting what they think is wrong. Say a poor man steals a loaf of bread to feed his starving family. Is that wrong? Keeping his family fed must surely take priority above everything else. Here's another one. A woman who attends to the desires of a man a day for their money. Is this wrong? Is this what you call evil? No, no; this is what you have to do to survive in this age. At the end of the day, it's about necessity and survival. Do you understand?"

Dowri answered, "I think I do. But what if either of them had to kill someone?"

"Well, if it was killing without reason, then yes. If that person refused to serve you food or killed someone you cared about, who's in the wrong there? Is it so wrong to avenge those you care about and seek retribution on those who have slighted you?"

"I suppose not."

"What I'm getting at is simple: people make mistakes. They judge others by their appearances and how they go about things. Samael was known to be a great fighter in his time. He had to be. He started as an outcast, a slave. He had to fight and kill to ensure his survival. Many of his northern kind saw him as an inspiration and followed him without question for the promise of glory. Then along came Orion, the so-called Saviour, who stood against him in the name of all things good. Hmph. What has this Saviour done for us? It took us nearly a thousand years for his message to get around, and yet there is still corruption in places. Dukes and princes trot around the land as they please, always born with money in their pockets. Never had to earn their way of living through blood and battle as Samael did."

"So, what you're suggesting is that the Empire would be better if we worshipped Samael instead?" Dowri asked.

"Oh, I'm not suggesting anything. Though, to be fair, having only one god to worship would make life so much simpler than worshipping four. And if there are those who blindly refuse to acknowledge this, then I say be gone with you heathens. Anyway," Valeran picked up his glass of wine.

"Help yourself, Dowri."

"Are you sure?" the servant asked. "I insist."

Dowri looked at the cup closest to him and picked it up.

"Have you ever drunk wine before?" Valeran asked.

"No, I haven't," Dowri confessed. "I've tried ale."

"I see. Well, have a sip. Don't be shy."

Dowri put this cup to his mouth. Valeran watched the servant take a sip whilst he did the same.

"What do you think?"

"It's strong, very strong. May I ask what it is?"

"Ah, this is Dragon Blood wine. The best wine in all of the realms." Valeran raised his cup in front of himself.

"Why is it called that?" Dowri asked before taking another sip.

Valeran then explained, "Well, some say that it was made with the blood of a slain dragon. But then again, the last dragon that roamed the continent died centuries ago. It is actually red grapes from the vineyards of Frankonia."

"My throat is a bit hot, though. It's like, it's like…."

Dowri struggled to put sentences together; his hands were beginning to shake. He dropped his cup onto the table, causing the map of Maldora to turn red. The squire looked at Valeran as he dropped down to his knees, clutching his neck.

"M… my lord, I can't breathe," Dowri tried to speak but started coughing. Blood began to froth from his mouth.

"Oh my. I forgot to tell you, Dowri. I added some Kraken's Curse to your drink," Valeran explained. "What you're experiencing right now is probably the equivalent of a dragon being dragged down below the sea by a kraken. Its tentacles wrapping around your throat, denying you air to breathe."

"H… help me!" the boy pleaded.

"Oh, I am helping you, my boy. Just in a different way," Valeran replied. He watched as Dowri's life began to fade. The boy's eyes turned white, and then he fell to the floor, reaching out to Valeran and grasping at his master's robes.

Valeran sighed and side-stepped the child. "I'm sorry I had to do this to you." He put his cup down on the stained table. "But I cannot risk any more people squealing before the emperor and his lapdogs."

The Master of Coin then picked up the Black Box and hid it within his cloak. He walked past his servant's body to the other side of his house, where he opened a window wide. He then closed his eyes and muttered a spell in a long-forgotten language. He opened his eyes to view the world from a different perspective. Now he was a bird, a crow. He flapped his wings and took off, shooting through the window, ascending high. Valeran could see the whole city below him as he flew out toward the city gates.

Onward to Bourgiatta, he flew. Onward to Destiny.

Chapter 17

The dungeons, beneath the Imperial Palace

AN HOUR HAD PASSED since Gerald and Brodus were caught. The captain put a bag over Gerald's head before they entered the palace grounds. When the bag was finally lifted, he was in a separate room to Brodus and by the sounds of Brodus's yelling, he was just a few cells away. He sat on a small roughly-assembled bed underneath a tiny barred window, the only source of light for a place that reeked of piss and sweat.

Gerald's mind was racing. *What will they want from me? What should I say to them? What proof do I have that this mad plan was concocted by someone else?* Gerald tried to ignore the possibility of him being killed for confessing, and push the images of his murdered corpse from his mind. If not by Brodus, then perhaps by someone else.

"None of this should be happening," he muttered to himself, shivering as the intrusive images burned into his consciousness. It was as if this was all just a dream. He squeezed his eyes shut, and counted to ten with a deep breath. Then he opened them, but he was still in the cell. His hands were numb from the cold air.

Suddenly, he heard the plodding of boots from outside They drew closer then stopped. The door opened. Gerald sat up as two soldiers entered, followed soon after by Captain Therin who was accompanied by another, much older, man. Gerald saw a golden badge on this man's jacket and assumed he was very important. The captain closed the door behind him whilst the older man sat on a stool that one of the soldiers had brought in with them.

"Hello again," Captain Therin spoke, but Gerald remained silent.
"Lord Chancellor," the captain continued, "this is Gerald Gilles, one of the two men we have been looking for."
Chancellor Gedric was eyeing Gerald as he sat on the stool. "I must admit, you don't look much like a thief."
He then turned to the soldiers behind him. "Would you give us a moment please, lads?" They lowered their heads before heading out through the door. The captain went to lean on the wall next to the door.
The chancellor turned back to Gerald. "Now then, let's begin. Do you know who I am?"
"Y…you're Lord Gedric. The chancellor and the Emperor's Hand."
"Good. So, Gerald, let's start with a simple question. What were you doing two nights ago?"
Gerald stared blankly at him.
Seeing this, the chancellor changed the question. "From what I have been told, you were once a student at the Imperial Academy, am I right?"
Gerald nodded.
"And you were caught making and distributing potions without permission from the Academy. Do you deny this?" the chancellor asked.
Gerald paused for a moment, then he replied, "No, it is true. I needed the money to pay my landlord."
"And that action led to your expulsion," Therin butted in.
"Now for the main question." Gedric leaned forward as he continued. "Were you not involved in the robbery at the Great Academy?"
Rather than test the chancellor's patience, Gerald sighed. "Yes. Yes, I was, my lord."
"That passageway beneath the Academy storeroom has

been kept a secret for years, no, centuries," the captain spoke again. "How long have you known about it?"
"I… I never knew anything about it until a week or so, before my expulsion," Gerald explained. "I was just searching for supplies when the headmaster and his guards entered the room. I hid behind one of the shelves and watched them open the passage trap door."
At that point, Captain Therin pushed himself off the wall and walked over to stand by the chancellor. "Right, I'm glad we got that out of the way. Now, here comes the more interesting question. Who ordered you to do it?"
"I… I don't know."
"You must be joking?" Therin looked at him with surprise. "You've known about this secret passage for some time, and you decide to just go with your friend and take whatever you want?"
"Brodus isn't my friend!" Gerald answered back. "I don't know him, and he tried to kill me. Unless you have forgotten that."
"Are you calling me stupid?" Therin was irritated. He was about to approach Gerald when Gedric raised a hand.
"Stand down, Captain," he ordered. The captain looked down at the chancellor before he backed away and sighed.
"Fine," he raised his hands.
The chancellor turned back to Gerald. "Listen to me, Gerald. What you have stolen from the Academy could have severe repercussions on the state and the continent itself." He paused to look at the door before he continued.
"You've heard about the tale of Samael and the Heart of Darkness?"
"Yes, yes, I have, my lord," Gerald answered.
"Well, I shouldn't be telling anyone outside the Imperial court of this, but those tales are true. The box you stole from the Academy contained what remains of him. His

spiritual self, trapped in physical form."
Gerald's face lit up with shock as if he had been splashed with cold water. "But that's impossible. W… why would you keep such a thing there of all places?"
"I've been asking myself that question for a very long time," Therin said, sharing his opinion.
"I'm pretty sure you can imagine what will happen if we don't get this thing back. Now, let's start again: where did you first meet your contact?"
Gerald gulped hard before he answered. "I don't know who he is. I remember receiving a letter whilst working at the Jolly Maid. I was told to meet him at the Black Rose on the other side of the city."
"I know that place," Therin responded as he pulled out a flask from his belt. "It's where the whores frequent. Very little comes out of there."
"So, you met him at the Black Rose. What then?" Gedric asked.
"Well, I was shown where he was sitting, then I was introduced to Brodus who was behind me with a knife. He said he saw me spying on them. Told me that he could've reported me to the headmaster if he wanted to, but then he said he had a job for me. He told me his plan, what he wanted me to acquire and said he would pay me well for it."
"What did he look like? You must've seen his face."
"No, I couldn't. We were in a very dark room. He was old, I think, by the way he talked, and he was leaning on a cane shaped like a snake even when he was sitting down. There was also a ring on his left hand. That's all I can remember, honest."
At that moment, the chancellor looked up at the captain and gestured to him. Captain Therin approached Gerald.

"Here," he offered his flask. Gerald greatly accepted it; he did not hesitate to quench his sudden thirst. It was just water that touched the back of his throat, but he was grateful. He drank until he had to pull away to breathe.

"Thank you," he said before handing the flask back.

"I think there's been enough talk for now, Captain," the chancellor called. He stood up from the stool and walked to the door. Captain Therin picked up the stool as he followed.

"Wait," Gerald spoke again. "Will I be pardoned?"

The chancellor paused for a moment before replying. "I appreciate all that you have told us. There will be a trial after the games. I will do all I can to ensure it will be fair. For now, it would be best that you remain here until the situation dies down."

After that the chancellor and the captain walked through the door, the last one of the two closing it behind him. The hard thud of the door echoed and was followed by silence. Gerald Gilles was by himself once again, confined beneath the Imperial Palace. His fate was now in the hands of others.

"Well, that was an interesting conversation," Therin recalled as he put the stool down.

"Where is Lord Valeran?" Gedric asked immediately.

"The last I saw him; he was leaving the palace courtyard—"

"I need you to go to his dwelling after we're done here. And take some men with you. In case he resists arrest," Gedric replied.

"What?" Therin looked surprised. "You want me to arrest the Master of Coin?"

"I'm not taking any chances. If he is the man behind all of this, then he has a lot to answer for. Gods only know how long he's been planning this."

"With respect, Chancellor, I know he is a Serpentine and all that comes with his name," Therin protested, "but what proof do you have that he is responsible for this?"

"More than enough by the end of today. Besides, I just need you to keep him wherever he is. I will inform the emperor of our findings afterwards. Now, let's go talk to the next one."

"As you wish," Therin acknowledged.

The chancellor and the captain walked down the dungeon corridor until they came to the last room. A guard rose from his stool next to the door.

"Lord Chancellor, Captain," he addressed.

"Open the door. We must speak with the prisoner," Gedric ordered. The guard took out a key from a pocket in his leather surcoat and opened the door.

"I must warn you, my lords, this one's a right stubborn bastard. Took three of us to keep him in here when he finally woke up," said the guard.

Gedric nodded to the guard before entering the room. The man known as Brodus was chained by his right arm to the bed he lay on. After closing the door behind them, Gedric and Therin stood with their backs to the wall, keeping their distance from the wild man.

"Do you know who I am?" Gedric asked.

"Like I give a shit." Brodus replied bitterly.

Therin asked, "We would like to know what you've been doing over the last few days and who are you working for?"

"Fuck off!" Brodus spat back.

"Thought you would say something like that," Gedric replied. "I imagine that your master has promised you something in return for your services. Gold? Women? Titles?" He took a step closer to the prisoner. "Well, it doesn’t matter really; you’ll never receive them regardless of whose side you’re on, so you might as well tell us who you are working for.”

“You think so?” Brodus looked at him, unyielding.

Gedric continued, “I can promise that you can either live out the rest of your days here. Or there is the shorter way out of your life. If you don’t mind the humiliation of the entire empire seeing you for the scum that you are. The jeering and the spitting from everyone just before we hang you.”

“Ha. You think you have it all, don’t you?” Brodus sneered. “Just when you think you had it all figured out, my master is already a step ahead of you.”

“Who is he?” Gedric demanded.

“You’re smart. Thought you would’ve squeezed everything out from that little shit,” replied Brodus.

“No picture is complete without all the pieces. Great or small,” Therin broke in.

Brodus replied, “I’m just a killer, you know. Kill this person, get paid. Burn this house down and all that.”

“Bullshit!” the chancellor called out. “Even lowly criminal scum such as yourself would know better than to involve yourselves with things beyond anyone’s understanding.”

Brodus looked the chancellor right in the eyes, then he spat at him.

“You talk a lot, old man. Bet you can’t ght as well.”

“He doesn’t need to,” Therin responded. “Shall we make an example out of him?” he asked Gedric.

“No,” he answered. “There is nothing he can offer us right now, willingly or not.” He then walked over to the door.

“`He knows more about the Heart of Darkness than you think,” Brodus boasted loudly behind Gedric’s back.

“I’m sure he does.” The chancellor looked over his shoulder as the door opened. “May the gods condemn your soul, traitor.” With that, he and Therin left the criminal to himself. The door to Brodus’s cell slammed behind them.

“I want to arrange to have that man executed after the games,” said Gedric.

“You didn’t even put as much effort as you did with Gerald,” said Therin.

Gedric replied, “I didn’t need to. His last words pointed out what I should’ve known all this time.”

“And you still want to arrest Valeran?” Therin asked.

“Absolutely. We shall inform the emperor at once,” said Gedric as they left the dungeons.

A sense of anger was burning inside of him. All this time that snake pretended to be weak and above the past ills of his house.

A cleverly concealed ruse.

The chancellor would tolerate it no longer.

Chapter 18

The Stronghold, Aberemrallt

THE DAY WAS CHANGING TO EVENING, the clear sky transitioning from light blue to a warm orange, whilst the sun slowly descended from east to west.

Arran was leaning on the balcony watching with keen eyes as the garrison of the Stronghold went about their day-to-day routines. The Stronghold was the pride of the Twin Blade Order, a small fortress within the city whose balconies extend all around above the courtyard, with a tower at each of the four corners. It had a dock of its own, allowing for ships bearing the order's banner to unload their provisions from the other strongholds.

Stable boys were piling old hay from the stables onto a cart to be taken away. Stewards and servants were going back and forth from the kitchen and sergeants were walking along the battlements. All this was happening as Arran began reflecting on today's events. Everything seemed safe and comforting to him, nothing out of the ordinary. Outside in the city, the daily routine of working, trading and gossiping went on. Perhaps he was just imagining things. He wanted to push them away so he could concentrate on the games tomorrow. He turned away from the courtyard and noticed Anwen walking towards him, appearing calm as usual.

"Someone told me you've been playing the hero today," said Anwen.

"It was nothing," Arran replied. "Just saw a man being threatened by another, that's all."

"My father doesn't take too well to people breaking out of

line."

"I've already had a word from him," Arran replied. "Said that I should leave it to the city guards next time."

"That's what they're there for," Anwen said.

"And being the captain's daughter means you wouldn't do the same thing either?" Arran asked.

"Whatever goes on among the citizenry shouldn't be our concern unless it's very serious." She leaned on the balcony, looking down at the courtyard. They watched as one of the many priests stationed in the Stronghold stood in the middle of the courtyard, whistling. A moment later, a large falcon came swooping down from one of the towers, landing and gripping its master's gloved hand. The satisfied priest walked away from the courtyard with his prized pet toward the stables, where the falcon would be returned to their birdhouse for the evening. Elsewhere, torches in the courtyard were being lit. There was even a small circular stone pit at the otherside, where servants placed piles of wood inside. Accompanying them was another priest, who - once the servants had done their part took a step forward, raising a hand over the pit and a moment later ignited the fire pit. Didn't even flinch.

"I suppose you're right there." Arran folded his arms.

"Say, didn't you serve someone before?" Anwen looked at Arran.

"Yes, I did," Arran nodded. "I was appointed to serve as a servant to Lord Rhodrik Wynne. He was the previous captain in charge of our company before your father."

"I've heard of Lord Rhodrik," said Anwen. "What was he like?"

"He was kind, dedicated to his vows," Arran began, "and sometimes stubborn, especially when I first met him as a boy. Oh, and a lover of beetroot." He shook his head. "He was reluctant at first to have a personal squire. Probably

trying to prove that he could do things himself despite his age. But he seemed to like me in time."
"You must have been a good servant to him," Anwen assumed.
"I was. He taught me how to hold a sword himself, how to write for him. His last gift to me before he passed away was Basil." He pointed to the stables. "So, what about you Anwen?"
"What about me?" She looked at him.
"Most women born with a father as a knight or a noble would spend their time sewing and learning to dance."
Anwen scoffed. "The only dance I care for is the one with a sword in my hand. Even though my father was against me holding one at first."
"The idea of a lady wielding a sword would scare most husbands, enough so that they wouldn't even dare sleep in the same bed," Arran chuckled.
"Knock it off." Anwen lightly punched Arran in the arm, but he didn't flinch.
"Marriage never crossed your mind then?" Arran asked. The girl just looked at him.
"Not really." She looked back at the courtyard.
Arran had learned over his years that once you have sworn an oath to a knightly order such as the Twin Blade, your options outside would be limited. A man who took the vow can only marry women of noble birth or those related to fellow members, if offered.
The same is somewhat said to women. Marriage between a man and woman within the order was forbidden. If a female knight chose to engage in marriage, she would have to relinquish her knighthood in exchange for the title of ladyship.
"My father decided to train me since I was his only child."

Arran replied, "I'm sorry about that. I don't have any siblings either."
"Something we have in common," Anwen acknowledged.
Arran nodded.
"What matters is tomorrow," said Anwen.
"The games," Arran replied as he looked up. He could see the peak of the coliseum from here. "A tradition that's been around for a long time."
"Are you nervous?" Anwen asked.
"No," Arran replied. "Maybe I will be tomorrow, maybe I won't. You never know. Regardless, I intend on going all the way, no matter who I face. You're lucky you won't have to face as many challenges as me and Gabriel."
Although female competitors were a recent addition to the Imperial Games, bouts and fighters in these categories were few, as the idea of women taking up arms was still seen as unpopular by the majority of people.
"Have you got a new sword then?" Anwen asked.
"Yes, I've spoken to the blacksmith here. He had plenty of spare swords in the armoury for use, and so I've found something with the perfect weight and blade."
"Hmm. You'd think that after two hundred and eighty years, more women would take up the games," Anwen pointed out.
Arran shrugged. "Giving everyone a chance to be a part of something in just a day is like trying to get a dwarf to feel comfortable with water. I heard someone say that once."
"Still, it feels like a lot of time has gone without much change."
"Maybe something will change, maybe it won't. Who knows?"
"It all starts with one person, just as it was with Orion. Otherwise, we wouldn't be here." "That's true," Arran

agreed.

"I must attend to my quarters," said Anwen. "Good luck to you tomorrow."

"You too."

With that, Anwen left Arran to himself on the balcony. Arran looked upward at the sky before retiring inside to prepare for morning to come.

Meanwhile…

Eafen stopped before the door of the chief archmage's office. He planned to inform him about his recent visions. The Chief Archmage of the Twin Blade Order was responsible for advising the Grandmaster in matters regarding magic. The man who occupies this life-long role also embodied the duties of overseeing the recruitment and indoctrination of new magic wielders. The young mage took a moment to tidy his robes before knocking on the door.

The hinges and handle were solid black. Above the latter there were two silver hands holding the symbols of the four elements: earth, wind, fire, and water. These were the elements that most known magic fell into. Eafen took a deep breath, reminding himself of what he wished to talk about and how to present it. He stepped forward and knocked on the door.

"Enter," a voice within the room answered.

Eafen pushed the door open and entered a room that took up half of the extended space built into the Stronghold many years ago. There were two spacious windows on the other side of the room. Outside, Eafen could see shadows starting to take form in the corners of the walls and towers belonging to the Imperial Palace. The walls were decorated with pictures of men who took on the mantle of archmage centuries ago. To his right, there was a large desk where a very sturdy man sat, writing with a quill on parchment. Behind him there was a shelf of books above his head. This was Chief Archmage Azurius Palovius Penno, wearing a clean dark green robe decorated with fine jewels on the sleeves. There was a tassel hat on the desk near a pot of ink.

"Ah, Eafen." Azurius put down his quill. "It is unusual of you to speak to me at this time."

"Yes, I know, Lord Azurius," said Eafen. "I hope I'm not disturbing you."

"Not really, have a seat." The archmage gestured to the chair.

Eafen walked over to the table and seated himself in front of his superior.

"So, my friend," Azurius began, "you have something to discuss?"

"Yes, I do." Eafen cleared his throat before he continued. "I would like to report that I, along with Captain Therin from the City Guard, was successful in capturing the criminals who stole... you-know-what."

"I've heard," Azurius replied. "Good work."

"Thank you, my lord."

"Have you received anything from the guard about where they hid the artefact?" The Archmage leaned forward as he asked.

"No, not yet. All I know is that they're both confined to the dungeons underneath the Imperial Palace."

"Hmmm. I would've preferred it if we were allowed to have some involvement in the interrogation. Still, it amuses me how quickly you were able to find them. In my youth, it took the authorities at least a week to find thieves and criminals in this city."

"Well, it was just luck that the criminal's paths crossed with mine today," Eafen scratched the back of his head. "I

had unexpected assistance from another of our brethren."
"Oh? Interesting." Azurius looked curious. "From our Stronghold or from the company that arrived from Gard Afon?"
"The latter, my lord. By the name of Arran Connaught."
"Ah, one of Captain Alric's men. Reliable man."
"I haven't met him yet. I will no doubt have the privilege to meet him soon."
Azurius nodded. "But I believe that's not why you are here?"
"No, I admit there's something else that troubles me," Eafen confessed.
"Go on," the archmage encouraged him to continue. "I was in the chapel today when I received a vision."
"A vision?"
"Yes. From the future."
"How far?" he asked.
"Not far. Tomorrow, during the coming Imperial Games. I'm not sure how to explain it. I was there, but through someone else's eyes."
"Through whose eyes?" the archmage asked.
"I don't know. Someone from our ranks."
"What did you see?"
"Chaos," Eafen replied. "As if something terrible is going to happen."
"I see," Azurius looked at him, pushing himself back in his chair.
"I know it seems hard to believe, but every bit of it felt real. Men fighting beasts and horrors I have never seen before. The Coliseum on fire. And," Eafen paused to pick his next words. "There was a massive portal before me."
"Hmm." The chief archmage seemed to be taking Eafen's words with a pinch of salt. "So why now?" he asked. "Have you seen anything similar to this before?"
"No. Nothing like this," Eafen confessed. "All I'm suggesting is that if this happens in the coming days, we

should inform the grandmaster and the chancellor ..."
"The grandmaster has already made arrangements with the chancellor in matters of security for the games. Those among us not participating will assist in maintaining order."
Azurius leaned forward, pressing his hands on the wood of the table. "Although the theft of the Black Box was unexpected, I cannot see this vision you are telling me as real."
"How so?" Eafen was curious, and surprised.
Azurius pushed back in his chair as he replied, "You have to remember there is a difference between visions of the past and the future. The former is easy because you are witnessing what has already taken place, as you have seen first hand at the Academy."
Eafen said nothing, but nodded.
"However, this isn't the case with deciphering the future. Fate is a malleable thing, even the littlest of things can change the outcome foreseen in one's vision. My predecessor had seen visions of the future, only a quarter of them were as he foresaw them. You've only just unlocked this rare gift Eafen, don't be surprised if what really happens, if anything does so in contrast to what you have foreseen."
"But it felt real," Eafen replied, "I believe that the robbery may be part of a bigger plot. One that's about to unravel on our very doorstep."
"Impossible," Azurius replied. "There has not been an attack on the capital for nearly two hundred years. For any enemy of the empire to attack us here, they would have already established territory on the way, raiding local towns for resources needed to lay siege to this city. That is if they haven't met any resistance on the way. And

yes, the loss of the Black Box is most troubling. But a box without a key is as useful to these robbers as a ship without sails."

"Sails can easily be made and replaced," Eafen countered immediately, "with the right material and knowledge."

"True, but the box where the Heart of Darkness is locked in is no ordinary box. Our order has taken steps since the construction of this device to ensure that it cannot be opened by either brute force or by any other form of known magic. We over the years have confiscated all material that explains what spells were used to seal it."

"But, lord Azurius, with respect to what we know of military strategy, aren't we not taught to expect the unexpected from our enemies? Especially those who fight for the dark lords?"

Azurius sighed. "Eafen. I wish I could believe in this theory, but there isn't enough proof to justify a possible attack. We would've known about it by now. Let us put this aside and see what happens."

Eafen replied, "My lord, you can't be—"

"Please Eafen, enough. The last thing we need is to stir up more trouble before tomorrow. If your visions come to you again, then I recommend you see the apothecary to inspect you. You may leave now."

Eafen swallowed hard, he knew he could say no more.

"Understood. Thank you, my lord."

He rose from his seat and made his way to the door. "You better get some rest too, Eafen. Tomorrow will be a big day," Azurius said as Eafen opened the door. He looked back at the chief archmage who resumed writing on his parchment.

There was nothing more to say to him, so he closed the door behind him. He walked along the corridor, but stopped at one of the windows. He stared out to the sea, where the moon now reigned above in the night sky. He hoped he was wrong about this, he really hoped. The only thing he could do now was rest his eyes and make himself ready for tomorrow.

Chapter 19

Friday 30th August
Outside of Bourgiatta Castle, Terradonia Province

THE SUN ROSE from the east over the fields that stood between Valeran and his next target: Bourgiatta Castle. It was an imposing sight to behold, built atop a knoll and casting a great shadow across the countryside, a masterpiece of Terran engineering. Bourgiatta Castle was commissioned for construction a hundred years ago by House Serpentine at the height of their power to keep the other city-states in check.

Pine trees swayed gently in a sudden light breeze from the east. Valeran was mounted on a black horse, staring at this marvel from the cover of nearby woodland. Next to him was a man also on horseback, dressed in the purple and yellow tunic of a soldier of the Imperial household. He was one of seven men clad in the same attire that stood behind them, awaiting their master's command.

"Is it time, my lord?" the rider asked.

Valeran continued to look out at the castle. From here, he could see one side of the castle's layout. Its design resembled that of a hexagon. Three gatehouses at the northeast, the south and the northwest points. Six large towers pointed out like arrowheads from each corner.

Valeran looked at the rider and replied, "Yes, it is time, Walder. Follow me."

"As you command, Lord Valeran," Walder acknowledged.

He gestured to the other riders to follow, then he fitted a helmet over his bald head.

Valeran led the party from the woodland and followed the

road toward Bourgiatta Castle. A large banner was draped on either side of the gatehouse, a maroon castle tower on a background of yellow, the colours of House Bastone. The mere sight of those colours made Valeran's skin crawl. House Bastone claimed to be a noble house, but Valeran knew the truth behind their origins. They were nothing but the descendants of lesser men. Foresters and farmers who rose up and took the castle for themselves and appointed one of their own to lead. *They won't be in power for very long when I'm done here*, he smirked to himself.

Along the road, they encountered a trade caravan. Three horse-pulled carts were on their way from Bourgiatta Castle. The man in the lead caravan spied Valeran and his men and indicated to the procession to pull over. The Master of Coin marched past them without pause. Valeran could see the eyes of the men and women looking at him.

"Remember, Walder," Valeran spoke again to his companion when they were out of ear range of the passing caravan, "keep your sword sheathed until I say otherwise. Hopefully, we'll be in and out before these fools realise what was taken."

"Very good, my lord."

The northwest gate was within reach. Two armed soldiers stood outside inspecting more merchant caravans, whilst men armed with bows were stationed on the walls at either side of the gatehouse. The men on the ground approached Valeran's group.

"Greetings," Valeran raised a hand before them.

"Who am I speaking to?" the first soldier asked.

"I am Valeran Serpentine of Ravenno, and Master of Coin. On behalf of the Imperial Court, I wish to seek an audience with the lord of this castle."

The soldier looked up and down at Valeran and his horse before turning to his entourage, then replied, "Lord

Aeolus hasn't informed us of your arrival, my lord."
"His Highness Emperor Otto V wanted me to keep this arrangement as discreet as possible. It is an urgent matter, one that I must address to Lord Aeolus in person without delay if you please."
The first soldier turned to his comrade. "Tell Lord Bastone that the Master of Coin is here to speak with him." The second soldier nodded and rushed through the gatehouse.
"Follow me, my lord."
"Thank you," Valeran replied, then gestured to his men to follow.

The first soldier led Valeran and his group through the gatehouse and into the heart of Bourgiatta Castle. Valeran could now see the castle's keep in front of him. It was nestled between two barbican towers with an inner wall. The whole thing was shaped like a diamond, with the entries to the centre by the two gatehouses at the north and south points. Surrounding this inner keep was a deep man-made ditch. As he rode in, Valeran continued to admire the feat of engineering that made this impenetrable fortress.

Stewards and peasants were everywhere, carrying out various labours to maintain the place. The leading soldier led the group to the stables, where they dismounted before proceeding to the southern inner gatehouse. Crossing the small drawbridge, Valeran saw a nobleman accompanied by two shield bearers. Valeran assumed this was Aeolus Bastone, the Lord of Bourgiatta castle. The man was tall and slender, with brown wavy hair reaching down to the sides of his well-built jaw. He wore a black vest over a sleeveless red tunic and black hose.

"Lord Valeran," the man called out, "this is indeed an unexpected visit. I haven't received a message from the capital of your arrival."

"My apologies, but there has been, shall we say, an incident in Aberemrallt which I would prefer to speak about without so many ears."

"Yes, that would make more sense. Come, I shall have my squires arrange for refreshments."

"Appreciated, my lord, but we hopefully won't be staying for long," said Valeran

Lord Bastone turned around and led the way into the inner keep; Valeran and his men followed him. With every step, Valeran could feel the key almost within his grasp He just needed to convince this fool to hand it over, and he would be closer to achieving his goal. Then they would all be bending their knees before him.

Back in the capital...

Captain Therin marched with six armed men from the City Guard. People all around stopped and stared as they made their way up Falcon street towards Monk's gate. The captain ignored their confused looks.

This was the second day in a row where he would be apprehending a would-be criminal. He never imagined a day when he would have to arrest anyone higher up the social ladder than the usual petty thief or murderer, let alone the Master of Coin. Indeed, his target, Valeran, was a Serpentine. His family history was full of plots and schemes to advance their position in the world, and It would seem that the old man was an apple that hadn't fallen far from the family tree. The sooner he got his hands on the old snake without causing too much trouble to the populace, the better.

Therin halted before the house at the end of the street where Valeran was known to reside. It was an old and outdated place compared to the other homes along Falcon street. The only thing that stood out was the front door, which looked new. The captain took a short breath before he approached it.

A few knocks on the solid wood produced no response.

He knocked again, then spoke.

"Lord Valeran. This is Captain Therin. Open the door, we need to have a chat," He stood back and waited but nothing happened.

"Lord Valeran. This is Captain Therin. Open the door. We need to have a chat," He stood back and waited, but nothing happened.

"Lord Valeran, are you there?" he called again, "We know you're in there. In the name of the Chancellor and his Imperial Majesty, I command you to open the door now."

He stepped back and waited but was met by silence.

"Looks like we'll have to fish the bastard out the old-fashioned way," he muttered and turned to his men.

"Right, you know what to do," he instructed two of them to come forward.

They each carried large hammers to break through the door. The other four men moved closer, standing next to Therin. They watched as the soldiers with the hammers took turns thumping and battering the door until they eventually managed to crack a hole through it.

This allowed one of them to reach in to open the door from the inside. They stormed into the house; Therin gestured to the rest of his men to follow. Placing a hand on his scabbard, he marched forward after them.

When the captain entered the house, his first sight was a single spacious room with almost no furniture, save for a few chairs and a round table. So dark, so quiet… Too quiet.

But then he noticed something on the floor. A puddle of dried blood surrounded the figure of a young man who lay face down on the ground. Therin knelt before the body and turned him over. Despite the face being stained maroon, he recognised the man as one of Valeran's servants. He continued to examine the body but found no stab wounds, so he assumed the cause of the person's death to be internal. *Poison, perhaps?* Therin wondered.

"Search the house, two of you in each room!" he commanded and watched as his men paired up. No stone would be left unturned. Every cabinet was opened, and every shelf swept for clues.

What are you hiding, Valeran? The captain asked himself as he turned his attention to the table. There was a map of all of Maldora laid out. It was stained and reeked of wine, yet Therin scanned it for clues. Was Valeran planning to leave the city at some point? How long had he been planning this?

A soldier approached Therin. "Captain?"

"Yes?" he answered.

"We've found something underneath the carpet." The soldier pointed to where his comrade stood. They dragged the rug away to reveal a trap door. Therin walked over to examine it.

"Right, does anyone have any picks on them?" Therin asked.

"I do," said one of the soldiers. "I'll get it open."

The captain stepped back and let the soldier with the pick fiddle away at the lock. He noticed something on the floor further into the house by an open window. He walked over and picked it up. The object was a single black feather, belonging either to a crow or a raven.

"I think I've got it," the soldier with the pick stated, and he and his comrade proceeded to lift the trap door.

The captain stepped back and saw nothing but steps leading into darkness. There were two torches attached to the inside of the door itself. Therin picked them up and ignited them before handing one to a soldier.

"Come on, let's find out what's down below," he said as he descended the steps.

The cellar was dark, damp and had an air of a strange incense. Shelves all around were filled with skulls, old books and bottles. A cauldron lay in the centre of the room, whilst a table was situated close to one of the walls.

"By the gods," whispered the first soldier that followed the captain down the stairs. "This room has sorcery written all over it."

"I don't like the looks of this," said the second soldier.

Therin kept his discomfort to himself as he looked around the cellar. He hadn't been expecting anything like this. What was supposed to be a simple arrest has become a surprising discovery. He had seen enough.

"I'm heading back. No one else is allowed to enter this place, understand?"

"Yes, Captain," the soldiers acknowledged the orders.

The captain walked up the steps. It was clear that Valeran had somehow disappeared. This wasn't the sort of news he had hoped to deliver to Chancellor Gedric and the emperor, but he had no other choice. The games were tomorrow, and Valeran and the Black Box were nowhere to be found. Things were going to get more complicated from now on.

Chapter 20

The Coliseum, Aberemrallt

ARRAN WAS GREETED BY THE ROAR of thousands upon thousands of cheering citizens as he and fellow Twin Blade members marched into the coliseum. A surge of pride coursed through his body and mind. All around him, horns were blowing away, and people were standing and waving. Arran and Gabriel were five rows deep in their column, led by Captain Alaric and knights on horseback. Arran knew that Anwen was at the front.

He saw Eafen on the far left of the column. Their group stopped in the centre of the arena, between a group representing the Knights of Frankonia and a group of dwarves from Myrgrad. Standing before them on a balcony above the arena floor was the emperor and his family, and other lords were present behind him. The emperor raised a hand, and the arena soon became silent.

"Citizens of Aberemrallt!" the emperor called out to the masses. "Today, we celebrate the continuation of our continent as a single entity. The Maldoran Empire is a beacon of unity and civilisation forged by our ancestors upon realising the benefit of standing together against the darkness. Against madness, against those whose barbarity brought nothing but misery. While those times are a distant memory, it is always important to remember and honour the sacrifices of those who came before us." The emperor paused for cheers before continuing. "Behold, standing before us today are dwarves, elves, humans and satyrs from all corners of our realm. You have been chosen to compete in the greatest of spectacles known to all. Each of you will compete to cement your own legacy. Today I, Emperor Otto V of House Valorn, declare the two hundred and eightieth Imperial Games open. May you all find your moment during these games and remember the values of honour, fairness and equality. Let the Games Begin!"

The emperor's words were followed by another roar from the crowd. The horns began to play. Another man walked up to the podium as the emperor took his seat.

"I think that's the mayor of the Aberemrallt," Gabriel said in Arran's ear.

"How do you know?" Arran asked.

"He caught my eye when we first entered, watching us from the window of the city hall."

"I see," Arran replied as their group began to follow everyone else out of the arena.

"Citizens of Llancarphig and beyond," the mayor stated, "We shall begin our glorious games with the first of our jousting events, featuring the greatest knights from the Twin Blade Order against those from Frankonia."

Moments later...

On the other side of the arena, Eafen was walking along the corridor. His visions still plagued him despite the Archmage branding them as unlikely. The only thing he could do right now was visit a friend. He stopped at the archway for one of the fitting chambers where he found Sir Ferrand Mosse. The veteran knight was sitting on a stool and in the middle of donning his armour with the help of his squires. Eafen couldn't help but stand in the doorway and admire the etchings on each part of his friend's armour, including the breastplate. This had been polished to near perfection.

The knight looked up at the mage. "Ah, Eafen, come to lend a hand then? I already have these two assisting me."

"I think your squires are doing a splendid job without anyone else's help," Eafen complimented. "Too many cooks around the same pot ruins the stew."

"Haha, well said," Ferrand chuckled. "Is this armour new?" Eafen asked.

"This armour belonged to my father. This was his last gift to me before he passed away years ago. It's been in my family for generations."

"It looks rather impressive."

"Thank you," Ferrand replied as he was handed his chainmail.

"So, you will be fighting first?" Eafen asked.

"According to the luck of the draw, yes. The sooner I start this joust, the better."

"Fools rush in, as they say. Considering your status in the order, couldn't you have requested to change places with someone else?"

"They wouldn't allow that," Ferrand shook his head. "Once you've been put down with an opponent, that's it. No favours or any excuses."

"I see," Eafen replied, hiding his disappointment.

"I thought you were supposed to be with the rest on the balcony?" Ferrand asked.

"Yes, I will be. I just thought I'd take the time to come and wish you luck," Eafen gave his best excuse.

"Thank you, friend," Ferrand responded as one of his squires finished attaching the last pauldron. "If you'll excuse me, I must make myself ready." The knight stood up from his stool to receive his helmet from one of his squires.

"Very well, I look forward to seeing you in action, Ferrand," said Eafen before leaving the room and making his way back through the corridor to his seating place.

Sir Ferrand Mosse was a capable fighter; Eafen had seen him in the courtyard training. It was likely that he would be the favourite in the jousting. But still, the vision played in the back of his mind. Especially the image of the man he had been friends with for so long lying dead on the ground. Eafen shook his head and carried on, for he was determined to let it go no matter what happened.

Arran sat patiently in the centre of the second balcony, watching as squires prepared the arena for the first joust. Above him on the next balcony were the citizens, whilst the next one down accommodated some officials and merchants. Gabriel sat to his left, while Callum and Anwen were to his right. They noticed the cloaked figure of Eafen walking up the steps to take his place next to Gabriel.

"Where've you been?" Gabriel asked.

"Nowhere far," Eafen replied as he sat. "Just speaking to a colleague of mine."

"Eafen, have you heard anything about those men from yesterday?" Arran asked.

"No, nothing to be honest. My best guess is that the Captain of the City Guard would rather retain knowledge of what happened until after the games."

"About what exactly?" Callum looked at Eafen curiously.

"Some things that shouldn't be spoken out loud, especially here," Eafen answered.

"Why did they come to you for help?" Anwen asked.

"Well..." Eafen paused for a moment before replying. "For the last few years, many of our older mages have been passing away one by one."

"Old men dropping like flies," Gabriel assumed.

"You'll have to excuse Gabriel," Arran butted in, "he's never been interested in magic."

"You're lucky Archmage Polovius is on the other side, sitting with the grandmaster and the emperor. He wouldn't take kindly to your words."

"I don't hate magic," Gabriel responded. "I just don't understand why only one in so many people have it and no one else."

"Magic is not something you can learn from either a book or from training in a courtyard," Eafen explained. "You have to be born with it to some extent. It's the same as nobility; you're either born into a noble family or a commoner like everyone else."

"Will you be quiet? They're about to start," Anwen broke in.

A wooden tilt had been erected from one side to the other of the arena. A spokesman in a fine brown surcoat stood at the halfway point raising his hand for silence before announcing.

"Ladies and gentlemen! Our first jousting contest will involve the following warriors." The man pointed to his left. The first knight, riding a horse as white as snow, wore silver armour under a cloak bearing the Twin Blade colours and emblem. "To my left, an experienced warrior with much to offer, representing the Twin Blade Order. I present to you, Sir Ferrand Mosse."

Arran and his companions stood up and cheered for Sir Ferrand. Eafen looked on smiling.

The spokesperson continued, "And to my right, hailing from the province of Frankonia, representing House Leroux, I give you, Sir Leon Leroux."

Half of the audience cheered for Sir Ferrand's opponent. This knight's cloak was red and black over his black armour, and he rode an ash-coloured horse.

"This will be interesting," Gabriel muttered.

"I have faith in Sir Ferrand," Eafen replied. "He's done

this hundreds of times."

Both riders stood ready at either side as the marshal raised his flag. Each knight received their first lance from their handlers. As soon as everything was clear, the marshal dropped his flag. Both knights began their first charge.

Arran felt his heart thump as the audience's anticipation grew louder. The moment the knights reached the centre, lowered lances met steel plating. Splitters of wood flew everywhere. Both knights remained in their saddles after the clash, their squires rushing out with fresh lances to replace the broken ones.

The second run soon followed, with Sir Ferrand charging again at full speed. Arran noticed his opponent was struggling to match Sir Ferrand's speed. *He won't last long*, Arran thought. He watched as the silver knight thrust his lance into the black knight with enough force to knock his opponent off the mount. The black knight landed hard, unable to get back up, let alone continue. The audience cheered as the marshal declared Sir Ferrand the winner. The silver knight raised his visor and shot a closed fist in the air.

"Your faith in him wasn't wrong, Eafen," Arran complimented.

Eafen smiled back at him. Then Arran saw Captain Alaric walk up the steps to them.

"Don't get too comfortable, you lot," he said. "Arran, Gabriel. You'll be fighting after the second joust. So, I would make my way to change if I were you."

"Well, you heard him," Gabriel said, rising to his feet.

"After you, Gabriel," Arran gestured as he rose from his seat.

He suddenly felt wobbly in both his legs and then a sensation of butterflies took hold in his stomach. Arran had been told by Captain Alric that you would experience these sensations as a result of nerves, especially because this was the first time he would be competing in front of an imposing audience. He noticed Gabriel was also wobbly in his legs momentarily. Arran waited for his friend to be a few steps ahead, and then he took a deep breath to calm himself before proceeding.

"Good luck, you two," Callum spoke.

"I think our opponents will be needing that more than us," Gabriel cockily responded, trying to hide his own nerves.

"We'll see about that," Arran replied. He followed Gabriel down the steps but looked back at Callum, Anwen and Eafen.

He raised a thumb at them and received a nod in return. Hopefully, fortune will favour him and Gabriel just as it did for Sir Ferrand.

Chapter 21

Within Bourgiatta Castle

"AS YOU CAN SEE LORD VALERAN," Lord Bastone spoke as he and Valeran walked, two of Bastone's personal guards with him, "I have the best men in the region guarding this castle from every direction."

Valeran took note of each soldier that he saw going about their duties. Walder and his men were following them through the corridors to the dungeons.

"Yes, very impressive," Valeran acknowledged. "However, due to the recent circumstances involving the Black Box, the emperor and the council fear that an attack here may soon follow. That someone will try and steal the key."

"Nonsense," Bastone rejected, "I have the best men in Terradonia keeping watch over this castle day and night."

Ignorant fool, Valeran thought, but continued to play along. "Of course, this castle is formidable. No foe would be stupid enough to come here unprepared. But if we could begin the plan to relocate the artefact now to its new location, we might be able to draw out our conspirators into the open."

"Hmm, an interesting strategy," Bastone replied thoughtfully.

"Well, I am no tactician," Valeran admitted, "but if you offer what our enemies desire as bait, they will come for it like wolves stalking a lonely lamb."

"How devious," Bastone commented. "Though

you could've sent me a message with his majesty's instructions."

"We considered arranging for a message. But then there was concern that your castle might already be infiltrated."

"Ha, not a chance," Bastone snorted. "I would've known if there was someone that didn't belong within my walls."

Valeran continued to ignore the Lord's hubris and glanced behind. Walder was still there. Listening and observing, ever quiet unless spoken to. They carried on down one of the castle's many corridors without another word, passing through the castle's dungeon, until they reached a flight of steps. At the bottom was a set of double doors with a carving of two figures: a knight and a horned demon, locked in hand-to-hand combat, teeth, claws and talons against steel.

A strange place to have such a well-crafted relief, thought Valeran. He watched as Bastone gestured to his guards to open the doors for them. They stood by as the rest of the party walked through before closing them shut. Valeran and Walder found themselves in the deepest part of the castle. A vast chamber supported by four circular pillars. Each was narrowest at the centre due to the way they were designed to curve when one looked at it from top to bottom or the other way round. They reminded Valeran of the pillars that supported the caves underneath the mountains near his home of Ravenno. These pillars were fitted with four torch holders each. Lord Bastone's men went to work, lighting the ones pointing to the centre, shedding light on a large box inside a cage made of iron. *At last,* Valeran thought. The prize was within grasp.

"And here it is." Lord Bastone pointed. "The key to the box that holds of the most loathsome of artefacts in all of the kingdoms of Maldora."

"And one which you'll never have to worry about guarding again, my lord," Valeran replied. "Shall we begin?"

Lord Bastone looked at Valeran eye to eye for a moment before looking at the cage, reluctantly, he sighed, "Very well." He approached the cage, pulling out a pair of keys on a ring from one of his pockets.

He opened the lock on the cage with one of the keys, before using the other to open the box itself. He walked out with the true key. Where the other two were made out of necessity and lacked anything elaborate, this new key that Bastone presented was something else. It was painted black with gold ridges and a red gem at one end. Valeran took the key from Lord Bastone with both hands. There was some weight to this artefact despite its small appearance. Just staring at the thing has him all excited within. Being another step closer to achieving his plans, to bringing back the greatest power to ever walk the face of this land. He licked his lips slowly, for he knew victory would be sweeter than any wine he had ever tasted before this moment.

At that point, Lord Bastone looked at Valeran with a suspicious face before speaking.

"Is everything alright, Lord Valeran?"

Valeran snapped out of his moment of awe and replied, "Yes, thank you, Lord Bastone. All is satisfactory.".

At that point there was a knock on the double doors.

"Please excuse me, my lord," Bastone walked over the doors and left Valeran in the chamber; his guards followed him but then stood by the door and watched over their guests.

Valeran paid no attention, for he continued to marvel at the craftsmanship put into such a crucial piece to his next plan.

Walder approached him and whispered, "We should make

a move, my lord."

Valeran nodded. He put the key in one of his pockets-still clutching it like a prized family possession, and looked at the double doors. Lord Bastone's guard stood by whilst his voice could be heard from the other side. Valeran couldn't hear what was said, but the tone employed by Lord Bastone was one of shock and concern. Valeran gestured to Walder and his men to stand with him. Just as this was happening, the doors opened again. Lord Bastone returned, but his face was blank, and Valeran noted more soldiers with him this time.

Valeran looked at his host with an innocent expression.

"Is there a problem, Lord Bastone?"

"You claimed to be relocating the key to another location, and yet I have just now received a letter from the chancellor stating that you have other intentions." He held out a scroll before him; the wax that sealed it was marked with the chancellor's emblem.

Curse you, Gedric! Valeran thought. He then opened his arms wide and replied, "Surely there's been a misunderstanding, Lord Bastone. The other lords are simply jealous of my talents and—"

Bastone cut him off with a harsh laugh. "Ha. Do you take me for a fool, Valeran? According to the chancellor, there is evidence to point out that you were behind the robbery at the Imperial Academy a few days ago. He has ordered your immediate arrest."

Valeran growled, "You dare speak to me like that? I am Valeran Serpentine, the Master of Coin, you idiot!"

"Not anymore," Bastone continued. "As of today, you are hereby stripped of your title and your lordship. You are now under my arrest. Fitting you come all this way and walk through my dungeons for that key, only to be better acquainted with my hospitality." He gestured to his men and his personal guard to surround Valeran and his company.

Bastone's men drew out their swords from beneath their tunics. Walder and his brothers did the same and took a stance.

Valeran sighed. "So much for subtlety,"

"I will only say this once: return the key to the box and order your men to stand down," Bastone commanded.

Valeran clenched his fists and growled, "You really have no idea who you stand against do you? I will not be silenced by a descendant of a lowly lumberjack!" Then, he thrust his arms forth, sending two of Bastone's men into the walls at either side of the doorway.

"By the emperor!" Bastone and his men were surprised by the power within this frail old man. "Stop him at once!" He pointed and ordered.

The rest of Bastone's guards charged forth; Walder and his men countered. A clash of swords followed. One of Bastone's men came forth at Valeran with a halberd. With a single swipe of a hand, Valeran sent the man flying into another wall. The foe hit hard on impact, most likely fracturing his ribs and spine. Walder was holding his own; he had already slain two soldiers and was on his third. The men under his charge were doing so as well. Valeran then glanced at Bastone; the man's face was white at what he was witnessing. He turned to the door and ran, but Valeran reached out with a hand and pulled him back into the chamber.

"No, you don't!" Valeran snarled as he held his enemy above the ground before him. Bastone started to flail around, trying to break free. Valeran then cupped his other hand and Bastone clutched at his neck, trying desperately to breathe.

"You were saying, Aeolus?" Valeran called him by his

first name.

"You… traitor!" Bastone choked. "Bloody bastard!"

"And you are a descendant of a thieving peasant! This castle was property of House Serpentine. All you ungrateful and ignorant little shits have been wanting to see my house fall since the days of our expansion. Now, it's my turn to see you all burn!"

With that, he clenched the hand that held Bastone's throat, snapping the man's neck. Valeran then released his grip, allowing his enemy to fall, the lifeless body thudded hard on the stone floor.

"Now what?" Walder asked bluntly as he was kicking one of the dead soldiers in the gut..

"Hide the bodies. With luck, we can still leave here before they realise what has happened."

Walder nodded, and he and his men started dragging the dead soldiers around the pillars. Valeran walked over to the broken body of Aeolus Bastone and picked up the parchment that was dropped during the fight. He opened it and scanned the contents. In thick, black ink it read:

Dear Lord Aeolus Bastone,

I write this letter as a matter of urgency, rather than pleasantry, in the hope you receive it in time.

I believe Valeran Serpentine has the Black Box in his possession and is heading for your castle.

In the name of his Majesty, Emperor Otto V, I declare Lord Serpentine a traitor to the state, and stripped of title and lordship.

Do not trust him. Do not let him leave with the key, whatever you do.

Arrest him on sight, but please do this quietly. I will be there as soon as possible.

Your old friend,

Gedric. Chancellor of All Maldora.

Valeran cursed under his breath. The chancellor must have sent a bird with this message just before he left. Who knows how far away he was. He looked at the carnage around him then stared back at Lord Bastone, his body laid still. He had planned on heading to Ravenno to seek a worthy body, but that plan may be out the window now that the chancellor and the emperor were onto him. Valeran then noticed an empty barrel in the corner that remained intact.

"Walder, put Lord Bastone's body in that barrel, quickly. And clean your swords. We're leaving." "What do we need him for?" he asked.

"A change of plans," Valeran replied. "We head back to the woods immediately."

He decided it was time for the hunter to become the hunted.

Chapter 22

The Coliseum, Aberemrallt.

THE ARENA GROUND WAS BATHED in a golden yellow, courtesy of the midday sun, expunging all traces of shadows except that beneath the arena seating. Arran and Gabriel stood alongside other young men in one of the tunnels waiting for permission to enter, all armed and prepared to do battle. Arran was holding his helmet in one hand and a heater shield in the other. He made the change from his round shield after inspecting and acquiring this on from the Stronghold's armoury after arriving. It was made from wood and overlaid with a metal plate, compensating for its extra weight with more protection. Everyone wore the same attire, but each carried a different weapon.

Gabriel stood next to Arran with his hand on the scabbard of his great sword. Rhodri on his left favoured a long poleaxe. Its blade and spike that jutted out at the top were intentionally blunted so that its impact would not cause any unnecessary injuries. Roff, the tallest member of the team, was gripping his own longsword close to the chest, muttering a silent prayer. His tunic barely covered the chainmail armour he wore underneath. In front of them were the brothers Jovarn and Bailin who were busy comparing their weapons. The former wielded a sword and round shield, whilst his younger brother favoured a mace. At the back were Donnal, Alan and Fabius Bastone. The last one had his back to a wall, busily adjusting his helmet. He also favoured a sword complemented with a round shield.

Gabriel leaned in on Arran. "So this is it, our first fight."

"Yes," Arran replied.

"I can't bear this delay much more."

Arran placed a hand on Gabriel. "Don't get too carried away now. Fighting together is what will earn us victory."

"Nobody likes a hot head, Gabriel," Jovarn chuckled.

Gabriel snorted. "You always think of me like that, don't you?"

Arran shook his head. He looked around the tunnel and noticed something about Donnal. He was at the rear of the group. The youngest member of their team, Donnal's freckled face was already starting to sweat as he gripped his scabbard tensely.

"Are you nervous, Donnal?" Arran asked.

Donnal jumped upon answering, "Uh no…it's just ...this is my first time."

"It's everyone's first time here," Roff replied.

"Come on, Donnal, suck it up." Rhodri walked over and squeezed Donnal's shoulder. "Just keep your shield up when you're out there, okay?"

"Yes, keep my shield up, okay I got it," said Donnal.

Arran nodded and turned back to the gateway. "What's the plan, Arran?" Gabriel asked.

"Just stay close together," Arran replied as he donned his helmet.

"Hey, Fabius," Gabriel called, "time to show off what you can do."

"The sooner we get this over with, the better," Fabius replied apathetically.

Out of everyone present, Arran questioned Fabius's commitment the most. Apparently, the only reason he was present was due to an agreement made between his family and the order where, for the last five generations, the first-born son of House Bastone would serve in their ranks in exchange for additional security for their castle. Not that his family couldn't afford a garrison of its own. At that point, the gate was drawn upward. Arran led his group as they marched in single file into the arena.

Barricades made from wooden logs were set up to mark out the boundaries of the fighting area. There were only two gaps to enter the squared arena. Arran looked ahead and saw their opponents; nine fighters entering from the other side.

He recognised them as marines hailing from Byzalia, for underneath their short purple capes, their polished armour was like the scales of fish, and their helmets had metal fins jutting out from both sides. While the knights were the dominant force on land, these men were their equivalent on the high seas. Arran took note of the variety of exotic weapons each opponent wielded. Double swords, a mace with a shield and tridents, the last one being the weapon of choice for many of them.

A spokesperson stood in the middle of the arena,

"My lords and ladies!" he called out. "It is time for the first melee of the day. Before you stand men from two great fighting orders. The team with the last man standing shall be declared the winner!" He cleared his throat then continued, "Our first team to my right," he pointed to Arran's group, "we have the young knights from the Twin Blade Order!" Arran and his group raised their weapons as the crowd cheered for them. The spokesperson called out again, "Today they will fight the men to my left, masters of naval combat, marines hailing from the islands of Byzalia." The audience again cheered as the marines made their voices heard.

"Now let the battle commence!"

A large horn was blown, its roar enticed the audience to add their voices in exchange for action.

"Let's go, form a shield wall!" Arran commanded.

Those with shields rushed forth and formed up with Arran, presenting their shields to the front. He found himself in the centre of this wall, whilst Gabriel, Rhodri and Roff supported the flanks. In response, the Byzalians mimicked them with a wall of their own. The two lines marched toward each other until they clashed in the centre. Shields locked and thrusted against each other. Swords were swung overhead, steel clanged against steel. Both lines held firm. Eventually, the Twin Blade were winning in the shield wall.

One of the warriors in the Byzalian wall buckled and fell to the ground before Arran. He capitalised and pointed his sword at him. Arran didn't need to actually touch the foe with his sword, just having his blade close to the chest would be enough to eliminate them. The other Byzalians broke off from the wall and took on a loose formation. Arran's group did the same and engaged the enemy. Arran glimpsed over to his right and saw Gabriel engaging a warrior wielding two pairs of swords.

Rhodri was close by; he was having trouble fighting one of the trident wielders. This one, however, was using a net instead of a shield that had snared around Rhodri's poleaxe. The warrior pulled on the net, dragging Rhodri down to the ground before tagging him with his trident. The crowd cheered at the elimination of the Twin Blade warrior. Rhodri was forced to roll away from the battle as part of the rules of the match. The warrior with the trident and net turned to face Arran. The two fighters locked eyes for a moment, even as their comrades clashed, and the spectators roared and cheered all around them.

Rather than be distracted for too long, Arran presented his shield in front; his opponent adopted a similar stance but swung his net around over his head as if trying to taunt Arran, just like a bull would be lured by a red cloth. Arran didn't take the bait. His foe then swung his net at him, it caught on Arran's shield. The warrior pulled on the net, trying to reel his prey in. But Arran dug his boots into the ground, refusing to be pulled in.

Using his own strength, he pulled his front foot back along with his shield arm. The trident warrior was struggling to maintain his own footing, until he eventually let go of the net. It dangled over the front of Arran's shield. Without it, Arran's foe gripped the trident with both hands and charged at him. Every thrust was deflected by the shield. Arran continued to parry these attacks until he decided to push forward. He swatted the trident aside and launched a foot, kicking his opponent in the abdomen with enough force to knock him off his feet. Without his trident and net, Arran's foe raised his hands in surrender as he pointed his sword down at him.

"I yield!" the Byzalian called out. Arran remained over his foe.

At that point, a horn had been blown and the fighting ceased. Arran looked around him. Most of his team appeared to be intact whilst the Byzalian warriors were on the ground, overpowered by the Twin Blades.

The spokesperson came forth again into the arena.

"Behold the winners of the first match: the warriors of the Twin Blade Order!"

The audience erupted with joy. Arran looked down at the Byzalian warrior he had beaten. He sheathed his sword and offered a hand to his foe. The Byzalian accepted and was pulled up.

"You fought well," said Arran.

The Byzalian replied, "Orion's luck was with you and your friends."

"I'll be saving that for the next one," the two warriors shook hands before the Byzalian took his leave with his comrades. Arran removed his helmet, and his face was met with warm air and dust.

Gabriel approached Arran. "Nice one Arran. So, who's buying us a drink then?"

Arran laughed and looked up, he could see Callum and Anwen clapping with the audience. He gave them a thumbs up and smiled before making his leave of the arena. Proud of his first fight, the first of many.

Chapter 23

Forest Hope, on the way to Bourgiatta castle.

Everything went quickly for Gedric as he dashed on horseback to Bourgiatta Castle. He departed from Aberemrallt the morning prior with ten horsemen from the City Guard chosen to escort him. They rode out through Sun Gate, crossed the river to the town of Paroy, then travelled northwest following the river until they stopped for the night at Luvera castle, opposite the River Tor to Gard Afon. Gedric wanted to continue, but the horses were tired and the Lord of Luvera had no spares to provide.

They left the following morning after a brief breakfast. He didn't waste time explaining to Tyrion, the Lord of Luvera Castle, about the situation. The last thing the chancellor needed was to spread panic, though the lord did speak of sighting men wearing City Guard attire heading toward Bourgiatta Castle.

So, he is already there? Damn it! he cursed silently. His only hope was that Lord Bastone would receive the message and have Valeran in custody before he could escape. He leaned further forward until his chest rested on the mane of his horse, enticing the beast to travel faster. Coming from a family who owned an estate, making its living off breeding and selling stallions to other noble families, he grew up around horses and thus, he hated the idea of pushing such creatures beyond their limitations. There was only so much a horse can do regardless of breed compared to man. Yet desperate times required immediate action. Gedric glanced over his shoulder, his own retinue was struggling to keep up.

"Lord Chancellor!" one of the men called out. "Please wait for us!"

He wished he could take things easy, but time wasn't with them. To him, the fate—no; the future of Maldora rested in his hands. I cannot fail, he told himself. He only needed to reach the end of the forests and Bourgiatta would be in sight. Just as he turned back to the path, Gedric pulled hard on his reins. The horse neighed as it halted; Gedric's fiery and determined eyes widened at what lay before him. Two wagons were turned over on the path. Both carts were dotted with arrows, the wheels were broken, and the ground was strewn with smashed pots, vegetables and bodies of horses and people.

This was a massacre, Gedric thought. By that point, the other horsemen managed to catch up with him, their horses trotting from behind. Some of the men dismounted to inspect the scene, whilst another rode up to the chancellor, expressionless upon seeing the wreckage.

"What in the name of the gods?" he asked.

"This was Valeran's doing," Gedric sighed with a tinge of despair. "We're too late for them."

A rustling from the bushes caught their ears. Before Gedric could say anything, the man next to him was struck in the face by an arrow. The soldier's horse was startled as he fell from the mount and thudded hard on the ground.

"Ambush!" another soldier cried out. The rest of Gedric's men pulled their swords, but another arrow was let loose, landing in one's back. The man dropped to his knees in agony, dropping his sword. Gedric heard cries as bands of men charged forth from both forests. They were surrounded. The remaining men stood their ground, their swords clashed with what weapons these assailants possessed. Gedric drew his own sword in time as one assailant came for him. The foe was covered head to toe in a hooded tunic, brandishing an axe as he attacked. Gedric deflected the first blow before slashing the man across the face. The assailant fell to the ground, clutching his hidden face as blood sprayed all over the soil. Gedric was about to lean in for a stab when out of the corner of his eye, a massive ball of fire flew across from the treelines. The explosion knocked his men and the attackers in all directions.

A few of his men survived. Some, however, were rolling on the ground as they were enveloped in flames. And yet more bandits spewed out of the forest. *This is madness*, he thought. This wasn't going to plan; he had no choice.

"Retreat!" he called out to whoever could hear amongst the chaos. He rode along the path, slashing at another assailant. But before he could escape, another fireball came out from the woodland. Landing in front of him, the force of the impact knocked the chancellor off his steed. He landed hard, dust and hot ash covering part of his fine tunic. His right shoulder screamed in pain. Gedric's vision was blurry and his ears rang painfully. He looked around and saw his sword on the ground. He winced in agony as he crawled toward his weapon. It was within reach when a boot landed on the hilt. Gedric looked up and saw the face of a bald man wielding what appeared to be an axe. He stared down at Gedric with not a shred of emotion. Just before Gedric could react, the man lifted his boot and kicked him hard in the face. His vision went black as he was knocked unconscious.

Out from the trees, Valeran strode calmly across the carnage of battle without regret. The ground smelled of scorched earth and charred flesh as a result of his magic. How he longed to finally put his magic to use. Horses were scattering like rats in all directions. All around him, his followers were poking their weapons at the bodies of the fallen men who had ridden into his trap. Valeran could've let his enemies ride on to their destination if he wanted to and continue onward, but he knew it would only be a matter of time before his sworn enemy would learn of his actions and catch up to him. He stopped in the middle of the road to admire his work. Walder approached, dragging behind him the body of his sworn foe.

"Is he still alive?" he asked.

"Yes, my lord," said Walder.

Valeran grinned. "Good, drag the other bodies into the woods and put our prisoner in the cart with Bastone's body."

Walder simply nodded and continued to drag Gedric's unconscious body with him. At that point, Valeran could see crows circling the forest waiting to feast on the freshly made corpses. Valeran turned around and walked back to the treelines. He continued to grin for he couldn't wait to show his newly caught prey the fate that awaited him and the rest of the world.

Chapter 24

The Dungeon, under the Imperial Palace

GERALD SAT WITH HIS KNEES drawn up on his bed, oblivious to the activity happening outside his cell. It had been a day and a half since he had been arrested and questioned, and now it was all but quiet. From the barred window he could hear the distant sound of horns and cheering of spectators as the Imperial Games began.

He had looked forward to seeing the action despite everything that went on prior. The action could have helped ease his mind had he managed to keep his head low for a little longer. With a swell of frustration, he pushed his head away from his knees until he felt the hard surface of the wall behind him and sighed heavily. There had been no word from the chancellor or the Captain of the City Guard, or in fact from anyone he knew and cared about. Just the occasional choir of moans from other prisoners sung between the footsteps of the soldiers watching over them.

He worried about everyone back at the Jolly Maid. *Nianna must be running around like a headless chicken searching for me.* Gerald knew she had a problem concentrating on her work when something wasn't right. Her father would be forced to spend time calming her down when he could be serving customers. Gerald gritted his teeth at being the cause of such a commotion. Already, the guilt had festered inside of him to the point where he wanted to scream, but sanity told him otherwise. It wasn't worth wasting his breath adding more noise to this place where he couldn't help but feel all but abandoned. *How in the hell would the Royal family sleep at night should every prisoner in this dungeon decide to moan and wail away together?*

The dungeon became unbearably warm as time went by. Despite this discomfort, Gerald was about to doze off when he heard footsteps outside his door. It creaked open and in came Captain Therin; the man's curly black hair had been combed into two long strands reaching down both sides of his face. He donned a fine doublet of royal purple with a pair of black trousers. There was also a sword sheathed in a scabbard, attached to the captain's broad belt.

Upon seeing it, Gerald sat up, pressing his back to the wall. He was confused. "What's going on?" he asked.

"It's alright, nothing to worry about," Therin raised his hands. "It seems you have your first visitor."

"Visitor?" Gerald tilted his head.

"Yes, lucky you. Normally, I wouldn't let anyone visit prisoners for at least a week. But you got someone who's desperate to see you." Therin turned back to the door.

"You can come in now,"

Through the door came Nianna. Arms folded; she didn't say anything upon seeing him. Her face bore the signs of stress and disgust; her hair was in a mess as if it had taken on a life of its own in response to her woes.

"Nianna?" Gerald muttered; it was all he could say.

The captain walked out of the room but came back in with a stool, placing it next to Nianna.

"Here, have a seat," the captain kindly offered. "Thank you, but… I'm not sure if I want it," Nianna's reply could barely be heard.

"Fair enough," the captain acknowledged. "I'll let you both have some time." He walked out of the room and gently closed the door behind him. An awkward silence followed. Gerald's eyes remained locked on Nianna. She then unfurled her arms, revealing his straw hat, which she chucks at him. It lightly bounces off of Gerald's chest

and falls to his feet.
He glanced down at it momentarily before looking back at the girl in front of him and sighed, "Nianna, you shouldn't be—" before he could finish speaking, Nianna stepped forward and slapped him hard on the face. Gerald grunted. He knew he deserved it.
"I knew something was wrong when you didn't follow me back to the tavern. And that bloody change in hair colour, must've fooled everyone except the Captain outside. What was I thinking, trusting your word last night?" Nianna spoke for the first time, there was a fiery anger building in her voice.
"I planned on getting back there," Gerald replied without hesitation.
"Then why did you run off the other way?"
"Those guards were looking for me."
"Looking for you?" Nianna's face twitched as she raised her voice. "Whatever you've been doing must be very serious for you to end up here, right under the emperor's palace. You said there was nothing wrong and yet here we are!"
"Alright." Gerald raised his hands. "If you can please just calm down, I can expl—"
"Calm down? Calm down?" Nianna spat back with a hint of venom in her voice. "I searched the whole fucking city for you, and the next thing I know one of my friends tells me that he saw you and some thug get arrested by the City Guard for Pete's sake! What the bloody fuck is going on, Gerald?"

In her frustration, she kicked the stool away from her, the thing clonked as it bounced back from the stone wall. Seeing her act so aggressively made Gerald lean back in fear. The two of them went silent again as they stared at one another. Nianna was breathing heavily following her outburst, eyes bewildered; she looked as though she could pounce on him at any moment. Gerald, on the other hand, remained calm in the face of this woman on the verge of tearing him apart.

He gave out a heavy sigh.

"Listen, I… I was asked to steal something from the Academy."

Nianna pulled back on her anger and took a deep breath, "Steal something? Like what? It wasn't some book or more of those potions that got you into trouble in the first place, was it?"

"It's complicated," Gerald replied. "I can't say any more without getting you involved."

Nianna raised her head to the ceiling and unleashed a heavy sigh, her arms dangling weightlessly by the hips. "Of course, it's complicated. But still, why did you do it?"

Gerald pushed himself back as he worked up his answer before leaning forward to reply. "I was offered this job by someone who desperately wanted the thing, no matter what it took."

"How much were you offered to do this? Or was it more about getting revenge on the Academy?"

"Both," Gerald admitted in a low voice. "But mainly for the gold I was offered to pay for staying with you and your father."

Nianna grunted. "How many times do I have to tell you, Gerald? You have done more than enough to earn your place with us. Why is it so hard for you to get that into your thick head?"

"Everyone has to pay their debts eventually, Nianna. I had to do something to compensate for the years I spent there only to be expelled. Heck, my parents don't even know about this."

Nianna continued to probe him. "Did you kill anyone while you were at the Academy?'"

Gerald straight away replied, "No, absolutely not! Stealing something is one thing, but I would never take another life,"

"One of your friends said two guards were found dead the morning after."

Gerald moaned as he lowered his head, "That was the work of the man I had to work with. If it had been my choice, I would never have involved myself with such people,"

At that point, the sound of horns from the Coliseum blew again. Gerald and Nianna turned their heads to barred window. Gerald noticed how the light from outside formed an almost perfect halo around Nianna, enhancing her beauty whilst he wallowed with his ugly deeds in the darkness. "My father and I always went to see the opening of the games. Since I was little. This is the first time we aren't watching the games together."

"I'm sorry about this," said Gerald.

"It doesn't matter, really," Nianna replied. "It's just men riding horses knocking each other out with sticks at the end of the day."

"Hmm, yeah, to us it is."

"Will they put you on trial?" she turned to him.

Gerald sighed. "No, not yet. I think they're going to wait until after the Games."

At that point, she turned back to the light. A tear trickled down her left cheek. Gerald pushed himself off the bed and approached her.

"Listen, Nianna. I know what I have done was wrong. I've seen things I shouldn't have, even had voices in my head occasionally since that night. But all I ever wanted was to be with you, to find a place away from here where we can be happy." He attempted to place a hand on Nianna's shoulder but sensing it she lightly swatted it away. Gerald continued, "I've already told them everything I knew, honestly. I'm going to find a way to clear things up. It may take a while, but I'll clear my name and things will be better afterwards,"

"How can you say something like that?" Nianna started to sob. "They could lock you up for the rest of your life, or send you on some errand to the other side of the world where you might never come back." Nianna's tears continued to flow uncontrollably as she placed the palms of her hands to her face. Gerald felt cold inside, for neither of them had any clue as to what fate awaited him. He gulped hard and tried to place a hand on her. She didn't stop him this time. Gerald leaned in and whispered in her ear, "I don't know what will happen to me. If the worst comes to pass, just move on. Find someone else."

"Oh, Gerald," Nianna sniffed as she shook her head. "You say you want to be with me, now you want me to forget you and pretend we never knew each other?"

"Do you still want me, Nianna?" Gerald asked.

"I ... I don't know," she hesitated. "I need time to think about it."

"I understand," he nodded.

Just then, they heard a knock on the door. It was time for them to part ways. Gerald looked at Nianna right in her innocent hazel eyes.

"I know this is a lot to take in, but be strong, Nianna." Gerald then wrapped his arms around her. Nianna did the same, hugging him tightly. Gerald let a hand run through her soft silky auburn hair, making every slow stroke count. The moment remained still whilst they embraced each other, but eventually, Nianna's grip on Gerald loosened.

She looked up at him and said, "Take care, Gerald."

Gerald nodded as he let go of her, just as he did, she pressed a light kiss on his freckled cheek before turning away. He watched as Nianna walked toward the dungeon door. It opened and Captain Therin stood outside waiting to escort her out. She looked back at Gerald, wiping away a tear, but gave him a forgiving smile. He smiled back as well. And then she walked out, and the door closed behind her. Nianna. The one girl who changed Gerald's life since he had arrived in Aberemrallt. The one who he swore to spend the rest of his life with until his last breath was gone. He returned to his bed, landing back-first onto the rough mattress, and let out a heavy sigh.

Alone again in this place of solitude, whilst the outside world moved on oblivious to him, all he could do was wait for his judgement.

Chapter 25

The Jolly Maid, Aberemrallt

"Here's to our first fight today!" Gabriel raised a tankard of cider.

"Cheers!" Everyone else followed suit with a roar of excitement.

It was evening. The Jolly Maid was ripe with activity.

Men and women were drinking and feasting eagerly. Most were happy and exultant while others seemed more content with enjoying their drink alone in the corners of the room. Maids were walking back and forth from the bar and the kitchen carrying trays of food and ale. Their hair of varied colours tied back with a headband so no strand touched the food and beverages they carried.

This was the first time Arran had set foot here. He was convinced by Gabriel, along with everyone else, to come and enjoy a drink to mark their first victory at the Games. A bit premature in Arran's opinion. but once Gabriel had an idea, he would go all in for it. The alternative was for him to walk back and forth in the barracks trying to find ways to entertain himself. *Better this than risk him becoming a nuisance to everyone*, thought Arran before they went.

There was a warm, cosy atmosphere at this tavern. It was spacious for a place close to the Imperial Harbour and next door to Market Square. There were long tables close to the white walls, whilst small round ones such as theirs, occupied the centre around the two pillars that supported the tavern's sturdy roof. Arran couldn't help but feel distracted by everything going on. In one corner sat a group of dwarves with excessive amounts of meat and flagons of ale on their table. He watched as the ringleader, with curly black hair and a beard to complement it, held with both hands a flagon that was the size of a rock. The dwarf raised the flagon above his head and poured the alcohol down his mouth whilst his comrades cheered him on.

"Chug, chug, chug!" they encouraged whilst banging their fists in unison on the table.

When the dwarf finished, though half of it was dripping from his mouth and into his beard, he slammed the empty flagon hard on the table and roared in triumph.

His comrades jumped up from their seats celebrating. Elsewhere, Callum was only a few metres behind Arran, sitting alongside some elderly folk in front of a fireplace with stone blocks arching over it. Callum was busy reaching out toward the fire and bathing his hands in its warmth.

"Oi, Callum!" Arran heard Gabriel call out. "Are your hands warm enough to play cards yet?" He and Rhodri chuckled.

Callum pulled away from the fire and sat between Arran and Rhodri. Eafen was next to Gabriel. The mage was more interested in the small painting on one of the walls.

The picture depicted Breia, the Goddess of the Earth and nature standing between the farmers from the kingdom of Gower and a group of Satyr tribesmen. Both parties were encouraged to approach one another and begin the first step of neutral respect. Gabriel gave Eafen a nudge to break his spell, and he turned his attention back round to the others.

"Right, shall we start?" Gabriel looked around the table before he opened a pack full of cards. He shuffled them vigorously before distributing them out to each player for a game of Monarch.

After the cards were dealt, marbles were placed in a small dish at the centre of the table. Gambling with actual coin was forbidden to members of the order, so as to avoid having members developing addictions or ending up in debt. The alternative was to use any object of inferior value to coin such as marbles. Gabriel took a sip from his cup before dealing out two cards each. Arran looked at his pair. An eight and a seven. He could either take his chance straight away or ask for another card. He looked up at Eafen who started off first.

"Six and a nine here," the mage called as he laid out his cards.

Better go for the latter, Arran thought.

"Draw me another card," he asked. Gabriel pulled him another card. Arran looked at it. An empress. That should give him a better chance.

"Mage and a five, I have," Callum plopped down his cards. Arran looked at Rhodri next when he heard the clunking sound of a fallen flagon at the neighbouring table. Ale spilled out across the wood tiled floor, giving it a new darker shade of brown. He turned around and saw a maid with tied back auburn hair standing before a party of men who were far less than sober. He counted four in tow.

"Oi you, you spilled my drink," one of the men spoke. A rotund f gure with long black hair, he swayed slowly side to side in his chair staring at the maid.

"That wasn't me," the maid objected. The entire room stopped and stared.

"Of course, it was you. Your arse knocked it off the bloody table," the first man slurred, pointing a f nger at her. "I want my money back!"

"Clumsy," the second man on the table called. There were few def ning features about him aside from his curly blond hair and a small goatee.

"That's women for you," said the third member who was by far the ugliest of the whole lot. Bald head and plenty of spots all over his face.

"I'm sorry, but you can't have your money back. I'll get you another drink when I clean this up," said the maid.
"Not good enough," the first man groaned and hiccupped.
"I know something she can do better," said the final member at the table, who had messy brown hair and a hooked nose. He snickered as he grabbed the maid by the arm, pulling her closer to him.
"Stop it, let me go," she beseeched the brown-haired man, trying to break away. The other three men started giggling at their friend's man-handling of her.
"That's it," Arran said out loud. He slammed his cards on the table, pushed off from his chair and approached the men and the maid.
"Took the words out of my mouth," Gabriel followed, along with Rhodri. Callum and Eafen remained at their table whilst the other three confronted the troublemakers. The man with the long black hair stopped laughing when he noticed the warriors approaching them.
Arran stepped forth. "I think you should let her go."
"You what?" the man with the messy hair looked at them blankly.
"Who the fuck do you think you are?" the first man sneered. "You're not knights, just a bunch of boys waving swords around."
"Yeah, fuck off you squires," the fourth man spat out. Distracted, he didn't notice the maid had broken free from his grip. He turned his head to the girl, only to receive a hard slap across the face. "Ow, you bitch!" He pressed a hand on his reddened cheek. Everyone else at that point had stopped whatever they were doing and were openly staring. Only the elderly men sitting by the fireplace were either ignorant of what was going on or had fallen asleep.
"Now you've done it!" The first man rose from the table

and sized himself up to Arran. Gabriel and Rhodri stepped forth to stand by their leader. Even Callum and Eafen rose from their seats.

"So much for a quiet evening," Eafen sighed as he picked up his staff.

"You picked the wrong night to be out for a fight, boy," the long-haired drunkard growled.

"I was about to say the same to you," Arran returned the response.

"Cocky little shit!" the man threw a sloppy right hand at Arran. He ducked underneath it and unleashed a strike of his own.

His fist struck him squarely in the jaw, sending the drunken man flying onto the table behind him. The wooden construct buckled under the victim's weight. Flagons of ale rolled off and stained more of the floor in dark brown. Everyone else gasped at the exchange. The auburn-haired maid made a dash to the bar whilst the other men looked at their friend who was out for the count and decided to retaliate. The brawl was on.

Gabriel squared off with Baldy, whilst Rhodri lunged forth to grab curly brown by the shirt and toss him into the table belonging to the dwarves. The one with the black hair and beard was knocked out of his chair. He looked at the man that landed on his table with furious eyes. The dwarf grabbed the curly haired man and started punching away at him. His comrades joined in. The whole gang went into a frenzy.

That left Arran with curly blond. Last to rise from his seat, he raised his fists up in front of him. Arran remained firm even as all hell broke loose around him. After a bottle went flying past the two, curly blond circled around the broken table and attacked. He launched his left fist at Arran. But Arran was able to dodge it. Curly blond came closer and struck again, this time with his right hand. The young knight blocked this attack then followed up with an uppercut. He caught curly blond on the chin; the foe backed away, almost losing his footing. But he recovered and went for Arran again. He moved low and attempted to tackle him. Arran was pushed back a few steps, but he never went down. He dug down into the floor with his feet, then brought a knee up into curly blond's chest. Arran turned slightly on his feet before finding the strength to push his attacker away. Curly blond crashed into the last untouched table.

A flagon of ale went flying into another man's chest. Arran realised that the next man staring at him was a Frankonian knight, the ale from the flagon changed the colour of his tunic from emerald to a murky dark green.

"You spill my ale!" the knight snarled as he rose from his chair. "Twin Blade cur!" He then unsheathed a sword from his scabbard that was hidden underneath a cloak.

"Shit," Arran muttered; he wasn't expecting to pick a fight with a senior knight here in the tavern, let alone with swords.

He had no choice but to unsheathe his own blade. The Frankonian lurched forward with a downward strike that forced Arran to roll to the side. He returned the strike with his own but was blocked by the knight. Caught in a deadlock, Arran was struggling.

The Frankonian, being stronger, was able to push him back a few steps. Arran recovered quickly and in good time, for his foe came at him with his sword two handed with another strike. Arran parried the attack, keeping his distance. He felt his back pressed against one of the pillars. An idea came to mind.

"Is that all you got?" Arran taunted his foe.

The Frankonian knight took the bait, he roared as he lunged forward leading with the tip of his longsword.

Moments before contact, Arran ducked out of the way. His foe's sword went right through the wood of the pillar. The Frankonian struggled to pull his weapon out. This was Arran's chance; he dropped his sword and charged the knight whilst he was occupied. He clenched his right hand into a ball and hurled it at him. The knight just caught Arran in the corner of his eye but could do nothing to stop him. Arran's fist landed hard on his foe's cheekbone and the Frankonian landed on his back, clutching his face. Arran stood before the knight, his hand bruising from after the strike. He was expecting the foe to jump back at him.

"Alright, you win," the Frankonian knight suddenly yielded, raising his hands up in defeat.

At that point, the action had died down. Gabriel and Rhodri had disposed of the men that harassed the maid, panting relentlessly. At least one of the dwarves was still standing, spinning around and laughing. Arran offered a hand to the knight, but winced as the latter reluctantly gripped it tightly before he pulled him back to his feet.

"Sorry about the drink," Arran apologised.

"I'll let you off for that," the Frankonian grunted. He walked back to the pillar where his sword was still impaled to pull it out. Arran walked over to where he dropped his sword and picked it up.

"What is your name, sergeant?" the knight asked after he freed his blade.

"Arran Connaught," he replied.

The knight nodded. "Reinald d'Allee. Knight of Frankonia. Remember that name, for I'll be watching you all." The knight then sheathed his sword and walked out of the door.

"Reinald d'Allee?" Gabriel was perplexed. "He's the..."

"The Green Knight," Rhodri cut in. "That's what they call him."

Arran looked around at the carnage; most of the men that started the fight were either knocked out on the floor or had fled the tavern. Ale, cider and leftover food stained the floor. The only other person standing was the dwarf with the black beard. His comrades were lying on the floor passed out whilst he stood amongst the chaos, slightly shaky in the legs.

"Well, that was fun," he burped loudly. "You showed him, lad."

"Wasn't intending to start a fight," Arran admitted.

"Arran? Wasn't it?" the dwarf recalled. "Brom… Brom Blackhammer. And my friends here. Well, they're too pissed for introductions."

"A pleasure to meet you," said Arran.

"I think it would be wise not to stay here any longer," Callum gulped, looking down at the mess.

"Yeah, before the guards show up," Gabriel agreed.

"Yeah...yeah... nice to meet you lads, too," Brom staggered.

"Oi!" Another voice came from the bar; it was the landlord—a man with wide shoulders and a round face to go with his short brown hair—standing with the auburn-haired maid. "I'm greatful for you stepping in for my daughter Nianna, but who's going to pay for this?"

Arran replied, "We'll put some of our winnings toward the repairs."

"Some of it?" The landlord looked at them, unimpressed.

"Hey, we didn't start this bloody fight," Gabriel broke in.

"Come on, let's get out of here."

"Definitely," Eafen agreed.

One by one they left the Jolly Maid, and back to the Stronghold they went before word got out about the brawl.

Chapter 26

Saturday 31st August, at an unknown place...

WEARY AND WITH A RHYTHMIC THROBBING in his head Gedric woke to the sound of a creaking cart being pulled by snorting horses, as they clipped and clopped on the ground. It was dark and his breath was hot. Blinking, he realised there was a cotton bag on his head, and that he was aboard the very cart being pull, for the wooden construct rocked gently side to side with the occasional bump. His shackled hands were bound to a cold metal chain. He sat up and pulled on it; the chain appeared to be attached to the cart itself. He noticed that his legs were also shackled.

Movement and vision limited, the only other sense he could use was his hearing. He calmed himself and listened again. He noticed how the wheels of the cart, along with the added sound of footsteps either side, echoed all around him. There was also the occasional sound of dripping water in places. Gedric realised that they weren't travelling on land, but underneath. Were they under the mountains?

It seemed likely as the air felt cool and had a chalky taste. Gedric looked ahead and noticed a light that grew brighter as he and his captors travelled toward it. The atmosphere changed, the cool air and darkness of the tunnel were replaced by a humid breeze, as well as the light of day. Birds squawked above and the murmur of voices and sounds of things moving. Their figures were still blurry through the cotton.

Abruptly the cart stopped, and the horses neighed. Someone climbed on board, the cart rocking at the unfamiliar weight. He was close by, undoing the lock on the cart for his chains. Two hands then grabbed him by the shoulders and forced him to stand up. He found the chain that bound his hands being pulled by those same hands. He was forced to stumble off the cart and follow in whatever direction the chains pulled him.

Gedric couldn't help but feel a sense of humiliation and anger, but also a growing tinge of fear brewing inside at the thought of having been ambushed and captured, blindfolded, chained and dragged around like a prized animal with no idea where he was being herded to. Was this it? Would this be how his life would end? Gedric Hermann. Chancellor to Emperor Otto V, to die here, blindfolded, at the hands of traitors and heretics? Just a few steps later, the figure that was pulling the chain stopped. In front, was another figure, though Gedric had no idea who it was. The one holding the chains pulled downward, forcing the chancellor to his knees. The ground was nothing but dirt and stones.

The chancellor heard the footsteps behind him. Then the bag was pulled off by that same person. Squinting at the brightness of the sun, he looked up and recognised the figures that towered over him. Valeran Serpentine, the former Master of Coin, the man who he suspected to be behind everything, was standing before him, grinning at his catch, his arms crossed. Next to him was a man dressed in the colours of Imperial attire. Gedric recognised the latter as the one who knocked him out during the ambush. All this time the chancellor had thought he was the hunter, the pursuer. Only to be caught, chained, brought forth and laid here at the mercy of the hunted.

"Well, well, what do we have here?" the snake smiled.

"Welcome, Chancellor."

Meanwhile...
The Stronghold, Aberemrallt

"Let me get this straight," Captain Alric began. He had Arran, Gabriel, Rhodri and Callum lined up before him in his temporary quarters. They stood shoulder to shoulder whilst he paced up and down the room in front of them, about to scowl them for what had happened at the Jolly Maid last night.

"You lot decide to go out for a drink, then you end up starting a bloody fight? Not to mention you left the tavern in a right bloody state!"

"But we didn't start that ght, Captain," Gabriel butted in.

"Did I ask you to speak?" Captain Alric shot a sharp look at him. "Keep your mouth shut unless spoken to!"

Gabriel gulped hard. "Yes, Captain."

The captain then moved on to the next person in the line. "Arran, I heard that you got into a ght with a Frankonian knight. Is this true?"

Arran risked a quick glance at Gabriel and Rhodri before replying, "Yes, Captain. Reinald d'Allee. He took offence when I spilled his drink by accident."

The captain gritted his teeth upon the mention of the knight's name. "And who drew swords first?"

"He did, Captain," Arran replied immediately.

Captain Alric looked at the rest of the men present, "Did anyone else see who drew first?"

Gabriel shrugged whilst Rhodri scratched his head, apparently someone from the Jolly Maid smashed a bottle over the latter when they were fighting the thugs last night. He had a small scar that stretched down his left cheek bone. Gabriel looked the most unscathed out of the three, except for a little bruise underneath the chin. Arran couldn't really rely on these two since they were caught up in their own battles. At that point, Callum cleared his throat and spoke.

"What Arran says is true, Captain Alric. I swear on my life."

Everyone looked at him. Arran made a little smile, grateful that at least one of his friends was able to back his claim. The captain stroked his chin before replying in his usual calm tone, "Well, at least you had sense not to cause any lasting injuries, otherwise the consequences could've been worse."

Arran quietly breathed a little, taking comfort in seeing the captain calming himself.

"Was there anyone else of noteworthy stature involved?" he asked the group.

"Well, um," Callum said again, "there was a group of dwarves led by a Brom Blackhammer..."

"Oh gods," the captain cursed. "Of all the dwarves..."

"You're familiar with him, Captain?" Arran enquired.

"Fought him before. One of the toughest bastards out there. He leads the dwarves of the Iron Hammer Order. If you're lucky, he'll still be too drunk to fight. And before you say it, Callum, I also heard that the fight involved a bunch of idiots harassing a girl from that same tavern. Under normal circumstances, you would be punished by the drillmaster. But considering that the three of you will have a hard fight today. I have no choice but to postpone your punishment until after the bout, win or lose. But I must warn you, cause any more trouble outside the Stronghold or during the games and you will be removed from the event altogether and sent back to Gard Afon to clean the stables. Am I clear?"

"Yes Captain," the four of them replied together.

"Good, now make your way to the coliseum, I expect you to get changed and be ready to fight. Dismissed, except

you Arran."
Arran was surprised to hear the captain wanting a word solely with him. He looked at Gabriel who was also surprised; the other two shrugged before heading for the door.
"I'll get the horses ready," said Rhodri.
Arran nodded, he watched as the others walked, one by one, out of Captain Alric's quarters. The door gently closed behind them. Arran looked at the captain, who looked glad that it was just them in the room. He walked over to a chair that was behind his desk and he gestured to Arran to sit in another chair across from his. Arran accepted and sat down. "So, Arran," Captain Alric started, "you've been around Anwen lately?"
"Captain?" Arran was surprised. "What are your thoughts on her, any?"
"Well…" Arran's words were stuck in his throat at that point. *What the hell? Is this some trick?* He thought. Was Captain Alric aware of his interactions with his daughter? He knew he had to be careful here. Too much flattery would most likely antagonise him, he had to be honest though about Anwen's abilities, so he cleared his throat before replying. "She's a good fighter, Captain. Someone that everyone can look to for inspiration. And she can handle herself in most situations."
Alaric nodded slowly. "Look, I know you've got something going on, but just some advice: don't get too close to her. It's hard enough for a woman to earn respect in a man's craft."
"I… I assure you Captain," Arran began, "there's nothing going on between me and your daughter. She's a good friend, one that I'm getting to know more of. That's all."
"Alright. And just for the record, you and your friends will drink from now on within the limits of the

Stronghold until I say otherwise. You're a knight in training, you have to start acting like one, all of you. Is that clear?"

Arran nodded. "Yes, Captain."

"Good, now go and make yourself ready. You and your team have another fight today, so you better be on your way."

"Yes, thank you, Captain," Arran rose from the chair and made his way to the door. As he closed it behind him, he was greeted by another figure. Eafen was leaning by the wall outside the captain's quarters.

"I noticed you didn't leave with everyone else, Arran," the mage spoke as he moved away from the wall.

"And you weren't present with the rest of us," Arran returned.

"I had chores to deal with; my apologies."

"Sure," Arran began to walk along the balcony to the stables. Eafen followed.

"I'm needed again at the coliseum," Arran added.

"Another fight?" Eafen asked.

"Yes, and I have a feeling who we'll be going up against,"

"Do you?" Eafen enquired.

"Say, have you seen Anwen, by the way?" Arran glanced over his shoulder to ask.

"She's already over at the coliseum. She's got her first fight today."

"Well, we better hurry up and get over there," Arran replied, as he walked down the steps and entered the courtyard. He saw Gabriel, Callum and Rhodri bringing the horses out. The latter, being true to his word, was holding on to the reins of Basil as well as his own horse, Summer, a brown steed of a lighter shade.

"Thanks, Rhodri," said Arran.

"Anytime," Rhodri nodded.

"Let's get going; we've got another match today," said Arran as he mounted up on Basil.

"Good," Gabriel replied as he mounted his own horse. "Time to blow off some steam."

Eafen stood by Callum watching the men mount up.

"We'll join you when we can," said Eafen.

Arran simply nodded and carried on. The young warrior led the way with Gabriel and Rhodri following him through the gates. *I wonder how Anwen is doing*, Arran thought as he and his comrades rode through the streets of the capital to the Coliseum.

Chapter 27

Somewhere in the Coliseum

ANWEN WAS ON HER KNEES before a small statue in one of the fitting chambers. It was shaped to resemble Volken, the Master of Fire, God of Warriors and Smiths.

The figure held aloft a sword in one hand and a ball of fire in the other. Anwen prayed to him to watch over her today in her first match. It helped her ease the nerves one can expect when dancing with swords before a great audience. Satisfied, she rose to her feet and reached for her helmet from the shelf. Next, she picked up her swords from the weapons rack opposite, fastening the scabbards to her belt. Sun and Moon, she called them. Each blade spanned the length of her fingertip to the elbow, and the guards were curved upward.

These swords were designed so that one of them would fix a foe's weapon in place, whilst the other would deliver the blow to the opponent's weak spot.

Anwen checked her attire again before she walked out of the chamber with her helmet under her arm. Two city guards waited by the doorway to the arena. The only light from torches that illuminated the corridor behind her and those which beamed in front from a small slit in the double doors. One of the guards was looking through the slit, talking to someone on the other side. The guard nodded and then both men glanced at Anwen before opening the double doors.

The sunlight flooded the corridor, reflecting off Anwen's gauntlets and every piece of her armour that wasn't covered by her tunic. So strong was the light, she raised her free hand over her eyes. She could hear the anticipation, the call of the crowd for action. She was hoping that her father would be there to watch, until he told her that he needed to have a word with Arran. Great idea, Arran, she thought. You and Gabriel go out for a drink and get involved in a fight. Typical men. She shook her head. Can't afford to be distracted by such petty things.

She could hear the anticipation, the call of the crowd for action. She was hoping that her father would be there to watch, until he told her that he needed to have a word with Arran. *Great idea, Arran*, she thought. *You and Gabriel go out for a drink and get involved in a fight. Typical men.* She shook her head. Can't afford to be distracted by such petty things.

She fitted her helmet before marching out to the arena where a spokesperson stood in the centre of the man-made ring announcing her name and that of her opponent, who approached from the other side. Anwen looked ahead and saw a woman clad in a full suit of dark silver armour. Her helmet was adorned with a pair of golden wings. She carried in one hand a heater shield like the one Arran used. Silver with gold trimmings, and well-polished, it was like a mirror reflecting back the sunlight. Carefully painted at its centre was a gryphon. Anwen guessed her opponent would be using a sword long enough to complement her shield in this fight against her.

The spokesperson announced her as Raina Osterbarn, hailing from Ostenburg and representing the Knights of Hothland, the land that the emperor and his family once called home before moving the capital from Reikenburg to Aberemrallt. Both combatants turned to the auditorium, where the emperor, his family and the members of the council sat either side of his makeshift throne. Below them, on a podium of its own and guarded by four soldiers, was the Unbreakable Will. The spear that once belonged to Orion pointed upward to the sky. It was traditional to have this sacred artefact present so that all might view its splendour. According to legend, the Unbreakable Will would sparkle brightly when in the hands of the one chosen to wield it.

The emperor rose from his throne and gave his approval by raising his hand. The two female warriors turned to face each other. Raina showed no emotion as she drew a long sword from her scabbard and took up a stance with a shield presented in front. Anwen followed suit, unsheathing Sun and Moon from her scabbards.

The spokesperson raised a small flag in his hand. "Let the fight begin!" He dropped his flag. A battle horn followed, and the crowd roared, anticipating the coming clash.

Time for Anwen to prove herself.

Chapter 28

The Ringspine Mountains, Hothland

"WELCOME, CHANCELLOR." Valeran stretched his arms out before his prisoner. "As you can see, we're very far from the comfort of the capital." He watched as Gedric's eyes briefly surveyed the mountainous landscape.

"Hothland," Gedric muttered dryly.

"You look thirsty, my friend. Walder, if you would please." Valeran gestured to Walder, who stood behind the chancellor. His servant pulled out a flask from his belt, opened it and offered it to Gedric. The chancellor was initially reluctant, but eventually, he sipped the water, then instinctively gulped it down until the flask was empty, and Walder withdrew the thing afterwards.

"Now go ahead, ask away," Valeran said as he turned his back to Gedric to admire his position in the mountains.

"How long?" Gedric licked his mouth. "How long have you planned for this?"

"For a very long time, my friend. From the moment I learnt about the history of my family's fortunes and misfortunes. How we once held power over almost half of the continent." Valeran looked down to the ground and sighed. "Only to end up as a puppet under the delusional emperors of House Volorn."

Valeran could hear Gedric resisting a chuckle before replying, "You let your family's misgivings get to your head, didn't you?"

Valeran snorted. "So what? Am I to simply watch and do nothing? As people like you continue to mock the name of Serpentine behind my back?"

"You self-serving serpent!" Gedric raised his voice. "I know you have the box and the key. Do you have any idea what will happen when you open it?"

Valeran turned sharply and sneered. "Of course I do! I know exactly what will happen, idiot! The world you know where people are treated as equals at the table of politics will end. I grew weary of stomaching your authority every time we shared a seat at the council table. Even kneeling before the foolish Hothlander usurpers who took what rightfully belonged to my house grinds my teeth to this day." He stopped to cough before reaching out a hand for water, presented by another servant.

"So, the old snake still has some bite," Gedric mocked. "Tell me, Valeran, has your master told you what he has in store for you and everyone else? Can you be sure your family will have a guaranteed place up the ladder above the chaos?"

Valeran glared at his prisoner as he drank from a flask. A moment of silence fell between the two, feeling like an eternity. The wind began to pick up, breezing and weaving among them. Valeran, more than ever, wanted to kill this man. To strip him naked and hang the fool from the top of the highest mountain. But his frown changed back to a sadistic grin. Death was nothing compared to fear. He preferred Gedric to suffer so he could delight in seeing the grief and frustration on his foe's face, knowing he had a lifetime to intervene.

"It doesn't matter who or what he will destroy," Valeran continued, "so long as I get to see my house in its glory renewed while I still draw breath. That is all that will ever truly matter to me. It is time you saw the face of this land's true master." He nodded to Walder; his right-hand man pulled Gedric up to his feet. Valeran turned and led the party into a cave deep within the mountain.

Vile bastard, Gedric thought as Walder goaded him into following his master. He could hear the sound of a cart moving. He glanced behind; he was sure it was the same cart that had brought him here. A hooded man was at the helm, steering the horse to follow the group into the cave. Something else caught Gedric's eye; behind the driver in the cart was a large barrel. With every ditch and stone the cart hit, the barrel would wobble.

What could he be hiding in there? The chancellor. Walder suddenly nudged him, forcing him to turn around as they entered another cave. The cave Valeran was leading them through was not lit with torches. Instead, the walls were illuminated by strange red rocks at every turn, giving out a small amount of heat with their glow. Gedric realised this was aerianeite, the raw crystal that gave warlocks their power over their respective elements. But there were also ones that gave out a dark purple glow alongside them as they descended further into the earth.

"I believe you are somewhat familiar with aerianeite, yes?" Valeran's voice echoed in the cave. "Every colour you see represents the magic of a certain element. Red, as you can see here, is for fire. My favourite colour aside from the green of my house banner. Azure for the wind, blue for water and green represents the magic of nature. The purple ones, however, are of a different sort of magic since they are not bound to a certain element. They are the product of magic made from the darkest of a man's mind. We call it dark aerianeite."

The tunnel exited into a large chamber, where a massive pit of boiling fluid was at the centre. A stone archway that acted as a bridge was above this pit. At this point, the group diverted. Walder forced Gedric into a cage large enough for a bear and locked the door behind him. Gedric was stuck there, forced to watch whatever came next.

"Pay close attention, Chancellor," Valeran called out as he stood over the pit. "This is how you bring a true god to life!" He then circled the pit and walked over to a pair of tables. Meanwhile, his followers were unloading the barrel from the cart. They brought it to the tables, undid the top and pulled out what appeared to be the body of a man.

"By Orion," Gedric muttered in dismay as he realised who it was. The tall and slender-built man being dragged and carried out by Valeran's men was Lord Aeolus Bastone. Face and skin translucent and pale like snow; his lifeless body was carried and placed onto the table in front of Valeran. The mad old man turned to the other table, where the Black Box and its key were laid out. He picked up the key and raised it above head height so Gedric could see him open it. Gedric's stomach turned with frustration and disgust. He grabbed and pulled on the bars of his cage,

"This is sacrilege! You bloody mad man!" he yelled at Valeran, but his voice fell on deaf ears. He rattled the bars furiously till Walder struck on one of his hands with a rod. The pain forced him back away as he clutched his wounded hand. He fell back down and watched as Valeran reached into the Black Box with his hands. A moment later, Gedric could see the Heart of Darkness in Valeran's hands. A swelling mass, still beating of what was once human muscle.

Walder walked over to the table and got to work ripping away Bastone's clothes. He began digging and tearing with crude tools into the man's body. Flesh squelched and bones cracked as they came into contact with rusty metal, and the air was suddenly tainted with the stench of blood. When Walder found what he was looking for, he put the tools down and reached into Bastone's body. The bald man pulled out what was the dead man's heart and placed it in a basket. Gedric gritted his teeth in disgust.

Valeran approached Walder, handing him the Heart of Darkness for him to insert into the body. After that, the latter gestured for the other henchmen to come forth. Armed with chains, they attached them to each of the deceased's limbs. They carried the body over to the pit, where a crane awaited.

Two of the henchmen operated the levers and pulleys of the machine, allowing them to hoist the body off the ground. They rotated the crane until the body was hanging over the pit. Just underneath the archway. Gedric observed as his nemesis walked along the bridge over the pit, stopping when he was at the centre. There was a gnawing sensation in the chancellor's stomach, watching the traitor standing over the pit, looking down at the body he had defiled.

"Begin!" Valeran called out with vigour. The henchmen began lowering the body into the pit. The old snake began muttering a chant in a language Gedric couldn't understand. His voice became louder as the body was enveloped by the hot fluid below. As Valeran finished, the pit momentarily ceased to boil. There was an uneasy quiet. Then a single bubble blurted out, followed by many more, causing the pit to foam up in the centre. The fluid roared and boiled into action again. Amidst it all, Gedric noticed something. A figure was slowly emerging from the steam and foam. *The body of a man?* Gedric thought. No, it was no longer a man. Its naked skin was now a fiery red, brimming with muscles. Its feet thudded hard on the ground as it surged forward away from the steaming pit. The head was clean of the hair that belonged to the previous being, though stubbles could be seen in its place. The being's eyes had a golden glow that complemented its sharp facial features.

Once out of the pit, it gave out a roar that no man or beast should be able to make, echoing all around the chamber. It sent a shiver down Gedric's spine like nothing before.

Samael, the Lord of Darkness, was reborn.

Chapter 29

The Coliseum, Aberemrallt

THE HORNS SOUNDED; Anwen approached her foe, swords twirling as she walked forward. The two warriors circled each other. The rays of the sun bore down and reflected off their armour. Anwen's opponent, Raina Osterbarn, wielded her longsword close to her shield, pointing outward, and she adopted a middle guard stance.

Eying Raina, Anwen realised that her foe had the advantage of being a few inches taller than her. Regardless, Anwen made the first move. She swung her blades at the opponent, and the shield met every strike with the occasional parry from the longsword. When space presented itself, Raina made a downward strike, but Anwen crossed Sun and Moon overhead like a pair of scissors to block. She gritted her teeth as steel grinded on steel. So fixated on the lock, Anwen failed to notice the movement of Raina's shield. Her foe used it to break up the deadlock. Anwen felt the shield strike her in the chest. She was knocked off her feet. Her armour clanged as she landed on the hard ground. A cheer from the crowd followed the action.

Anwen was on her back but quickly rolled over to her knees, still clinging to her weapons. She looked up at Raina; the Hothlander remained in her stance, ready to strike again. *She's not taking any chances*, Anwen thought as she carefully rose to her feet, eyes focussed on the foe before her. She could rush Raina, take her by surprise with another flurry of strikes, but she remembered something; her father's words from when she first began her training. *Don't rush into every fight head-on, Anwen. Think before you leap.*

The worst thing a warrior could do in a situation like this was to give in to their temper when things weren't going their way.

Anwen raised her swords in front of her, ready to fight again. Raina moved a little closer with the intent of finishing the fight. Anwen realised the best way to beat Raina was to strike where she couldn't protect herself with the shield. She took two steps forward and feigned an attack. Raina grunted loudly before leading forth with her shield. She had taken the bait; Anwen grinned.

Raina lunged with her sword, rather than blocking again, and Anwen stepped to one side. Her opponent went forward in her last direction, almost losing balance. Raina turned around and charged again, this time with her shield. Anwen fell back as Raina closed in. The latter swung her sword over the shield, aiming for Anwen's head. She ducked the first swipe, then the second. On the third strike, Raina switched to bringing her sword downward. Before impact, Anwen turned on her back foot. She twirled around, bypassing Raina's sword, then struck with Moon in her right hand at her foe's exposed back, followed by Sun. The tips of her blades scratched her foe's armour. The Hothlander flinched from the force and went down to her knees. The audience was awed at the clever manoeuvre, which seemed to have infuriated Raina, for as soon she got back up, she retaliated, leading with her shield. The two female fighters clashed again.

Every strike from one blade was parried or deflected by the other. At one point, Raina's fatigue and aggressive approach got the better of her, for she went for another downward strike. Anwen sidestepped it and lunged into her foe's chest, jabbing quickly with one of her swords on Raina's armour below the breastplate, then stepping back before the shield could be brought to bear.

The horns blew again, and the spokesperson called for the fight to cease. Both fighters stepped away from each other. Anwen didn't take her eyes off her foe but eventually sheathed Sun and Moon. The spokesperson returned after speaking to a panel of judges.

"A marvellous display of strength and skill from these women!" he called out. "However, the winner of this bout…" there was a pause before he replied, "is Anwen Dorwin of the TwinBlade Order!"

Anwen's hand was raised in triumph by the spokesperson.

The audience roared in delight. Pleased with the outcome, she removed her helmet to breathe, the sun drying her sweat-drenched face. Someone walked toward her. It was Raina. The Hothland warrior removed her helmet, revealing pale skin, with golden blonde hair reaching down just past the jawline, matched with hazel eyes. She offered a hand to Anwen, which she gratefully accepted.

"You're very good with those swords, Anwen Dorwin," Raina complimented.

"And so are you with your weapons," Anwen smiled.

"May we fight again sometime." Raina let go of Anwen's hand and walked away.

Anwen nodded before taking her to leave as well. As the two fighters left the arena, Anwen stopped and looked at the audience; she saw her father sitting next to Eafen and Callum. They were clapping and cheering with everyone else. What made her heart burst with pride was the smile on her father's face. She waved to them before leaving.

"Well, that was a good fight, I'd say," Callum commented gleefully to Eafen, who sat next to him.

Eafen raised a hand to cover his head from the sun's rays. "Yes, indeed."

"Too bad Arran and the others missed it," said Callum.

Eafen turned his head to Callum. "Didn't you say she had sparred with Arran and Gabriel before coming here?"

"Yes, they did. If Anwen could hold off two men, she could beat anyone. Well, almost anyone, I think."

Eafen chuckled, and they turned their attention to the next bout. This time, two knights entered the arena from opposite sides, preferring to fight on foot rather than with horse and lance. He looked over to where the emperor and his council resided. He saw the figure of Captain Therin, who was leaning on the balcony barrier, observing the next clash. Below the royal balcony was the Unbreakable Will. The spear was upright on its podium, surrounded by Imperial soldiers and fellow TwinBlade Knights.

At that point, Eafen noticed something that made him forget about everything else around him. It appeared to him as though the Unbreakable Will was sparkling, much like before in the chapel, only this time it was coming from the real thing and not his vision. He looked around; Callum was busy talking to somebody else. It was as if the spear was somehow communicating only to him, even at this distance. He stared at it, mesmerised by the shine. Once again, the mage's vision was engulfed by a flash. Everything around him seemed darker like he was sitting in a twisted perception of reality. He saw at the far side of the arena, a massive portal had opened, swirls of black, red and purple. The voices of the audience were blurred out by ones he couldn't recognise; whispers and sadistic cackles were filling his mind. Was he going mad? No, he couldn't be. Was his worst nightmare about to become a reality?

"Are you alright, Eafen?" a familiar voice was heard, instantly causing another flash, and he returned to reality. He looked at a very puzzled Callum. "You look like you've seen a ghost."

"No, I've seen something worse than that," Eafen replied, breathing heavily. He wiped his forehead with a sleeve upon realising that he was sweating.

"Like what?" Callum asked.

"Something is about to happen. It's hard to explain. I need to speak to someone. Please excuse me," Eafen rose to his feet, making his way out of his sitting area. Still a little giddy from the visions.

Callum hesitated before getting out of his seat as well.

"Eafen, wait up!" He followed the mage as they made their way to the royal observation point.

Eafen frowned. He wasn't expecting his newly acquainted friend to follow him, nor did he need the assistance. But he simply carried on. He hoped there was still time to avoid a catastrophe.

Chapter 30

Valeran's camp, Hothland

THE MASTER HAD RETURNED. The God-like being standing tall for all to see. Steam rose from Samael's red skin, chiselled as though from stone. He took a massive heavy breath, his first in what must have felt like an eternity before exhaling. Humming triumphantly, Valeran could barely hold back the excitement as he descended the bridge when he burst out loud.

"Behold! Our true master has returned." He then gestured to a servant, who approached Samael with a cloak of black and red with gold trimmings. The Dark Lord grabbed it and threw it over the shoulders.

"You've done well so far," he spoke for the first time in a soft yet malevolent voice, flexing his hands and arms. "Finally ... It is good to feel again. To have flesh and bone once more."

"It is all because of you, my lord," said Valeran. "To finally stand before a god, it is—"

Samael raised a hand before Valeran could finish. He turned to face the old man and towered over him. Suddenly, the old man's excitement left him, replaced by a sense of dread that made him feel cold inside.

"I'm not fond of flattery or grovelling. Understand?" Samael replied.

Valeran gulped immediately. "Uh, yes, of course. My apologies, Master."

"Tell me, Valeran, are we within the mountains?" Samael asked.

`Yes, we are, Master," Valeran told him. "Just under

Mount Otto in Hothland."

"Ah, Hothland. Mount Otto," the red God reminisced. "Here was where it all began. I have fought many battles within the heart of the Ringspine Mountains. My glorious victories, always shadowed by the defeats." He clenched his fists hard. "Especially the time when I last clashed with my old enemy… Orion." Samael involuntarily growled, as the name of his arch-enemy, passed his lips.

"Hundreds of years ago, and yet here we are," Valeran offered.

Samael walked along the wall of the chamber over to the cage where Gedric still lay in shock. The chancellor scurried away from the bars as the red titan looked down and studied the man that had long been a thorn in Valeran's side.

"And who might this man be?" Samael glanced over his shoulder at Valeran.

Valeran approached him. "This, my lord, is…"

"My name is Gedric Hermann." The man somehow found the courage to cut Valeran off, which surprised him. "Chancellor to Emperor Otto V, that…" he coughed, "is all you will get from me, Demon."

Samael snorted as he continued to stare at the man, then he grinned. "You are def ant, even as a god stands before you. I respect that." He leaned forward until his head was a few inches from the bars of the cage, casting a large shadow over the prisoner.

"I shall let you live," he whispered to him. "So you may see your world burn before me." He followed it up with a sadistic smile before he turned back to Valeran. "It is time for the next phase of my plan."

"My lord?" Valeran responded eagerly.

Samael turned away from him and continued to walk around the chamber. Valeran followed him like a puppy staying close to its mother. He couldn't help but notice his lord had a hand in front of him, trailing along the hard surface of the carved wall. He assumed that Samael was just getting a feel for his surroundings, but upon closer inspection, it didn't look that way though. *Was he still weak? Impossible*, Valeran thought. Upon closer inspection, it looked as if he was looking for something. And then Samael spoke again over his shoulder.

"You will return to the capital, and you will bring me the Unbreakable Will."

Valeran stopped dead and gulped. *I'd completely forgotten about that bloody thing*, he thought. As he took in his command, Samael continued to walk alongside the wall. He quickly moved to close the gap between the two.

"With all due respect, my lord, the Unbreakable Will is most likely to be right in the heart of the coliseum," Valeran replied while using a handkerchief to wipe the sweat from his forehead. "It will be surrounded by the emperor's best soldiers with the Imperial Games happening as we speak. There will also be knights and warriors from every corner of the continent. I do not, unfortunately, have the resources to take the weapon in the middle of the day. Surely, it would be better to wait until the games are finished? By then, we would have gathered enough power to strike."

Samael suddenly stopped. The palm of his hand still pressed on the chamber wall as he appeared to Valeran's eyes contemplating this idea.

He replied coldly, "Your strategy would've worked in another time," he then carried on walking, "but time will soon be our enemy. Attacking even the most neglected of garrisons will draw in the attention of the emperor and his armies."

"But most of the Empire's best troops are stationed in the

capital," Valeran protested, "It will take time for them to mobilise, which we can use to establish our presence."

Samael glanced over his shoulder and growled at him. His tone made Valeran pause, realising that he might have overstepped his place.

"As I said, it will only be a matter of time before we are discovered," Samael resumed his walk. "By attacking the Empire at its heart now and seizing the Unbreakable Will, the enemy will be in disarray, leaving the rest of the land vulnerable."

"But still, my lord," Valeran continued, "we don't yet have an army big enough to march all the way to the capital, let alone lay siege to it. My encampment is made solely of cultists."

At that point, Samael stopped at a particular point in the chamber. His hand hovered over something carved into the wall. Valeran noticed it was a symbol of some sort.

A goblet outlined in gold with a fiery eyeball peeking over the top. He watched as his master waved his hand over it, muttering a spell before thrusting his palm into the stone wall. A moment later, Samael pulled his hand away, and the goblet symbol glowed, then the wall slid open before them to reveal—to Valeran's astonishment—another room.

"You want an army, Valeran?" Samael asked coldly. A heartless smile crossed his face, followed by a twinkle in one eye. "Watch me bring you one."

He walked into the newly opened room confidently. Valeran stood in awe. *How could I have missed that symbol?* he wondered. Not long after he had entered the room, Samael returned. In his hands, he carried an unusual object. Valeran approached his master to inspect it and couldn't believe his eyes. It was a bronze sphere. Like the box in which Samael's heart was kept, there were carvings of skulls and other figures all over the object. The top half of it looked as if it could open up like the petals of a flower when blossoming.

"Is that what I think it is?" Valeran's mouth was trembling.

"Yes, the Sphere of Confinement," Samael replied. "Within it lay the souls of all the warriors that served me before. Every creature that ever terrorised this land. Trapped and dormant. I say it is time to awaken them."

"I thought they cast it out into the North Sea," said Valeran

Samael laughed. "Another lie to keep those who came before looking in the wrong direction. It has always been here. I know this because it contains a fragment of my soul."

He raised the Sphere of Confinement above his head and began another chant. Valeran stepped back and watched as the markings on the ancient relic began to glow a dark orange. The top half opened up just the way Valeran assumed it would. A swirling mass of black smog emerged from the sphere. It circled around Samael before diving down to the ground. The mass changed its form to that of a puddle before Valeran. Out rose a mysterious figure draped in black robes. *It must be some kind of shade*, thought Valeran, watching as it hovered a few feet above the ground right in front of Samael.

Unfazed by its presence, the Dark Lord simply nodded while holding the Sphere of Confinement above his head. The shade let out an almost inhuman, feral scream as it flew low around the chamber. Valeran caught a glimpse of what was beneath the hood. Nothing except a skull that belonged to a man long deceased. Its eyes glowed a deep vermillion.

Suddenly, the ground beneath Valeran's feet became unstable. He looked down and saw a skeletal hand burst out from beneath. He jumped at the sight, landing on his backside as the figure of a warrior crawled out from the ground. Clad in a tunic so filthy and torn in places, Valeran couldn't tell who this warrior once fought for before meeting his end. Soon, more skeletal beings emerged from the ground as the shade continued to fly, cackling away. Another shade emerged from the sphere to join its kin. All the while, Samael grinned at the entire spectacle. Valeran continued to gaze in awe of his master's power over the dead.

He knew this was only the beginning.

Chapter 31

THERIN LEANED on the balustrade as he watched the games from the comfort of the auditorium, the seating area having been reserved only for the emperor, his family, and those most trusted of officials and lords and ladies. Since the games had begun, he had donned a dark blue cotehardie with a pair of black trousers. Attached to his belt was a sword sheathed in a red scabbard just in case something out of the ordinary were to happen.

Despite the calm presence he displayed in front of everyone around him, there was a sense of uneasiness within. The things he had seen from the last few days continued to play out in his mind. The captain hoped to receive word from the chancellor about his mission soon, and Therin couldn't help but find it strange for both Gedric and Valeran to be chasing each other around the Terradonian countryside over a stupid key. A game of cat and mouse.

Therin would have thrown the thing into the sea and been done with it. He took a sip of wine from the cup next to him, staring down intensely at the two knights in the arena who clashed, sword on sword. The audience cheered and awed with every strike and parry made. *How I wish I were down there, taking my frustrations out in a duel right now*, he thought.

"Is everything alright, Captain Therin?" a familiar voice caught his attention. He turned and saw Lady Eleanor standing close to him. "You seem uneasy."

Damn it, am I so obvious to you, Eleanor? Therin thought, as he turned to the elven noblewoman. She wore for this occasion what Therin considered to be her finest dress yet. A purple tunic outlined with gold, she even had golden leaves sprouting out from her shoulders. And as for her hair, she chose to have it braided, with the remaining pulled back up into a ponytail that rested on her slender shoulder. Topping it off, was a green and bronze headpiece that balanced on her forehead.

Therin sighed. "Would you feel easy when there is a man you thought you knew, who sat at the same table as you running loose somewhere in the countryside? Making plots and schemes? I should've stopped him sooner."

"There's no need for you to be hard on yourself," Eleanor assured. "Valeran was a secretive man. It was hard even for me to tell what was going on in his head."

Therin quietly snorted. "What if the stuff I saw in his house was just scratching the surface? Heck, do we even know who he really is?"

Eleanor placed a hand on his shoulder. "Well, he can't hide forever. If he even sets foot in Terradonia, he won't have far to go before Gedric catches him."

Therin nodded as he resumed staring out at the arena. Watching the audience react enthusiastically as one knight exchanged the winning blow against the other. Prince Frederick walked over to join him. He wore a bright red tunic with purple outlines for today's festivities.

"There goes your favourite, my prince," said Therin.

"Damn," the prince replied plainly. "Can't believe I bet on him."

Therin grinned. "Some you win, some you lose, my friend."

Frederick raised an eyebrow. "I'd like to hear you say that if you and I were down there now. I would like to see what you look like in a suit of armour."

Therin laughed lightly. "Is that a challenge, my prince?"

"Well, we can always wait for the next games if you want? Provided I'm still a prince, and you don't feel too old to do this anymore," the young prince replied.

Therin barely held back a chuckle upon hearing those words. "We don't have to wait for another five years," he taunted.

"Now, now, boys. Behave yourselves," Eleanor broke in; Therin and Fredrick just chuckled.

At that point, another person came forth. It was Duran, holding a flagon in one hand. Gedric had assigned the young servant to the captain in his absence. "More wine, my Prince, Captain and lady?" he asked.

"Thank you, Duran," Therin offered his cup for a refill. At the same time, one of the guards walked up to him and whispered in his ear.

"Captain, there is a man by the name of Eafen waiting outside for you. He says he has urgent news."

"I'll be right there," he said to the guard, then he looked at Duran, "Hold on to my cup for me please, Duran."

"Yes, Captain."

"My prince, my lady, if you'll excuse me," he addressed Fredrick and Lady Eleanor before walking across the auditorium floor to the doorway.

Another guard was present. He opened one of the double doors for the captain. Standing outside was Eafen, whose face looked a little pale around the cheeks. He was accompanied by another person dressed in the blue and red tunic of the TwinBlade Order. Judging by his slightly bulky frame in comparison to Eafen's slimmer appearance, Therin assumed he was more a scribe or steward than a fighter.

"Eafen," Therin began, as the door closed behind him.

"Captain Therin," the mage replied.

"Has the sun all of a sudden drained you of your colour?" he asked as a light-hearted joke.

Eafen rolled his eyes, then he replied, "I apologise for interrupting, but there's something I need to tell you."

"Go on," Therin encouraged.
"I've had another vision," Eafen continued, "I believe we are in danger."
Therin was taken aback. "What?" He looked at Eafen's comrade, who stared at Eafen with equal surprise as himself.
"I know this sounds out of the ordinary," Eafen explained, "but I fear something is going to be happening at some point today. I believe someone is coming for the Unbreakable Will, and they won't be alone."
Therin raised his hands. "And you are sure about this?"
"If I had received the vision sooner, I would have informed you immediately. I swear by the gods, what I speak is the truth," said Eafen.
Therin raised an eyebrow. "So, you're assuming we are to be attacked? By whom?"
"Most likely whoever the criminals we captured were working for," Eafen replied.
Therin looked around the corridor before continuing. "Since you helped us discover the thieves, I'll let you in on this one. We believe it was Valeran Serpentine who orchestrated the robbery."
"The Master of Coin?" Eafen's friend spoke for the first time with shock.
"And you are?" Therin asked.
"This is Callum. He is with the Pwynt Afon branch of my Order, Captain," Eafen explained.
"Um, yes well, an honour, Captain," said Callum, he bowed his head slightly before him.
Therin eyed the man for a moment before returning to Eafen. "We have people tracking him down as we speak. But I don't think an attack is going to happen any time soon."
"But we need to move the Unbreakable Will before—"

Therin frowned. "Are you mad? We can't just move the spear. People will notice."

"Please, Captain," Eafen begged. "You're the only one I can trust on this."

The captain sighed again. "Look, I'll station more troops to keep an eye on it. If something comes up, I'll have the spear removed while the public is occupied. However, if this turns out to be a farce, you will owe me, both of you."

"Me as well?" Callum's eyes widened. "I have no knowledge of any of this at all, Captain."

"And you will keep it that way," Therin commanded. "Now, unless you two have anything else to report, I have an event to watch. Now go, and don't do anything stupid."

Eafen sighed with frustration but nodded, accepting the captain's decision. The mage headed back the way he came, Callum followed after taking another look at the captain. With that, Therin turned back to the auditorium. Upon closing the doors behind him, he noticed that a lot of the nobles were looking at him as he walked across the auditorium floor, even the emperor himself.

"What exactly was that all about?" His Highness asked as he leaned forward.

"Nothing, your Highness," Therin responded immediately. "A minor criminal issue reported, nothing to worry about."

His Highness eyed the captain for a moment, but then he shrugged and sat back on his throne. Everyone else resumed their usual conversations.

Could he be onto something? the captain thought. Eafen's ability to see into the past was what allowed Therin and Gedric to learn about this brewing plot. If what the young mage said was true, then he needed to act. But he felt the need to know more about visions. He heard stories in the past of people with these abilities; people who ended up losing their sanity over such visions. Only half of them were ever realised. The captain looked around the room for someone who could have more insight, and then saw him, the Chief Warlock of the TwinBlade Order, Azurius Penno. He was speaking with another nobleman and lady. The captain straightened his cotehardie before striding toward him. He swiped his cup of wine from Duran's hand when he presented it. He nodded to the servant as he approached the Master Warlock.

"Afternoon Lord Azurius," Therin called.

"Ah, Captain Therin," he addressed him, "I heard that one of my students was helpful in your recent investigation."

"Yes, I have Eafen to thank," Therin replied. "Speaking of which. There's something I would like to speak to you about."

"Really?" Azurius was curious. "Well, what do you wish to know?"

He nodded to the nobleman and lady, who nodded back and continued their conversation elsewhere.

Therin cleared his throat before he asked, "How common is it for someone to receive a vision?"

"A vision?" Azurius asked.

"Yes, you know," Therin continued, "the stuff people claim to see in their dreams or even during the day."

Azurius put down his wine glass and pressed his hands together. "Visions, while fascinating, are not as common as you might think. Yes, the odd person may see something that they can't quite explain. But it is more likely to occur with someone who is gifted with the ability to harness magic."

"Such as yourself," said Therin.

Azurius chuckled a little. "Yes, such as myself. However," he raised his voice on the last word when the roar of the crowd almost made it impossible for Therin to hear him. "Few amongst our kind will ever receive a vision from the gods, let alone ones depicting forthcoming events."

"What if someone of significant talent were to be granted a vision from the gods of something bad that could happen anytime? Would that not be something we should consider heeding?" Therin enquired.

Azurius pursed his lips before replying. "In any other occasion, then yes it would be a sign that we should take into consideration. But let's be honest, Captain." He then raised his arms out wide. "Does this look like we are heading toward a disaster? Why would the gods choose now to deliver us an ill omen?"

Therin shrugged. Deciphering the will of the gods and other deities was not his area of expertise. Though he felt like the Master Warlock knew more or should know more of what was going on.

"You make a fair point, but then again, there could be other things that might sway fate the other way around. Maybe the gods are testing us?"

"The gods are always watching us in one form or another, Captain Therin," said Azurius.

"I'm sure they are," Therin leaned in and whispered. "A little bird says that something might happen today. Don't suppose you could ask your grandmaster to spare some more men to guard the Unbreakable Will? Just in case something unusual happens."

Azurius frowned at the captain. "I will see what we can do. Though I doubt the accuracy of such information. Now if you will excuse me." He turned away from the captain and went toward the balustrade.

Therin watched him walk away before turning back to Duran and Prince Fredrick. The latter was in the middle of a conversation with a young noble lady. He patted the prince on the shoulder and whispered in his ear.

"Better bring some more men to watch below."

"For what reason?" the prince asked.

"Let's just say I have a feeling something unusual could happen today"

"I thought it was your job to ensure our security, Captain?"

"Just wanted to let you know. We might be expecting some unwelcome guests."

"I thought Valeran was in Terradonia?" Prince Frederick was confused.

"That's what Gedric and I thought," said Therin. He looked over the prince's shoulder toward the arena; the crowd was awaiting the next bout to begin. "And I've got a bad feeling about all of this."

Chapter 32

IT HAD ONLY BEEN A FEW HOURS since his resurrection, yet Samael had bolstered Valeran's forces substantially. Valeran Serpentine stood atop a cliff with his master, and they watched as their army continued to grow; rows of freshly-risen skeleton soldiers, the bulk of the new force, stood in tight square formations. These fleshless bodies were lifeless, unflinching, except for the occasional clamber of bones and chittering of jaws. Orbs of dark red or green glowed in their eye sockets. Every single one of them wore different battle attire from the next. The dead cared not for whose banner they once served under, and neither did Samael. Their bodies were just one of many tools to him, armed with whatever weapons they were given or still clung to from the previous conflicts.

Shades flew low over the heads of the foot soldiers. Like crows and ravens, they circled the camp tirelessly. Some guided newer skeletons into place, others acted as lookouts for intruders. Behind him, Valeran could hear the thundering sound of large feet that made the ground tremble beneath his own. That sound belonged to the horde of massive beasts emerging from the cave after centuries of slumbering inside the Sphere of Confinement. Minotaurs, massive bull-like beasts whose dark bristled bodies were grown to stand upright. Their crude, jagged horns looked sharp enough to pierce any armour. Following them were the golems, creatures of clay or stone, shaped to look like giant humanoid beings and brought to life through the power of magic, imbued with elemental infusions such as fire or ice.

Scuttling in between these giants were the ghouls; small, hunched-back, and hideously naked beings save for the pieces of cloth around their waists, with no flesh covering their mouths, revealing the crude teeth underneath. Individually weak and cowardly according to past records, these fiends made up for it by throwing themselves upon their enemies in overwhelming numbers.

Valeran felt the air grow colder where he stood; he pulled on his own robes and grasped his cane tightly. He watched as black clouds slowly massed over the mountains. A spiral was forming before them, with the blackest of clouds at its centre. Valeran noticed that his Master was also staring stoically up at this phenomenon. Samael now donned a suit of armour that invoked awe and terror. His sleeveless breastplate was adorned in golden scales that almost resembled the face of a dragon upon closer inspection. Curved spikes of bronze jutted upward from the pauldrons. Under one arm, he held a reddish helmet with more horns that faced outward.

"Is this storm part of your plan, my lord, or is your nemesis trying to expose us?" Valeran asked.

Samael snorted out loud. "Even if so, it doesn't matter," he spat on the ground in front of him. "I've always questioned how much power Orion truly has over the Heavens. The same can be asked of the other gods. Do they really have the final say on how big the tides should be? Or when men can reap the best harvest?"

Valeran looked at him with puzzlement. "My lord?" Samael's views of the world continued to surprise him. Never in this old man's life did he think he would hear a being supposedly as powerful as Samael questioning the limitations of a god.

"It won't matter, though," Samael continued. "After today, the power they all have over life, death, the

Heavens and the Earth shall be but a memory." The Dark Lord lifted his helmet and slid it over his head before turning to Valeran. Once again, he felt small inside as his master towered over him. It was as if Samael was staring into Valeran's very soul.

"It is time," said Samael.

"My lord?" replied Valeran hesitantly.

"You will lead the attack on the capital and capture the Unbreakable Will. Let nothing stop you," Samael commanded as he led the way back down to the camp. Valeran followed closely behind like a puppy following its mother.

"May I ask, my lord, why do you need this weapon?"

"Why should you know?" Samael countered as he walked.

"Well, it is said that the Unbreakable Will is the one thing… No, the only weapon that could… kill you." Samael suddenly stopped his tracks and turned to face Valeran. Once again, Valeran's questions were rewarding him with nothing but fear as the red titan in gold armour stared down at him.

"I am aware of its power. I've experienced its potential firsthand," Samael growled. "More than any man, woman or child in this lifetime or the next. I have many reasons for wanting it. Primarily so that no one else can use it against me again. Any more stupid questions?"

Valeran struggled to string together an answer. "N…No, of course not, my lord. Forgive me." He bowed before him. Samael continued to stare him down. He eventually grunted before turning back to the path he was walking.

Valeran felt that there was more to the conversation than what was revealed. It made sense to keep something that could be used against oneself away from his enemies. He resumed following his master until he stopped before a group of shades, four in total. In the centre of this gathering was a pile of dark aerianeite stones from the caves. Another shade approached, followed by two robed cultists. They carried a small open cauldron, its contents bubbling over the top. The leading shade looked at Samael, awaiting further instruction.

"Begin," he ordered in a stoic tone.

The fifth shade pointed to the pile of dark aerianite at the centre, and the cultists brought the cauldron forth. They tilted the thing, and blood – fresh blood from a recently sacrificed goat, lamb and pig mixed together – poured out onto the stones. Steam rose, and the rocks glowed intensely. Sparks pricked in places, followed by a purple flame. Valeran struggled to keep his eyes open as the flames roared.

When the fires died down, he opened his eyes, and the old man again found himself in awe. Standing before him was the largest portal he had ever seen invoked. The great vortex was a maelstrom of dark colours swirling around relentlessly. The shades that surrounded the portal were busy murmuring a continuous ritual. Most likely to maintain the tear, in reality, Valeran thought. He looked at Samael, and to his surprise, he noticed a tiny smirk on one side of his Master's face. He watched unopposed with arms folded. Valeran looked back at the portal and saw something in the centre. At first, it was so minuscule he couldn't tell what it was. However, the thing became clearer as the image grew bigger. Valeran squinted hard until he realised what it was.

"The coliseum?" he muttered. "Indeed," replied Samael.

It was the arena in Aberemrallt in its entire splendour. He could hear horns blowing in the distance as well as people cheering. He could even see the Imperial Auditorium and the podium where the Unbreakable Will was positioned before them with soldiers guarding it. So entranced he was by the vision that he jumped upon feeling a hard hand grasp his shoulder.

"What a nice place to hold a tournament, don't you think?" Samael whispered in Valeran's ear. "Would be a shame if someone came along to make a mess of it. I think it's time we show them what true power looks like. Go forth, Valeran Serpentine, prove yourself and bring me my prize."

Valeran gulped hard. Never before had such a burden been placed on him. He risked a glance over the other shoulder and saw his master's army gathering. All the skeleton soldiers, ghouls and other monsters: a thousand living and undead eyes staring, waiting for him to make the first step toward the other side. Among them, he saw Walder at the forefront of this massive unholy force. At least he had someone he could trust to watch his back, Valeran thought. Samael lifted his hand from Valeran and pointed to the vortex. Valeran took a deep breath, gripped his cane and marched forward. He reached out with his free hand, watching as the swirling vortex enveloped itself around it. Seeing it as safe, Valeran followed with his whole body as he entered the portal. This was his time. The opportunity to seek revenge against the Empire had come, and he wasn't about to squander it.

Onward to power, onward to glory.

Meanwhile, in the coliseum ...

The draw gate slowly lowered behind Arran and his team. Another day in the heart of the arena and battle beckoned. Standing before them were a group of dwarves hailing from the mountain city of Veldor. This would be an interesting matchup. The foes stood ready, clad in bronze-like armour from the head all the way down to the toe. Their faces and beards were covered by metal masks that portrayed them as goblins or demons. Some of these warriors carried a round shield, painted in light green with a brown outline, whilst holding a long blunted polearm or a hammer since axes were deemed too dangerous to use in these fights. One of them, in particular, wielded a long two-handed war hammer. This was their leader, Brom Blackhammer, the dwarf Arran and Gabriel had met at the tavern. He stood out in front of his brothers, ready to fight. Arran looked at Brom's face, the warrior eyed him and his team as he spat on the ground before putting on his mask. It covered everything except for his long black beard.

Arran followed suit. As his team organised themselves in a line formation, he thought back to what Captain Alric had told him. Although they had an advantage over the dwarves in height, the strength of the dwarves and their body weight being nearer to the ground meant getting too close to any of them would be a terrible idea. It was best to keep a reasonable distance and use his superior height to get his sword over the dwarven shields. He looked at his team. Gabriel was to his right, followed by Robart, Rhodri and Roff, while Jovarn, Donnal, Bailin, Fabius and Alan were on his left. Each man was spread out to make use of space. The horns sounded; the two sides slowly closed the gap. Arran looked at Brom. The dwarf leader swung his war hammer around in front of him. The young warrior gripped his sword firmly.

But from behind the dwarven line, something was stirring at the far side of the arena. At first, it was tiny sparks igniting close to the ground that then intensified. The biggest of these sparks triggered a flash that blinded everyone within range. With it, a massive portal appeared out of nowhere. Everything else at that point ceased, warriors stopped in their tracks, and the audience was shocked and awed at the unexpected interruption. Everyone, including Arran and Gabriel, was motionless as they stared at the mysterious phenomenon. The dwarves turned around, and they, too, were frozen by the sight, momentarily covering their eyes until the light dimmed.

Arran pulled off his helmet when he saw something in the centre. Among the swirls of this vortex, there was a silhouette of a man-shaped figure, but Arran had to strain his eyes to identify it. This new anomaly soon revealed itself. Arran blinked his eyes as he saw what appeared to be an old man in dark robes stepping out of the portal. The old man was standing tall as he stepped forward confidently.

"Oh, I'm sorry!" the man shouted out loud. "Am I interrupting something?" There was a moment of muttering among the audience, then complete silence.

"Allow me to present myself to my lords and ladies," he bellowed. "I am Valeran of House Serpentine. Like many nobles who came before me, I served the Imperial Court even though my House were once masters in their own right. I bent my knee before your emperor, swallowing my own pride for the sake of this kingdom and my family. But no more! I am not here to save anyone from this rule. Your dynasty is only content to stay safely within the shores of this continent, denying other houses their right to ascend to the top. Behold, Your Majesty." He pointed a finger at the podium where the emperor and the nobles sat.

"On behalf of my new master, the true lord of this world, Samael, the first king of Nordland, the conqueror and destroyer of kingdoms, I carry a message to you all. I bring the beginning of the end!"

With that, the old man raised his hands above his shoulders, and from behind him, more figures began to emerge. Arran was frozen to the ground; he couldn't believe what he was seeing. Rows and rows of what appeared to be soldiers. But when he looked closer, he realised they weren't men. They were the undead. Skeleton warriors were marching out from the portal, the sound of their footsteps in unison. But beyond them followed silhouettes of more enormous creatures. Arran looked around him. He was still surrounded by his comrades and the dwarves.

"I think we're in for a bigger fight now, lad!" Brom Blackhammer shouted to him.

"Arran!" Gabriel shouted to him as well. "What do we do?"

"We stand our ground!" Arran responded. He gulped down hard. They were staring into the face of the coming apocalypse.

"Orion help us," he muttered under his breath.

Chapter 33

"SOUND THE ALARM! NOW! Get the people out of here!" Therin ordered one of the guards.

"Yes, Captain," the man replied, before he rushed off to the doors to relay the message.

A moment later, an alarm bell rang from one of the towers overlooking the arena. Another soon followed on the opposite side, reverberating around the entire coliseum. Captain Therin watched as the people panicked. Like frightened rats, they scrambled for the nearest exit. The nobles with him in the Auditorium were almost paralysed. Yet, Emperor Otto was standing firm in front of his throne, his fists were clenched, his face was red. Empress Deidre stood by him, shocked, with a hand over her mouth. Therin approached the divided monarchs.

"Your Majesty, you must leave here at once," he suggested.

"Leave?" the emperor shot a glare at the captain.

"We have been betrayed and outmanoeuvred by this treacherous snake, and you want me to leave with my tail between my legs?"

Therin continued to plead, "Sire, it's too dangerous to stay here…"

"I don't care, damn it!" the emperor barked back furiously. "This is what Valeran wants. Can't you see? I show my arse to him and everyone else, it'll justify everything that madman said. I am staying until the threat has passed. Contain this attack immediately. That's an order."

I suppose you have a point there, Your Majesty, Therin admitted.

"My love, please." The Empress had snapped out of shock and clutched on to her husband's arm. "We must put our trust in our officers."

"I shall not abandon our people!" The Emperor rejected. "You and Frederick will return to the palace and send reinforcements."

"Father," Prince Frederick protested, "I wish to stay as well."

"You're not dressed for combat," Emperor Otto countered. "And neither are you! At least I have a sword," The prince pointed out as he put his hand on the scabbard hidden under his tunic.

"It'll take more than a prince's sword to stop this madness," said Therin.

"Incoming!" a soldier shouted.

Therin turned around just in time to see a massive fireball that was launched from the arena ground heading for the Auditorium.

"Get down, now!" he shouted as he dived for cover, and everyone followed suit. The fireball struck the roof above them, part of which broke off and crashed down to the floor.

Therin found himself on the floor, coughing from the freshly risen dust that momentarily impaired his vision. There were bits and pieces of stonework everywhere. Flames began to flicker to life, catching whatever was flammable. One of the tables bearing fruit and wine had collapsed due to a fallen pillar splitting it right down the middle. The royal family thankfully appeared unharmed. The captain rose to his feet and looked around until he saw movement under a pile of rubble.

"Oh no!" Therin muttered; he had a feeling who was underneath. "Eleanor!" he called, then rushed to the debris. He was about to lay a hand when the rubble erupted like a volcano. From out of the debris, Kleif roared in anger. The dwarf's favourite tunic of red and black was dulled by the dust, giving him a ghostly appearance. As Kleif pushed the broken stonework aside, Captain Therin saw the figures of Lady Eleanor and Duran rise up. The dwarf must've placed himself between them and the falling debris.

"Are you alright?" Therin reached out a hand to each of them.

Eleanor coughed as she took his hand. Her plait had come undone, and there was a scratch on one cheek. Duran slowly rose to his feet, looking so shaken and wobbly that he might collapse right there.

"We could've been worse, if not for Kleif," Eleanor said.

"Right!" Kleif yelled furiously. "That bastard's done it now! When I get my hands on Valeran Serpentine, I'll squeeze the life out of him"

Now that would be something to watch, Therin thought.

"No," the emperor replied with a dusty voice. "He must stand trial for this madness before anyone can execute him."

"Assuming we can get to him," Therin replied, as he helped Elanor to her feet. "Everyone must vacate now!" the captain commanded.

He watched as the nobles exited the remains of the Auditorium one by one. The emperor shot Therin a look before eventually swallowing his pride and followed the others, the Empress in tow. The captain headed over to the balustrade, or what was left of it anyway.

He watched in dismay as monsters of all sizes poured out from the portal, one of which caught his eyes and ears. A flock of humanoid beings flew around the arena, screeching and cackling away. These creatures, as Therin observed with disbelief, were female in their appearance, with nothing to cover their dark-toned breasts. They flew around on pairs of black wings and had bird-like talons instead of feet. The captain recognised them as harpies—creatures that thrived on delivering pain and terror. He was soon joined by Prince Frederick, his face etched with shock and outrage. They watched as Valeran remained where he stood in front of the portal, like a rock amid a flowing river of death and destruction. The madman launched another fireball in their direction; fortunately, it flew up so high into the sky it passed over the highest arena seating, destined to land somewhere else in the city. *I really don't want to know where that one's heading*, Therin gulped hard. So did Prince Frederick, realising that they would have their hands full this day.

Therin turned to Frederick. "You get the people out of here, I'll coordinate the defence."

Frederick stared at him and sighed. "I'll be back to assist, I promise." The prince turned and left the captain.

Therin smiled a little as he took one last look at the chaos before deciding to vacate the Auditorium. He saw a lieutenant along with two soldiers standing by the doorway.

"Lieutenant," the captain addressed.

The Lieutenant turned to salute him. "Captain."

"Get archers positioned around the arena, I want them to target the large beasts and the flyers. And get every soldier and knight you can find out there," Therin instructed.

"Yes, Captain," the lieutenant replied without hesitation before heading off.

"Gods help us," Therin muttered under his voice.

Weary, filthy, and with nothing but a blanket for warmth. Gerald had spent the day in his prison eating, pacing and sleeping. His sense of guilt had made him so depressed that the only way to avoid the feelings was to sleep. He would only wake up when a guard presented him with a tray of food, at least twice a day. When undisturbed, he would fall into a slumber where his dreams would switch between good and bad. Days when he would dream of a quiet life living in the countryside with Nianna in a little cottage somewhere. Just a small place for them, no one else. To eat, sleep and make love together.

Every time he indulged in this fantasy, it followed with the gnawing sense of guilt that stalked him like a cruel, vicious shadow. It would rip him away from his desired dream, forcing him to wake up now and then. Today, however, he woke to the sound of voices and footsteps louder than usual. He got off his bed and went over to the bars of his cage. The sounds were above this floor. Something was happening, but he had no idea. He scanned the surroundings. Not a guard in sight. He went over to the barred slit where the only ray of light existed. There were men running back and forth bellowing instructions. A bell was ringing from one of the towers. He couldn't understand what was going on until he concentrated on listening. He heard something about the coliseum being under attack.

But that was impossible? Another thought entered his mind. *Where is Nianna?* The idea of her being in harm's way took the guilt he felt to a new level. It made him feel colder inside. If something happened to her, he would never forgive himself.

Just then, he heard a guard shouting, "Incoming!" He turned back to the barred window and looked up at the sky and saw a massive fireball. At peak hight, it was above even the tallest towers in the city. Now the fireball was descending at a frightening pace, aiming straight for the palace. Gerald shitted himself at the sight. He backed away from the view and crouched himself into a corner. The sound of the fireball drew ever closer. He closed his eyes and prayed to the gods and his beloved for forgiveness and accepted his fate. If death was to be his punishment, so be it. The fireball landed and exploded. The impact sent his whole body launching forward. He rolled before crashing into the prison bars, his face pressed into the cold hard iron.

A moment later, he opened his eyes. The temperature of the dungeon had risen dramatically. There was sweat across his bruised face and he found himself lying flat on the cell gate that buckled before the force of the fireball. By some miracle, he had survived. Pieces of wood and stone lay everywhere. The fireball had created a massive crater in the side of the palace. This would've been an opening for escape if not for the intense heat.

Luckily, Gerald found something on the ground. A pair of keys that must've fallen to the floor after the impact. He crawled off the iron bars and picked them up. He found the strength to get back on his feet and walked as quickly as he could to the dungeon door. He fiddled with the keys until one of them clicked inside the lock and the door opened. He rushed out of the dungeon and into a hallway.

As he made his way through the hallway, he occasionally hid behind a pillar to avoid the guards; though in his mind, putting out the raging fire was probably a bigger priority over any prisoner at this point. It took a few minutes before he found himself in the courtyard. None took notice of him as he rushed out of the opened gates. Men were rushing back and forth through the gates, bringing buckets of water to douse the flames.

When he was in the clear, Gerald stopped and took a

deep breath. He looked ahead and was horrified. He saw in the distance that the coliseum was in flames. The rumours were true, the place was under attack. He couldn't stop now and he so jogged into action. The thought of Nianna in danger drove him to push himself, to ignore everything else. He ran in the direction of danger, clinging on to the faint hope of redemption.

Staring into the heart of the vortex, the mighty Samael sat on a throne carved from stone. Eagerly, he watched the onslaught that was taking place on the other side of the portal. Flexing his large red hands over the ends of his seat, he was flanked by four cloaked figures, two on each side. All was going as he had envisioned. While the majority of his army was sent through the portal to aid Valeran in acquiring the Unbreakable Will, he still had a sizable force here ready to carry out the next step of his plans. He watched as Valeran, his new servant, toyed with the enemy. One of the shades closest to Samael lowered his head to his master's level and spoke. This shade, unlike the others, wore a mask made of iron. It featured small holes where the eyes were supposed to be, and a nose-shaped protrusion resembling the beak of a raven. It whispered in Samael's ear with a hoarse voice as if speaking through a metal tube.

"This Valeran appears to be enjoying himself… A little too much perhaps?"

Samael raised a hand at the figure. "Patience, my subject. He will deliver one way or another."

The cloaked figure remained silent for a moment, then, "Shall I prepare your weapon, my lord?"

"You've worked on this device for quite some time. Will it work?"

The shade paused for a moment before replying "It will."

"Then bring it to me," Samael ordered.

The shade retreated to the cave, while the others remained where they stood. The other shade closest to Samael spoke, this one had the voice of a female snake.

"This plan is quite dangerous, my liege. The last time you got into contact with…"

"Yes, I know, I have felt its power many times, long before you began to feast on your mother's breasts. Now, keep your mouth shut unless you have something useful to say."

"My apologies, my lord," the shade bowed.

Samael stared at the servant, then returned his focus to the portal. *It is only a matter of time*, he thought.

Only a matter of time.

Chapter 34

ARRAN COULDN'T BELIEVE HIS EYES. The impossible was happening right before him as a horde of skeletons and beasts charged him. Bells were ringing from the high balconies. He looked around and saw that the rest of his comrades were in a similar stance, unsure whether to fight or flee.

"Arran!" he heard someone call out his name. He glanced over his shoulder, and there was Anwen, followed by Captain Alric, and a stream of other warriors rushing out from the arena gates to their aid. The sight gave him hope and a new sense of bravery within.

"Band together!" he called out to them. Gabriel was first to respond, followed by Robart, Rhodri and then the rest. He heard Brom Blackhammer calling for his dwarf kin to rally behind him. This was a bleak situation, a forlorn hope that they could hold back this forsaken tide alone. But the chances of survival by running would be even slimmer. To him, they stood between these horrors and the people still trapped here.

Arran raised his sword high and cried, "For the Order!"

He led the charge. His eyes were fixated on what was in front of him. There was no turning back. The lines clashed, steel clanged with steel and battle cries rang out. A skeleton warrior came charging at Arran, thrusting a spear, two-handed, at him. He knocked the spear aside with his shield, then jabbed his sword at its ribcage. With no armour protecting the lower area, a blow like this would kill a normal man, but the thing just went through. The skeleton looked down at where the sword plunged, then back at Arran.

Well, that didn't work, Arran realised. The skeleton suddenly lurched forward, its jaw wide open. Arran instinctively jumped back, pulling his sword out of its ribcage, as the thing tried to bite him. The skeleton growled with a tone that was neither human nor animal. He noticed its eyes glowed a violent red. There must be a spirit possessing the body, Arran thought. *Maybe if I were to separate or destroy the skull...*

The skeleton grasped its spear and thrusted at Arran as he thought about what to do next. He parried the attack with his shield before backing away, goading the thing into attacking again. The skeleton took the bait and let out a horrible shriek as it lunged at him a third time. Once again, Arran swiped the spear with his shield, the tip of the foe's weapon broke on impact. Now was his chance. He lunged forward and jabbed his sword into one of the attacker's eye sockets.

The creature dropped its broken spear and grasped its hands around Arran's sword arm whilst letting out an agonising screech. Eventually, something popped out from the other socket. The glowing red eyes appeared to be some sort of spirit resembling a floating ball. It hovered above the skeleton before flying off, back to the portal. Without its host, the skeleton collapsed into a pile of bones before him.

Arran was relieved, but then another skeleton came charging at him, wielding a two-handed axe. Arran turned to face the new threat and braced. Suddenly, from the corner of his eye, Brom Blackhammer rushed in and knocked the skeleton to the ground. He brought his war hammer down and crushed its skull. The evil spirit that possessed the skeleton shrieked in agony before abandoning its vessel.

The dwarf turned to Arran and yelled over the deafening screech, "That's how you stop a skeleton, lad. Smash the skulls!"

"Thanks!" Arran called back, but the dwarf had already

turned away in search of another foe.

All around him, he saw nothing but absolute chaos. As men, elves and dwarves were locked in singular and grouped combat against the forces of the undead. In the distance, he saw Anwen with her father, they stood back-to-back guarding each other against whatever came at them. Not far from them was Eafen, standing beside a knight in full plate armour. Arran recognised him as Sir Ferrand, the knight who competed in the tourney yesterday. The mage was unleashing fireballs of his own on the monsters that tried to get close to them.

So that's his power then? Arran thought. He couldn't see Gabriel or the others amongst the melee, so he rushed over to fill the gap between Anwen and Eafen, hoping Gabriel would join him as well. Another skeleton came at Arran, bringing down a crude great sword at him. Learning from the first encounter, he sidestepped the downward attack and counterattacked immediately.

The skeleton was sluggish in its movement and response, unable to stop Arran as he thrusted his sword into one of its eye sockets. A dark purple spirit screamed angrily before shooting out from the skull, leaving another pile of bones to drop to the ground before him. Arran was about to move on when something poked him from behind. He turned around sharply, raising his shield. He expected another skeleton, but instead, it was Gabriel, holding his longsword up high ready to strike.

"Gabe!" Arran eased his guard slightly. "Arran!" Gabriel jumped a step.

"Not looking good, how are you holding?" Arran asked.

"I'm fine, just bloody fine," Gabriel shouted back with sarcasm.

"Anwen, Eafen!" Arran called out to the others.

"Arran," Anwen replied, she rushed over to them.

"Glad to see you two haven't got yourselves killed yet," said Captain Alric as he followed close to his daughter.

Gabriel called over the noise of battle as he decapitated another skeleton warrior by the skull.

"I know things are bad, but can someone explain how and why we are fighting a literal army of the undead?"

"It's the portal," Eafen replied, before letting out another fireball at a golem in the distance. "Valeran Serpentine has somehow summoned a portal from another place."

"Who?" Gabriel answered.

"The man who just renounced his allegiance, you idiot!" Alric raised his voice.

"So, we need to cut off the portal to end this fight?" Arran asked.

"Assuming we can get to the bastard." Alric replied dryly. "I don't think he's the one creating it though. It must be something or someone from the other side."

"Look!" Anwen shouted and pointed toward the portal. Everyone turned and saw it. A large beast emerged from the portal, it towered over the traitor Valeran. A pair of crude horns jutted out from its head. The monster began to plough its way through the battlefield. Goring and knocking soldiers living and undead aside with its horns as well as the massive spike club it wielded two-handed.

"What the hell is that?" Gabriel stared with disbelief.

"It's a minotaur," the captain answered,

"Haven't been around for a thousand years," said Sir Ferrand.

"It's coming this way," said Arran

Gabriel looked at the captain uneasily. "How are we supposed to kill that?"

"Spread out and go for the legs. But keep out of its reach," Captain Alric ordered.

The minotaur was soon upon them. Arran noticed that

the eyes of the beast were fixated on something else. Gabriel was first to attack the minotaur, despite his unease. He ducked low as he approached from the side. Then he cried as he swung his longsword at one of its legs. The minotaur flinched, but soon turned his attention to Gabriel. He swatted him aside with an open hand as if he was just an annoying fly. *Holy shit!* Arran gasped as he watched Gabriel roll backward before landing flat on his back. The monster turned its attention to Arran who stood before it, bringing the club down at him. Arran barely managed to roll out of the way before the minotaur's weapon slammed into the ground, the resulting impact creating a small crater where Arran once stood.

The minotaur raised its club again when it was hit by one of Eafen's fireballs. It growled in agony as it tried to put out the flames that caught on its bristled chest. Arran then saw Anwen and Captain Alric attacking the beast in a pincer movement. They circled the monstrosity, looking for an opening. The minotaur lashed out, thundering the ground with its club, but the father and daughter duo managed to evade its attacks. Anwen eventually closed in while her father distracted it. She stabbed the beast in its thigh with her swords, then attempted to climb up the limb, but the minotaur shook its leg until she was kicked off. Alric attacked the other leg with his sword, but the monster seemed to have expected this and lowered its head and rammed one of its horns at him. The captain was momentarily impaled, clutching his chest as he was lifted off the ground before being cast aside.

Anwen had just risen to her feet and her face went pale and her eyes widened with shock.

"Father!" she cried out.

Arran watched with equal horror as Captain Alric's body landed hard on the ground, his blood already creating a pool around him. Instead of taking advantage of their paralysis, the minotaur resumed to march past Arran as if nothing had happened. He watched as it strode unopposed toward the podium.

"Arran!" he heard Eafen call him out. He looked at the mage. "It's going after the Unbreakable Will; we have to stop it!"

"I'll stop it myself!" Sir Ferrand answered the call. The veteran knight charged at the minotaur head-on. He slashed away with his sword at the beast, trying to delay its advance. The monster swung its club at him, catching the knight on one of the protruding spikes. Like Captain Alric, Sir Ferrand was lifted off the ground and sent hurling across the battlefi ld.

"No!" Eafen yelled. "You foul monster!"

He summoned another fireball and launched it without hesitation at the minotaur. Somehow the beast was aware of the attack and evaded the flaming ball. It growled at Eafen before reaching out at him with his club. The mage immediately rolled out of the way. He continued to summon more fireballs whilst dodging the monster's attacks.

So that's why it's here, Arran realised. Valeran brought this monster to do all the dirty work and steal the spear for him. Arran looked back at Anwen, who had rushed to her father's side. Gabriel had recovered at that point and joined them once more. Arran clenched his sword tightly; his moment of surprise and horror becoming that of pure anger. He roared at the top of his lungs as he went after the minotaur with reckless abandon.

Arran sheathed his sword and picked up a spear that lay on the ground on the way. He instinctively hurled the thing at the monster. The spear landed squarely on the monster's back. It winced upon feeling the spear tip dig into its bristled skin. The minotaur turned toward Arran, pulling the spear out of its back. If it wasn't angry before, it certainly was now. The beast pawed the ground with its hooved feet, then it charged full speed at Arran, intent on goring him. The earth trembled under Arran's feet, but he held his ground.

"That's right you fucking piece of shit! Come and get me," Arran muttered under his breath.

He waited until the very last moment as the minotaur closed in, then he did the unthinkable. He unstrapped his kite shield and slid it along the ground, the outer part of it facing upward, then he rolled to the side. Unaware of what he had done, the minotaur slipped on Arran's shield. It fell flat on its face, dropping its massive club to the side.

Arran recovered quickly and rushed toward the monster, its back turned and vulnerable. He clung onto one of its legs as it attempted to get back up. Then he climbed up the limb like he was doing so with a tree, until he was on its back. Realising something was clinging to it, the minotaur shook its body violently left to right, but Arran clung to its bristled hair tightly.

He climbed further until he was in reach of the beast's neck. He unsheathed his sword and roared as he jabbed the blade into the back of the minotaur's head. The beast thrashed about relentlessly, but Arran kept pushing his sword deeper into its skull. Eventually, the minotaur succumbed to its fate. Arran felt the monster's struggle fading. It went down on both knees, then fell to the ground.

Arran pulled his sword out of the minotaur's head and surveyed the carnage. Weary and almost exhausted, he discarded his helmet and wiped the sweat from his forehead. It was still unclear who was winning, as the battle cries and clashing steel continued to ring across the battlefield. He saw some of his comrades were either dead or wounded. The fight was starting to take its toll. He realised he was standing just before the Unbreakable Will. The mighty spear remained on its podium, untouched. As he dropped down to the ground, he was confronted by another foe. A group of creatures were surrounding him. Hunched backs and hideous ape-shaped heads. Arran knew of them as ghouls. Foul things that once terrorised men in ancient times.

They slowly closed in on him. Arran raised his sword two-handed and walked backwards until he was before the steps. If this were to be his end, he would take as many of these fiends as possible before letting them pass. The first ghoul shrieked and charged. Brandishing a one-handed sickle. Suddenly, the creature was struck by a bolt of lightning and reduced to a smouldering carcass. Arran was as stunned as the other ghouls. He thought it was Eafen casting a lightning spell but looked behind him.

The Unbreakable Will was crackling with energy and let out another lightning bolt. It was enough to make the little monsters scatter in fear. Arran decided to sheath his sword and walk toward the spear. He hoisted it out of its stand and raised it high. The weapon was surprisingly light in his hands and Arran somehow felt rejuvenated. He looked beyond the battlefield to the portal. He now wielded the most powerful weapon in all of Maldora and he intended to make good use of it.

He rushed forth into the fray, the Unbreakable Will in hand. Every time he swung or thrusted the spear, lightning would crackle out of the tip, incinerating every vile thing in his path. Warriors who noticed him holding the weapon began to cheer and fight back with a new sense of vigour. Pushing further through the chaos, he was almost in range of the portal, but the mass of bodies fighting in front of him stopped him. The madman Valeran stared at him with a serious look. He flung another fireball over the massed melee, aiming for Arran, but another bolt of lightning was fired from the Unbreakable Will, exploding the flaming ball in mid-air. Tiny sparks rained down on the battlefield, but Arran didn't flinch. He twirled the spear in his hands. Aiming for Valeran, he threw is with all his strength.

Arran watched its flight over the bodies of men and monsters. Everything and everyone paused as it flew. Valeran's face turned pale, yet by some miracle he was able to dodge it. The Unbreakable Will flew right past the traitor and entered the portal instead. Arran's confidence turned to dismay. He had thrown away the spear and missed. But then the portal began to dissipate. Streams of bright lightning replaced the dark swirls. And then, with a great flash, followed by a deafening boom, the portal exploded violently, knocking back Arran and everyone else.

The entire coliseum was enveloped in white.

Chapter 35

ARRAN SQUEEZED HIS EYES SHUT moments before the flash engulfed his vision. A shockwave followed and he was knocked back like a rock before a massive tidal wave, and he braced for the impact that never came. He expected to land hard, maybe break bones if lucky and if not, well, he would be dead, and yet it was as though he was light-weighted and all he could hear was a constant buzzing sound in both of his ears.

Arran slowly opened his eyes, and to his surprise he was in a completely different place. Though he found himself on his back, the surface felt cold, solid and smooth, like marble. He stared at what should have been a cloudless sky, but in its place a canvas of white. Sitting up, he looked around. He was still in the coliseum—only the place was devoid of colour, save for white. Objects like the pillars were outlined in a tinge of grey to differentiate one thing from the rest. There was no one else present. He saw none of the scars he would expect to see following the battle that took place. No corpses, no craters, not a single weapon left abandoned. Arran could hear nothing aside from the pounding of his own blood and the noise as he shuffled about and rose to his feet.

Arran called out, "Hello?" His voice echoed all around him. He scanned his surroundings until he saw something, or more likely, someone, stirring on the ground before him.

He recognised the person by his robes as he approached. "Eafen?"

"That's quite an echo." Eafen winced as he sat up, his voice magnified the echo.

Arran looked around with his arms out wide.

"I don't understand. We're in the arena, but it's all white."

Eafen twisted his head to view his surroundings. "Yes, very white indeed."

"Do you think we are…" Arran struggled to finish his question, "dead?"

Eafen shrugged. "No idea. This could be the first stage before entering the afterlife, for all we know."

Arran sighed. "Great." It was then that they heard slow footsteps, followed by the humming of a hymn that Arran recognised. He turned to stare at a familiar figure approaching them.

"Who is that?" Eafen squinted.

Arran didn't answer. He was frozen in place as he watched the druid in brown robes approach them before stopping. Just like before, she carried with her a lantern that pulsed a bright blue.

"I remember you," Arran said, "from the stables at Everdale."

"Arran Connaught and Eafen Faughn," said the robed lady. The first time Arran had ever heard the mage's full name. She spoke with a very soothing tone clearly meant to ease a troubled mind.

"Where are we? What has happened to the arena?" Arran asked.

The lady simply raised a hand. They watched as she put the lantern down. Its pulsing light changed from blue to dark green. Next, she removed her hood, revealing a clean, pale, young face, eyes as blue as a calm sea. Her hair, brown like her robes, stretched down to her waist.

"I know who you are," said Eafen as he stood next to Arran, then dropping down on one knee bowing before the lady. Arran looked at him before realising who they were in the presence of. He too knelt before her. They stood before Lady Breia. The first Earth mage, one of the original quartet. Goddess of Nature, the Earth and Fertility.

"Lady Breia," Arran cleared his throat. "Forgive me, I—"

"Please," the Goddess raised a hand and smiled. "There is nothing to forgive."

"But I..." Arran hesitated. "I cast the Unbreakable Will into the portal. It was supposed to have killed the traitor Valeran. I failed." Arran sighed, then he spoke again. "May I ask, my lady. Is this real or a dream? Are we among the perished?"

Breia shook her head. "No, Arran. We have taken this opportunity to enlighten you both of your predicament."

"Enlighten us?" said a confused Arran.

Eafen was also taken aback by this. "What do you mean by 'we'?"

"By we, she refers to herself and me on behalf of the great four," a new voice answered.

Arran and Eafen looked past Breia as another figure

entered. At first, the mysterious person appeared all black as if he were someone's shadow, but as he walked closer, the surrounding light unveiled his features. It was a man cloaked in a pure white, hooded robe outlined in gold. There was an aura that followed this person, shining a brilliant silver. He approached them, oblivious to his surroundings with the confidence of a person willing to help another in time of need.

"What you are both experiencing is the two of the Great Four communicating with you within your minds," he explained. "An unconscious mind is easier to approach rather than one distracted by the outside world."

Arran's eyes were as wide as his mouth when he replied, "You're Orion."

"That didn't take long to answer," the white-robed figure chuckled as he pushed back his hood, revealing the face of a calm man, whose hair and beard were long, wavy and dark brown. His grey eyes gave Arran the impression that this being could see into his soul. This was Orion. The first of the Mages, Master of the Wind, Saviour and God of Truth and Reason.

"I can't believe this is happening," Eafen said out loud.

"You should," Orion replied softly.

"But what about the spear?" Arran asked. "I remember it flying past Valeran and—"

"We know, it's alright," Orion assured them. "You've done nothing wrong, my friend. Your actions have ensured that innocent lives caught up in the attack were spared."

"For now, I guess," Arran muttered as he turned his head away, even though it was probably futile to hide his doubts from the great saviour who stood before him.

"So, if we are here in this reimagining of the real world," Eafen enquired, "where is the Unbreakable Will?" Orion and Breia looked at each other for a moment, the former nodding his head to let her explain.

"It is in the hands of our greatest enemy."

"Samael?" Arran answered.

"Yes," said Breia. "He has been brought back to flesh and bone once more."

There was a moment of silence as Arran and Eafen looked at one another, taking in this ill news. Arran clenched his fists as he took in a deep breath.

"There is a war coming," Orion replied. "He and his servants are, as we speak, preparing for battle."

"What can we do to stop this?" Eafen asked.

"There is no stopping the war," Breia answered, "but

you two can still help avoid disaster by retrieving the Unbreakable Will."

"That won't be easy," said Arran.

"Nothing on this scale is ever easy," said Orion. "But have faith. Help will come when you need it most. It is time for you both to return to the real world. We will speak again soon, Arran Connaught and Eafen Faughn. Good luck to you."

With that, Arran and Eafen watched as Lady Breia raised her lantern in front of her. The pulsing light grew bigger, to the point where it engulfed the realm without shattering the lantern.

"It is time for you both to awaken," Breia's parting words echoed in Arran's mind as the gods disappeared from his vision.

Valeran found himself lying on his side when he came around. A migraine pecked away at his mind like crows at a corpse. He struggled to his feet. His vision was disorientated, but when it cleared, he was shocked at what he saw. The whole arena was littered with corpses. Loyalist men as well the skeleton soldiers.

The bodies of the golems were broken into lifeless pieces, whilst the more flesh-made beasts lay scattered, leaving behind a charred smell. He looked down at his feet and saw Walder faced down on the ground. The old man picked up his cane and used it to prod his servant before turning him over. The fanatic's eyes were as white as ice. He cursed under his breath. For years Walder served Valeran in the shadows without question or pause, only to perish here. Valeran then remembered the objective. He looked around, but the Unbreakable Will was nowhere to be found. All he could see was the warrior who threw it at him. He lay on the ground, helpless, unconscious.

A rage stirred in him. Furious that he was so close to acquiring the prize, only to be taken from him by this upstart child. He was about to consider grabbing a blade to slit the boy's throat, but he soon realised that some of the loyalist bodies were stirring. It seemed the blast only killed off his army and left the loyalists knocked out. Outnumbered and defeated, he decided his immediate lust for revenge would be pointless. He murmured a spell under his breath and in an instant, transformed into a crow, flew upward to the sky and headed north. Valeran swore he would return to avenge this humiliating defeat in this city. One day.

Chapter 36

GEDRIC CLUTCHED HIS CLOAK tightly, for the weather had become bitterly cold even though it was only autumn. Samael's minions had brought his cage out from the cave into the open and exposed him to the harsh wind, though he didn't know why. Perhaps so he couldn't devise a way to escape without everyone watching him, but more likely to taunt and torture him whilst he was helpless and incarcerated.

Most of the activity outside the cave seemed to be concentrated around the gathering point where Samael was. The Dark Lord sat on his throne surrounded by shades, his eyes fixated on the portal before him. Where was Valeran? Did Samael send him through that portal to retrieve the Unbreakable Will? He wondered how Therin and everyone else were doing, though he wouldn't be surprised if the Imperial garrison in the capital would be taken aback by the unexpected attack. At that point, sparks appeared around the edges of the portal.

Every creature in sight stopped whatever they were doing and stared at the anomaly. Samael sat upright upon seeing it. Gedric squinted as he leaned closer to the bars, trying to understand what was happening. Suddenly, something sped out from the portal, though Gedric couldn't tell what it was, as the portal immediately shattered violently with a flash of white. Gedric couldn't maintain his vision and turned away from the light, covering his eyes. When the light receded, he turned and saw that the portal was no more. In its place was a spear, impaled tip first into the ground before Samael, cracks spreading out from the entry point like spider webs along the granite surface.

The chancellor realised that it was: the Unbreakable Will. Strands of blue lightning were crackling all around the blade and upper pole of the weapon.

From the moment of its arrival, bolts sprang forth from the spear in every direction, catching the few shades and ghouls that were close by, their inhuman screams echoing long after they were reduced to dust and charred bones. Every other creature jumped back and took cover. To Gedric's surprise, Samael was unphased. He rose from his throne and walked toward the Unbreakable Will. The chancellor eyed the Dark God and noticed that he was wearing something. On both, his hands were two large black gauntlets ornate with gems and stones.

As if alerted by his appearance, the Unbreakable Will directed its lightning bolts from the ghouls and shades to the Dark Lord. But Samael raised one of the gauntlets in front of him. The first bolt ricocheted off the gauntlet and dissipated. Another soon followed in an endless stream. Samael brought both of his gauntlets together to resist this attack. The stream of lightning pushed him back a few steps, but Samael held firm, his bare feet pressed down into the ground underneath him. Samael grunted as he pushed off his back foot, closing the distance between himself and the spear with every massive step. The lightning intensified, its strands taking on a darker shade of blue.

Once within a stone's throw, Samael growled as he reached out with one gauntlet for the stave of the spear while holding back the lightning with the other. Eventually, the lightning grew weaker and ceased. Gedric stared with utter shock at what he had witnessed. Samael had done the unthinkable, the unfathomable. He had managed to get close enough to the Unbreakable Will and overpower it with his own. The Dark Lord raised the spear above his head for all to see. He roared and laughed at his most outstanding achievement. The sight left Gedric cold, helpless and shaken within. He had witnessed not one but two impossible feats accomplished today, at the detriment of all he cared for, and there was nothing he could do about it.

The cries of battle were over in an instant. Moments after the great flash, all was still and quiet. Fires continued to burn, and the coliseum grounds were littered with broken weapons, banners and bodies. Humans, elves and dwarves lay strewn alongside the skeletons of the possessed undead and every other monstrosity that had emerged from the portal only to meet their end. Some bodies were nothing more than blackened outlines. A light breeze blew across the arena, picking up dust and ash before dispersing it everywhere.

Anwen was on her side when she woke, smears of dirt and blood across her face and a throbbing sensation in her head. She looked up and found herself staring at the skeletal remains of a ghoul on its back. Its hideous skull stared back at the girl; the stench of charred and melting flesh made her gag and cough as she backed away from the mess. Anwen rose to her knees and looked around the battlefield, turning her head frantically until she found her father. Captain Alric lay not far from her. He was on his back, arms and legs out wide, staring at the sky.

Anwen cursed under her breath and tried to run to him, but her legs gave out, and she collapsed to the ground. Unwilling to give up, she crawled and dragged herself towards him and found herself staring down at a hole in his gut. The horrific result of being gored by the minotaur.

"Father?" she muttered. "Come on, wake up!" She grabbed her father and shook him. He gasped for air when her hands touched him, followed by a cough of blood.

Anwen leaned down and wiped the blood from his mouth. "It's okay, Father, I'm here."

Captain Alric tried to say something, "A...An... Anwen. Thank the gods you're still alive."

"Hang in there." Anwen found the strength to try and stand. She then pulled her father up by the collar of his shirt so she could get behind and drag him away by his tunic. She glanced over her shoulder, one of the gateways was close by. She decided to drag him there and seek help.

"Ar...Arran," Captain Alric was trying to speak again. "Where is Arran?" he asked.

Anwen hesitated. "I don't know. Just hold on, I'll get you out of here."

"There's no time," Alric replied. "Y...You need to find him."

Anwen didn't reply. She hoped that Arran was alive, but right now, her father needed her the most. She surveyed the battlefield again as she dragged her father along. She couldn't see Arran, Gabriel, or even Eafen amongst the other bodies. Suddenly, she felt something catch the back of her boots. She lost her balance and fell, cursing as she landed on her back.

Anwen felt something crunch against the back of her neck, something bony. She twisted her head and realised she had landed on the lower remains of a skeleton warrior. The force of her fall had caused the bones in one of its legs to snap. But this wasn't what caused her fall. Anwen looked forward and realised she had tripped over the body of a soldier. A member of the City Guard, recognisable by the purple and yellow tunics. The soldier's attire was soaked red from the many gashes and stab wounds all over his body.

Anwen swallowed hard, then quickly rolled away from the bodies and rushed back to her father.

"Father?" she called, but Captain Alric was murmuring something and didn't seem to hear her. His skin was pale and almost covered in dust.

"Please stay with me," she muttered. She then grabbed him by the collar and dragged him to the nearest wall to the gateway.

"Anwen?" someone called out for her, and she looked up and saw Callum. The scribe and one of Arran's friends stood in the gateway, looking baffled upon seeing Anwen and her father in their current state.

"Callum. Help me with my father, please."

Callum snapped out of his stupor and rushed to them. He knelt down before her and Captain Alric.

"What happened?" he asked.

"A minotaur gored him," Anwen replied, her throat dry and cracking. "We need to get him inside and to help."

"Anwen…" Callum was lost for words. "I don't think he's going to make it. Look at his face."

"Shut up!" Anwen barked back at him. "Don't you dare say that."

Callum's eyes widened and his face went pale as Anwen glared at him.

"He's right," Captain Alric spoke again, "I'm as good as dead."

"No, stop it," Anwen looked back at her father in disbelief. "I'm not letting you die here."

"You can't stop death, Anwen," said Alric. "Just as you can't stop the night taking the place of day."

Anwen pursed her lips, refusing to shed a tear. "This isn't how it should end. Not like this."

"Never thought I would see a day like this either," Callum added.

"We don't get to choose how or where we start our lives." Alric spluttered, he placed a hand on Anwen's cheek.

"And we don't always have the luxury of choosing when they will end. All we can do… Is to keep living, keep fighting, loving, learning whenever we can before…" he was interrupted by another cough; more blood spurted out from his mouth. Callum moved in to hold Captain Alric's other hand.

"Please, no," Anwen whispered as she shook her head. Deny it all she could, her father was slowly fading away. It was becoming harder for him to keep his eyes open, let alone fixated on her. She briefly glanced up to the sky and thought, *Orion, please. Don't let my father join Mother. Not yet…*

Arran opened his eyes again to see a blue sky instead of white. Crows and ravens squawked and flocked around the battlefield, searching for a free meal. Smoke and burning flesh flooded his nostrils, making him cough as he turned over to his hands and knees. He heard men's voices, some calling out orders, others crying out in pain. He looked up and, despite his blurry vision, saw a soldier approach him.

"We've got another one here!" the soldier called out before kneeling down to Arran.

"Are you alright?" the soldier asked, reaching out a hand. Arran took a firm grip and pulled himself up. He almost fell back to his knees as his legs felt weak, so he held onto the soldier for support.

"Easy," the soldier said, "you were pretty close to the blast. Anyone else would be dead."

Arran found the strength to ask, "Any survivors?"

"Yeah, surprisingly. Those who haven't been gutted by the undead."

Arran glanced around. Some soldiers and knights were coming around from the shockwave. Like Arran, many of them struggled to stand on their own legs. Others, however, no longer had legs to stand on. He saw Eafen, who was on his knees before the body of a fallen warrior. He gestured to the soldier to help him as he moved toward the mage.

When Arran found the strength in his own legs, he let go of the soldier and walked over to Eafen. When he reached Eafen, he found himself staring down at the body of Sir Ferrand, the knight who was knocked aside by the minotaur's spiked club moments ago. His armour had been crushed by the force of the weapon. Eafen carefully removed the knight's damaged helmet. But underneath, they saw that his eyes were pearl white.

Arran leaned in and placed a hand on his friend's shoulder. "He's gone, Eafen."

"I know," Eafen murmured in a low voice. He put a hand over Sir Ferrand's forehead to close his eyes. "I saw all this happening in a dream. And here we are. I could've saved him and everyone else if only the people I trusted believed in me."

"He was a good man, Eafen. A great warrior. There's nothing more we could do," said Arran.

"Arran!" a familiar voice called out. He turned to see Gabriel rushing over to him. There was a smear of blood over his torn surcoat.

"Where are Anwen and the captain?" Arran asked.

Gabriel said nothing; instead, he pointed to them.

Anwen had her back to the wall clutching onto her father. Callum was there holding one of the captain's hands, whilst the other hand was placed over the massive hole where his stomach should've been. Despite feeling sore all around, Arran left Eafen and made his way to them. When he got to them, he fell to his knees.

"Anwen, Callum," he called to them.
"Arran!" Callum was surprised when he looked at him. "I thought you were dead."
"Is he…" Arran asked Calum when suddenly Captain Alric coughed and uttered his name. "Arran?"
He knelt down before Captain Dowrin to better hear him.
"The flash?" he coughed again. "What did you see?"
"Does it matter?" Arran asked. "You need to rest, Cap–"
"Of course, it does, lad," Alric butted in. "I saw you carry the spear… The white flash. The gods must have something planned for you. Why else would you have survived it?" Everyone looked at Arran as he paused for a moment. The captain was no fool. There was no point lying to him now, he thought. He cleared his throat and answered.
"I saw Orion. And Breia. Me and Eafen. They came to us."
Alric barely had the strength to ask, "What…Did they tell you?"
Arran gulped before he answered. "That there is a war coming. That we need to get the Unbreakable Will back. They told me that he's returned."
Anwen's teary eyes widened. "Samael? No," she replied in a deniable tone, "it can't be."
Alric nodded before coughing again. "You listen to me, Arran. You do what your heart tells you is right. You hear me?"
Arran reached for the captain's hand that Callum held. His heart felt heavy, more than ever, as a single tear rolled down his right cheek. "I… I don't know if I can do this," he admitted.
"Not alone, you won't. Keep your friends close to you, Arran. And…don't forget about family. You're going to need all the help you can get. I believe in you."
Arran nodded. "Yes, okay."

"Please, Father," Anwen begged him. "don't leave us. Just hang on a little longer."
The captain looked his daughter in the eyes and said, "I'm sorry, Anwen." He coughed again, tears streaming down both cheeks, followed by blood trickling out of his dry mouth. "This is it for me. Your mother would be as proud as I am of the woman you've become. I love you, Anwen."
"I love you too, father," Anwen sobbed, blinking and wiping away frantically at the river of tears from her face.
Next, he turned his head to Callum. "Callum, you keep reading, you hear me? You find anything that would help; you tell Arran about it."
"Yes, Captain," Callum replied with silent tears whilst struggling to clear his throat. He was starting to show tears.
"Good luck to you all. I know you won't let me down..." said Captain Alric. Then, after a moment, his eyes began to close. His grip on his daughter's hand loosened, and his head dropped forward. Anwen screamed and cried. She clutched her father even tighter.
Arran stared at the captain, almost paralysed, failing to suppress the tears that trickled down his face. He realised that a burden had been placed upon him and his friends. For the first time in his life, Arran felt lost inside.
Suddenly, a hand was placed on his shoulder. It was Gabriel standing over him, wiping his nose and face, as he, too, couldn't stop himself from feeling the same.
"We should head back with everyone else," he said. "Not yet," Arran replied. "Give us some time, Gabriel." All he and everyone else wanted to do was sit there and mourn their loss.

One hour later...

Please be there...please, Gerald thought as he reached Market Square after searching outside the coliseum. He had no luck finding Nianna or her father among the chaos that had befallen the city. People were running in every direction away from the entrance of the arena. He saw black smoke billowing over the roof and ascending toward the sky. He pressed on through the panicking populace and across the bridge, and by the time he crossed over, there was a deafening explosion. He risked a glance back at the coliseum, but all he saw was a massive ball of blinding light enveloping the place. He was tired, and his body ached from the running, but finally, he found himself in Market Square. He noticed as he walked that the stalls, save for a few, had been abandoned. Everywhere he turned, people were closing their doors shut and pulling their blinds over the windows. Never before had Gerald witnessed the city caught in the clutches of fear like this. It all felt so bizarre. Then a thought came to him.

Was this the Black Box's doing? Was all this why it was kept underneath the Academy? He gulped hard when thinking about that accursed thing but decided now was not the time to reflect. He finally reached the Jolly Maid. A sign on the door was hanging: "Closed for today," it said. *What the hell happened here while I was away? Nianna's father would never close his tavern during the Imperial Games,* Gerald thought.

He glanced over his shoulder, but no one was watching him—at least, no one in plain sight. He knew Brodus was locked away in a separate cell in the dungeons under the Imperial Palace. *Good riddance to that bastard,* Gerald thought as he started knocking on the door three times and waited. No one answered. He knocked again, putting more emphasis each time his fist banged on the wooden door.

A woman's voice sighed on the other side. "We're closed for today. Come back tomorrow."

Gerald recognised the voice on the other side. "Nianna, it's Gerald. Open the door."

"You're just wasting your time," Nianna replied.

"Oh, for fuck's sake," Gerald muttered under gritting teeth. "Listen, Nianna," he knocked again, "I'm not lying. Open the bloody door!"

At that point, he heard another sigh from inside. Gerald was about to step back and figure another way in when the door quickly opened. Still leaning on the frame, he lost his balance and almost fell on top of a frustrated Nianna.

The girl's eyes widened. "Gerald!" She dropped her broom and grabbed Gerald by the shirt collar, then pulled him inside and slammed the door shut. She turned to him; her hazel eyes sharpened as she looked at him.

"What the bloody hell are you doing here, Gerald?"

"Long story, you don't want to know," Gerald replied.

"I think I'm entitled to know why you're here instead of living out your sentence underneath the Imperial Palace," Nianna snapped.

"Oh, I'm sorry," Gerald replied. "A big flipping fireball came crashing down, and I miraculously survived. Yet you'd rather I stay and get roasted by another?"

"I didn't mean that," said Nianna.

"Of course, you didn't," said Gerald. "What exactly happened?"

Nianna shrugged. "I've no bloody idea, Gerald. One minute I'm sweeping up this mess, and the next thing, someone comes running down the street shouting that we're under attack. Bells go off, and everyone's running to their homes."

"Right." Gerald raised his hands and sighed. "Where's your father?"

"What's going on in there?" came the voice of Nianna's father as he walked through the kitchen doors holding a wooden spoon in one hand. "I thought I told you not to let anyone… Gerald?" His eyes widened. "What are you doing here?"

Gerald pursed his lips before he answered. "Long story, let's just say my sentence was cut short."

Nianna's father put a hand over his face. "Just what I bloody need right now. You go off and do something stupid and end up arrested. Now you've come crawling back here? Do they know you've escaped?"

"Not yet," Gerald replied. "I'm pretty sure putting out the biggest fire in Aberemrallt in the last hundred years is more important than catching me."

Nianna's father gritted his teeth. "Of all the days. Still, you need to get out of here before the authorities come looking for you."

"Father, please," Nianna intervened, "I know things are bad outside, but just let him stay for a bit."

Her father paused for a moment before sighing. Gerald knew the man would only relent when his daughter intervened. "Fine, but just stay away from the bar. Might as well have you in the kitchen with me."

Gerald shrugged, "That's good enough."

At that point, Nianna's father turned away and headed back into the kitchen, mumbling something under his breath. Gerald took a moment to look around the tavern; it was only now that he realised that the place wasn't the way he last recalled. There were broken chairs and tables all piled up in one corner, along with a mopping bucket near the fireplace.

"So, uh," he looked back at Nianna, "did someone start a war here or something?"

Despite the stress that etched her face, Nianna fought back a chuckle as she pursed her lips. "It's a long story."

"Fair enough," Gerald smiled for the first time since

being arrested. At that point, Nianna reached out and hugged him as tightly as she could. Gerald was somewhat surprised by this, but then he put his arms around her.

"You stupid fool," she muttered.

"I know. I'm sorry," Gerald replied.

"You better stay here tonight," said Nianna.

"Thank you," said Gerald. He kissed her on the forehead. Despite the guilt within and the madness going on outside, he felt safe in Anwen's arms, in this place he called home. For now.

Chapter 37

VALERAN PUSHED HIMSELF HARD whilst in his crow form as he rose over the peak of the Ringspine Mountains. With the encampment in sight, he soared down the mountainside, flapping his wings to slow his descent and flexing his talons to balance himself.

Once landed, he changed from bird to man before falling to his knees. Huffing and wheezing, he crawled momentarily on all fours. Suddenly, he felt the presence of another being. Valeran looked up, and Samael stood over him with a malevolent grin across his red face. Valeran noticed that his master was wearing a black jewelled gauntlet on each hand. One of them, to his surprise, gripped the stave of the very spear he was sent to retrieve. Tiny sparks danced along its tip.

"My lord..." he gasped. "The Unbreakable Will! But how?"

"That I can happily explain. If our lord will permit me," came another voice. Male, yet cold and metallic in tone.

Valeran turned his head as he looked at a shade standing next to Samael. Only this wasn't a shade as Valeran knew them. This figure wore a long, dusty, black coat with a hood covering his head and an iron mask covering everything but a pair of golden eyes. Underneath the coat was a black buttoned-up jerkin and trousers with a belt made up of tiny silver skulls around the waist. For hands, this figure had a pair of silver talon-like claws. Each metallic finger—curved inward—was the length of a tiny dagger.

"Valeran," Samael spoke, "meet Metarro. Expert in the magic art of manipulating metals. He can bend any metal to his will. And even bring certain constructs to life." He nodded to Metarro.

"These gauntlets you see are made with a combination of runes, a few spells and the rarest metals." The man with the iron mask gestured to the gauntlets. "The result is that he who wears these will be impervious to the power of the Unbreakable Will. I call them the Gauntlets of Control."

Valeran's eyes widened. If only he had access to this device, he could have completed his task sooner. "So, the spear is now under your control?" he asked.

"Yes, Valeran. Thanks to you for allowing its delivery to me," said Samael.

"My lord I…."

Samael cut him off with an open hand. "No time for grovelling. The enemy knows we exist, and we must follow up our attack with expansion." He called for two fanatics to help Valeran up.

"Expansion?" Valeran asked, perplexed as he rose to his feet. "But most of our forces were sacrificed in the assault. Had I known the weapon's full potential, I would've taken a different approach."

"It doesn't matter," Samael replied calmly yet firmly. "We can raise more corpses and monsters to fight and replenish our losses when needed. Our enemy's best troops are based in Aberemrallt, which leaves the rest of Maldora ripe for the picking. Come."

He turned away and walked to a large stone table with Metarro trailing behind. Three other figures stood idly around the table awaiting their master's orders, all covered in dark and tattered cloaks.

Valeran followed, even though his legs felt like dead weight. He reached the table and sat next to Samael. The Dark Lord stared at an old map of Maldora, unrolled, laid out and held in place by a stone at each corner. The old man watched as, one by one, the other figures threw off their hoods. For the first time, Valeran could see what was hidden beneath the cloth.

The closest to Samael was an elven woman wearing a purple cape that flowed down her boots. For protection, there was a pauldron that resembled dark grey scales on each of her shoulders. She sported two pieces of black scaled leather, one overlapping the other to cover each of her breasts. Around her belly button was a tattoo of a single purple eye with a pink pupil. A long silky grey skirt clung tightly to her legs. Valeran took note of how pale her skin was, like ash. Her blood red eyes, sadistic smile and wild strands of black hair portrayed her as unruly and devious. In her hands was a staff with a large shard of dark aerianeite jutting out at the top that glowed and hummed quietly. The elven woman stroked her staff as if it were a beloved pet.

Next was a satyr, whose fur and facial hair was a mixture of black and grey. From the chest down to the hips, he was covered in rags and strips of pelts, the upper part held together by a cross of chains with a humanoid skull at the centre. This wild beast flexed his biceps and pulled a dagger-like blade with serrated edges out from a scabbard strapped to his back.

Last was an impressive specimen clad in dark steel and crimson red armour. This warrior wore a helmet with dragon-like wings jutting out of its sides. The figure sat comfortably on a small rock while wiping down the blade of a terrifying longsword. When he rose from his seat, Valeran was amazed at how tall he was, only a few inches short of Samael.

"Shall we begin?" Samael looked around. Each of his commanders nodded without question.

"Varraddon," Samael addressed the knight in red armour, "you will take a force and launch a surprise attack on Soulman's Gate. You must seize and hold this position. Resistance should be light, but you can expect reinforcements from the capital to march their way north to you, do not engage the enemy on open ground. Understood?"

Varraddon replied, "I shall make preparations at once, my lord."

As he spoke, Valeran noticed a pair of fangs. *So, he is a vampire?* Then he realised who he was. Varradon the Terrible. Samael's right-hand man for most of his campaigns, delivering fear and terror to the hearts of his enemies.

"Ulgor," Samael looked up at the satyr, "I want you to raid the villages surrounding Ostenburg Castle and the town of Luden east of our position. Terrorise the populace and deal with anyone foolish enough to oppose you."

So, this was Ulgor the Dark, Valeran realised. Master of a thousand ambushes, born with the rare trait of black fur. He personified the dark nature of the satyr. His hatred of humans was the driving influence for his blood-thirsty rampage across the land. None could tame this savage beast in either peace or war. No one except for Samael.

"Ulgor will enjoy the slaughter," the dark satyr snorted. "Ulgor pillage and destroy the town of Luden. Bring back loot and slaves for Master." Ulgor then shot a look at Valeran; two bloodshot red eyes bearing nothing but hatred made Valeran recoil a bit.

On one side of his face, Samael lifted a small smile. Clearly, this beast of unbridled rage and hatred could be counted on to do his bidding, where bloodshed and terror were involved.

"Shanira will accompany me in attacking Reikenburg. The defenders won't be expecting us."

"Ah, the old capital," the elven mage spoke. "So

many memories. A little predictable if anyone cared to remember the previous sackings."

"I don't care what the enemy thinks we will do. I will make Reikenburg the centre of our war effort as done before. And if I can't have it, I will simply burn it to the ground." Samael looked at Valeran and Metarro. "As for you, Valeran, you will head east with Metarro to Old Argantis."

"Old Argantis?" Valeran was puzzled. "That's past the Ringspine, east across the sea."

"Then you had better find a boat. You will assist Metarro in his task of awakening an ancient power and await my further command. Do you understand?"

"Uh ...y ...yes, my lord, I shall follow," Valeran gulped hard, feeling as if he was put under the spotlight in front of everyone else.

With that, Samael waved everyone away. The war council was over for now. Valeran was about to leave until he heard Metarro behind him.

"Well, this has been a fascinating day, hasn't it?" Valeran sighed. "I must admit, I'm surprised to still be here."

"Yes, well, let's see how long that will continue," Metarro spoke.

Valeran turned to Metarro and tilted his head at him. "What do you mean?" he asked.

Metarro chuckled a little before explaining, "Our lord is someone who takes loyalty and success very seriously. One minute he will reward you, but the moment he senses any fault in one's efforts, he'll come down on them faster than an avalanche. Best to obey orders and fulfil them without question as quickly as possible. If you want to remain in his good graces."

"Do you know what his plans are?" Valeran asked. Metro

shrugged. "I've been entombed inside a prison for the last five hundred years, and I have only just been informed that he wants these relics. I can assure you, my friend, that when Samael has a goal, he won't stop until he's achieved it. And when he does, the world will know of it."

"I see," said Valeran.

"Anyway, we've dabbled on enough here. Time to pay Old Argantis a visit." Metarro gestured to Valeran to follow.

"Yes. To Old Argantis then," Valeran murmured to himself.

This was going to be quite a journey if taken so by foot. Valeran couldn't understand why he and Metarro were commanded to go east, far away from where his knowledge of the central provinces would prove vital.

And what exactly would be waiting for them? *What did lord Samael mean by "ancient force"? Another relic like the Unbreakable Will or something similar?* He wondered, for Old Argantis was the centre of the once great Argantean Empire but had been abandoned for hundreds of years since The Fall. He only briefly ventured near that once great city and its ruins whenever he travelled between Aberemrallt, Ravenno and Arivinium.

Whatever his master and Metarro sought, Valeran would follow without question. For he couldn't afford to lose favour with him now. Better to follow Metarro and go beyond the ruins than wait for the Imperials to catch up.

And so, the war had begun.

Chapter 38

Sunday, 1st September
The Stronghold, Aberemrallt

GREY CLOUDS LOOMED in the morning sky over the western side of the city, a grim sight for an even grimmer day. The air, as a result, felt colder, a complete contrast to the warm weather from yesterday. There was a light breeze that blew over the Stronghold and down into the courtyard. From one of the towers, a bell rang endlessly.

Arran took it as a sign of the gods and their sympathy toward mortals as he leaned on a balcony overlooking the courtyard. A day of chaos, followed by one of grief. Below in the courtyard several caskets were laid out. Each covered with a banner of the order and placed on top of a cart. Knights, sergeants, monks, mages and stewards alike were arrayed in a semi-circle around them.

Arran left the balcony and walked quietly down to the lower ground. He found Gabriel and Callum with Anwen and Eafen in front of one of the caskets. That must be the one Captain Alric's body was in. He stood next to Gabriel. Neither spoke. Among the caskets stood the grandmaster of the order, Lord Robert O'Hare. He was flanked by Chief Mage Azurius and by another senior knight. Out of the three, Lord Robert stood as the tallest. He was lean, with a mane of black hair that was starting to go grey in places. His tunic was decorated with various sigils indicating his position and his deeds. When the bell stopped ringing, he stepped forward.

"Knights, soldiers, comrades," he addressed the gathering. The grandmaster had a way of getting everyone's attention with very little effort. "Yesterday was a tragic and disturbing day. We are gathered here to bid farewell to those who took up arms against the unexpected invaders and sacrificed themselves to save others, even those brave souls who weren't participants in the Imperial Games. They demonstrated the true traits of what it means to be a warrior. Courage, determination, loyalty and self-sacrifice." He paused for a moment to allow everyone present to take in his words of wisdom. "Brothers and sisters of the TwinBlade Order, I ask that as you journey with them to the Tomb of Heroes where they shall be finally put to rest, that you remember them not for the cruel fate that befell them, but for who they were. Their dedication and their attributes. Only by embedding our memory of them in our hearts and minds will they be able to join the gods and those who came before in the afterlife. For faith and truth!"

"For faith and truth!" Everyone in the courtyard responded.

"Chief Mage Azurius shall lead you and the deceased out of the city."

"As you command," the mage replied.

The bell rang again. Horses were led out of the stables, each with a pair of squires escorting them. They attached their harnesses to the shafts that jutted out from each cart. A group of soldiers formed by the gatehouse, ready to march in front of the first cart.

Arran muttered as he watched, "How did all of this happen?"

Gabriel replied, "No idea. None of us could've seen it coming."

"I did," Eafen broke his silence. Everyone except for Anwen looked at him. "I had visions of this. Yet nobody listened."

Arran sighed, unable to continue the conversation. He looked over to Anwen. She stared at her father's coffin undistracted. Her facial expression froze in place. It seemed like nothing mattered to her but this moment, watching the carts leave one by one.

"Arran Connaught," he heard the grandmaster call his name; he was approaching them.

"Grandmaster." Arran straightened himself up before the grandmaster, the others did the same.

"I need you, along with Gabriel and Eafen to come with me."

"My lord?" Arran asked.

"Emperor Otto and the council have requested an audience with us at the Imperial Palace. Get your mounts ready, we leave here immediately."

"What about the funeral?" Eafen asked.

"You will have time later on to pay your respects. Anwen and Callum will not be needed, they will go with the rest to the tombs."

"Thank you, Grandmaster," Anwen replied.

Grandmaster O'Hare nodded at her then looked back at Arran. "Let's get going."

"Yes, sir," Everyone answered.

The five of them separated as ordered, but Arran noticed something. He stopped and looked behind. Anwen remained in her spot watching the carts.

"Anwen," he called out to her. The girl looked at him. A tear travelled down her cheek.

"I'm sorry for your loss. He was a good man, your father," was all he could muster.

"I know," Anwen replied, wiping the tears away from her cheek.

Arran nodded and left her be. He wanted to say something, but didn't know what. Time for grief would come later.

Sometime later…

After traversing the streets. Arran, Gabriel and Eafen made it to the Imperial Palace with the Grandmaster and his retinue of other knights acting as escort. Upon dismounting, they took note of the large crater in the courtyard. Black scorch marks etched the area of impact. Now they stood in a hall that was bright and clean within, despite the lack of sunlight from the outside world. Before them was the emperor who sat on his throne. His hands were clutching and releasing the arms of his chair. Standing either side of him were the members of the council; Captain Therrin was to his Highness's left, whilst the Crown Prince stood to his right. The room felt tense. These people wanted answers. To know what happened in yesterday's battle.

The emperor began, "So, these three men were the closest to the Unbreakable Will?"

Grandmaster O'Hare responded, "Yes, among the few that used it to turn the tide of the battle, Your Grace. I present to you Eafen Ulrin, Gabriel Stowark, and Arran Connaught."

The emperor didn't take his eyes off the men. Arran felt that he was staring more at him than anyone else. "So, who among you cast the Unbreakable Will through that portal?" the emperor raised his voice.

Eafen and Gabriel turned their heads to Arran. The whole room was looking at him. He cleared his throat before giving an answer. "I did, my emperor."

"You?" The emperor's eyes narrowed at him.

Arran nodded.

The emperor leaned forward. "I would like to know what was going on inside your head when you hurled that spear. Do you have any idea what you threw away during

that engagement?'
Arran replied, "Yes, Your Imperial Majesty."
The emperor turned his growing rage to the grandmaster. "Is this what you train your squires and knights to do, Robert?"
The grandmaster replied, "In case you have forgotten, your highness, I was with you on the balcony when the attack happened..."
"I don't care where you were yesterday, Grandmaster!" The emperor rose from his chair as he barked back. "You and your order are supposed to be the best knights in the entire Empire, second only to the Griffon Knights! I allow you to provide security for the Games and the Unbreakable Will, as traditionally agreed by my family for generations. And you lose it to a horde of barbarians and foul creatures!"
Unable to bear the argument, Arran spoke out in defence. "I had no choice, your majesty. I felt that the best course of action was to disable the portal and deny the enemy reinforcement. I take responsibility for my actions."
"Speak only when spoken to, sergeant." Grandmaster O'Hare shot a look at him.
"No choice? No choice?" Emperor Otto stared at him. "With respect to my emperor," Captain Therrin intervened, "the situation could've been far worse if the battle continued."
A moment of silence befell the hall. The emperor looked around at everyone as they looked at him. He sighed and slumped back into his throne.
"So, is there anything else that needs to be said regarding yesterday?" he asked.
This time it was Eafen who spoke. "There is, sire."
"Go ahead," the emperor commanded.

"As most of you saw, there was an explosion of light that followed after the spear went through the portal." Just then, an interruption came from a dwarf who stood at the far-left side of the table. "And thus, destroying everything that isn't human, elf, dwarf or whatever is considered decent. What does this have to do with the situation?"
Eafen cleared his throat. "I know you might find this hard to believe, Lord Kleif Stonebearer, but the explosion of light had transported my consciousness and that of Arran to the spirit realm."
"And what did you both see?" Grandmaster O'Hare inquired.
"Whilst in this realm, we were greeted by the gods. Orion and Breia came to us. They said something about this battle being part of a coming war."
"Is this true, Arran? Did you see the same thing as Eafen?" the grandmaster asked.
"Yes, Grandmaster," Arran answered.
"Preposterous," the emperor muttered. "Why would the gods grant so late a vision to a minor mage and an upstart initiate?"
"Well, it doesn't take a genius to figure that out," Lord Stonebearer spoke again. "This attack couldn't have been an isolated incident."
"What about the spear?" Therrin asked. "Did they tell you where it is now?"
Arran watched as his friend paused before answering. "The spear apparently is beyond our reach and that of the Great Enemy."
These words surprised Arran, though he didn't show it when he looked at Eafen. The mage had told a half truth.
"The Great Enemy?" the emperor asked. Everyone else looked at each other, puzzled.
"You are referring to Samael?" Captain Therrin asked.

"Yes. I believe that the man called Valeran is working alongside him, for whatever purpose I cannot say."
At that point, the Crown Prince leaned forward and spoke. "So, just to summarise, we have been attacked by a madman in league with one of the most powerful deities in the history of Maldora. Most likely a declaration of war against our Empire. And we have no idea of where the Unbreakable Will might be?"
"Pretty much," Captain Therrin answered.
The emperor growled. "This cannot stand," he declared. "If this is to be the start of a war, then so be it." Just then the doors opened behind Arran and a lone messenger rushed in. "My emperor," he called. "I bring terrible news."
"Now what?" Grandmaster O'Hare eyed the messenger.
"Speak now," the emperor demanded.
"We've just received reports of activity from Albruck Castle. It appears that the garrison there has been attacked." "By whom?" Grandmaster O'Hare questioned.
The messenger looked around at everyone before replying. "We are not sure, my lords, but people south of the garrison have told our men stationed close by that they saw Imperial banners being replaced by black flags along the walls."
"It looks like we have an idea of where the bastards have been hiding," Grandmaster O'Hare responded. "If this information came from people south of the garrison, then the enemy must've struck from the north, within the heart of Hothland Province."
The councillors muttered to themselves. The emperor's expression went from anger to bewilderment. Arran himself wasn't sure what to feel regarding this new information.

As if snapping from an illusion, the emperor rose from his seat again and replied, "Everyone is to prepare for war immediately. Grandmaster O'Hare, I want you to call upon all of your knights across this realm and rally them to hear at once. Therrin, I want a war council to be held later today. Everyone is dismissed."

"What about these men?" Kleif pointed to Arran and his friends.

"These men will stay put. Grandmaster O'Hare, I command you to court-martial these men for the loss of the Unbreakable Will."

"What?" Gabriel muttered under his breath.

"Yes, my lord," the grandmaster replied without attempting to reject His Majesty's word.

"This is ridiculous." Eafen was perplexed. "You can't be serious."

"He is. We're done here." The grandmaster gestured to his men to make their leave.

Arran was shocked and speechless. War was coming to their doorstep, yet he and his friends were being punished for his actions. He was last out of his group to leave the hall; the councillors were still muttering behind his back.

A war was coming, and he had no idea what part he would play in it.

Midnight, at the Jolly Maid...

Gerald tossed and turned in his bed. Despite the warmth, he was cold inside. Although glad to be back home, he knew it was only a matter of time before someone recognised him. His close friends might happily turn a blind eye, but if a city guardsman spotted him, then he would be in trouble. The

Jolly Maid was still recovering from the other night. And he couldn't help recalling that the sheltering of fugitives was illegal by Imperial Law and would result in the closure of the establishment. He couldn't bear being responsible for this fate.

Frustrated, Gerald rose from his bed and walked over to the windows. He pushed them wide open and stared outside. The streets should be filled with activity going on until dawn. Music and laughter were usually heard from all over the city when the Imperial Games were about, but tonight the square was quieter than usual. The chaos of yesterday had silenced the city's proud spirit. The feeling disturbed him greatly.

If only there was some way to make things right, Gerald thought. He remembered the look of the men and women who marched out of the arena today. The expression of one person, Arran Connaught, stood out the most. An idea came to mind though. If he could join the order and assist this man, he would be able to atone for his wrongdoings. It felt like a sensible course of action.

But what if he didn't recognise him? What could he offer other than his mediocre medical skills? He wasn't skilled at fighting. There was the risk that the knights would simply hand him back to the City Guard and throw him into another filthy dungeon. A light breeze touched his cheeks. The curtains fluttered. Gerald was about to close the windows when he felt a presence behind him. He turned around and found a hooded figure standing before him.

"What?" he jumped back. "Who are you? How did you—"

"Shh," the hooded figure hushed him. "It's alright. I am not here to harm you."

Gerald stared blankly at the stranger. This person was covered in a brown cloak from head to foot.

She spoke again, "I know what you are thinking."

"You... know what?"

"You want to make things right?" she asked.

Gerald stared at the woman for a moment before slowly nodding.

"Every path, every decision, has its risks and rewards. No matter how you look at them."

Gerald sighed. "All I want is to stay here with Nianna. But I'm worried about what will happen if I do."

"I understand." The stranger pointed to the window. "Look outside again."

Gerald followed without question and looked outside.

"Now, tell me what you see?"

"Well, there's nothing special," Gerald began. "It's quiet. Wouldn't be so if not for the maelstrom of chaos that happened."

"You have no idea what true chaos looks like," the hooded woman replied.

"I really don't want to know."

"Things could've taken a turn for the worse."

Gerald nodded. Things could've been far worse for everyone as well as himself.

"Many brave souls had thought to save innocent lives yesterday. But it also allows the stage for another battle to begin. One that you can help steer, in your own way."

"Me? In my own way?" Gerald looked over his shoulder at the woman.

"Yes," she said.

He turned away from the window. "Look, I'm no hero. I've made some bad decisions. I stole a stupid black box from the Academy. All this has happened… Because of me."

"If we did everything right all the time, how would we learn? A friend of mine once told me that there will be choices we will make that we cannot take back, no matter how long we dwell on them. It's what we do afterwards that matters."

Gerald looked down at his feet as he leaned on the wall.

"If I stay here, Nianna and her father will lose everything the moment the City Guard finds me."

"And?" the woman asked.

"If I go to the order, they'll simply throw me in prison again. Unless there is someone who could help me."

"Arran Connaught," the woman whispered.

Gerald looked up at her. "How do you know him?"

"I know a lot of things, Gerald," she grinned. "Tomorrow, he, like you, will face a decision regarding himself and those he cares about."

"Well, there's your hero then. Why not send him to make things right?"

"Because no one person can do everything. Even the bravest of souls are prone to doubt. He, like you, cannot fight the forces of evil on his own. Seek him out and you will find redemption."

"Really?" Gerald asked.

The strange woman nodded. Gerald looked out the window again. For the first time since the robbery, Gerald felt a feeling of hope that he could still make amends. He looked down at the square, plotting out the route he must take. He felt a soft hand on his shoulder.

"Take the sewer before you reach the bridge," she whispered in his ear. "When you find Arran, tell him to go to the mountains near Ravenno. There you will find a cave under the tallest peak. I will be there to show you the way. Good luck."

With that, the soft hand left Gerald's shoulder. He turned to find the mysterious woman was gone. Not a trace of her left behind. Gerald took a deep breath. He decided that he

would take one of the two risks. If there was a chance that he could do good, he would take it. But first he wanted to leave something for Nianna. So, he opened a draw under his cabinet and pulled out a parchment of paper, an ink pot and a quill. He sat down quietly, lit a candle beside him and wrote his farewell.
For tomorrow he would begin his quest.

Chapter 39

Monday, 2nd September

THE STRONGHOLD WAS ALIVE with activity once more. Only this time, there was a sense of urgency in the air. Squires and sergeants occasionally went in and out of the mess hall, oblivious to one another. Sounds of men could be heard outside, along with the clanging of weapons forged and stockpiled in the armoury. Horses snorted and whined as they pulled carts in and out of the gatehouse. And all the while, Arran sat alone at a table in the mess hall, sipping a cup of water.

Apparently, they were now at war with the Great Enemy, though no one had told the people of Aberemrallt of what had transpired or anything about the coming conflict. The last thing they needed was panic over a menace that no one knew enough about, Grandmaster O'Hare had said as they rode back from the Imperial Palace. What bothered Arran the most was the order made by the emperor and the council.

The loss of the Unbreakable Will to the enemy had rewarded him with nothing but a court-martial. He wasn't allowed to leave the Stronghold without permission from his superiors, nor could he take his horse, Basil, out of the stables. Even his opportunity for knighthood would be postponed. With his company captain gone, he was lost. Unable to do anything of significance, let alone the plans the gods had laid out for him, he brooded as he sipped until someone pulled a seat opposite him and sat. He didn't need to lift his head to know it was Gabriel by the shape of the shadow he cast over him. He too, was in low spirits.

"So, this is how a war begins?" he asked.

"Seems that way," said Arran.

"One moment, a horde of monsters attack us from absolutely fucking nowhere. We saved the day; now we're stuck here while everyone else is preparing for a war with you know who."

Arran took another sip, taking in his friend's disbelief.

"Was it true, then?"

"Was what true?" Arran looked at Gabriel.

"That the gods spoke to you and Eafen the other day?" he said.

Arran looked down at his cup, which was now empty. He pushed the cup away and sighed. "It is. At least I believe what I saw was real."

"What was it like?" Gabriel asked. "What happened?"

Arran pursed his lips. He wasn't really in the mood for explaining things that were beyond his understanding. He and Eafen had already confessed before the grandmaster and the emperor yesterday. It wasn't like they would be going anywhere anytime soon. Arran glanced left then right for anyone else present, then he leaned forward and spoke.

"It is true; they spoke to us."

"Who?" Gabriel leaned in closer.

Arran's eyes narrowed. "Orion and Breia. Didn't you remember what Eafen said before the emperor?"

"Oh, right of course," Gabriel realised. "But is it true that the Unbreakable Will is beyond anyone's knowledge right now?"

Arran gritted his teeth and looked down at the table, whilst his friend waited patiently for an answer. He didn't understand why Eafen lied to the others yesterday. Perhaps he wanted to preserve some grain of hope that the most significant relic in all of Maldora could still be recovered.

That, or he was saving them from a far more humiliating sentence. He looked up again at Gabriel, who presented him with another cup of water.

"Cheers," said Arran as he took the fresh cup. He sipped the contents as before, letting the cold fluid soothe his dry throat. He drank half of this cup before putting it aside. He whispered to his friend.

"You're not going to like this but they told me it's now in the hands of the enemy."

"As in… Samael?" Gabriel asked.

Arran nodded slowly. Now it was Gabriel's turn to grit his teeth. "Shit," he muttered.

He was going to speak up until another figure appeared. The silhouette of Eafen Ulrin loomed over the table where Arran and Gabriel sat.

Gabriel was the first to look at him. "I should've guessed you would lie," he said coldly. "You mages are always keeping shit to yourselves."

"I only spoke a half-truth," Eafen replied. The mage sounded as if he had anticipated Gabriel's response. He pulled up a chair and sat at the end of the table. "Our fates could have been worse if I had told them the full truth."

"Makes sense," Arran muttered.

Gabriel, however, wasn't impressed. "But it still goes against what we stand for. Heck, the word truth is in our motto for goodness sake."

We all have our moments of dishonesty, including you Gabriel, Arran thought. He didn't want to say that out loud, knowing that it would make things worse.

"What we write and use for a motto, and what we actually do can be two different things," Eafen continued, "And for a reason. Sometimes it's better to either lie or tell only half of what's true. Truth and honesty are like double-edged swords. Or in my case, like playing with

fire."
Gabriel was frustrated, yet he held his tongue. He stared up at the mess hall ceiling and sighed.
"So, we're just going to sit here whilst everyone else prepares for battle?"
"Seems that way," Arran submitted. He barely had the will to do anything at that point, let alone care. Why would the gods themselves place such a task on his shoulders when he was forbidden to leave the capital?
Gabriel sighed whilst Eafen continued, "By the time our forces have mobilised, along with the Imperial Army, Samael could've taken most of Hothland. If they've already taken Soulman's Gate..."
"Then half of the continent is completely unaware of what's happening and therefore at Samael's mercy," Arran injected.
Gabriel joined in once more. "Well, if they're blocking us off at that gate, then all we need to do is send troops through Gower province and enter Hothland via Frankonia. Hell, we could ask the Arganteans to transport our troops to Nordland and attack from there."
"Yes, but still, by the time we use either path, Samael's army might have broken through and invaded south," Eafen stated.
"If he wanted to come all this way to invade here, that is," said Arran. "We don't even know what his objective is or why he wanted the Unbreakable Will."
Gabriel looked at Eafen. "I thought Samael was prone to its power?"
The mage shrugged. "He hasn't survived this long by making the same mistakes over and over."
At that point, an idea occurred to Arran. "Say, Eafen, how do you know Kleif Stonebearer?" he asked.
"Who doesn't?" Eafen replied. "He's the Head of the

Dwarf Embassy as well as the Master of Masonry. He and his army of architects oversee the construction and maintenance of all buildings within and around the capital, from the smallest house to the coliseum itself."

"I see," Arran acknowledged.

"What are you thinking?" Gabriel tilted his head to him.

"Dwarves are known for making tunnels under the mountains as well as their craftsmanship and masonry, right?"

"And tunnels we have plenty of, lad," boomed a voice that caught everyone's attention, followed by the thudding sound of footsteps on the mess room floor. Arran, Eafen and Gabriel looked at the front doors and were surprised. Approaching them was Brom Blackhammer, wearing the same attire as when they last met at the Jolly Maid. Arran noticed the dwarf bore a fresh scar that stretched from his right cheekbone down to the side of his jaw.

"Brom?" Gabriel was stunned.

"That's quite a cut you have there, Blackhammer," Arran remarked.

"Yeah, it stings like hell, but here I am," the dwarf replied confidently.

"Here for what?" Arran asked.

"Well, here to give my condolences for your losses. And I have been hearing that one of you held the Unbreakable Will. Though you can tell me more about such things over a drink."

Great, Arran sighed, *another person to slate me for losing that fucking spear!*

Regardless, he offered Brom a seat next to him. The dwarf took it and sat, shifting his backside left and right until he was comfortable. Brom then looked past Gabriel and called out to someone.

"Oi, you. Yes, you. Fill me a flagon of beer or whatever you got in those kegs if you will."

"Isn't it a bit early in the day to be sating your thirst for alcohol?" Eafen enquired.

Brom snorted. "Nothing eases the mind like a pint, lad. It's the one thing to keep you sane in these strange times."

Everyone else looked in the same direction at a man who was wearing a brown cloak with a hood over his head. He stood by the large barrels that were stacked in the corner of the mess hall. Taken by surprise, he hesitated a little before fulfilling Brom's request. Everyone observed as he took an empty tankard and filled it slowly.

I wonder who he is, Arran thought.

"Come on now, we haven't got all day," the dwarf called out.

Arran watched as the strange man walked over to them with a tankard. There was something not right about him, aside from the unwelcoming stench that became more apparent as he came closer. Arran wasn't sure what to make of this person. It made sense that he didn't know everyone present in the garrison. The stranger handed the drink to Brom.

"Cheers," said Brom as he accepted the drink from the stranger. Suddenly the stranger's hood slipped down from the back, revealing a dirty freckled face and scruffy hair that was a mixture of red and brown.

"Urgh." Eafen raised a hand over his nose. "That's definitely not the familiar scent of someone who has been cleaning out the stables."

"Good grief," said Gabriel as he shook his head.

"I know you," both Arran and the stranger spoke at the same time.

"Yes, I recognise you as well. You're Gerald, the man we caught the other day," Eafen realised.

"Who?" Gabriel looked puzzled at everyone. "What the fuck is going on?"
Eafen stepped in. "This man here was involved in stealing the Black Box. I've no doubt you stole it for Valeran Serpentine?"
"What?" Brom spat out.
"You bastard!" Gabriel growled as he rose from his seat.
"Alright, hold on," Gerald backed away, "I can explain."
"We're court-martialled because of you," Gabriel barked at him.
With no choice, Arran stood up and intervened. "Calm down, everyone."
"Why aren't you rotting in a dungeon?" Brom demanded, casting aside his tankard and clenching his fists. "I lost many of my brothers the other day."
"Keep your voices down, damn it," Eafen forced himself into the argument. "They'll hear us outside."
"Good, we should let them know there is a traitor amongst us," Gabriel bragged.
"Alright, alright," Gerald admitted. "I'm sorry for your losses. Look, I get it; you're all pissed off. I had no idea what I was getting myself into. Yes, I helped steal the stupid box. And I was put in the dungeons underneath the palace. For a day and a half."
"So, why are you here, Gerald?' Arran asked. "And how did you manage to get inside the Stronghold?" "Well," Gerald cleared his throat, "long story short, I got here through the sewers."
"That explains the reeking stench," Gabriel mumbled as he put a hand over his nose.
"All to seek you out," Gerald pointed to Arran. Arran stared at the fool. "You came all this way, through the stinking sewers, to see me?"
Gerald pursed his lips. "I need your help to clear my

name. I know I don't look like the heroic type, but I want to redeem myself. So, whether you like it or not, I'm here to help."

"How?" Brom asked. "What can a no-good, treacherous welp such as yourself offer to solve our problems?

Gerald sighed. "Well, I'm no fighter, but I was trained to use medicines and know how to wrap bandages. And I'm good with keys and locks. That was how I helped steal… you know what in the first place."

"A lock picker and a healer rolled up into one, heh?" Brom mused.

"He can learn to fight while accompanying us," Eafen stated.

"To do what?" Gabriel asked bluntly.

"Isn't it obvious?" Eafen explained as he rose from his seat. "A war is coming, and we have an idea of where the Unbreakable Will is".

"Do we?" Brom raised an eyebrow at the mage. Eafen continued, "And we all seek atonement for our failures and misgivings."

Gabriel's eyes narrowed. "Are you suggesting the five of us—complete strangers—two sergeants, a mage, a dwarf, and a thief embark on some quest?"

"What would you do?" Eafen asked.

The frustrated Gabriel threw his arms up in the air, "I don't know. But if we're caught leaving here, we'll be stripped of our ranks and thrown into prison with this idiot. And don't you dare suggest we go through the sewers." He pointed at the newcomer.

Gerald took a moment to sniff himself. "It's not that bad."

"Yeah, right," Gabriel snorted.

"What say you, Arran?" Eafen turned to him. But Arran's expression was blank. There was doubt in his mind about this plan.

He sighed. "I don't know. Why would you need me to lead? I'm the one who cast the Unbreakable Will away."

Eafen replied, "We're all guilty of something, Arran. But doing nothing will only magnify the situation."

"It's now or never, lad," Brom added.

Arran Connaught looked at everyone at the table before scanning the entire mess hall. Miraculously, no one else was around, despite the noise created by Gabriel and Brom's uproar. This was a significant risk, he knew. To abandon his post in the capital and journey to Hothland with his closest friends and strangers alike for a relic that he carelessly threw away. To fight the Greatest Evil the world had ever known to save all he cherished. *What would Captain Alric say about this? What about Anwen?* He took a deep breath before replying.

"Alright, I'll lead. The five of us will set off today to retrieve the Unbreakable Will."

"With nothing to lose," Gerald added.

"If he's in, so am I," Gabriel stated. "Wherever you go, I'll follow."

"I was half expecting you to reject," Arran admitted.

"Piss off," Gabriel added. "You'll need everyone you can trust if we're going to set things right. Alric said to not take this journey alone. And besides, would you trust him over me to watch your back?" He pointed a thumb at Gerald. "Hey," Gerald replied, "I know I'm not a warrior like you, but give me a break."

"Same here. I, Brom Blackhammer of Veldor, shall help you slay everything in the name of honour and justice. By my ancestors, I'll march with you into the pits of Hell if that's what it takes."

"Thank you," Arran acknowledged as he rose from his chair. "First things first, I need to speak with Anwen. Eafen, see that you arrange for a way to escape undetected. Gabriel, you get our weapons and provisions ready." He parted from the table but glanced over his shoulder. "Oh, and give Gerald a wash while you're at it."

"You're not serious, are you?" Gabriel replied. "And what about you?"

Arran just smiled. "Me? As I said, I need to speak with Anwen. I won't be long."

Arran left the other four in the mess hall. He hadn't seen Awen since yesterday, but he had an idea of where she might be. Moments later, Arran found himself in the chapel of the Stronghold. There, he saw Anwen sitting still in the front pew before a statue of Orion.

The room was all but empty. Arran could only see the back of her head, so he walked up the aisle. He had only been in the chapel once to pray for good fortune before his first battle in the games. When he reached Anwen, her head was bowed in prayer. Her heavy eyes opened upon sensing his presence. She looked up at him.

"Hey," Arran muttered.

"Hey," she quietly returned.

"How are you feeling?" He couldn't resist asking though he knew nothing good would come out of it.

"I still feel heavy inside," she admitted calmly. Her voice sounded weak to Arran. "What happened at the palace?" She asked.

"Nothing good," Arran replied instantly. "Gabriel, Eafen and I are forbidden from leaving this fort. And now we are at war."

"I heard the chaplains speak about the declaration. We're not even allowed to tell anyone outside about it. I'm sorry for you three."

"It's alright. But listen I need to speak to you," he briefly scanned the chapel, but no one was present, save for a few priests talking in the far corner. They didn't seem bothered by him or Anwen.

Arran looked back at Anwen and whispered, "Could we talk in private?"

The girl's eyes narrowed. "Why?"

"Something I want to say that shouldn't be said out loud."

Anwen sighed. "There's a storeroom next door that's open most of the day. Come on."

She rose from the pew. Arran followed her down the aisle and out of the chapel. She turned left and walked a few steps before stopping at the door. She and Arran waited as a group of servants passed by. The room was tightly packed, shelves upon shelves filled with boxes of candles, tools, sacred oils, and other things. There was a single window to the outside positioned high above the shelves. Anwen went in first, whilst Arran closed the door behind them.

"Okay, go ahead," she began.

"Right. Eafen, Gabriel and I are planning to leave the city today."

Anwen's face went from weary to puzzled. "What? Why?"

Arran explained, "We're going to retrieve the Unbreakable Will. We think it's somewhere in Hothland."

"You think?"

"That's what Orion and Breia told Eafen and me."

"Are you mad?" asked Anwen.

"Look, that spear is the key to this. If we can get it back, we can use it to stop this war before it can begin."

"They say that when you start a war," Anwen stated, "few live to see the end of it."

"Yes, but there's no doubt the enemy will be busy fighting us in different places. They won't be expecting the likes of us sneaking ahead behind their lines."

Anwen put her hands in her hair and sighed. Her expression went from grief to frustration. "My father is dead. You've been court-martialed by the grandmaster. There's a war about to happen, and you want to risk further punishment by going against His Majesty's orders? Charge off against an enemy we know little about on a mad quest to recover one stupid spear?"

"Everyone is going to be heading in that direction, anyway," Arran countered.

"I know what this is about, Arran. You think you'll be able to redeem yourself, but at what cost? You'll be killed, either by them or by our allies for deserting," Anwen protested.

"By them, you are referring to the same monsters that killed your father. Don't you want to avenge him?"

"Not the way you want to do it," Anwen spat back.

"Oh, come on. Do you think we're stupid enough to just charge right into the jaws of death? Look, Eafen and Gabriel are planning our route as we speak."

"Who else is coming?"

"Well...." Arran paused before answering. "Rodrick and the others are still wounded. I still need to talk to Callum. He might not be a fighter, but I'm sure some of his knowledge of things will come handy once we're outside the city. Brom Blackhammer is here and willing to aid us."

"Brom Blackhammer?" Anwen asked. "The dwarf you were fighting two days ago?"

"Yes, and another person, I'll introduce you to them."

At that point, Anwen sighed and turned her back to him. Arran's arms slumped to his sides. "You're not coming, are you?"

"My father would never approve of it," Anwen mumbled over her shoulder.

"I know, but he's not here."

"We'll get hanged for this." she protested.

"No way," Arran objected. "The Imperial army will need every man and woman available to fight. Why execute a handful of good fighters just because they disobeyed orders?"
Anwen turned around and stared at him coldly. "Because what you are about to do is reckless and stupid. Forsaking your oath and position for a personal quest."
"It's better than doing nothing." Arran countered. "Can't see us standing shoulder to shoulder with everyone else in a meat grinder fight."
There was a moment of silence between the two. Arran occasionally glanced over to the door whenever he heard footsteps. Fortunately, no one else disturbed them.
He sighed when he looked at Anwen again. "If you want to stay here, that's fine. I'll respect that. My only request is that you take care of Basil for me."
Anwen tilted her head. "You want me to have your horse?"
"I can't take him with me. The guards will know it's me, even if I dress up as someone else."
"I can't take him," Anwen refused, "he's loyal to you." "If anything should happen to me, set him free. I don't want him to wait for me. I better go." Arran headed for the door, but Anwen stretched her arms to stop him. "Wait!" she whispered.
"Yes?" Arran looked down at her. Right into her emerald eyes.
"I can't see myself riding your horse. And neither can I imagine Basil without you." She sighed. "I'm coming with you."
"You sure?"
"Someone has to come along to keep you, idiots, out of trouble." She put a hand on his chest.
"It takes an idiot to bring out the genius, I suppose,"

Arran joked.

"Does that make me smarter than you?" she teased.

"Depends. If it's a sword fight. I can match you. Or maybe this…."

At that point, Arran then put his arms around Anwen. Before she could protest, he pressed his lips onto hers. It surprised her, but she soon embraced the warm sensation that flowed through them both. She weaved a hand through his hair and pulled Arran closer, enticing him to continue holding on.

Satisfied with the kiss, their lips soon parted, Arran looked into Anwen's sparkling eyes. A little smile etched across her face. Arran had been so caught up in the moment that he didn't realise they weren't alone. He looked over Anwen's shoulder and saw Callum, who stood mesmerised by them, holding a box of scrolls.

Arran broke the silence. "How long have you been there?"

Anwen turned around and blushed upon seeing Callum.

"Wha .... oh." Callum bucked backwards as if prodded by a hot pitchfork. The box slipped out of his hands in a thud on the stone floor, scrolls rolling away in every direction.

"Oh gods," he cursed. "I'm sorry, I…." He sighed as he kneeled down to pick up the box.

"It's alright, Callum," said Arran. Anwen just chuckled. They helped him gather up the stray scrolls.

"You won't be telling anyone about this, will you?" Arran eyed him.

"No," Callum looked bluntly at him. "Of course not. I suppose we only have one life and might as well make the most of it."

Arran looked at Anwen, then back at Callum; they might as well explain. "There's something else you should know. But you can't tell anyone else."

"What's that?" Callum looked puzzled.
"We're planning to leave the city today. Are you up for another adventure?"
"What?" Callum responded flabbergasted.

Epilogue

AFTER EXPLAINING THE plan to Callum, Arran and Anwen left the storeroom unnoticed. It took some convincing, as Callum initially saw the whole adventure as suicide. Arran had to remind him that his vast knowledge of different subjects would be helpful, followed with a choice. Stay in the city to act as a contact or join them in their quest. Eventually, Callum chose to accompany Arran and Anwen and help in whatever way he could. They departed to gather their essentials and met with Gabriel and the others in the mess hall.

An hour later, Arran found himself strapped underneath a cart whilst everyone else had either disguised themselves or hid in one of the barrels on top. The decision to strap someone beneath the cart came about when they couldn't fit any more barrels topside. So, Arran and Gabriel played rock, paper, scissors to determine who would be strapped underneath. *Should have picked rock*, he frowned as he knocked and banged his head against the wooden subframe as grit and wet dirt sprayed and soaked his clothes and face. Every now and then, he would spit out said dirt should it ever make its way into his mouth. Worse was the occasional pile of horseshit that the cart would travel over, forcing Arran to pull his chest in even more and turn his head sideways to avoid the freshly made muck from touching either his face or his clothes. *Still, better than travelling through the sewers*, he thought.

Gerald and Callum would be guiding the cart with Arran's horse, Basil, and another pulling it. Apparently, Eafen had found a way to alter Gerald's appearance so that the city guards wouldn't recognise him. How he accomplished this in so little time, Arran could only wonder.

His body shifted back and forth with the straps every time the cart stopped, moved or changed direction. His eyes were fixed on the cobbled roads as they travelled through the city, yet he could distinguish the sounds of everyday life. Children running and playing games, men and women gossiping. The occasional voice of an out-of-tune bard singing outside some tavern. Plodding hooves, whining of other horses, and the familiar marching footsteps of soldiers passing by. Merchants were boasting about their sales, though not as enthusiastic as Arran had come to expect, but considering what just happened the last two days, he didn't blame for being a bit more cautious.

Finally, they reached the last gate. The sounds of the city were slowly fading away, replaced by the cries of birds, the buzzing of bees and the collective voices of farmers and livestock living outside Aberemrallt. Eventually, the cobblestone roads were replaced with that dry dirt. The cart stopped after traversing a hill. Arran could hear Gerald leaping off the cart, who then tapped on the wood and spoke. "You can come out now," he called.

About time, Arran thought. He undid the straps one at a time, allowing himself to drop onto the ground. He crawled out from underneath the cart; Gerald and Callum were the first to greet him. Arran was the only one in the group who hadn't seen the disguise that Eafen had concocted, hence why he was surprised to find Gerald's hair had gone from half ginger, half brown, to now black as coal. He also donned a scruffy beard, while Callum wore a straw hat which had seen better days.

He couldn't resist asking, "How did you manage to change your hair colour so quickly? And the beard?"

"That beard belongs to me!" A growl came from one of the barrels, and out came Brom. The dwarf crossed his arms and was grumpy. Arran noticed that his beard had been snipped halfway. Realising what had happened, he suddenly exploded in laughter.

"Oi, stop laughing, ya nob head!" Brom roared. "It's not bloody funny!"

Eafen then appeared, pulling himself out of another barrel before helping Anwen out of the one next to his and Brom's. He then jumped out and walked around the cart to explain, "As you can see, Callum and I borrowed a sample of Brom's hair to concoct a drink that temporarily changes Gerald's hair colour. We also had to borrow some hairs from his beard."

"Borrow it?" Brom looked at the mage with disdainful eyes. "You forced me to sit down and let you snip it off. No dwarf should ever let anyone cut his beard off without his permission. Whatever the reason. It's dishonourable."

"Oh, shut up, will you?" Gabriel intervened. He wore a straw hat as well to hide his blonde hair and covered his blue surcoat with a dirty old cloak. "It's just bloody hair; it'll grow back in time."

Brom simply grunted. He wasn't pleased with forfeiting half of his beloved beard.

"This thing's getting really itchy," Gerald admitted.

"If you're done with it, I'll have it back," the dwarf demanded.

"Seriously?" Gerald was amused. He removed it by undoing a string tied around his ears.

The dwarf grabbed Gerald's mop of beard hair and stashed it in his backpack. Even Eafen and Anwen struggled to suppress their amusement at that. The latter had donned a brown hooded tunic with a black leather ringed belt around her waist. She could easily deceive anyone into thinking she was a priestess, Arran thought. After a moment, Arran stopped laughing and looked around. They were atop a hill overlooking the fork point of the Tor River. The sun was well above them. Its rays of light pierced through the gaps in the clouds. Looking back at their path, he could still see the capital. He stared at the splendour of its walls that still amazed him to this day. Everyone else was doing the same. He couldn't blame them, for all he knew, this could be the last time they would set their eyes upon it. Peace would be a rare luxury from now on. Gabriel walked over to stand by Arran.

"So, what's the news?" Arran asked.

"Well, apparently, messengers have been sent by the emperor to every province to marshal all troops to Hothland at once. The knight orders of Hothland and Nordland have already packed their things and headed straight for Soulman's Gate, so they're ahead of us. Our brothers should be pouring out of Aberemrallt right now."

"We need to get to Soulman's Gate before they do," said Arran.

"Do you intend for us to attack those walls head-on?" Eafen interjected.

"No, but we'll worry about it when we get there."

"It'll be a long way to that place," Gerald commented.

"Then let's not waste any more time," Arran replied. "If we continue on this road, we'll cross the river to the town of Paroy. Then we'll head north. Avoid Luvera Castle and continue past it."

"Still not sure how we're going to get inside," said Anwen.

"We'll find a way," Eafen reassured them. "The gods will show us."

"I hope you're right about this," Gabriel commented.

"Let's go," Arran concluded.

Everyone hopped back onto the cart, ready to move again. Arran took one last look at Aberemrallt. There was no turning back now. He took in the cold air as the wind brushed across his face before turning away. He walked to the front of the cart, where Basil waited patiently alongside Frey, Anwen's horse. He patted their backs before climbing aboard. Arran took charge of driving the cart this time, but he wasn't alone; Anwen had decided to join him at the front. They smiled at one another before he whipped up the reins. And then they were off.

A fellowship of six, brought together by fate, guided by the gods, onto a journey of peril, adventure and redemption.
The quest for the Unbreakable Will had begun.
To be continued...

Author's Notes

SO, YOU GOT TO THE END? Congratulations! Now, I imagine you have a hundred questions about what went into the writing of this novel.

First off, there were several inspirations for this story before I decided to put them onto paper. The first inspiration that came to mind was a computer game called *Myth: The Fallen Lords* by Bungie Inc. The game is set in a fictional world, following humanity's struggle against an all-powerful group of warlocks commanding unending hordes of undead, whilst learning that the conflict is all part of a never-ending cycle between the forces of light and dark. The story is told from the first-person perspective of an unknown protagonist as he writes about his experiences in a journal. This, along with the music that plays between each entry, was my first inspiration for this story.

So why this name? Why call it 'The Maldoran Chronicles: The Unbreakable Will'? Again, for simplicity's sake, because I liked the name of it.

As time went by, the second half of the title seemed to become much more pertinent. I mean, I never thought I would be completing and publishing my f rst novel in the after a pandemic. I suppose this is what perseverance means: carrying on, no matter what life throws at you, until you have achieved what you set out to do. And there's no shame in taking a step back. Hell, I had a few months' (well, more than that) absence from writing after finishing the first draft, mainly because I was struggling to find anyone to help me refine it. And when I looked back on my work, let's just say there were many moments where I was like "Wow, really? What was I thinking back then?"

I could go on, but there's a lot of things. So I will leave it there for now. If you want to learn more about what went into this story and the world of Maldora, I encourage you to check out the website frostbridgepublishing.com. I've also got a Facebook page ready to follow for future updates.

I hope that you, the reader, have enjoyed this novel. I look forward to continuing (or actually starting) the adventures of Arran Connaught and company. How will they fare in their quest to retrieve the Unbreakable Will? How will Arran handle the pressures of leading this band of individuals? What plans does Samael have for Valeran and the rest of Maldora? Will Gerald overcome his sense of guilt? And what other characters will our heroes (and villains) find on their merry way? Until then, stay safe.

And hopefully, I'll have another story to share with you.

Hwyl Fawr! (That means goodbye in Welsh)

Glossary

Kingdoms, places and geographical features

The Universal Era: Abbreviated by the initialism U.E.., the Universal Era defines the year in context with the rest of world history.

Aberemrallt: Capital of the Maldoran Empire, situated in Gower province. This city initially began as a minor settlement at the mouth of the River Emrallt that fed the area of sea known as Prince's Bay. It is the current seat of power for the Vorlorn Dynasty. It is also home to the Imperial Academy and to the Stronghold, Headquarters of the Twin Blade Order of Knights.

Alvaria: A large island off the western coast, Alvaria was discovered around the year 89 U.E. the First Era by the elves. It was believed that the elves had migrated from the coast due to constant harassment from human tribes. Their first settlement on the island was Rheonne, named to honour their first queen Rheonna I, thus beginning the colonization of the entire island that would become the Kingdom of Alvaria by the Year 112 U.E.. Since then, they were rarely interested in the affairs of other kingdoms. Settlements outside their domain included the cities of Ayos and Myar'Groath. Elves are known for their elegance and their love for the arts. In battle, their archers are among the finest, for their shots rarely miss a target. They are also keen learners, and scholars in the art of magic.

Bourgiatta Castle: A fortress in the heartland of the Terradonian countryside, built by House Serpentine during its height of power. Outside of Ravenno, this bastion was the centre for House Serpentine's military campaigns until their masters were overthrown and replaced by the ancestors of House Bastonne, the current owners of this mighty fortress.

Byzalia (or sometimes called Byzalium): Colonised and founded by the people of Argantis in the year 177 U.E., Byzalia lies south of the island of Lanpenthoes. When the main island of Argantis was destroyed in 482 U.E., many of the surviving citizens sailed south and took refuge among the colonies and from there, the kingdom of Byzalia was established in 483 U.E.. Since then, Byzalia had honed its naval prowse in response to compeititon from its rival kingdom Lapenthoes over trade and territory. Despite these developing feuds, the two domains did contribute massively to the Battle of Old Argantis, where their combined naval expertise proved invaluable in defeating a large Nordish fleet.

Frankonia: Situated in the far central west, Frankonia is a kingdom that neighbours the island of Rheonora. It is separated from the lands of Gower and Satyrom by the river Bergemont, and by the steppes of Zarmania to the north. Frankonia was settled by a tribe known as the Frankoni, who were originally part of a larger tribe known as the Langomann, who, after laying the foundation for the neighbouring kingdom of Hothland, continued to venture east to the heart of The Ringspine Mountains. Frankonia is known for its wine and being the founding place of chivalry, thus its knights are renowned for honouring this code.

Gard Afon Castle: Situated on an elevated hill overlooking the River Tor. This castle was originally a hill fort built by the neighbouring Terradonians during a period of aggressive military expansion westward. This expansion was met with resistance from the local Gowern tribes who banded together to attack and overwhelm the fortification. With the Terradonians driven out, the victorious Gowerns chose to keep the fort, rather than raze it to the ground. The hillfort that would eventually become a castle would change hands over the decades until it was gifted to the Twin Blade Order by the Maldoran Empire for decades of service.

Gower: Located west of Terradonia. The lands of Gower were settled by the migrating Gowern tribes who built their settlements upon the hills. These towns soon evolved over time into hill forts, and then castles as lords grew in power, seeking to protect their surrounding lands (Gard Afon Castle is one such example). Gower is known to be the land where Orion was born many centuries ago at a time when feudal tribes reigned. After the death of Orion, and his ascension to godhood, many of these tribes joined together, forming what would become the Kingdom of Gower. The decades that followed its founding were anything but peaceful, as the kingdom was plagued with internal and external conflicts.

Hothland: A kingdom based in the centre of the continent, Hothland is surrounded on all sides by The Ringspine Mountains. Geographically, there are only three ways in or out, making it a very comfortable place to defend. The kingdom was founded by King Otto I (also known as the Dragon Hunter) following the battle of Dhulbragh between Orion and Samael. Its capital, Reikenburg, is situated in the centre, where the noble ruling families would reside, especially the current ruling House of Vorlorn. The latter now rules the Maldoran Empire from the city of Abermerallt. It is also where the headquarters for the Knights of Hothland is situated.

Old Argantis: First discovered by Jason Argantius who journeyed out to explore the sea aboard his ship *The Argan*. Jason was named king following the establishment of the first settlement. Its capital was Argantia and its people were known as Arganteans. From this island, they flourished in naval trade and commerce. Their Empire stretched all the way south to the islands of Lapenthoes and Byzalium that they colonised and even took to the mainland of Terradonia, conquering the coastal cities of Kosantoes and Arivinium, the birthplace of their founding father. They proved themselves to be the finest sailors at the time. The Arganteans enjoyed many decades of prosperity until the destruction of Argantis itself, when a volcano underneath the surface erupted with a force so powerful that the entire island was broken apart, leaving only its highest points above the water. The few who survived sailed to either Arivinium or to the colonies of Lapenthoes or Byzalium.

Lapenthoes: Originally the first and the largest island colonised by the rising kingdom of Argantis. When the great city was destroyed in 482 U.E., many surviving citizens fled by ship and made Lapenthoes their new home. The kingdom of Lapenthoes was established a few months later. Lapenthoes is known for its deposits of gold beneath the island, and its naval capabilities are on par with its southern neighbour, the kingdom of Byzalia. These two emerging island kingdoms would clash over trade and territory for many decades.

Mandelheim: Stretching from the Frysen River across the northern tip of The Ringspine Mountains, Mandelheim is the home of the dwarves. Since the beginning, the dwarves built their settlements close to and within the mountains, including the Citadel of Myrgrad. Experts in mining, iron making and building, their architecture and goods are among the finest in all of Maldora and sought after by those willing to be on the good side of the dwarves. Mandelheim is divided into strongholds, each ruled by a Dwarf High Lord, each of whom answers to a High King elected from among the members of The Council of Dwarven Lords and Kings. These strongholds would, over the years, expand into the heart of the mountains themselves. The largest of these is Myrgrad. The dwarves are no stranger to conflict, as the Dwarven strongholds have spent years fending off hostile adversaries such as the Zarmanian tribes to the west and the men of Nordland to the east. By the year 1266 U.E., The last Dwarven High King Ulfric XI signed a treaty with the Maldoran Emperor Theodoric I, thus completing the unification of the continent of Maldora under the namesake Empire, which to this day retains a certain degree of independence.

Nordland: This kingdom is situated in the far north-eastern corner of the continent. The first people to settle in this land were the Skraveni and the Drakoni who divided into smaller clans following their settling of the region. Experts in seafaring and raiding, many of the clans would raid one another and, when the opportunity presented itself, raid other distant regions by land and sea. Fierce and aggressive are the warriors born in this harsh landscape; even their women have been known to take up arms. They were known to travel by sea on their famous longboats to as far as the coastlines belonging to the Elven Kingdom of Rheonora. It is the birthplace of the infamous warrior who would become the Dark Lord Samael, who united many of the Northmen in promises of conquest, whilst attacking those who opposed him during his rise to power. Situated in this kingdom is the stronghold of the Knights of the Wolf, established to counter the taint of Samael in the region. While the land, particularly in the eastern part, was unsuitable for farming, they made up for this by trading animal pelts.

The Ringspine: A massive collection of towering mountains that resemble an almost completed ring in the centre of the continent. Many mages and scholars claim that the mountain range was formed when a great comet crashed into the continent long before life existed.

Satyrom: Situated to the southwest of the Kingdom of Gower, this vast realm of woodland is home to the satyrs, a race of beings who are half human and half goat due to the abnormal development of hooves and horns. These people were a confederation of tribes that lived in isolation from the rest of the known world. Having lived most of their lives in these woodlands, they became experts in shadow warfare*, striking any foe that wandered too close to their heartlands, then retreating back to the safety of the woods before any retaliation could be made.

Zarmania: Nestled in the northwestern corner of the continent, Zarmania is considered the youngest of all the kingdoms of Maldora. The kingdom was named after the foremost of several nomadic tribes from the Frigid Steppes who settled the area of what would become the kingdom of Zarmania. This tribe was famed for their cavalry tactics, especially in their wars against the dwarves and other kingdoms further south. The people who made their home in this land initially did not worship the four elements, as magic is seen as a mysterious thing to them and anything related to what they believe as sorcery was forbidden. Instead, they worshipped—and continue to do so to this day—two deities that take the form of two horses, one that watches them during the day and the other watching during the night.

Deities

Aegonius (known also as Aegon): Lord of Water, God of the Sea and Sanitation. Aegonius is worshipped by sailors in hope of safe sailing, and by those who are enthusiastic about sanitation. One of the first magic wielders to be discovered by Orion. They clashed in an epic duel where neither had the upper hand before becoming friends afterwards.

Breia: Goddess of Nature and Great Lady of the Earth element, often representing fertility, good harvest and nature. Known as a kind and caring being, Breia dislikes violence and bloodshed and is always willing to protect the natural world. Breia is unique in that she is the only human deity worshipped by the satyrs because of their shared connection to nature.

Orion: The Lord of the Wind and God of Reason and Truth, Orion was considered the first to master the wind element. Many mages have considered him to be the first of their kind. The kind and generous son of a farmer often used his power to levitate objects and control the wind to help those around him. His accomplishments include the many battles with his adversary Samael whilst wielding the Unbreakable Will. In their final confrontation at the battle of Dhulbragh, he perished and is now revered as a saviour. His tales of courage, self-sacrifice and commitment to the less fortunate, as well as his magical prowess, inspired the movement of the religion known today as the Faith Elementi, where he, alongside others, are worshipped as gods.

Samael: The Lord of Darkness and the arch nemesis of Orion. This being rules all things beneath the earth. Little is known about his origins save for rumours that he began his life as a slave. Eventually, he broke free and rose to power when he discovered he could control magic. He used his newfound powers and his unrivalled skills as a warrior to unite many of the Nordland tribes whilst destroying those that dared to oppose him. His final battle with Orion, during which he wielded his sword: The Black Dread became a thing of legend. When he was defeated by Orion, many believed he was finished. *How wrong they were...*

Volken: Lord of the element of fire, God of Soldiers and Smiths. Known for his fiery spirit and sense of honour, Volken does not hesitate to punish those who commit dishonorable acts. Many soldiers pray to him before going forth into battle. Since metalworking involves the use of fire, many blacksmiths look to him for inspiration.

Military Orders

The Knight of Hothland: Founded only a few years after the kingdom of Hothland was born, these knights initially pledged an oath to serve and defend the kingdom from all threats outside and within. Their oath has since been reformed to include their service to the emperor whenever he calls for them. On their banner of black and white is a large red griffin, hence the reason they are also called the Griffin Knights. They are the only known order to breed and train griffins as mounts for the best knights within their order.

The Knights of the Wolf: Also known as the Knights of the North, this order was founded by a handful of knights who saw it their duty to establish their presence in a country with a history of falling under the yoke of the Dark Lord Samael. They are so known for their ferocity in battle that even other fellow knightly orders are intimated at the prospect of facing them. Their banner is a silhouette of a wolf howling on a f eld of grey that is outlined in silvery blue.

The Twin Blade Order: Formerly known as the Knights of Gower when founded in the year 575 U.E. tasked with defending the kingdom and acting as the main mobile force for any Gowern army. It was renamed in the honour of its greatest hero, Sir Owain Meylor, who was famous for his style of fighting with two swords following his battles with the returning Samael, hence the name. This order, since its reformation, has been tasked with rooting out all followers of the Dark Lord. Their emblem features a pair of crossed swords upon a field of dark blue that is outlined in red, with the four elements shown above them.

Other

Aerianeite: A mysterious element found in the heart of The Ringspine Mountains. The main characteristics of this crystal include a constant glow and the ability to enhance sentient beings with magical powers. It is claimed to be responsible for the birth of the many races in Maldora such as the dwarves and satyrs due to contact with the source and the mutations that would occur over the generations.

This stone is known to be found in the following colours:

White – the most common colour often associated with mages who specialise in the wind element.

Blue– the rarest colour, this type of aerianeite is used to enhance the powers of water-based magic.

Red – found mainly around the once active Mount Wodun and around the northern half of The Ringspine

Mountains. This type of aerianeite is used to enhance fire-based magic.

Green – found commonly under the southern mountains of The Ringspine, aerialite of this colour is used to enhance the power of earth-based spells. It also has the ability to rejuvenate plant life when in contact with soil.

Yellow – the result of aerianeite exposed to lighting, these crystals are used to enhance the power of lightning-based magic.

Dark violet – known as dark aerianeite. The origin of this colour is unknown, yet there are claims that it is the result of experimentation with more than one of the other types of aerianeite. Others say that this darker source is the by-product of a warlock's dark side, allowing him to utilise powers that are deemed unnatural.

* **Shadow Warfare**: The collective term used in Maldora to describe the use of tactics such as ambushes, hit and run, the raiding of key strategic (or most cases vulnerable) places and other such tactics that don't involve directly attacking an enemy on the battlefield

The Black Box: An artefact forged by the finest o dwarven craftsmanship and imbued with the most potent containment spells known. This device was made for the sole purpose of locking away the Heart of Darkness.

The Heart of Darkness: Named so, for it is the only part of Samael's anatomy that appears to have survived the destruction of its host's body. It was later retrieved and placed in the artefact that became known as the Black Box. Though some tales are told of its existence, many scholars and Imperial authorities would denounce it as nothing more than a dark myth or a story some parents would tell their children.

The Imperial Games: A quinquennial event. The games were first made official in the year 1270 U.E. by Emperor Julian II as a means of bringing the various cultures and kingdoms of Maldora together. The games would take place in the capital city of Aberemrallt, or any other settlement with the resources and capacity to host such a spectacle. Events include archery (both mounted and dismounted), racing, jousting, armed mêlée combat and wrestling.

The Unbreakable Will: A weapon of immense power, this spear was forged by the hands of a dwarven smith at the request of Orion to help him counter the powers of his nemesis Samael. The spear holds a shard of aerianeite beneath the blade. This weapon has been sought after since the fall of Orion, and at one point was believed to be lost or destroyed until discovered by the Knights of the Twin Blade Order, becoming its most sacred of relics.

Printed in Great Britain
by Amazon

21996116R00198